PENGUIN BOOKS

FAMILIAR ROOMS [illegible]

Caro Fraser was educ[illegible] ttending Watford School of A[illegible] ter for three years, then read law at [illegible] was called to the Bar of Middle Temple in 197[illegible] ipping lawyer, before turning to writing. She is the auth[illegible] other novels, five of which are part of the highly successful, critically acclaimed Caper Court series. She lives in London with her husband, who is a solicitor, and her four children.

Familiar Rooms in Darkness

CARO FRASER

PENGUIN BOOKS

PENGUIN BOOKS

Published by the Penguin Group
Penguin Books Ltd, 80 Strand, London WC2R 0RL, England
Penguin Group (USA) Inc., 375 Hudson Street, New York, New York 10014, USA
Penguin Books Australia Ltd, 250 Camberwell Road, Camberwell, Victoria 3124, Australia
Penguin Books Canada Ltd, 10 Alcorn Avenue, Toronto, Ontario, Canada M4V 3B2
Penguin Books India (P) Ltd, 11 Community Centre, Panchsheel Park, New Delhi – 110 017, India
Penguin Books (NZ) Ltd, Cnr Rosedale and Airborne Roads, Albany, Auckland, New Zealand
Penguin Books (South Africa) (Pty) Ltd, 24 Sturdee Avenue, Rosebank 2196, South Africa

Penguin Books Ltd, Registered Offices: 80 Strand, London WC2R 0RL, England

www.penguin.com

Published by Michael Joseph 2003
Published in Penguin Books 2004
1

Printed in England by Clays Ltd, St Ives plc

Harry Day

Poet, playwright and author, whose talents spanned generations

Although latterly best known for his novels and plays, it was as a poet that Harry Day achieved his first literary success. His collection of poems, *Before the Dusk*, was published in 1949 under the pen-name H. M. W. Day (his middle names were McCardle Wentworth) when he was just nineteen. The poems were mainly lyrical, often tinged with a wistful melancholy, and set out to deal with spiritual and temporal themes by magnifying life's trivial issues and its mundane and harsh realities. Following National Service he took a variety of jobs, including night-watchman and carpet salesman, to finance his writing career, and over the next decade he continued to publish regular volumes of poetry, always to critical acclaim.

In 1958, as Britain came to terms with its post-war identity, Day found a new voice as a playwright. He abandoned his poetic pen-name and wrote his first play, *Crying Out Loud*, as plain Harry Day. The play ran for a sell-out season at the Royal Court theatre and was voted Best Foreign Play on Broadway in 1959. In this year, too, he met and married the actress Cecile Patterson, who played the leading role of Christine in the first production. His second play, *Foremost First*, established him in the front ranks of the new social realists, along with Wesker, Delaney and Osborne. The critic Kenneth Tynan wrote of Day: 'Social realism, for Harry Day, is not merely a dogmatic formula. Amongst all other contemporary English dramatists, he uses it as a uniquely powerful means of conveying true theatrical emotion.'

For the next fifteen years Harry Day continued to write for the theatre, but in the mid seventies his career took another direction. Following his divorce in 1975, he began to move in a new circle, socializing with pop stars, fashion designers and artists, and in 1976, in a quest for spiritual enlightenment, he travelled to India, where he wrote *Pale Journey*, the first volume of the celebrated Green Juniper trilogy. The novel, set in both India and England, was an instant bestseller, as were the subsequent two volumes, establishing Harry Day as the new guru of young, enlightened, middle-class English intellectuals. Day remained in India for five years before returning to England in the early eighties.

Throughout this decade Harry Day's output as a novelist was prodigious, and each new publication was eagerly acclaimed, though there were critics who maintained that much of his work was superficial and lacking in integrity. His eighth novel, *Adventures Of . . .*, shortlisted for the Booker Prize, was his least commercially successful.

Harry Day's novels often touched on the subject of drugs, a theme prevalent in the Green Juniper trilogy, and indeed he admitted, in later years, to considerable experimentation with a variety of substances, including LSD and mescaline, and was a lifelong proponent of the beneficial effects of marijuana. In 1987 he was arrested for possession of cocaine, and spent three months in Brixton Prison, an experience which he turned to good account in his subsequent novel, *June to September*. This novel saw a return to his early lyrical poetic style, and although well received by faithful Harry Day enthusiasts, it marked the beginning of a decline in his popularity as a novelist.

His literary energy remained undiminished, however, and it seemed that advancing age drew him ever closer to young people. He co-wrote a number of plays for the National Youth Theatre Foundation, published two volumes of comic verse for children, and, somewhat bizarrely, was a regular contributor to the eclectic music monthly *Rox*. He was a lifelong rock-music enthusiast, and could frequently be spotted at the Brixton Academy and other rock venues.

A minor stroke in 1996 forced Harry Day to limit his activities, and his time was spent largely at Gandercleugh House, the Suffolk home which he shared with his second wife, the actress Briony Nugent, and at his house in France. He lost none of his conviviality, and continued to throw parties and to entertain a wide circle of friends and admirers. Throughout these years he returned to his first love, poetry, but the lukewarm reception of his 1997 collection, *New Bearings*, discouraged him from further publication, though he continued to write until his death.

He is survived by his first wife, his son Charles, his daughter the actress Bella Day, and by his second wife.

Harry Day, poet, playwright and author, was born on 6 November 1930. He died of cancer on 22 December 2002, aged seventy-two.

I

It was an August afternoon, and a party was in progress at Gandercleugh, Harry Day's country house in Suffolk. Guests mingled on the oval lawn, and the air was warm with talk and laughter, drowsy with the sound of wood pigeons from the deep woods beyond. Harry was already very ill; he knew this would be the last summer of his life. The knowledge lay dispassionately within his heart, unconnected to his present and continued existence. Harry Day would be alive right up until the moment of his death, and that seemed sufficient. He did not feel unwell. In fact, he felt far more robust than his appearance suggested he had any right to be. He sat on the terrace in a cane chair, an elegant but frail figure, a glass of wine in one thin hand, surveying the scene. He paid great attention to detail, scrutinizing the company, the faces, attentively trying to glean the depth of every moment. Some of the guests he knew well, some hardly at all. At the moment he was paying particular attention to a tall young man who stood a little way off at the edge of the terrace, leaning on a stone cupid, talking to Francis Cleverley, literary editor of one of the Sunday heavies and an old friend of Harry's. The young man was very handsome, with dark, curling hair and a strong face. He was listening closely to Francis, nodding now and again, smiling occasionally. Though he was half a head taller than

Francis, his very body seemed to curve in towards the older man in a kind of physical deference. Circumspection pervaded every aspect of his young being. He must be a journalist or a reviewer of some kind, thought Harry, to be sucking up so assiduously to an old bore like Francis.

'Tired, darling?' Briony, Harry's wife, rested a light hand on his shoulder. He glanced up at her. She was dressed in peach-coloured trousers and a pale silk top. Her skin was clear, her eyes luminous, make-up perfect. Nobody would have guessed she was nearer fifty than forty. She possessed a wholesome radiance, and even the fine lines round her eyes and mouth when she smiled were part of her charm. When he looked at her at times like this, Harry saw what everyone else saw: Briony Nugent, household name, sitcom queen, subject of endless women's magazine interviews and *Radio Times* covers, the darling of the middle classes. What would they all think, he wondered, if they could know her as he did?

'Far from it,' replied Harry.

'Just be careful how much you drink.' She indicated the glass in his hand. 'Remember what the consultant said.'

'Bugger the consultant.' He knocked back the remains of his drink. 'Who's the young man talking to Francis?'

Briony glanced across, and Harry watched her, observing how her look of mere inquiry switched swiftly to one of predatory sexual assessment. How marvellously predictable she was. 'Not a clue. Don't you know? It's your party.'

'Anthea put together the guest list. It's what I've got an agent for. I've never even heard of half the people who review my books.'

Briony plucked at the sleeve of a passing man. 'Ralph, darling, who is the very good-looking young man talking to Francis?'

Ralph glanced towards the end of the terrace. 'That's Adam Downing. He's a freelance, does reviews for the big Sundays, and for the *Spectator* and the *Literary Review*, the odd feature here and there. You'll have seen his name.'

Harry nodded. 'Yes, indeed. How odd that I haven't met him before. Darling, would you tell Mr Downing I should very much like to meet him?'

Briony gave her husband a swiftly considering glance. 'Of course.' She sauntered to the end of the terrace. Francis Cleverley looked up at her approach and they bent towards one another to exchange light kisses. 'Francis, darling, forgive me for interrupting –' She turned to Adam with a smile. 'You're Adam Downing, I believe?' They shook hands. 'Harry would so much like to meet you. Would you mind, Francis?'

She led Adam along the terrace to where Harry sat, and made introductions. Harry put out a hand and Adam shook it. 'Do sit down,' said Harry, gesturing to a chair on the other side of the little table on which he had placed his empty glass.

'This is quite a thrill for me, meeting you at last,' said Adam, his eyes alight with sincerity. 'I've always been such a great admirer of your work.'

'I'll just go and see that everyone has everything they need –' Briony was about to head off in the direction of the lawn.

'While you're at it,' said Harry, 'pass one of those

bottles from the table. Mr Downing and I could both do with a refill.' He gestured towards a long trestle table, manned by a uniformed maid, at the end of the terrace nearest the house.

Reluctantly Briony did as Harry asked her, then left to attend to the other guests.

Harry poured them both a glass of cold Chablis. Their talk skimmed briefly over current literary events, then homed in where it belonged, on Harry and his work. One of the more beguiling aspects of being an ageing celebrity, thought Harry, was the way people liked to talk about you. And how well Adam did it too.

After thirty minutes and two glasses of wine, Adam felt emboldened. 'Mr Day, can I ask you –' He twiddled his glass diffidently.

'Call me Harry. I feel we've become rather good friends, don't you?' Harry's glance ranged speculatively over Adam's handsome features.

Adam gave a self-conscious laugh. 'If you say so. I wanted to ask why you've never written about your life.'

'An autobiography? You know, my dear boy, living one's life is such a labour, it always surprises me that anyone can take the pains to go back over it all.'

'But a life such as yours – such fantastic scope! All the literary disciplines you've mastered, the people you've known – it would be a fascinating story.'

Harry waved a hand. 'My publishers have asked me, of course. But, d'you know, I don't much interest myself any more. I don't care to look back. I'm living on time which, if not exactly borrowed, is certainly fairly minutely proscribed. I haven't the health and strength to undertake an autobiography now. Anyway, I don't think I could bear to tell the truth about myself. I suspect that if ever I were to embark on such a project, I'd only finish up telling dreadful lies. I'm an inveterate liar. It must go with the territory of being a writer of fiction. Now you –' He smiled as he touched Adam's sleeve, '– as a journalist, you are accustomed to taking the objective view, the scrupulous view. I'm of the belief that a biography is far more likely to paint a thoroughly honest portrait of an individual than that individual ever would of themselves.'

'But a person writing about himself is in possession of every scrap of information – intimate details, recollections, unrecorded experiences. How could any biographer hope to better that?'

'Well, that's just it, you see. Which of us is prepared to tell the entire truth about ourselves? I should think the average autobiography is as likely to be an exercise in concealment, or at any rate careful dissimulation, as a full and frank revelation. A biographer, with adequate access to the people and materials relevant to a person's life, is far more likely to come up with a truthful and rounded picture of that life, wouldn't you say?' Harry reached out for the wine and extended the bottle towards Adam, who shook his head. Harry replenished his own glass.

'But it still finishes up being merely a point of view,' said Adam. 'No matter how many papers and letters and diaries a biographer has access to, no matter how many interviews he or she conducts, the end product is merely a distillation, surely. The essence of that individual, the true essence, their own voice, is always going to be lacking.'

Harry smiled. 'It's a subject that interests you, I can see. Would I suit you, as a subject? Would you care to write my life?'

Adam was a little taken aback. 'I didn't mean to be presumptuous –'

'You haven't presumed anything. I ask the question because, naturally, it's something that has preoccupied me of late. I'm dying, you see – pancreatic cancer, very difficult to treat –' He waved a thin hand in nonchalant acknowledgement. 'And naturally that predisposes me to concentrate on the business of living, for the moment. Setting false modesty aside, I'm aware that I'm a ripe subject for a biography. The vultures will start circling as soon as I drop.' He shifted uncomfortably in his chair. 'I don't care for the idea of my life being raked over, becoming the subject of speculation and lies. I think that's rather terrifying.'

'Why should it be? Why should any biography not be quite candid and fair?'

'Fair? Now that's an interesting word . . . fair. *Honest* might be more appropriate, wouldn't you think? Surely a good biographer wouldn't scruple to tell the truth about his subject, whatever he might discover?'

'Well . . . yes, naturally. But I think you have to have respect for your subject. Anyone who undertakes to write the life of another person must surely already have a certain admiration for them, or their work, to want to do it in the first place. I'm not talking about hagiography, necessarily, but when a person achieves success or distinction because of certain talents and abilities, or work they've accomplished, then it can't serve much purpose in chronicling the development of that person's life to expose all kinds of irrelevancies, merely because they happen to be salacious and good for publicity.'

Harry nodded thoughtfully. 'It's an interesting question, certainly, the nature of truth and its usefulness.'

Briony approached them. 'I'm sorry to disturb you both, but it's time for Harry's medication. I think you should come indoors for a little while, darling.'

Adam, taking his cue, stood up.

'I have enjoyed talking to you, Adam,' said Harry, as he, too, got slowly to his feet. 'We've touched upon a fascinating topic. You must leave your phone number with Briony. I'd like to discuss it with you some more.'

A fortnight later, Harry invited Adam Downing to lunch. The late-August air was still balmy, and they ate outside on the terrace, just the two of them. Harry told Adam that Briony was in London.

'A busy girl, my wife. She'd stay down here all the time, if I let her, but I insist she doesn't let her work drop. She's in great demand at the moment.' Adam murmured something that sounded like mild agreement. Harry paused and surveyed Adam's features with lazy pleasure. 'So, Adam, tell me all about yourself. Tell me about your family, where you went to school, that kind of thing.'

'My family? Well, not a great deal to tell there. My mother died when I was quite young. Eight. My father was a good deal older than she was, and he didn't quite know how to cope with me. So I was sent to boarding school – which I didn't much mind.' Adam ran his long fingers repeatedly over the edge of the wrought-iron table as he talked, his glance not touching Harry's. 'My father's business meant he spent a good deal of time in the States, so more often than not I went to my aunt and uncle in the holidays. My mother's sister. Very kind people.' He smiled. 'I think of them as my real family.'

'And your father?'

'My father . . .' Although Adam smiled in his customary gentle and deprecating manner, Harry could read the darkness in his eyes. 'I think my father tried to return to the life he'd led before he married my mother. It was what he knew best. I didn't really fit in – a small boy, somewhat lost, in need of something he wasn't sure how to give. I don't think he was very good with children. That is . . . I think he was waiting for me to turn into someone he could make sense of – an adult, I suppose. But by the time I did, it was too late. He died when I was in my first year at university. He was in the States at the time. Very sudden.' Adam frowned, fingers moving back and forth, back and forth on the table's edge. 'That was when I found out he'd remarried, about two or three years before. He hadn't told me. He simply hadn't told me – or my aunt and uncle. I don't know why.'

'So you suddenly found you had a stepmother?'

Adam looked mildly surprised. 'I never thought of her as that. I suppose she was. She just took the money and ran. I don't think about her. I don't think about him much, as a matter of fact.'

The silence stretched over long seconds.

Harry gazed reflectively at Adam, remembering his own choices in life as a young man, wondering what had set Adam on the path which had brought him here today. 'What made you become a journalist?' he asked.

'Something to do with English being my best subject at school, I imagine. I was always passionately fond of literature. I mean, I was happy enough as a boy, but I suppose I was – well, somewhat solitary. Reading has always been a passion. I thought I wanted to teach, had ideas of becoming a fellow, staying at Oxford, but I'd already begun to write the odd review, articles here and there . . . I sort of slipped into journalism, and I've stayed there.'

'Being a freelance is quite a lonely occupation. Don't you mind that?'

'No. No, I enjoy solitude. I like my own thoughts, my own company. I've been on the staff of a couple of big dailies, had quite enough of working for large organizations. The way I work now suits me very well. I've always wanted to be a writer, and I suppose I thought going freelance would give me more time to work on something of my own. But it hasn't quite happened that way. I'm too busy. That's the trouble with journalism. No end to writing.' Adam laughed. 'Not that I should complain.'

'No, indeed. I see your name everywhere.' Brenda, the middle-aged woman who acted as Harry's nurse and housekeeper, appeared bearing a large tray, which she set down on the table.

They talked on over lunch. Afterwards, as the afternoon grew cooler, they moved indoors to the morning room to have coffee. It was a room of battered grandeur, reminiscent of a London club, comfortably furnished in a masculine style. It was here that Harry did his writing, working at a large desk which stood in one corner, surrounded by ceiling-high bookcases. They sat in large armchairs, Harry with a tartan rug over his thin legs, feet resting on a leather footstool.

'I wonder,' said Harry, stirring his coffee, 'whether I couldn't be instrumental in helping you to achieve your ambition of becoming a writer.' He looked up at Adam and smiled.

Adam returned the smile hesitantly. 'I don't quite understand.'

'I was serious when I said I wanted someone to write my biography, to begin it while I am still alive. Someone of my own choosing. I should like some control over my reputation's destiny. Is that conceited, do you think?'

Adam paused before replying. 'I don't think so – no more so than putting the rest of one's affairs in order before the end of one's life.' He felt a tingle of apprehension.

'How very well you put it.'

'Given the way that unauthorized biographers tend to plunder the lives of famous people after their deaths, I should think it would be regarded as quite a prudent action.'

'Prudent, yes. I feel that.' Harry glanced at Adam. 'What d'you say? Think you're up to the task?'

'You want me to write it?' Adam felt a thrill of excitement, then laughed. 'It's very flattering, but you don't really know me very well, to entrust me with something like that.'

'Think of it as professional rather than personal, Adam. We have talked. I know you well enough to think we could work together for such time as I have left. And thereafter –' Harry lifted his hand, then let it fall. 'I feel pretty sure you would finish the job admirably. I've read a good deal of your work over the past week or so. I like your style. I think you're acute, intelligent, reflective. And you seem to have an understanding of my work that is almost scholarly, if you don't mind my saying so.'

'Well, look, if you're serious –'

'Never more so. I think you would make an excellent biographer.'

'I've never written a full-length book before.'

Harry spread his hands. 'You're a journalist. My life just happens to be a longer story than most that you write. I would give you full access to my papers, my diaries, such as they are, my correspondence. And, of course, you would have the fullest cooperation of my friends and family. Without that, I don't think any biographer would get very far. If you accept the commission, it would be understood among my circle that there should be no contact or cooperation, after my death, with anyone else attempting to write about me. Only you.'

Ring-fencing, thought Adam. He wants to protect his territory. Why me?

'You look doubtful,' said Harry.

'No,' said Adam with a start. 'Not at all. I was thinking. I'm just . . . astonished. And –' Grateful? Yes, bloody grateful. The biography of Harry Day would have to be worth a six-figure advance from a publisher. Apart from that, it would add a new dimension to his career. Being a freelance was fine, but it could be a shaky existence. The money this would bring in would be invaluable, to say nothing of establishing his reputation for future similar projects. If he could bring this off . . . Yes, he believed he could. A rush of excitement shook him. A life like Harry's was a gift. The man had done so much, known so many people. It was bound to sell well. '– and grateful,' finished Adam. 'That you should ask me.'

'It'll write itself,' said Harry. 'All I have to do is tell you what happened.'

Adam nodded. What could be simpler? It wasn't as though he was going to have to trawl around, picking up a cold trail, researching. Harry was still alive and kicking, and what greater help could a biographer have than that of his subject? Yet he had to ask the question. 'Why me? Why not one of your old friends, someone like Francis Cleverley, for instance?'

'Because . . . because I don't want this book to be written for all the old bores who knew me, knew those times. I want it to come from someone with a different perspective, someone who might find it all genuinely intriguing.'

'When do we start?'

'As soon as possible. I don't have a great deal of time left. Better make the most of me while you've got me.'

At that moment the door opened and a girl came in. Even dressed in combat trousers, boots and a sweatshirt, she was ethereally pretty. Adam recognized her instantly as Harry's daughter, Bella Day, a twenty-something actress who had made a name for herself in a recent British gangster film, which had enjoyed unexpected success in the UK and the States. Adam, schooled from an early age in old-fashioned courtesies, rose from his chair. Bella gave him an amused glance, and crossed the room to her father.

'I'm off now, Daddy. I've got a hectic weekend ahead.'

Harry stroked her hand and gestured in Adam's direction. 'Bella, I'd like you to meet Adam Downing. He's a journalist, and he's going to be working on my biography. Adam, this is my daughter Bella.'

'Really?' She shook Adam's hand and surveyed him with mild curiosity. Adam couldn't tell from her expression whether she approved of the notion or not.

'So in due course he'll want to spend some time talking to you and Charlie about your blighted existence with me.'

Bella smiled at her father. 'Blighted's the word.' Her attention had switched entirely away from Adam. 'Are you going to be all right till Briony gets back?'

'Of course. Brenda sees to everything. Briony will be back the day after tomorrow.'

'Right.' Bella slipped on her denim jacket, pulling her curling blonde hair free from the collar. 'I'll be off. I'll ring you next week.' She bent and kissed the top of his head.

She didn't glance at Adam or say goodbye.

When she had gone, Adam sat down. 'She is quite amazingly beautiful,' he said, unable to help himself.

Harry smiled, evidently pleased. 'Isn't she? I feel she's going to be a tremendous success as an actress. I hope so, at any rate. I should like to be around to see it, but there . . .' He rearranged the rug across his spindly knees. 'Now, what were we discussing?'

And they began once more to talk about Harry and his life.

That evening Adam put a bottle of champagne in the fridge with which to celebrate when he told Megan the news. Then he began to prepare supper. Fridays had turned into a kind of ritual now. Either they went out with friends to a wine bar and then a restaurant, or else Adam cooked, he and Megan ate, then they talked or watched television for a while, went to bed, made love. The rest of the weekend they spent together, mostly – seeing friends, going out, idling in bed with the papers . . . He had slipped into this couple business without really noticing at first. So much of the relationship had happened that way. It was restful, easy, like Megan herself. They had been living together for four months now, having met two years ago at a media event which Adam had been covering, sponsored by a car magazine. Megan worked for the PR company which had set up the event. He had seen her across the room and liked her instantly. She reminded him of some kind of woodland creature – a squirrel, or chipmunk, one of those anthropomorphic female Disney animals. She had soft, dark hair falling to her shoulders, big, bright eyes, and a small, sensual body. She drove a snappy VW, she was trendy, vivacious, and possessed the kind of up-to-date, superficial understanding of books, plays, people, films and events which passed for intelligence. At thirty-one, she was older than she looked, something which she worried about more than she would ever have admitted to Adam.

The business of living together had seemed a logical

extension of going out with someone for two years, but Adam was still finding it hard to get used to. Until Megan, girlfriends had always been largely peripheral. Now there were days – days when he had a great deal of reading to do, or was working on a difficult piece – when he would look back longingly on the quiet, connected days of complete solitude which had characterized his bachelor life. Having to consider another person, to take account of them in the evenings, allow their time and troubles to overlap your own, made extended periods of concentration difficult. But one adapted. One always adapted. Most of the time it was more fun to have another person around, someone with whom to share domestic trivia, as well as more momentous events, such as the Harry Day coup.

Megan came in, kicked off her shoes, and was immediately and enthusiastically embraced by Adam.

'What?' she asked, leaning back in his arms and trying to read his face. 'Tell me.'

When Adam told her his news, she tried to seem as pleased as he evidently was. Despite her degree in media studies, Megan's grasp of literary matters was tenuous. She rarely opened, let alone read, the review copies of books which Adam occasionally passed on to her, preferring the lighter pleasures of the pretty pastel chick-lit paperbacks which she picked up at W H Smith's or from girlfriends. Although Harry Day's name resonated in her consciousness in the same way as, say, that of Ted Hughes or William Golding – literary giants who had straddled both her own and her parents' generations, but who seemed to have more to do with theirs, really, and had been a bit of a yawn at GCSE – the momentous importance of Adam's news was somewhat lost on her.

She stood in the kitchen, listening as Adam expanded on the topic of Harry Day, his iconic status, the immense significance of being asked to write the life of someone about whom no one had ever written at length before.

'Why you?' she asked, picking bits out of the green salad as he took the champagne from the fridge and popped it.

'I don't honestly know.' He handed Megan a glass. 'Well, that is – he said he'd read some of my pieces and liked them.'

'Even so.'

'He also seems to have some idea that having a young biographer might help. So that he won't just be relegated to the old-literary-fart department.'

'I don't see what difference it makes. Anyway –' Megan realized that now wasn't perhaps the right moment for a questing analysis of Harry Day's motives. She raised her glass and grinned. 'Here's to Harry Day, and his life's story. Congratulations.'

'Thank you,' said Adam. 'It's going to make a bit of difference on the money front, I can tell you. Let's go through.' He took the bottle and they went through to the living room and settled on the sofa.

'How much?'

'I haven't spoken to Giles yet, but we have to be talking six figures.'

'Adam! That much?' Suddenly Adam's news took on significance.

He nodded, gave a smile of satisfaction and propped

his feet up on the coffee table. It was most pleasant to be reappraising his immense good fortune by discussing it cosily with Megan. 'I should get a quarter of it up front. Of course, we'll have to find a publisher first, but something tells me that won't be difficult.'

'I am *so* pleased for you, clever man.' Megan snuggled against him.

'It's a fantastic opportunity,' said Adam, returning to his theme. 'If this is a success, I can stop reviewing other people's books and write my own. No more crawling to commissioning editors, chasing money month after month.' He leaned his head back and sighed. 'I can start doing the kind of work I've always wanted to. It's time that's the problem, see – buying time. When you're a freelance, you're always after the next piece of work, you're never able to devote yourself to anything that takes sustained effort, like a novel, say, or a play. If I can pull this off, then it'll earn me enough to be able to do anything I want.' He stared at the ceiling, his mind drifting. 'I could write a life of Baudelaire. I'd really, really like to write a life of Baudelaire. Just think of having enough time to go off, do the research, read the books. No more deadlines, no more anxiety . . .'

'We could put down a deposit on a house.'

House? What was wrong with the flat? He'd lived here for six years and had no particular wish to move elsewhere. Baron's Court had much of the convenience of Fulham and Chelsea, without being as expensive. Being a freelance journalist was often a solitary occupation, and Adam liked being able to emerge from his isolation and wander the familiar streets. He knew the shopkeepers and the restaurant owners, and enjoyed the sense of community.

He drained his glass slowly, then nodded non-committally. 'I'd better get the commission first.'

'So, what happens? When do you start?' asked Megan.

'I'm going to speak to Giles over the weekend. As I said, I don't think finding a publisher will be a problem, since the project has the blessing of Harry himself. Then,' Adam shrugged, 'it's a question of spending time with Harry, talking to him and his family and friends, going through papers, letting the thing take shape. Harry seems to have fairly clear ideas about how the book should develop.'

'Then I don't understand why he isn't busy writing his autobiography.'

'He's very ill. In fact, he's dying.' Adam's voice was reflective. 'From what I can gather, he hasn't got much more than a year left. A task like that would be too much for him. This way, he's allowed a certain amount of input. He also knows the thing will get finished after he dies.'

'Sounds a bit controlling to me, as though he's just going to tell you what to write. Don't you mind that?'

Adam was not prepared to acknowledge that he was too grateful for this rare opportunity to start cavilling about lack of artistic freedom. 'I'm sure it won't be anything like that. I'm lucky to have his help.' Adam drained his glass and rose from the sofa. 'I'm going to start supper.'

Megan stayed where she was, sipping her drink, thinking happily about what a difference the money would make. They might even be able to think about getting married.

Giles Hamblin, Adam's agent, was delighted when he heard Adam's news. It was generally known that Harry Day was on his last legs, and Giles knew of several people who had tentative ideas about a biography, ready to cash in as soon as the old boy kicked it. Adam was going to pre-empt them all. When the word got out that family and friends were talking to no one but Adam, the others would just fade into the woodwork.

He set about putting together a deal with a leading publisher, carefully keeping Adam's rights to serialization, and by the end of the month, when he signed the contract, Adam received fifty thousand pounds, a quarter of his advance, the largest sum he had ever put into his bank account. The sense of freedom and elation it gave him to bank the cheque was very pleasant. Not that he was going to live off that alone. No, he would continue with his reviews and arts features, depending on how much time the biography permitted.

Adam spent much of the next two months in Harry's company. On a number of occasions he spent several successive days at Gandercleugh, sleeping in one of the guest bedrooms, spending long days in the morning room with Harry, breaking for lunch or for Harry's medication and rest. He made many, many tapes of their conversations, going back through Harry's childhood, his time spent in National Service, his career as a young poet, his post-war theatrical successes, his heady years as a celebrity playwright in the swinging sixties, his first marriage, the birth of his children, the divorce, his spiritual journey to India, the novels, the drugs, the spell in prison, his second marriage, his return to poetry, the reflective later years . . . It was all beautifully chronicled, embellished with wonderful anecdotes and reminiscences. All Adam had to do was fashion it into a third-person narrative.

Briony was not always there – her work took her up to London for long spells – but when she was she would occasionally join them, her chair next to Harry's, his hand clasped in one of her own, and help out with accounts of events since their marriage. She was the fondest, tenderest, most devoted of wives, it seemed to Adam. But at times when he sought to draw her out on her own, when Harry was resting, she would generally make some excuse to keep the conversation short. Adam got the impression that, although she was more than happy to help out where Harry was concerned, she didn't care to reveal too much about herself. For all the warmth and ease of her manner, there was, when they were alone together, a distinct reserve.

The rest of the time Adam spent in London, working his way through a long list of people drawn up by Harry, who had all known him at different times in his life and had an engaging range of recollections and stories. The material was abundant. Adam had no time to go off at any tangent of his own, even if he'd wanted to.

In early December Harry became briefly too unwell to continue with the collaboration, and Adam took the opportunity to try to pull the material together, going through the various interviews which he had transcribed from tape to computer. Megan was away for a few days, and he welcomed the uninterrupted solitude as a chance to get a proper overview of the material he had gathered so far.

It was a laborious task. When he had finished, he knew he should have been pleased with what had been accomplished so far, but instead he felt an odd sense of dissatisfaction. Something about the biography thus far wasn't quite right, but he couldn't put his finger on it. He thought about it for some time, going on one of his habitual long walks around the local streets and parks. The truth was, nothing so far gave any new insights into Harry Day. Apart from Harry's own recollections of his childhood, Adam was aware that everything, every fact, every anecdote, every name and every face, had featured somewhere previously. Much had been written about Harry during his lifetime. This biography, apart from re-hashing that, should cast new and fascinating light on its subject. It didn't. So far, he wasn't telling anyone anything that hadn't been told before.

He decided to speak to Giles about it. They met for a drink at a riverside pub near Giles's office in Hammersmith. Giles was some twenty-five years older than Adam, and an ex-journalist. As Adam's agent, he had naturally been ecstatic at Adam's good fortune in securing the chance to write Harry Day's biography, particularly since he would be creaming off a healthy ten per cent, but he had always had certain reservations about Adam's sense of independence in the matter. It seemed to Giles that Adam was too enthusiastically admiring of Harry, too prepared to take the old man's word as gospel, to try to delve deeper and find those little hidden pockets of dirt which made a person's life interesting. He listened to Adam's misgivings, and said as much.

'Well, where is there to go?' Adam spread his hands. 'I've only got what Harry's told me. None of his friends and acquaintances have come up with any dark secrets or interesting aspects of his past. They all think Harry's a wonderful guy. Fine, he's had some run-ins with the odd theatre director or critic, but nothing electrifying. Above all, nothing new.'

'What about his family?'

'Apart from Briony, his wife, I haven't got round to them yet. I've been too busy making the most of what time Harry has left. Besides,' Adam lifted his beer and took a sip, 'I should think they'd be the last people to start dishing the dirt. If there is any, that is.'

'What about his first wife, Cecile Patterson? You might unearth something interesting there.'

'I doubt it,' sighed Adam. 'According to Harry, they're the best of friends. She even gets on with Briony. All is sweetness and light. Maybe it's the truth. Maybe I just have to accept that he's a genial old man of letters who, apart from being busted for drugs and once landing one on the literary editor of the *New Statesman* at a drinks party, led an average life. Christ, what am I saying? Everything he's done, everything he's ever been, should be interesting enough. But somehow it's not.'

'Because everyone knows it all.'

'Quite.'

'How is he, by the way?'

'Harry? Improving slightly. I rang Briony yesterday. If

he's better next week, I'll go back to Gandercleugh and pick up where we left off. But it's just a matter of weeks now, I suspect.'

'Well,' said Giles thoughtfully, 'maybe the real problem is the fact that Harry's still around. It's something of a constraint, you know. Not just on the people who know him, but on you. You naturally feel reluctant to go to work properly.'

'Properly?'

'As you said, what you've got so far is superficiality. It's a life, but it's the life he wants you and the world to know about.'

'But what if there isn't anything else? What if what you see is what you get? Anyway, I'm not deliberately aiming to unearth anything discreditable. That's not what I mean. I just –' He broke off, uncertain, exasperated.

'Adam, you're a journalist, a would-be biographer. It's your job to dig deep, to investigate, use your instincts, follow up hunches. You're writing about someone who's lived on the planet for over seventy years. You want this biography to be more than a lengthy publisher's blurb. You have to go to work.'

'Giles, what d'you think I've been doing for the past two months?' He sighed. 'Perhaps it's me, the way I'm approaching it. Maybe I should make it more literary – what d'you think? Go more extensively into his work, and the way it reflects his life. I mean, I do that to a certain extent, but perhaps I should make it more academic –'

'Adam, don't be such a bloody Cambridge graduate. Be more forensic. We're talking about a human being here, warts and all.' Giles finished his beer. 'Just give it time. Harry's too substantial a presence right now. He's dominating what you do. Wait until he's a ghost. That's my advice.'

Two weeks later, a ghost was what Harry Day became. Nothing remained of him except a jar of ashes, volumes of assorted poetry, plays and novels, a circle of grieving relatives and friends, three fulsome broadsheet obituaries, and a drawerful of tapes and notes in Adam's flat.

2

The memorial service for Harry took place the following May, at the Actors' Church in Covent Garden. Adam went, naturally. He already knew many of the faces from the work he had done so far on the biography, and could have chatted to any number of them, but Adam was not the mingling type. He preferred to sit at the back of the church on his own, observing.

When the church was buzzing and full, and it appeared that proceedings might shortly commence, Bella hurried in through the door at the back. God, late for her father's own memorial service, she thought. She could see members of her family up at the front, and was about to head down the aisle to join them when she noticed Adam, sitting alone. She hadn't seen him since the funeral, when they had exchanged only a few words. She hesitated, then slid into the pew next to him.

He glanced at her in surprise.

'You don't mind if I sit here, do you?' asked Bella, with a tentative smile.

'Of course not,' replied Adam.

They sat together in silence for some seconds. Adam wasn't certain how to open the conversation, or even if they were meant to have one. Then Bella spoke, eyes fixed ahead, voice low. 'I didn't really want to come to this, you know. I didn't want to go to the funeral, either. I just hate death, all the mournfulness.'

'This shouldn't be too bad,' said Adam. 'It's meant to be a celebration of your father's life. Or so it says here.' He lifted the order of service which he'd been handed on entering the church.

'I suppose so. Anyway, I'm meant to be reading something, so I have to be here.'

Apart from their brief meetings at Gandercleugh and at Harry's funeral in December, Adam had only ever seen Bella's face in photographs in magazines. Now, sitting next to her, he was enjoying the reality of her beauty, particularly the tiny flaws, which somehow enhanced the delicacy of her face and rendered more vulnerable the large grey eyes and childlike mouth.

She glanced around the church and sighed. 'Christ, I could kill for a cigarette.' Then she turned to him, giving Adam a considering look. It was like being bathed in the radiance of some gentle light, thought Adam. She really was lovely, like an elegant urchin, with that luminous skin and ragged blonde hair. 'I still think it was weird, Dad asking you to write about his life. I mean, I don't mean to be rude, but he would have been better off doing it himself. Don't you think?'

'He left it too late. He knew he'd never finish it.' Adam was silent for a moment, then added, 'When we first met, I asked him why he didn't write his own autobiography, and he said, "Because I couldn't bear to tell the truth about myself."'

Bella smiled. It took long seconds for the smile to die away. Adam watched her mouth, fascinated. She looked at him again. 'Why d'you think he asked you, in particular?'

'Oh, I don't know . . .'

'I mean, you're very young.'

'Am I? Is thirty-three young?'

'I should hope so. I'm twenty-nine. God, is this thing ever going to start?' She tapped her bag impatiently. Adam glanced down at her hands, at the polished oval nails, the slender fingers.

'I think he asked me because I'm a good listener. Because we got on well. And because – well, maybe you're right. Because I'm young. I think he found it reassuring.'

'Not having to look death in the eye, you mean.'

'Not straight in the eye, no.' Adam smiled. 'I think he thought, too, that I wouldn't judge him, or his life. That I'd just write it.'

'Was he right?' He felt the touch of her glance again, lingering, appraising him.

'I'm not sure.'

'What do you mean?'

'Well, I still don't know enough. There's everything he told me, of course. I've interviewed an endless number of people. But I still don't know everyone else's side of things.' He gestured vaguely around the assembled members of the service of thanksgiving for the life of Harry McCardle Wentworth Day. 'Ideally I'd like to hear everyone's version of events. I have this theory that the voices which are still alive and talking at the end of someone's life don't tell the whole story. The ones that have fallen silent along the way, the people from forgotten parts of a person's past – they tell another kind of truth. If you can track them down.'

Bella was about to say something when a hush fell in the church. Bella and Adam glanced up. A portly, tall man with a trim grey beard and a flamboyant waistcoat beneath a red velvet jacket stepped forward to the front of the gathering. He welcomed everyone, and embarked upon a neat, amusing résumé of the life of the deceased, finishing with a reminder that 'Harry would want this to be a day of laughter and irreverence, and not of melancholy reflection.'

'Who *is* that?' whispered Adam to Bella.

She leaned close to catch his words, and he drew his breath to take in the scent of her.

'Andrew Nugent, my stepmother's brother. He's on the radio a lot.'

Adam thought the voice was familiar. He sat back and watched as the proceedings unfolded. He had never been to a memorial service before. A variety of well-known guests, writers and actors paid tributes to Harry. There were amusing anecdotes and recollections, readings from his novels and poetry, and an extract, read by one of Harry's rock celebrity friends, from one of his *Rox* columns recounting a hilarious, stoned two days at Glastonbury. Bella read, both amusingly and touchingly, a letter written to her by her father in her teens while he was in Brixton prison. Two of Harry's favourite rock songs were played – 'Bat Out Of Hell' and Neil Young's nine-minute-long 'Ambulance Blues'. A nervous ten-year-old great-nephew read one of his comic poems, and after an hour and a quarter, to the strains of 'Hey Jude', people made their way out of the Actors' Church into the flagged churchyard and the mild May afternoon.

Bella and Adam drifted apart, Adam to talk to fellow journalists, Bella to members of her family. Adam glanced in her direction several times, and once found her looking at him. When their eyes met, it gave him a wonderful jolt. He hadn't had a crush like this in a long time. Hopeless, of course. But sometimes, the more hopeless the better. Something that needn't interfere with real life, just repose idly in one's dreams.

Bella eyed Adam again surreptitiously. He hadn't made much of an impression on her at their first meeting, except for his ultra-good manners, but seeing him again today, she was intrigued. What struck her most was his gentle diffidence. She could read most men's eyes and find the same predictable things there most of the time – that came with being well known – but Adam Downing was quite inscrutable. Except for his smile, which was sweet and warm. Charming. That's what he was. Charming, but not in the up-front, look-at-me way she was used to. He was like a very polite, grown-up schoolboy. And he was, in a tweedy kind of way, bloody gorgeous. Uh-oh. Here she was, doing it again. Why couldn't she just meet people, and like them, without always wanting to seduce them?

She crossed the churchyard. 'Are you coming with the rest of us to Gandercleugh?' she asked Adam.

'I haven't been invited.'

'I'm inviting you. It's family and old friends, but as you're Harry's biographer, you should be there.'

'I rather think that if she'd wanted me there, Briony would have asked me,' said Adam diplomatically.

'What's it got to do with Briony?'

'Well, she's Harry's widow . . .'

'I'm Harry's daughter.' Bella regarded him for a few seconds, wondering what he was thinking. 'Don't you want to come? I'd have thought it would be invaluable to you, seeing the family all together. Give you marvellous insights, a chance to schmooze up to one or two and get them talking.'

'I don't like the idea of being an unwelcome intruder.'

'Some journalist!'

'On top of that, I don't much feel like driving all the way to Suffolk and back in a day.'

'Stay the night. You've done it plenty of times before.'

'Absolutely not. I mean, thanks, but no. If I want to keep in with your stepmother, this is not the right way to go about it.'

'Well, there's a hotel in the village you can stay at.'

There was a delicious pleasure to be had in arguing on such a familiar level with this gorgeous creature. 'Why do you want me to come?' Adam asked.

She looked surprised. 'I thought it might be of help to you.' She could tell that he was wavering. 'Don't worry. If you come as my guest, Briony won't utter a murmur. We have a most harmonious stepmother-and-daughter relationship. Besides, you'd be doing me a favour. My car's in dock at the moment, and if you take me, then I won't have to go with my brother Charlie and his fiancée. She is a total pain.'

'You just want a lift, in fact.'

'Not at all. It's a mutually advantageous arrangement. You get to meet the assembled family at close quarters, and I don't have to listen to Claire banging on about her wedding.'

A two-hour drive to Suffolk, just himself and Bella.

'All right. What's this hotel like?'

'Bog standard. You know, coaching inn turned Trust House Forte.'

'I'll have to pick up one or two things first.'

'Fine. I'll tell Charlie.' She swept away to speak to her brother. Adam glanced over with curiosity at Charlie. He had seen photographs of Bella and her twin brother in Harry's study at Gandercleugh, and found it hard to reconcile the son to the father. Charlie was fair, like Bella, but unlike either Bella or Harry he was big – tall and broad. He looked bulky and prosperous in his pin-striped suit, every inch the barrister, with that ruddy, buffed-up, peculiarly English handsomeness. Adam could picture him as he must have been at eighteen, a roaring prop forward in the school's First XV, and the man he would be thirty years from now. He had the air of one bred to warm his arse at drawing-room fires, and to condescend to women as a means of getting them to sleep with him.

The girl standing with Charlie had to be Claire. Adam could tell because she had her arm through his. Why did it look so silly, so proprietorial? Claire was tall, a drawn-out beauty with a narrow face and lazy-lidded eyes which made her look bored. Maybe she was. I mustn't be determined to dislike her, just because Bella does, thought Adam.

As Bella talked to her brother, Adam saw Charlie's eyes flicker in his direction. Eyes just like Bella's, but with an expression that was flat and hostile, quite unlike the warmth and curiosity of Bella's. Adam glanced away. He guessed that any information concerning Harry Day the father would be more likely to come from Bella than from Charlie.

Bella came back. 'That's all settled.'

'I have to go home and get my car and things. Where shall I pick you up?'

Bella scribbled the address down on a piece of paper. Beaufort Street, Chelsea. Of course. Adam smiled. 'I'll pick you up in an hour.'

Cecile Patterson, Harry's first wife and the mother of Bella and Charlie, stood near the church entrance, watching Bella talking to Adam. She was tall, with a serene, patrician air. Though she was now in her sixties, the evidence of her former beauty was still clear in her fine bones and deep-set eyes. She was elegantly dressed in a linen coat and high heels, a long silk scarf at her throat, and her grey hair was stylishly cut. She turned to Briony, who was standing next to her, smiling and murmuring at guests as they passed. Both wives had agreed that a united and friendly front was the best PR strategy. Briony had come into Harry's life rather late, only ten years ago, and Cecile in no way regarded her as a usurper. If anything, she had been relieved that Harry had remarried before old age could throw back on her the possibility of responsibility for him. Both women had a strong regard for one another. Being involved with Harry and his life was a complex and taxing business.

'Who's the young man talking to Bella?'

Briony glanced across. 'That's Adam Downing. Haven't you met him?'

'No. Should I have?'

Briony gave Cecile a meaningful look. 'He's Harry's biographer.'

'My God.' She stared at Briony. 'I didn't know Harry had one. When did this come about?'

'I thought Harry might have told you. He took him on last autumn. Harry had this idea that if he got in first, with the biographer of his choosing, then it would forestall muck-rakers. A preventative measure, if you like.'

'Well, there's something to be said for that . . .' Cecile fingered the scarf at her throat, gazing at Adam. 'Downing, Adam Downing – I think I know the name.'

'He's a journalist. He does literary stuff, and the odd feature here and there. You'll have seen his pieces.'

'But why him in particular?'

'Harry took a fancy to him.' Briony's eyes met Cecile's. 'And he seemed to feel that young Mr Downing was just the thing – high-minded, scrupulous, a little naive, and, of course, an ardent fan of Harry's work. Someone who would do exactly as Harry told him.'

'That,' said Cecile, nodding, 'is just what is wanted. But he is a journalist, when all's said and done. And Harry's not around now to tell him what to do.'

Briony shrugged. 'Harry's steered him on a certain course, and I think he'll stay on it. Much of the work must already have been done over the months before Harry died. Anyway, he's not that kind of journalist. He doesn't seem endowed with much investigative curiosity.'

Cecile pondered this, then said with mild disgruntlement, 'Well, if he's writing about Harry, one would have thought he'd have been in touch with *me* by now.'

'I gather he's been leaving the family till last. Expect a phone call any day.'

'At least I'm prepared.'

'Now, you're sure you won't reconsider and come to Gandercleugh this afternoon? Lots of old friends will be there.'

Cecile shook her head. 'Kind of you, but I think I've seen enough faces from the past for one day.'

Adam went back to Baron's Court, packed a few things in an overnight bag, hastily finished off and faxed a piece which he'd promised to file with a magazine by the evening, and set off on the short drive to Chelsea.

Bella was on the phone when he arrived. She opened the door, cigarette in one hand, phone to her ear, and waved him in, pointing in the direction of the kitchen. Adam went obediently through. The kitchen was roomy and cheerful, and overlooked a long garden. Adam stood looking out, waiting for Bella to finish her phone call, which was mildly argumentative in tone and appeared to be about clothing and dates.

'Right,' said Bella, when she had put the phone down. 'I'll get my bag.'

They set off in Adam's Fiat. Adam had decided to maintain the driver's prerogative of preoccupied silence, requiring Bella to initiate conversation. But for half an hour or so she seemed quite happy to stare at the traffic, lost in her own thoughts.

By the time they reached the M11, just as Adam decided he couldn't face the prospect of an utterly silent journey and was about to speak, Bella sighed and said, 'It is *so* wonderful to go on a car journey with someone who doesn't insist on making conversation all the time, I can't tell you.'

Adam was bemused. The remark seemed to deserve some kind of a reply, but in itself suggested she would prefer him to remain silent. Steering a middle course, he asked, 'Would you like some music?'

'Yes, that's a nice idea. Let's see what you've got.' She fished through his CDs for a few moments, and then put on Fauré's Requiem.

'Do you mind if I smoke?' she asked.

'Yes,' said Adam.

Bella leaned back in her seat and closed her eyes. Because Adam wasn't sure whether she was asleep or just sulking, he didn't like to say anything more. So much, he thought, for the warmth and intimacy which two people could develop during a two-hour car journey.

Twilight was gathering by the time they reached Budleigh, the village which lay a mile away from Gandercleugh. Adam drove slowly down the High Street. Bella opened her eyes.

'Whereabouts is this hotel?' he asked.

'At the end of the High Street.' Bella wriggled upright in her seat. She pointed. 'There.'

Adam parked the car outside the hotel and went in.

A moment later, he came back to the car. 'They haven't got a room. Mid May, and they're fully booked.'

Bella yawned. 'It's not a very big hotel. I suppose most of the guests decided to stay over. Don't worry. I told you, Briony will put you up.'

Adam said nothing. He didn't really relish turning up

uninvited in the first place, and certainly not to beg a bed for the night. He and Briony got on well enough, but . . . He tapped the wheel. 'I don't suppose there's another hotel in the area?'

'Not for miles,' said Bella.

Adam sighed and started the car.

'Stop worrying so much about Briony,' said Bella. 'She's not worth it.'

'You sound as though you have mixed feelings about your stepmother.'

'Not really. I just meant that she's not as likely to make a fuss as you seem to imagine. I think Briony's a good thing, generally. Charlie and I were grown up and had left home by the time Daddy married her, so she hasn't had a great deal to do with us. But she made him happy, so . . .' Bella shrugged.

'I'm surprised your mother never remarried. She's a very attractive woman.'

'She was pretty much taken up with us when we were little. I don't remember her going out with men, not then. I know she had a couple of relationships while we were at boarding school. Friendships? Affairs? Children don't know, do they? There was one man she was seeing for several months . . . we met him one half-term, I remember. Alistair something. He looked like a possibility. Charlie and I even discussed what would happen if she married him, but he disappeared from the scene, and she never mentioned him afterwards. She's always been very busy with work, has a good social life. She seems pretty much content as she is. I get the impression that one marriage was probably enough for her.' She leaned forward a little as they came in sight of the stone gateway. 'Here we are.'

Adam drove up the familiar driveway to Gandercleugh, then turned his car round so that he was parked facing the road, ready for a quick getaway. Despite Bella's airy assurances, he had his doubts about being made welcome by Briony. He had spoken to her only twice since Harry's death, in relation to some letters, and her manner, though polite, had hardly been cordial.

Adam followed Bella into the house, and at that moment Briony came out of the drawing room. She glanced in surprise at Adam.

Bella, taking off her coat, leaned forward to kiss her stepmother briefly. 'Briony, you know Adam Downing, don't you? He drove me here.'

'Hello, Adam. This is a pleasant surprise.' Her expression was only moderately warm.

'Adam was going to stay at the hotel in the village, but it's fully booked. We can find a bed for him for the night, can't we?'

'Oh, I imagine so. Come through – everyone's in the drawing room.' Briony led the way, adding, 'It's just family and *very* old friends.' Adam decided this was probably a reproach, though he wasn't entirely sure.

When he had secured a drink, Adam wandered to one side of the room and watched his hostess doing her stuff, vintage Briony Nugent. Given the circumstances and the nature of the gathering, she had had to dampen down her famous sparkle to a sorrowful shimmer, but she none the less exuded remarkable charm. Her guests adored her. Warmth and sincerity clung to her like perfume. What

Adam admired most, he decided, was the way she kept the deceased Harry to the forefront of the proceedings, even though she knew she was the star. It was a remarkable performance.

Adam had met most of Harry's old friends before, but there were one or two new faces. He chatted and made arrangements to speak to them at greater length. All this time he was aware of Bella's presence in the room. She acted like a gentle magnet, drawing his eyes back to her time and again, suffusing him with the giddy pleasure of infatuation. It was, he knew, immensely disloyal to Megan to feel like this. Not that it counted. It was rather like having a crush on Julia Roberts, or someone similarly out of his league.

Bella came over. 'I noticed you working the room. Was everybody nice to you?'

'Mmm. People like talking about Harry.'

'About themselves, you mean. Still, I suppose it amounts to the same thing.'

'Will you be able to make time to talk to me about your father over the next few weeks, d'you think?'

'If you can pin me down. I've got a new play opening soon, and I'll be pretty busy with rehearsals. You've got my number – give me a ring.'

Adam nodded in the direction of Charlie. 'What about your brother?'

She glanced across. 'Why don't you ask him? He's had a fair bit to drink, so maybe now's as good a time as any. Have you spoken to my mother?'

'Not yet. I'll have to get in touch with her soon. She and your father seem to have remained on very good terms after they split up.'

'Oh, immensely civilized, that's my family. Good at keeping up appearances.'

'Right,' said Adam, who realized he was becoming somewhat too fascinated by the delightful contours of Bella's upper lip. 'It's getting late, so I'd better start trying to make some headway with Charlie.'

Charlie was talking to relatives. They were all sitting down, Charlie standing up. He looked as though he was enjoying himself, performing for his elders. Adam could imagine him in court, the same confident, assertive, rather overbearing figure. He waited for a lull in the conversation, then introduced himself.

'I'm Adam Downing.' He put out his hand and Charlie shook it.

'Bella's friend?'

'Well, more your father's friend. Bella and I have only met a couple of times.'

Charlie frowned. 'Downing, Downing . . . Did you know my father very well?'

Adam would have liked to kick him. 'Yes. I was working on his biography when he died, as a matter of fact.'

'Not quite the same thing, you know.'

'With him. We were working together.'

'Ah.'

'It's something he very much wanted me to complete –'

'I take it this was authorized?'

'I have his notes. Tapes. I can assure you, your father was fully cooperative. It was his idea.'

Charlie nodded, then glanced suspiciously at Adam. 'And?'

'And I would very much like to talk to you about your father at some point. If you can find the time. I'm sure you could make a valuable contribution to the book.'

Charlie reflected for a few seconds and then said, 'I don't see why not.' He took a hefty swig of his drink and smiled. The charm of his smile was quite transforming. He looked very like Bella, only big and masculine. 'I take it Bella is happy with this?'

'Yes. She seems very willing to help.'

'Mm. And my mother?'

'I haven't spoken to her yet. I intend to. Of course, I have to rely heavily on your family's goodwill. When your father was alive –'

'Yes, yes, I can see your problem.' Charlie studied Adam quite candidly for a few long seconds. Then he fished inside his jacket pocket for a card and handed it to Adam. 'Give me a ring in chambers.'

'Thank you.' Adam pocketed the card.

Charlie nodded. Adam nodded in reply, and they parted.

By ten-thirty, Adam reckoned he had made the most of the evening's opportunities. A large number of the guests were already departing – presumably the local hotel was the kind of place where they kicked out the punters and pulled down the shutters at eleven on the dot – and Adam hoped he'd be able to get to bed fairly soon. Even though tomorrow was Saturday, he had an article to write which he'd been putting off for weeks, and he'd have to make an early start.

'Since you're staying,' murmured Bella in his ear, 'you can do some clearing up. Come on.'

Adam helped Claire and Bella to clear up plates and glasses. Briony was at the front door, in the throes of extended leave-takings.

'Just put things on the table and by the sink,' said Bella. 'Someone will see to them in the morning. Come on, I'll find you somewhere to sleep.'

Bella showed him to a bedroom at the end of a corridor. From a shelf in a closet she took some bedding, and handed it to Adam. 'There you are. Sleep tight. Bathroom's next door.'

'I know.'

'Of course – you've stayed here before. Well, goodnight.'

'Goodnight,' said Adam.

He made up the bed, went for a pee, washed his face and cleaned his teeth, and undressed. He got into bed and flicked through his notebook, looking at the handful of names and addresses he had culled that evening. What would they have to tell him? Probably not much more than their own version of what Adam already knew. He brooded on this. He didn't want this book simply to be a gathering-together and regurgitation of known facts. There must be people out there who knew another reality, not just the writer and his successful career. He wanted to make the silent voices speak. But first he had to find them – if they existed at all. He sighed and chucked the notebook aside.

He was just about to switch off the bedside light when he heard the gentlest of knocks on his bedroom door. As he glanced up, Bella came in, closing the door behind her. She was wearing a short robe, and beneath that, he noticed, only a pair of silky, flimsy knickers. That much he absorbed in the few seconds it took her to cross the room. She sat down on the edge of the bed and smiled. Adam was too astonished to know what to say. He was trying not to look at her breasts, only half-hidden by the sides of the open robe. He failed and his glance slipped, catching a tantalizing glimpse of nipple. He looked hastily back at her face.

'What is it?'

'I came to see you. I was thinking about you.'

He nodded, nonplussed. He longed to stretch out a hand, though whether it was to touch her breast or pull her robe closed, he wasn't sure.

'I was thinking that you're nice. That it's a waste, having you two rooms away, and not making love.' She stretched out a hand to brush a lock of dark hair from his forehead.

Adam said nothing, incapable of sensible thought.

She leaned across, put her mouth to his, and kissed him. He scarcely moved, kissing her back only a little. After a few seconds she drew away. He just lay there.

'Don't you want me?' Her eyes held the glimmer of faint amusement, and behind that, fear.

'It's not that.'

'What is it, then?' She spoke very quietly.

'I don't think you should do this. Give yourself away so easily. Why would you want to do that?'

She frowned a little, then her smile returned. Though the fear had not quite gone away. 'I said. Because I like you. Because I can tell you like me. Because I thought it would be fun.'

It would be fun all right, thought Adam. He closed his

eyes for a second. 'That's not what I meant. I meant you should think more of yourself. You're worth more than this. You hardly know me.'

'Prude.'

'No.' He paused. 'I live with my girlfriend.'

She said nothing, plucking at the bedcover with her fingers. He stared at her, trying to see past the loveliness, the injured air, to whatever insecurity had brought her to his room. Did she always give herself so easily to any man she vaguely liked?

'Oh, well.' She shrugged, about to rise.

Adam put out a hand and held her arm. He leaned forward and drew her to him, and kissed her for a gentle, brief and dizzying moment. Her response was too warm for him to handle. He drew away.

'That was just by way of compensation. To me, I mean. For not –' He stopped.

'Taking advantage of me?' Her voice was wry.

He nodded. 'I had hoped to elevate you to pedestal status and leave you there.'

'Oh God.' From where he lay, Adam could see the swell and curve of one delectable breast, the nipple stiffened. If she didn't go now –

She stood up and pulled her robe together.

'Don't be cross,' said Adam, studying her face.

Bella ran a hand through her cropped, soft hair, shook her head, and left the room.

Adam lay awake for a long time, reflecting on the odd occurrence, trying to derive some consolation from the knowledge that at least he had done the right thing.

*

Next morning, Adam awoke at six to the steady cheeping of the alarm on his mobile phone. He dressed and went downstairs quietly. The household still slept. The front door had been locked by some process which Adam couldn't fathom, so he went through to the kitchen. Pausing to leave a note on the table for Briony, thanking her and explaining that he had to leave early, he walked through the scullery to the back door. The large metal key was still in the lock. He turned it, and stepped out into the chilly dawn. He made his way to the front of the house and crossed the gravel driveway to where his car stood. The engine coughed a couple of times before starting, and he glanced up at the house, hoping he hadn't woken anyone. But no one appeared. He put the car in gear, and headed back to London.

3

Three weeks later, Adam was sitting with a photographer in the lobby of a West End hotel. They were there to interview an American Pulitzer Prize-winning author who had kept them waiting for over half an hour. Adam picked up a copy of *Hello!* from a nearby table and flicked through it. Bella was featured twice in *Diary of the Week* – once, attending the premiere of yet another lottery-funded British no-hoper movie, and then at the opening of some Sloaney friend's new jewellery shop. You could see why photographers loved her. He stared intently at both pictures of her. In one she was laughing with two other girls, and in the other she was talking to an actor called Bruce Redmond, saying something in his ear. He was smiling. It looked very intimate.

Adam folded the magazine and showed the page to Dan, his photographer. 'Bella Day. What d'you think?'

Dan considered the pictures. 'Yeah. Wouldn't kick her out of bed, that's for sure.'

Adam closed the magazine and sighed.

When he got back to his flat that afternoon, Adam played back his messages. The third was from Bella. After the night at Gandercleugh, he had hardly expected to hear from her again.

'Adam, this is Bella Day. You didn't say whether or not

you had my mother's number.' There followed Cecile's phone number, and nothing more. That was the content of the message.

He sat down and went back, for the thousandth time, over the conversation they had had in his bedroom at Gandercleugh. Not really a conversation, more a fragment of one, mere words, two people not quite making sense to one another. Leaving the fact of Megan aside, his response to her availability had been instinctively truthful. She was insecure, flaky, and she had come on to him purely out of boredom. How many other men did she offer herself to on first acquaintance? Dozens, probably. A strange girl. You would think someone as beautiful as that would have a stronger sense of self-regard. He could wish the incident had never happened, given that he wanted to be able to talk to her easily and equably about what it was like being Harry Day's daughter. Then again, it had possessed a bizarre eroticism which he found difficult to put from his mind.

That evening he and Megan lay on the sofa after supper, Adam flicking through television channels, his shoes off, feet on the coffee table.

'I still don't know what to wear to Jo's wedding,' said Megan idly.

'When is that again?'

'In two weeks – July the first.'

'I may be in France that weekend.'

'Oh, Adam! You've known about it for ages. I've accepted for both of us.'

'Sorry about that. But she's your friend.'

Megan said nothing for a moment. She had wanted very much to attend this wedding with Adam. At an old schoolfriend's wedding, being part of a couple had a special importance. It was all very well being a single thirtysomething on the London scene, but when the chips were down, in the old church setting and at the reception afterwards, she'd look very much like remaindered goods if she had to show up on her own.

'Why might you be in France?'

'I pitched this idea to the commissioning editor on one of the Sundays – about farmers who've abandoned this country to go and farm in France. I suggested it months ago, and he's only just come round to the idea. So I may be away for a week or so.'

'Can't you go later? I could take a couple of weeks off, come with you. It would be more like a holiday.'

Adam considered this. 'I could, I suppose. There's no particular hurry. I'll think about it.'

'Anyway, I thought you were meant to be getting on with this biography thing?'

Adam sighed. 'I know. I really should. Actually, Bella Day rang today and left her mother's number. You know, Cecile Patterson, Harry Day's first wife.'

'Oh, right.' Megan had lost interest, and was watching the television.

Adam wondered why he didn't ring her now. He'd been hanging back on this book, hadn't got in touch with any of the people whose phone numbers he'd taken down at Gandercleugh. His diffidence had something to do with that business with Bella. Well, he'd sorted that out in his mind, so he might as well get on with it.

He got up and went into his room, picked up the piece of paper on which he'd written the number, and rang it.

The voice which answered was light yet husky, very precise. 'Cecile Patterson.'

Adam introduced himself, and mentioned Bella.

Cecile was warm and expansive. She said she would be delighted to assist Adam, and that he was most welcome to visit any time next week. She began to talk about Harry, unbidden, and went on for a good ten minutes. Adam started to jot down notes, but stopped. He could get it all again when he went to see her. He suspected she was somewhat lonely. She talked in the eager way that lonely people did.

He arranged to visit her at her home in Dulwich the following Wednesday, at two in the afternoon. As he went back through to Megan, Adam wondered whether he would glean from Cecile anything more than the superficial facts of this period of Harry's life. She sounded too civilized, too much at ease with the past, to bring out any hard and bitter truths.

He sat down next to Megan. She half-turned, nestled against him and kissed him, unbuttoning the top of his shirt. 'Do you want to go to bed?'

'Let's do it here.'

'On the sofa? Bed's comfier.'

'Comfy,' replied Adam, 'is not what I want.'

'Cosier.' She slipped her hand beneath the waistband of his trousers.

'Nor is cosy.'

Undefined thoughts, vaguely connected with Megan's friend's wedding, drifted through Megan's mind as Adam undressed her. They were to do with the pleasures of being part of a couple, and of patterns taking the shape of stability. Adam's own thoughts dwelt on the sensual pleasure of sexual familiarity, quite different from the erotic charge of first encounters, and tailed off, when his mind became incapable of coherent thought, into the question of how long it took for familiarity to lose its delight and become merely boring.

Cecile lived in a semi-detached house in Dulwich, in a street which she described as a quiet backroad. As though Dulwich contained any other kind, thought Adam, as he got out of the car that afternoon. The early summer air was blank and still, awash with suburban melancholy. He felt its genteel oppression as he walked up the pavement to Cecile's house, through the gate, up a short flight of steps, and pressed the bell.

Cecile answered the door, dressed in loose trousers, a long cardigan with a brightly coloured scarf at the neck, and house slippers. She smiled at Adam. 'Do come in,' she said. Her voice was husky, languid, with nicely accented vowels. Although she no longer appeared on stage, and very rarely on television, it was a voice which kept her much in demand with producers of a certain kind of Radio Four drama.

She made Adam coffee, and they sat in the front room with a plate of chocolate digestives on the table between them. It was not the kind of room Adam associated with an old person. The floor was of polished wood, the walls white, hung with pictures, and the furnishings a tasteful blend of whites and neutrals. But then Cecile, as he had realized from glimpses of her at Harry's funeral and memorial service, was not a typical old woman.

'I don't use this room a great deal. The other one,' she gestured vaguely behind her, 'is a dreadful clutter. Full of clothes, you know, and my sewing machine and paraphernalia. I do some dressmaking – just for a few clients, friends, really. And myself, of course.'

Adam nodded, then took out his tape recorder and set it down on the table next to the biscuits. 'Shall we start?'

'Of course,' said Cecile. 'Fire away.'

'Tell me about the early days with Harry. You first met when you were cast in *Crying Out Loud* at the Royal Court, didn't you?'

'Oh, we met before that, you know, when I was playing with the Birmingham Rep, and Harry came to see one of the plays – I can't recall what it was. Anyway, the director was Donald Weir, and Harry was a friend of his. Donald was terribly temperamental, and not at all the kind of person one liked working for. But a job was a job in those days . . . So that was when we first met. Then the following spring I was in *A Taste of Honey* at the Wyndham's, and he came to see me, and I suppose he thought I would be good for the part of Christine in *Crying Out Loud*. So he suggested me to Bill Prior, the director. The last thing in the *world* I expected was that Harry would ask me out. But he did . . .'

'Do you remember what you did, the first time you went out together?'

'Oh, yes. I wanted to see *At the Drop of a Hat* – you know, Flanders and Swann – at the New Lindsey. It was the most wonderful smash. But it was sold out, and anyway it wasn't really Harry's kind of thing. So we went to a Tennessee Williams play which had just opened, *Camino Real.* Harry loved it and I thought it was dire. I think time has proved me right, and Harry wrong – please, do have the last biscuit. And after that,' she clasped her hands between her knees and smiled brightly at Adam, 'we began to see one another on a regular basis and . . . well, we went on from there.'

'Tell me about your life together after that. You appeared in his next play, didn't you?'

For an hour Adam sat listening as Cecile recounted as much as she could recall of her marriage to Harry. He noticed that she scarcely mentioned Bella and Charlie.

'And then, you know, we divorced.'

'Was that a difficult time?'

'Oh, in some ways. He was not a particularly provident person, you know, Harry, when it came to money, and so on . . . The children were very young, and things were quite hard, financially. But emotionally difficult? No. We had rather gone our separate ways some time before that.' Cecile stared abstractedly at the back of her hands, and just as Adam was about to ask another question, she went on, 'Harry really was a bit of a puzzle, you know. He started out as a rather mature person in a lot of ways, but as he got older, he seemed to become more juvenile. Like someone living their life backwards. Maybe it had something to do with the fashions of the times – manners, and so on. When he was a teenager, just after the war, you know, there was no such thing as youth, really. People reached the age of twenty-one and became grown-ups. Men in their early twenties behaved terribly like men in their forties. They dressed the same, by and large. No such thing as fashion for teenagers or young men in those days. Well, not until teddy boys, all that kind of thing.' She glanced at Adam's cup. 'Would you like more coffee?'

'No, thank you.'

'Harry, when I met him, was a serious grown-up. He was twenty-nine, he was a playwright, he'd published books of poetry . . . I was only nineteen, of course. At the end of the fifties, the early sixties, society began to change. Things became looser, less well-defined. The younger generation got invented. I think Harry decided he wanted to belong to it. He'd never had much of a youth, you see, between being a schoolboy and being grown-up. Straight into National Service, bang into his first job . . . He refused point-blank to go to university, you know. That was a sort of rebellion against his father. Anyway, by the time he was thirty-five, or thereabouts, Harry decided to be the young man he'd never had the chance to be. He embraced it all – pop music, flower power, marijuana, modern art, modern fashion. Oh, and how he enjoyed being a celebrity. Back in the fifties, that was the last thing he thought about. When he was writing those early plays, he was utterly dedicated, he wanted to reveal the reality of the kind of life he'd seen. You know, coming from a fairly privileged, middle-class academic background, the life Harry led – the life he forced upon himself, after leaving the army . . . Well, it was a complete revelation to him. Living amongst working-class people, doing pretty menial work, no money . . . It was a kind of moral imperative with him to show to the middle-class world he came from exactly what life was like for most people, hard and basic and not at all genteel. He disliked Coward and Rattigan . . . though of course that's all become fashionable again now, hasn't it?'

'What d'you think changed Harry's idealism?'

'Oh . . . Success. Success is very seductive. A successful playwright can't go on living in a bedsit in Soho, even if that is where he gets most of his material from. And the world of the theatre draws you in, strokes your fur, makes you purr. Directors, actors, wealthy patrons – it was very hard to stay an angry young man under those circumstances, you know. Though God knows, some tried. I mean, look at Osborne. Poor old thing. What an effort that must have been . . . Not that Harry was ever a celebrity as such, not like Colin Wilson, say. But he had a following. He was writing ideal material for all those up-and-coming young actors from the provinces – Tom Courtney, Peter O'Toole, Albert Finney . . . Did you know that Finney and I were in Birmingham Rep together? He played Hotspur in Henry the Fifth and I was Katherine . . .' Cecile paused for some seconds, her eyes fixed on her own past. Then she resumed. 'The trouble was, by the end of the sixties, that working-class theme was rather played out. People had moved on to other things. Mainly due to the removal of the Lord Chamberlain's powers of censorship, I suppose. There was a great sea change, culturally and morally. We had *Hair* and *Oh! Calcutta!*, nonsense of that kind. Well, by the early seventies, Harry wasn't writing much at all. A few plays for television, that was about it. He was very much caught up in his own busy social life. He drank a lot, I remember. I suspect he was making up for all that lost time.'

'Lost time?'

Cecile shrugged. 'As I said, he had his youth to live all over. Those years he spent in Soho, surrounded by artists and writers and God knows who else, largely blind drunk from morning to night so far as I can tell, and Harry toiling away abstemiously . . . It was as though he was making up for not having taken part in all that. Oh, the seventies, that was Harry's decade for riotous living.'

'And you?'

Cecile frowned, the first indication she had given of any impatience. 'Well, I had the children.'

It was the first time she had mentioned them.

'So you were at home with Charles and Bella, while Harry –'

'Led his own life, more or less.'

Adam hesitated for a few moments, searching for tactful words. It was past four o'clock, and she had been talking for a long time. She was probably tired. 'It must have been difficult, Harry beginning to behave in that way, when you both had young children to care for.' He wanted to add that it seemed odd, too, that Harry should go off the rails just when the twins were born, having been apparently solid and dependable up until that point. But he didn't. He waited.

'That's men for you, isn't it?' She smiled at the banality. 'He was wonderful at the beginning. We'd waited a long time for a family. He was there at the birth. That wasn't the done thing in those days, you know. Harry insisted. Everything went well with Charles – he was born first – but I had such a dreadful time with Bella. Anyway, when it was all over, Harry went home and celebrated with friends. And he carried on celebrating from that day forward. Well, it seemed that way. He wasn't there much. He always said he was seeing television people, made excuses of that kind, but he was mostly out on the spree. Just never home. I'm sure it was partly my fault. I was so bound up with the children. They say that, don't they? That women can become so involved with their babies that they shut their husbands out. Maybe I did that . . .'

She talked on for another twenty minutes or so, until Adam's tape ran out.

'I don't think we can do any more this afternoon. It's really been invaluable. Thank you for your time. May I come back and talk to you again, if I need to?'

'Oh, of course. I rather liked talking about those old times. I don't revisit them much, you know. I keep telling myself that I shall save up all my memories for my extreme old age, and take them out and inspect them *then* . . . Though, of course, that way one might well be dead before one gets round to remembering anything properly.'

'I wonder,' said Adam, 'do you happen to have any photographs? From the time when you and Harry first met?'

There was an almost imperceptible hesitation, a slipping of her gaze, and then she said, 'Of course. Let me fetch some.'

Cecile went to a desk which stood below the window. It was late afternoon by now, and school children trailed along the street outside.

'You might be able to use some of these in your book . . .' She drew out two large albums and brought them back to the table. She sat down and opened the first, smiling. As she turned the pages of the album, Adam realized how much it would please her to think of her young self living again in the pages of some biography. There were many pictures of her, theatre stills, mostly, from the fifties and early sixties, showing a tall girl with wavy blonde hair and well-defined features, and the figure of the times, with a nipped waist and pointed breasts. He could probably use no more than one in the biography. The ones which interested him more were the casual snapshots, Harry and Cecile with various theatrical celebrities, some forgotten, some still well known. There was Harry in his youth – smiling eyes, handsome, rather roguish features, light-brown hair slightly receding, the same spare, muscled body, slight in stature. There, evident in these early photos, was the quiet dynamism which Adam had occasionally sensed in those long talks with the older Harry, in the days before his death.

Cecile sat back in her chair, let Adam take over the page-turning. She seemed tired. Adam told himself he would go soon. He paused at a picture larger than the others, which had the look of having once been in a frame but later stuffed away out of sight in the album. It was of Cecile and Harry on their wedding day. A group of people outside Kensington Register Office, Cecile in a smartly tailored dress, short gloves, hat brim shading her eyes, laughing, clutching a small posy of flowers. Harry in a loose-jacketed suit, trousers with turn-ups, scarcely any taller than his wife in her high heels. Adam immediately recognized Lucian Freud and Francis Bacon among the group, and felt a little thrill of excitement.

This was definitely one he could use. He turned the book towards Cecile.

'This photo of your wedding – can you tell me exactly who everyone is?'

Cecile leaned forward. She gave a quick frown of surprise when she saw the photograph. She took it from Adam's hand and gazed at it for some seconds. She recited names, one by one, without hesitation, then handed it back to Adam.

'What about this man?' He pointed at the image of a young man with dark, slicked-back hair, who stood just behind Harry, slightly shorter than him, staring at the camera with unsmiling eyes.

Cecile glanced briefly at the picture again. 'I really can't remember. Some photographer friend of Harry's, I think. I didn't know him well.' She leaned back in her chair, evidently fatigued. Adam could read the subtle signals telling him that his time was up. He stared back at the picture. His instinct told him that Cecile knew very well who the man was, but was choosing not to say.

'May I take this picture?' he asked. 'And a few of the ones of yourself? I'll bring them back, of course.'

Again, an instant's hesitation – but she agreed. She selected some of herself and Harry, and Adam tucked these, together with the wedding photograph, into his bag.

Cecile picked up the other album. 'There are some more here,' she said, opening it as though, despite her tiredness, she suddenly wanted to postpone Adam's departure. 'They're mostly of the children.'

Even the picture of the infant Bella had a potent effect on Adam. He smiled at the sight of her in a smocked baby dress, sitting on a rug with her brother, toes bare, curls brushed. She had been lovely from the word go. He progressed through the album, hardly glancing at Charles, the sturdy toddler, or Harry and Cecile, the proud parents. It was a revelation to see Bella grow through the years as he turned the pages, the features changing imperceptibly, the wide-eyed childish innocence turning gradually into fresh, scarcely aware sexuality. He wouldn't ask for any of these now. He knew he would have to come back another time, once he had spoken to Charles and Bella. He would go through these pictures at greater length then. He had enough for the time being.

Adam thanked Cecile for the coffee, and for her time and patience. She stood at the front door as Adam made his way to his car, waved as he set off, then went back inside to clear away the coffee cups. The photograph albums still lay on the table. With a faint sigh, almost one of reluctance, Cecile sat down and drew them towards her, turning the pages once more. She dwelt on the pictures of herself as a young woman. Such pleasure one could take in the enduring image of one's loveliness. It almost obliterated the yearning pain of its brief, illusory transition. She contemplated a picture of herself, with a group of other people, in the foyer of the Royal Court. It was the opening night of *The Entertainer*, quite an occasion. Olivier had actually asked to play that part . . . There was a man who had always known what was good for him, unlike a lot of actors she knew. She gazed at herself, remembering the rustling feel of that dress, her first Dior, very chic. That was something girls missed today – the sensuousness of petticoats, that feeling of femininity . . .

She closed her eyes, suddenly recalling, for no particular reason, the scent of cologne, Four-seven-eleven, and rouge in those little round green cardboard pots. How funny. What days they had been, the days of Harry's early success. The people they had met. Dylan Thomas, trying one of her Sobranie Black Russian cigarettes and then cadging half a dozen. Robert Helpmann – so courteous and kind to her at some party where she felt out of place. What had been the occasion? Was it with some of Harry's bohemian friends? Probably. Not that Harry had stayed bohemian for long. After the huge success of *Foremost First*, which Michael Langham produced, Harry had bought his first car, a Vauxhall Sniper Gazelle, of all things. A thousand pounds, it had cost. An absolutely enormous sum of money in those days. She remembered driving to see that revue with Tommy Cooper and Shirley Bassey, *Blue Magic*, in the days when you could park just about anywhere in London in the evenings, and then for supper at a jazz club . . .

No one ever told you, when you were young, that it wouldn't last. Well, maybe they did, but you never listened, never believed. People would laugh, nowadays, at the suggestion that the fifties had ever been a time of glamour, of wonderful innocence mixed with perfect sophistication. For them, the decade was an Osbert Lancaster joke. But in certain innocent ways the fifties had been glamorous and shining. She knew. She had been there.

The next day Adam spent the morning on the phone to two commissioning editors, trying to whip up a bit of interest in an idea for a series of articles on women's prisons, and chasing up money for articles for which he hadn't yet been paid. In some superstitious way, he didn't want to eat into the large slice of the advance which presently sat in his bank account. What if he never finished this biography? The thought of having to pay the money back haunted him. It was difficult to find time for both the biography and his freelance work, but he had already determined that he would spend that afternoon following up the mystery man in the wedding photograph. He had a feeling that it might not be time wasted.

Armed with the photograph, he set off for the London Library. Painstakingly he looked up books on fifties and sixties Soho, trying to assess which ones would produce most in the way of photographs. The list he finished up with was dispiritingly long, covering both biography and topography, and it took him some time, tramping through the echoing rows and stacks, to track down volumes which looked as though they would be any good.

He sat in the hush of the reading room, turning the pages in search of photographs, soon feeling thoroughly nauseated by black-and-white fifties images of depressing streets, battered faces, smoky nightclubs and dreary pubs. Until he opened the fourth volume. He had hardly flicked through the first few pages, not much expecting to find anything, when there was a picture of his man, flanked by a very young Jeffrey Bernard with his coat collar turned up against the shiverings of another morning hangover, and Jeffrey's brother, Bruce. Once again the anonymous man was staring directly at the camera in a defiant fashion, one that made everyone else in the photo redundant.

Adam's eyes flicked to the caption. *Bruce and Jeffrey Bernard with the photographer George Meacher.*

George Meacher. The name rang bells, but not very clear ones. Perhaps he was dead. Most of the people from that era seemed to be, except for George Melly. Adam flicked through to the index and looked up the final listing for Meacher. According to this book, an account of Soho life from the thirties to the sixties, George Meacher had still been alive and kicking at the time of the book's publication in the early nineties, so there was reason to hope he was still around. Adam turned back to the photo of Meacher with the Bernard brothers, and studied the gimlet eyes. Meacher had an indestructible look about him. Adam closed the book, and thought for a few moments. Perhaps Giles could help him.

In his former career as a journalist, Giles had started off as a staff reporter on the *Express* – a job that seemed to have consisted of endless drinking at Poppins and other Fleet Street watering holes. Adam enjoyed the sense of vicarious nostalgia engendered by Giles's tales of Fleet Street's golden age, before the diaspora, when idleness and drunkenness had apparently gone hand-in-hand with journalistic brilliance. Giles, partly because he enjoyed the company of writers and artists, and partly because he would drink anywhere with anyone, had been a frequenter not only of Fleet Street boozers but of Soho pubs, so there was a very good chance that he knew something of George Meacher, dead or alive.

Adam rang Giles when he got home.

'Meacher? God, what a poisonous little man. What's the interest in him?'

'He was a friend of Harry Day's. At least, I think he was. Back in the fifties.'

'Might have been. I wasn't knocking around Soho then. Still in short pants. I knew Meacher, though. I used to avoid him like the plague.'

'Is he still alive?'

'Well, he was when I last saw him, a couple of months ago. Horrible little piece of work. He was quite a good photographer in his day – well, right place, right time – but he had a vicious tongue on him. I hated the little bastard. So did plenty of people. Some of them found him amusing. I didn't. He was two-faced, and a cadger.'

'How can I get in touch with him?'

'Well, you could stand outside the Coach and Horses for a couple of days. He's bound to turn up. I haven't got a phone number, or anything like that. I don't even know where he lives. Don't know him well enough. I just see him in pubs now and again.' There was a pause. 'Leave it with me. I'll see what I can do.'

The next day Giles rang Adam.

'I've tracked him down, and he's agreed to meet you.'

'Giles, you're a genius. When?'

'He said he's usually in The French House at opening time. You can find him there. Be prepared to buy him lunch as well as a criminal amount of alcohol.'

'Great,' said Adam. 'I take it he knows what it's about, and will be happy to talk?'

'Oh, yes,' said Giles. 'Only I wouldn't expect the unvarnished truth. He's a horrible little liar.'

4

Bella had arranged to meet Charlie for a drink after work. She was in rehearsals for a new production of a Joe Orton play at the Ambassador's, and the walk to Charlie's chambers in the Temple took a mere ten minutes. They met in this way as often as Bella's schedule allowed – sometimes for lunch, sometimes for a drink. Despite the differences in their enthusiasms and temperaments, the relationship was a close, affectionate one, grounded in constant companionship throughout childhood, including the progressive co-educational boarding school in Hampshire which they had attended together until the age of fourteen, and which Charlie had wholeheartedly hated. Charlie was a boy who liked structure and discipline, and the liberal ethos of the place, which had suited Bella entirely, made him uneasy and miserable. Bella had been something of a protector and comforter during these years, until Charlie, using a combination of wheedling and threats, had persuaded his mother to send him to Uppingham, which he had heard about from a boy whom he had met during the school holidays, and which Charlie thought sounded much more his type of school. He had flourished there, discovering like-minded souls who enjoyed rugby and bossing people around, and was genuinely appreciative of a hierarchy based upon seniority and sporting prowess as much as intellectual and creative ability.

They always went to the same wine bar in Essex Street, and Charlie was generally there before Bella. He was rigorously punctual, even with social appointments, a quality in which Bella was deeply deficient. This evening, however, Charlie was twenty minutes late. Bella sat with a paperback book, trying to pretend she was unaware of the frequent glances she attracted from every man in the place. Even when she felt, as she did today, that she was at her bedraggled worst, in old jeans, trainers and an outsize Barbour (one which had belonged to her father and which she had sentimentally retrieved on her last visit to Gandercleugh), men always looked at her, while trying to pretend at the same time that they weren't. She knew she should be used to it by now, but it was most annoying not being able to glance around in an ordinary kind of way, for fear of making unwished-for eye-contact.

Suddenly there was Charlie, sliding into a chair opposite Bella and slapping down a rolled-up copy of the evening paper. He was out of breath. 'Sorry I'm late. Rowley heard today that he's been made a QC, so we had a couple of glasses in chambers by way of celebration. I could hardly say no.'

'Why didn't you ring me on my mobile to say you'd be late?'

'Don't grumble. I'll get us a drink.' Charlie took off his coat and went to the bar.

Glancing up, Bella saw a man standing near Charlie at the bar, dark-haired, wearing a raincoat, his back to her. For a moment she thought it was Adam Downing, but he half-turned and it wasn't. To her relief. She still felt angry and a little embarrassed at the recollection of that evening at Gandercleugh. No man had ever turned her down before. Not that she made a habit of propositioning men, but when, in propitious physical and social circumstances, there seemed to be raging mutual attraction, she could see no good reason for not taking the initiative. In fact, given the way most men seemed to be somewhat in awe of her – Bella always thought it quite ludicrous to be thus perceived, but accepted it as her inevitable lot – it was often positively necessary to do so. Of course, the way he had behaved didn't do him any favours – it merely marked him out as a prig. She had reassured herself on this point often enough. The girlfriend factor could scarcely be counted. On Bella's scale of morality, playing away, provided it didn't inconvenience or upset anyone, was perfectly acceptable. Notions of fidelity were boring, and conventions there to be broken. No, she didn't think much of Adam Downing. Which didn't prevent her from mentioning him almost as soon as Charlie had sat down with two glasses of wine.

'Did Adam Downing ever get in touch with you? The journalist who's writing the biography?'

'Not so far. I gave him my card that evening, but he hasn't rung.'

'Maybe he's lost interest in the project, now that Dad's dead.'

'Quite the opposite, surely?'

Bella shrugged. 'I rang and left Mother's number and address on his answering machine, and he never rang back to thank me.' She wasn't sure whether she had hoped or expected that Adam would call her back. She only knew that the unsatisfactory balance between them had to be redressed somehow.

'Oh, he's been in touch with Cecile. I spoke to her last night. He went round to see her the other day and spent a couple of hours there. I think she enjoyed it. She even lent him some photographs.'

The knowledge that Adam hadn't abandoned the project, and would therefore have to make contact with her again at some point, pleased her. Bella took a sip of her wine and leaned back with a sigh.

'How are your rehearsals going?'

Bella gave a groan.

'It's an Orton, isn't it?'

'*Funeral Games*. Which about sums it up.' She took another sip of wine. 'No, actually, it isn't too bad. I just find it hard to get my head round the humour. De-frocked priests and bodies in the cellar. Still, according to my agent, appearing in a radical revival of a lesser-known play by a sixties icon is good for my image. God knows what the critics will make of it. It has some fairly iffy lines.'

'I thought that was the point of Orton.'

'Yes, well – political correctness seems to have brought things full circle.' The dark-haired man in the raincoat went out. Bella was still half-thinking about Adam. It was annoying how he stuck in her mind. 'Getting back to this biography . . . Are you all right about it?'

'What d'you mean?'

'I mean, there's no guarantee that it's going to be some kind of hagiography. Awful word. What if Adam Downing unearths all kinds of things we'd rather not see in print?'

Charlie laughed. 'Come on. Dad led a fairly unconventional life, but most of it has already been well covered. I don't think there are going to be many surprises. I'd be more worried if he'd led an apparently quiet, blameless life.'

'And you think you'll be all right talking about him?'

'Why shouldn't I?'

'You're a barrister – you should know. When people start to ask you questions, all kinds of things can come out. I mean, you might surprise yourself. It might be upsetting, talking about him.'

'I don't think so.' Charlie shook his head, wanting to change the subject. 'Listen, we have to talk about the house in France.'

'What's to talk about?'

'I mean, it's great, Dad leaving us both the house, but I want to know what we're going to do about it.'

'Do?'

'Well, it was fine for Dad – he and Briony could go and spend as much time there as they wanted, more or less. Now it's just sitting there.'

'What are you talking about? We can use it. I fully intend to. We'll work something out between us.'

'Yeah, well, that's all right for you – you'll get out there far more often than I will. The point is, I'd honestly rather we sold the place and split the proceeds.'

Bella was astonished. In her mind, the house in France was sacred territory. Harry had bought Montresor back in the seventies, after he and Cecile had split up, when it had been just an abandoned, ancient farmhouse in the Lot. It had taken Harry years to put it into shape, gradually turning the rooms into marvels of exposed wood and stone, building the swimming pool, bringing the orchard back to life, planting the vines that now covered the trellis which shaded the long terrace. It was there that the twins had spent most of the time they had had with Harry. Gandercleugh was for occasional weekends, half-term holidays, and Bella had never much liked its gloomy atmosphere. Besides, it was Briony's now. Montresor was summer holidays, sunshine, her childhood. How could Charlie possibly want to sell it?

He read all this in her eyes as she stared at him.

'Don't look like that. Frankly, Bell, I need the money.'

'You can't need the money! Not that badly. Not badly enough to sell Montresor.'

Charlie sighed. 'Claire's found a house near Lewes. She's set her heart on it. A Georgian manor house. Three acres, lots of rooms, tennis court, swimming pool . . . If we're going to be able to put in an offer, I need the capital.'

'Why does she need a Georgian manor house, for God's sake? Can't she start married life somewhere more modest? Most people do.'

'Well, she says that if we want a family, we need a proper family home. We don't want to be moving in ten years' time. She wants somewhere she can feel settled.'

'She wants somewhere she can swank about, more like. Why do you let her put that kind of strain on you, Charlie? All these expectations . . .'

'To be honest, Bell, that's not really your concern. I'd like to buy the house, too. That's why I need the money. If you're so keen to hang on to Montresor, why don't you buy out my half?'

'With what? What makes you think I've got that kind of money? Just because I've made a couple of half-decent films doesn't mean I'm rolling in it. Do you know how much this Orton play pays? You don't want to, believe me. It's all I can do to keep the flat in Beaufort Street going.'

'If we sold it, you'd get your share of the capital, and you could buy somewhere in the same area. Something smaller, but still a holiday place.'

'That's not the point, and you know it. I *love* Montresor. Another place wouldn't be the same. I couldn't bear to sell it.'

Charlie shrugged slowly. 'I don't really see that we have any alternative.'

'Well, you could tell Claire to lower her sights a bit, for a start. You're going to be working your arse off for the rest of your days to keep up with her!' Bella drank the remains of her wine. 'Oh, and don't forget the school fees. Eton for the boys, if I'm not much mistaken.'

'Don't be so bloody rotten about Claire. Stop going on as though she's pushing me into this.'

'Well, isn't she?'

'You may not much like her –'

'No, I don't, as a matter of fact.'

'– but the fact remains, she's going to be my wife, and we both want this house.'

Bella looked at her watch. 'Shit. I'm going out in an hour.' She sighed. 'Look, Charlie, we'll have to talk about this some other time. I've got to rush.' She leaned over, kissed his cheek, and got up. 'It's not worth fighting about. We'll sort something out.'

He watched her leave. There wasn't any other way of sorting it out, so far as he could see. All right, the Lewes place was a bit big. The prospect of the mortgage was frankly terrifying. But he couldn't face having to tell Claire they couldn't afford it. She wanted it so badly. And when it came down to it, he had to do what was best for himself and Claire.

A light wind whipped through Leicester Square gardens as Adam walked up from Charing Cross towards Soho. It was fifteen minutes before noon, but the general vacancy of the streets and the proliferation of delivery vans gave the place a yawning, not-yet-started feeling. Which, Adam reflected, was the way of such an area, where the real day didn't begin until the pubs got going.

With ten minutes to kill, he strolled around the stalls in Berwick Street Market, then made his way to Old Compton Street and The French House. It had not been open long, and both doors at either end of the bar were open to the street, the sash windows up, airing the place from the night before and subjecting any early drinkers to a stiffish breeze. Adam stepped in and glanced round. He had expected to find George Meacher tucked away in the alcove, surrounded by the mournful nostalgia of the dozens of black-and-white photos which covered the walls, depicting Soho in days of former glory. But the small figure, instantly recognizable to Adam, was seated round the other side of the bar, taking the brunt of the gusts of fresh air from the street outside, and tapping the ash from the end of his cigarette with soulful absorption. A glass of Scotch stood before him on the bar.

Meacher took another drag on his cigarette and made some quiet remark to the barman, who, busy counting change for the float, murmured in reply. Then Meacher looked up and saw Adam.

Adam's first impression had been of a small, seedy man, rather pathetic in detail – the grey, thin hair combed greasily across the scalp, the too-long trousers, twice or thrice turned up so that the hems bulged, the dingy woollen overcoat – but when he met Meacher's gaze, only one word sprang to Adam's mind. Poise. Meacher might be old, beaten and worn, but he had poise. He sat with one elbow on the bar, smoke rising from the cigarette between his leathery, yellow fingers, his legs crossed, one grizzled brow raised, and seemed to transcend his shabby clothes, his wretched shoes, his entire situation. He might as well have been Noel Coward.

'Mr Meacher?'

The eyes, in contrast to the pouched, dull, battered old face, were dark and sharp as they surveyed Adam.

'My name's Adam Downing. We have a mutual friend – Giles Hamblin. He told me I might find you here.'

'Ah, yes – Giles. He did mention you.' The voice had a cultivated edge to it, and was light and rasping from constant smoking. Adam drew up a stool and sat down. The barman, having finished his count, moved away to pour the change into the till. 'You're writing a biography of Harry Day.'

'That's right,' said Adam.

Meacher nodded, smoking. 'I knew Harry.' He eyed Adam reflectively. 'I knew Harry way back. Last saw him back in the seventies. How did you track me down?'

'His first wife.'

Meacher let out a creaking laugh. 'You're joking!' He sounded genuinely disbelieving.

'She didn't mention you by name –'

'I'll bet she didn't.'

'– but she was showing me some photos, and I saw you in one of them. Their wedding photograph, actually. You and Francis Bacon and some other people.'

'So.' He stretched his arm out to crush his cigarette into the tin ashtray, his wrist thin beneath the frayed, slightly soiled shirt cuff. Adam could detect the sweetish, stale odour of unwashedness.

'I take it you're willing to talk about Harry, then?'

'Yes. Oh, yes.' Meacher drained his drink.

Nice timing, thought Adam. He gestured to Meacher's empty glass. 'Another?'

Meacher's smile creased his face like rubber as he reached into his pocket for his cigarettes. 'Thanks. Make it a double.'

Fifteen minutes later, Adam was buying him another. To avoid the draught from the street, Adam had suggested moving to the alcove, snug with cigarette smoke, which Adam knew would give him the mother of all headaches later.

'So it was before you went freelance that you met Harry?'

'Oh, well before that. I was working for a studio, going out and taking photos of people in the street, that kind of thing, charging half a dollar a photo. It was a cheapskate outfit, run by an old codger. He'd only the one camera.

Harry got a job in the dark room. That's how we met. It was '51, we'd both just done our National Service. We used to go out to the pub together after work, and we got on all right. So after a while we figured it would be cheaper to get a room together. I was earning six quid a week, God knows what Harry was getting – half that, probably. So we took a room together, a sort of bedsit, with breakfast thrown in.' Meacher pinched the end of his cigarette and took a final drag before stubbing it out. 'Forty bob a week, one big attic room, bed either corner, washstand, odds and ends of furniture, and one prize bitch of a landlady.' There were four spent butts in the ashtray already.

Adam tried to picture Meacher and Day, young men in their early twenties, and the meagre life they must have led together in the wake of the war. 'How long did you live together?'

'Year and a half. Something like that. Then Harry got his own place. But we still knocked around together, knew the same people, went to the same places.'

'What was he like back then?'

'Harry? You mean to look at? Well, you must have photos.'

'I want you to tell me how you recall him. The way he looked, how he was, everything.'

'Average bloke. Not too tall, but with more muscle on him than you'd think to look at him. Mousy brown hair. Quiet. Women liked him, but he wasn't too bothered. He preferred writing his poetry of an evening. I'd often come in, and there he'd be, battering away on his Remington. Dire shit it seemed to me, half the time . . . Went down well with the arty-farty types, though. Old David Archer took him under his wing, and he knew a thing or two about poetry. He spotted Dylan Thomas before anyone else. Harry was always hanging round Archer's bookshop in Greek Street. I think he was meant to be employed there at one point . . . Not that anyone ever bought a book there. It was more like a club, people dropping in, most of them sponging off Archer.' Meacher lit another cigarette. 'Soft old sod. He always liked helping people on the quiet. He put a fiver in an empty matchbox once, put it in my pocket, but I chucked it away, didn't know what was in it. Only found out later when he said something. A bloody fortune, gone. Jesus, we were always skint in those days . . . I remember taking back beer bottles to get the money on them. Had to hock my suit more than once. Haven't exactly come a long way since.' He took a swift, bottom-of-the-lung drag on the remains of his cigarette. 'And you know, Harry could have had money if he'd wanted. His father would have seen him right, provided Harry took the kind of job he wanted. But Harry never did. He liked to go his own way. I admired that. His mother used to send him the odd twenty now and then, and that was a real bonanza. We'd go to Wheeler's for lunch, crack a few bottles of Chablis, then go on the piss for the rest of the day. Not that Harry was ever a great drinker, but the people he liked being with were. They'd all come running when Harry had money. You were never short of friends in Soho if you had a bob or two.' Meacher shook his head and drained his glass. 'We'd spend all afternoon in the Colony Room, letting the afternoon drift away. Bloody lovely times.' Meacher stared reflectively into the bottom of his glass.

'How do you get by now?' asked Adam, hoping Meacher wouldn't be offended by the question.

But he wasn't. 'Pension. I've got rooms round the corner, they don't cost me much. Landlord owns the Greek place at the end of the street, he feeds me now and again. He's all right.' Meacher shook his head. 'There was a time when I made a half-decent living, doing shoots for the glossies back in the late sixties. Gritty realism. Birds in mini-skirts and long boots standing around bomb sites. But I was never ambitious. Not like Harry. Which is probably why I'm still here.'

Adam knew it was his cue to buy Meacher another double, but he didn't think he could spend another half-hour in this little alcove bathed in the miasma of smoke from Meacher's endless cigarettes. 'Would you like some lunch?' he asked.

Meacher blinked in surprise. 'Upstairs?'

'Unless there's somewhere else you'd rather go.'

'No, upstairs is fine.'

Adam stood up. 'I'll go and ask the barman if they've got a table.'

'I'll have another while I'm waiting,' said Meacher swiftly. Adam bought him another large whisky.

The restaurant upstairs was a small room, made to look bigger by a mirror at one end, and Adam and Meacher sat at a corner table by the window, overlooking the street. It was Monday, and there were few other diners. Adam set his tape recorder on the windowsill.

They talked over lunch about Harry's early Soho days, the poetry, the jazz clubs, the characters who came and went. It was all interesting enough, but uneventful in terms of Harry's career. When he wasn't writing poetry, Harry appeared to have taken a variety of menial jobs to pay the rent and fund his social life.

'Old Harry, he did most things. He was a scene shifter in one of the theatres for a while, he washed up in a café in Charlotte Street. Washed up in a number of places, in fact. The best-paid job he got was in the lampshade department in Selfridges, but one of his artist friends got drunk one lunchtime and decided to pay a call on Harry at work, and that was the end of that job. Not that he minded. I think he was pleased – he was bored out of his brain there. There was something good about all those ups and downs. Nobody liked life to get too predictable. It was like a balancing act, me and Harry. When I was on my uppers, he usually had a bit extra to spare, like money from his mother, or from flogging a poem. And when he was out of work, I might be a bit flush, say from doing some porno negatives for someone, that kind of thing. There was always something.'

Meacher had put away sweetbreads on brioche, followed by a rack of lamb, and had consumed the better part of a bottle of Burgundy. He was now leaning back in his chair in a state of comfortable satisfaction. Adam guessed he didn't eat well, nor often. He caught the waiter's eye and ordered another bottle.

'And then Harry had his big success,' said Adam, steering Meacher.

'That's right.' Meacher gave a little inward belch. 'He

surprised everyone. Most of the people in Soho were real no-hopers, always talking about the book they were going to publish, the picture they were going to paint. That was just drink-driven drivel, half the time. They weren't going to do anything, and they knew it. You generally knew who the people with real talent were. Francis, Lucien Freud, Johnny Minton . . . They kept quiet about it. They could drink themselves rotten with everyone else, but then they'd go home and you wouldn't see them for two weeks. And they'd be working, doing their thing. The others just kept on drinking and talking, pissing away the days. Including me.' Meacher looked rueful. Adam refilled his glass. 'My mistake was staying alive. They cut out half my fucking lung, you know, and I'm still here. Sometimes I wish I wasn't. If I'd been smart, I'd have died twenty years ago, and they'd be having retrospectives of my work at the V&A. I did some good stuff when I was working for *Vogue*.'

'Maybe they will, some day.'

'What?'

'Have a retrospective.'

'Hmmph.' Meacher squared his shoulders miserably and frowned. Adam wondered if he was losing the momentum here, if he'd let the old bloke drink too much.

But Meacher sighed and his face cleared. He drew out his cigarettes. 'Anyway, Harry did it. He pulled it off. He wrote his play, and he got out of the Soho trap. He was lucky, really. He could have gone under, like so many of them. But he wrote his play, he was in the right place at the right time, and when it was a big hit, I thought – bloody good luck to you, my friend.'

'Didn't you begrudge him his success – just a bit?'

'I'd be lying if I said I didn't envy him. But he saw me right. He paid back everything I'd ever lent him, which was quite a bit, over the years. I'd never have asked him for it, but he gave it to me. And it wasn't like he shot off like a rocket, or anything like that. He was still part of the Soho scene, still knocked about with the same people . . . Till he married Cecile, of course.'

'And the last time you saw Harry was in the seventies?'

'That's right. He had his reasons for not seeing me again after that.' Meacher glanced up and looked directly at Adam, and there was a new expression in his dark eyes. It amazed Adam that the old man could knock back so much and still appear so lucid.

'What were those?'

A long and rigid silence developed. As Meacher drew on his cigarette, Adam realized that the old man was debating within himself. He waited.

'You know his kids were adopted, don't you?'

'No,' said Adam. 'I didn't.' In trying to register the sense of this startling piece of news, Adam's mind moved swiftly over every reference Bella had ever made to her father. Not once had she ever suggested anything like this. Then something stopped his train of thought dead. 'That can't be right.'

'No?' Meacher drained off his wine and poured himself some more. The waiter brought the menu for dessert.

'Cecile. She talked about when Bella and Charlie were born – about how she had a difficult time with one of them.'

'Did she now?' Meacher scanned the menu. His face expressed the unshakeable confidence of someone who, while accustomed to lying, was for once in possession of the truth.

Adam sat back and stared at him.

Meacher put out his cigarette. 'I think I'll have the treacle tart,' he said to the waiter.

Adam shook his head at the waiter and handed back the menu. 'Just coffee, please.'

Meacher savoured the tension he had generated, before saying, 'I don't know what story she's made up for herself all these years, but that's all it is. A story. The fact is, Harry and Cecile couldn't have children. He told me one evening when we were having a drink together. About twice a year Harry always used to ring me and suggest going out. I think he felt a bit guilty where I was concerned, felt he should keep in touch. Anyway, it all came out. He told me how badly it was affecting Cecile, and that they were thinking of adopting. But even back then in the seventies it was hard to find nice little white babies to adopt, and that was what Cecile was desperate for. So Harry thought I might be able to help.'

'Why you?'

'I'd done my National Service with a fellow who became a GP in Camberwell, and he was always happy to do the odd favour for the right money. Help out girls in trouble, that kind of thing. A lot of the girls in Soho had me to thank for putting them in touch with Gerald. Anyway, it had occurred to Harry that Gerald the GP, as I always called him, might be able to circumvent the old adoption process, maybe find a private client, so to speak, and the whole thing could be done without the social-services people, all that stuff.'

'And?'

'And that's what happened. Gerald the GP found some woman in south-east London who was pregnant and didn't want to be, the Days paid a few thousand, plus the private-nursing-home bills, and we all got what we wanted. I took my cut, of course, kind of a broker's commission, Gerald the GP took his, Lottie of Lewisham was rid of her little problem and a couple of grand better off. Harry and Cecile, of course, got double what they'd bargained for, an instant family, and they were happy with that. I didn't hear from Harry again.' The waiter set Meacher's pudding down, and Adam's coffee. 'I think that was more to do with Cecile than Harry. She wanted everyone to think they really were her kids. She and Harry went abroad for a few months before the woman was due, so no one was any the wiser.' He shrugged. 'It was their affair. Maybe Cecile thought if anyone found out they were adopted, but on the sly, they'd be taken away from her. I don't know. So she told you she'd had a difficult birth, did she?' Meacher snickered. He picked up his spoon and dug into his treacle tart. 'Thirty years on, and still keeping up appearances. Only nowadays they call it being in denial, don't they?'

Adam sat thinking, taking apart, then putting together again, the pieces of this story. Meacher sat hunched over his pudding, eating with slow relish. When he had finished, he picked up the empty cigarette packet from the table and flipped the top open forlornly. Adam gestured to the waiter and said, 'Twenty Marlboro. Put them on the bill.'

The cigarettes came. Adam watched as Meacher unwrapped the fresh packet and lit one. He thought about what Giles Hamblin had said of Meacher.

Meacher winked at Adam through the smoke. 'I fancy a brandy to round off the meal.'

Adam asked the waiter for the wine list. Meacher perused it thoughtfully, then ordered a triple Armagnac.

'Anyway,' he said to Adam, 'that's a nice little story for your book.'

'If it's true.'

Meacher didn't look in the least offended. 'Oh, it is. Take my word.'

'What about Gerald the GP? Is he still around?'

'No. Long dead.'

'If it's true that the children were adopted,' said Adam slowly, 'you would expect Harry and Cecile to have told them at some point. You would tell children that they were adopted, wouldn't you?'

'Would you? I don't know.'

'His daughter has never mentioned anything about it. Harry's obituary simply referred to his children, nothing about adopted children.'

George Meacher shrugged. 'Sometimes you start off lying – and I suppose silence can be as good as a lie – and you get to a point where it's more of a problem to tell the truth than carry on lying. You do what's best.'

The waiter brought the bill. Adam stared at the total. Either this was an enormous amount of money to be conned out of for nothing, or it was worth every penny. He had no way of knowing. He handed over his credit card.

'The thing is, I can't put something like that in a book

without verification. Forgive me – but you could be making it all up.'

'True.' Meacher tapped the ash from his cigarette, nodding.

'I can't ask his children. I mean, it's not something you –' He stopped, sighed. 'Anyway, if it is true, I don't think they know, somehow.'

'Mmm. That's a bit of a problem.' Meacher grinned.

Adam signed his credit-card slip and put away his wallet, tape recorder, pen and notebook. 'Thank you for your time and trouble.'

'Always a pleasure.'

Adam looked across at the happy, well-fed Meacher, bathed in a haze of cigarette smoke, his triple Armagnac still before him. Then he got up and left.

Meacher crushed out his cigarette and went to the gents' for a long and gratifying piss. Then he returned to the table, picked up his cigarettes and his brandy, and went downstairs to the bar. He perched again on the bar stool where he had been sitting when Adam first came in.

'Who was your friend, then, George?' asked the barman, wiping glasses. 'Not often someone buys you lunch upstairs.'

'Some journalist,' replied Meacher. He lit another from the new pack of Marlboros. Talking about Harry and their times together in Soho all those years back – it had been strange. He never much thought about life then, when he had been young. Suddenly it seemed as clear as yesterday. All the chaotic times fused into a single image – himself, coming down Old Compton Street in the bright, clear late morning, head a bit thick but going to be all right, Robert Colquhoun sitting on the step of the Golden Lion in his tweed coat, smoking, thinking about nothing, waiting for opening time, for that blessed, raw sound of the bolts dragging back and shutters going up, and the first of the day. He could smell the room he and Harry had shared, almost feel beneath his hand the wooden knob on the cupboard where they kept their bread, maybe a lump of cheese wrapped in greaseproof paper. No fridges then. Bottled beer. Sometimes oysters at Wheeler's when one of them was flush. Sometimes a plate of corned beef and pickles in the pub. What a life. Those years. Here he was, still in this place, still in Soho, alone. People bought you drinks all right, people still talked, but it wasn't like back then, when you still thought you were going to make something of your life, when the next drink, the next conversation, the next exchange of witty banter, seemed worth living for. The next day, the next drink. Friends. And everyone growing old and thinking time wasn't paying any attention, with the present turning into a past that some journo was going to write about. And here he still was, sitting in the French, waiting for someone to come and buy him a drink. Someone like Adam.

'Fucking idiot,' he muttered. About whom, he wasn't quite sure.

Adam walked back down through Chinatown to Leicester Square. It was busier now, the day in full flight. He sat down on a bench in the gardens, and tried to think. He hadn't a clue what to do. Not a clue. He watched the pigeons stepping in aimless circles. In his heart, he believed every word Meacher had told him. There was the possibility it was a piece of malicious mischief-making, but Adam didn't think so. Yet he couldn't possibly put such a thing into print without talking to Harry's family, without verifying the story. And how was he to do that? Cecile had actually talked about giving birth to Bella and Charlie – he could hardly go back and confront her with Meacher's story. Or could he?

He thought about Bella. Maybe she knew. Maybe Charlie did. Maybe Cecile had told them ages ago about the adoption, but for some reason they had all agreed to collude in keeping it secret. Why? Well, why did anyone do anything? Perhaps they simply didn't see any need for people to know. Yet if he proceeded on the assumption that Bella knew, and asked her about it, there was always the horrible possibility that she *didn't* know . . . And then he would be right in it. If Bella and Charlie didn't know, didn't they have a right to? Even so, it seemed incredibly presumptuous of him to take it upon himself to tell them.

Leaving the dilemma of the family aside, he couldn't help feeling a certain appalled elation. This was exactly the kind of new information about Harry which he'd hoped might turn up. He wondered how much Harry would have welcomed him making the discovery. He'd certainly never once mentioned George Meacher, and that, given that they'd shared a room together for some months, had to amount to some kind of concealment. Adam remembered Harry saying, about a month before he died, 'It would be interesting to see what you make of my life. A pity I won't be around to read it. Maybe it would surprise me.' And he had smiled in that way Harry had. Was that some sort of challenge to Adam to unearth this kind of secret? A licence to find out the truth . . .

He had no idea. He didn't know where to go from here.

5

'Does this look all right?' Megan twisted in front of the mirror, trying to survey the back of the dress she had bought for Jo's wedding.

'Fine. Very nice,' said Adam.

She turned and surveyed Adam. 'I wish you'd dress up a bit, sometimes.'

Adam was wearing his one and only suit. 'I don't do dressing up. Come on. We're going to be late if we don't go now.'

They left the flat and set off in Adam's Fiat for Epsom.

The narrow road where the church was situated was lined with cars. Adam squeezed the Fiat into a space on the verge between a Jag and a Land Rover, and he and Megan made their way to the church.

Adam had no particular expectations of the occasion. He was prepared to be mildly bored, since he knew no one and assumed Megan would spend most of her time talking to old school friends. He had his doubts about the relevance of his presence there at all. It was only as they nudged their way into a pew on the bride's side, and Megan began to introduce Adam to the various couples around them, that he understood his role. It was bemusing. He had never, until this moment, thought of himself as being anyone's appendage. He was part of a unit. The entire congregation, he realized, consisted of little family units. That was how everyone was identified. The bride and groom were their own about-to-be unit, there were aunts and uncles, mothers and fathers, grandmothers and grandfathers, themselves little units forming a much bigger one. There were young-married-couple units – a lot of them, it seemed – with toddlers and very new babies. The sense of being identified according to which unit you belonged to, even down to the business of being ushered to the correct side of the church – bride or groom? – was peculiarly strong. Adam decided he didn't care for it. When he and Megan were with people socially in London, although they were together, so to speak, he was not conscious of being identified as a couple. Here he felt his entire existence was defined only by his relationship to Megan.

'This is Adam,' Megan said, introducing him to people. In context, these innocuous words seemed to have 'and he's mine' automatically tagged on at the end. He knew the thought was unfair to Megan, but he couldn't help it. He didn't like being seen as someone's accessory, or other half. He realized, with sudden misgivings, how happy Megan seemed to be in the cosiness of it all.

He smiled politely at the various people Megan introduced him to, but had nothing to say. It simply wasn't the right set-up for conversation. While Megan chatted to a red-faced young woman in the pew behind, who was struggling to contain a boisterous one-year-old on her lap, Adam kept himself amused with a quick riffle through the Book of Common Prayer.

Suddenly there was a rustling and murmuring and

turning of heads. Adam assumed this heralded the entrance of the bride. Odd, he thought, since the organ music was still pootering tunelessly along, instead of blasting out something triumphal. He turned round, along with everyone else, and was astonished to see Bella entering the church with Charlie and Claire and a few friends. What on earth were they doing here? Megan would certainly have mentioned if any of her friends knew the Day family, so presumably they were here on account of the groom. He gazed at Bella, musing on the coincidence. She looked, Adam thought, utterly amazing. She was wearing a suede skirt of a dusty shade of pink, a cashmere top of the same colour, and boots. No hat. Her raggedly cut blonde hair was longer than when he had last seen her. But it wasn't the way she looked that went straight to Adam's heart – it was the expression on her face. Conscious of the attention she was attracting, she looked defensive, yet provocatively proud and endearingly apologetic all at the same time. Adam found himself smiling as he turned back to his perusal of Psalm 21.

'That's Bella Day!' whispered Megan.

'I know,' said Adam. Ever since he'd had lunch with George Meacher, he'd been debating how best to tackle the ticklish issue of Meacher's unlikely story about the adoption. Seeing Bella here today, delightful though it was, only served to remind him that he had to do something about it soon. Today, however, would definitely not be a good day.

At the end of the wedding service he filed dutifully from the church with Megan by his side.

'Oh, there's Imogen!' squeaked Megan, sighting a long-lost friend among the guests. She trotted across the grass in her kitten heels, leaving Adam on his own. He stood aimlessly on the gravel path for a few moments, chattering guests milling around him, then decided to wander off and soak up the morose charm of the ancient churchyard.

He surveyed the time-worn epitaphs on the headstones, reflecting with pleasant melancholy on his own mortality, and came at last to a little cluster of smaller headstones in the mossy turf beneath a very large yew. As he walked around these, he suddenly came upon Bella, leaning on the other side of the yew tree, smoking.

'Hello there.'

She turned, eyes widening in surprise. Her smile lit him up inside. 'Adam! How extraordinary to see you here. Are you a friend of Toby's?'

He shook his head. 'I don't know anyone. My girlfriend's an old friend of the bride's. They were at school together. I'm merely here as a decorative accessory.'

'Poor you.' She dropped her spent cigarette on to the grass and ground it in with her heel. 'Oh, well, you can always talk to me.'

'I take it you and Charlie know the groom.'

'Toby? Yes, we were at school together, years ago. It's quite astonishing how respectable he's become, considering the kind of teenager he was.'

There was a moment of speculative silence.

'We'd better be getting back. I think everyone's heading off to the reception.'

She nodded, and they walked back through the churchyard together. Close to her, Adam was faintly conscious of her scent, and thought how perfectly like a new summer's day she smelt.

Megan caught sight of Adam and Bella coming round the side of the church together. Adam said something to Bella, then they parted. Something about the serenity of his expression gave Megan a little pang of unfathomable anxiety.

'You were quick enough off the mark there.'

'She's the only person here that I know,' said Adam.

'I wasn't being serious. Anyway, you must introduce me later.' She glanced in Bella's direction. 'She's sickeningly gorgeous, isn't she?'

'If you say so,' said Adam, with an affectation of boredom. He smiled at Megan and kissed her face lightly.

Bella, standing near the church door, caught sight of this brief gesture. So that was the girlfriend. Well, they seemed very fond of one another. Not that Bella particularly cared.

The reception was held in a marquee in the large gardens of the bride's home. Heat under canvas, the tent-warmed scent of newly cut grass, always reminded Adam of school sports days – the familiar, involuntary flicker of excitement . . . or was that just the thought of being only a few yards away from Bella?

Throughout the meal Adam made polite small talk to a landscape gardener and an old schoolfriend of Megan's. During the speeches, which were to do with people and events he knew nothing about, he felt a growing sense of detachment. He had been up late the night before, and the wine and the closeness of the marquee were making him sleepy. He longed to get outside and stretch his legs. His glance strayed in the direction of Bella, who was sitting three tables away, and stayed there. She seemed utterly absorbed in what the best man was saying, and so he let his gaze dwell on the curve of her half-parted lips, her cheek, her hair . . . From contemplation of her loveliness, his mind moved idly to thoughts of Harry and Cecile. He saw now how utterly unlike either of them she actually was. Much as he disliked thinking about George Meacher, he couldn't help it. Looking at Bella now seemed to make sense of everything Meacher had told him.

Little bursts of clapping and laughter broke his train of thought and he looked round to find Megan gazing pointedly at him. He let his glance stray on as though he hadn't noticed.

When the speeches and formalities were over, little knots of people began to move between tables, finding friends and talking. Music began at the other end of the marquee. Adam leaned back in his chair and took a huge gulp of rather flat mineral water. He would be driving in an hour's time. He wished it were sooner.

'Adam Downing, isn't it? I've been expecting to hear from you.' Adam looked up to see Charlie smiling down at him, resplendent in full morning dress, glass in hand. He sat down in the chair which one of Adam's neighbours had vacated. 'How's the book coming along?'

'A bit stalled at the moment, I'm afraid.'

'Oh? Why's that?'

'Earning a living is rather getting in the way. But I hope to be getting down to it soon. I will be in touch.'

'Good, good. I know Harry was really keen for the book to happen . . .'

Suddenly Bella appeared and laid a hand on Charlie's shoulder. 'Toby's looking for you.'

'Is he? Better go and see what he wants.' Charlie gave Adam a nod, and went in search of Toby.

Bella sat down. Adam smiled at her. They both began to speak at once.

'Go on, you first,' said Bella.

'No – please. After you.'

'I was going to ask why you were staring at me all through Alan's speech.'

'Was I?'

'Yes.'

'I was thinking.'

'Oh?' She waited for the usual flattering elaboration.

'About you. Largely. About you and your family.' He glanced around. 'Look, this isn't really the time or the place, but I need to have a talk with you.'

Bella gave Adam her best soft, sensuous smile. She always felt terrifically sexy after a few glasses of champagne. She had already decided she couldn't let this one get away, girlfriend or not. He was too good-looking, too much of a challenge. It would be fun to seduce someone so achingly conventional, to find the animal beneath that literary exterior. That night at Gandercleugh had just whetted her appetite for the challenge. 'Sounds serious,' she said.

'Well, it is, actually. I know you must be very busy, but I was wondering if we could meet up in the next few days.' Just the thought of trying to tackle the subject made him go cold, but it had to be done. It could be that he was worrying needlessly.

'Mmm, I'm sure we could manage that. Why don't I come over one afternoon after rehearsals?'

'I don't want to put you to any trouble. We could meet in town, if you prefer.'

'It's no trouble, honestly.'

Perhaps it would be better if she came to the flat. It wasn't the ideal thing to discuss in public. 'What about Tuesday, then?'

'Fine. Tell me where you live.' He told her his address. 'I'll be round a little after four.'

Adam gazed after her as she threaded her way through the crowd of guests. Just three days in which to work out how to broach the information which he had bought from George Meacher. If he had three years, he didn't think he'd find the right way.

Bella dressed with care on Tuesday. Normally she wore any old thing to rehearsals, but that day she put on a blue cotton shirt tied above her midriff, showing an expanse of smooth, soft skin, and a pair of Versace hipster jeans. Not too dressy, simple but sexy. All day she felt elated. Then, on the way over to Baron's Court in the taxi, she was suddenly assailed by a dipping, familiar sense of depression. No use pretending to herself that this was going to be anything special or different. Bella knew herself too well. It was just the pattern repeating itself. Always the same old thing. She would meet someone, and decide she wanted them. It didn't matter that she didn't really know them. All that mattered was getting what she wanted. She would go after them, just as she had with Adam that first night. He'd turned her down, and it had made her mildly delusional, giving her a heightened sense of need. That was what she craved. Connection, the other person's desire. It was never the actual person she wanted, not in the long run. What she really yearned for was that high, the hit that came from flirting, touching, taking . . . That lovely rollercoaster that started with a shared glance, and ended up in bed. Nothing, nothing was ever as good as that first time. The shock of the new. The high curve. And after that – downhill all the way. Because she never cared enough.

Adam was probably going to be another one just like that.

She stared dejectedly out of the taxi window at Baron's Court cemetery rolling by. In America they had clinics for people like her, serial seducers, people who couldn't sustain nice, proper one-on-one relationships without getting bored, or resist gratifying their own impulsive desires. She never had the patience to wait for any man to take the initiative. The ones who did weren't the ones she wanted. It was always the ones like Adam – the ones who were spoken for, or apparently not interested. Even gay men – the ultimate challenge. She swallowed a sigh. One day she'd get some serious therapy, sort herself out. In the meantime, she might as well just get on with being the way she was. Someone might turn up along the way, someone with whom she could go the distance. It might even be Adam. Maybe he was the one. In which case, sod the girlfriend. And sod the therapy. Maybe she and Adam would live happily ever after.

In this confused state, Bella paid the taxi, got out, crossed the road, and pressed the bell of Adam's flat.

Adam was too wound up about the potential conversational minefield to pay a great deal of attention to the way Bella looked. Pretty as ever, he thought, as he let her in, but his thoughts shifted swiftly and nervously to what lay ahead.

'Coffee?' he asked as he led the way through to the living room.

'A drink would be even better. I've had a gruelling day.' She sat down on the sofa, kicked off her shoes, and tucked her bare feet beneath her. Nothing like a little alcohol to get things mellow. She looked up at him and felt a shiver of pleasure.

Adam glanced at his watch. 'What would you like?'

'Any old thing – a beer will do. Cold, if possible.'

He went into the kitchen, and while he searched out beers in the fridge, Bella jumped up and wandered through to his study, which lay off the living room.

Adam came back through, realized where she'd gone and followed her in, a chilled bottle of lager in either hand, mildly annoyed at this invasion of his private sanctum.

She was perusing his bookshelf. 'So this is where you toil away.' She plucked a copy of *The Penguin Book of Journalism* from the shelf, glanced through it, then put it back. 'Don't you find it lonely?'

'No. Never.'

She turned and took one of the bottles. 'Thanks.' She raised it to her lips. He was looking a bit distracted, clearly not yet in the kind of mood she required. Oh, well. Give it time. She went back to the living room, brushing past Adam, and sat down on the sofa. She sat to one side, leaving room for him, but Adam sat in a chair opposite, nursing his beer between his hands. He seemed preoccupied, nervous. Maybe he did have some hidden agenda, after all. She smiled to herself.

'So –' She put up a hand to ruffle her hair, 'what's this serious thing you need to talk to me about?'

'I have to warn you – what I'm going to talk about, you may not find easy.'

She let her hand drop to her lap. Whatever was going to happen here this afternoon, it was not the seduction of Adam Downing by Bella Day. The atmosphere and the man were too intent, too serious for that. Her mental focus shifted.

'I take it this is to do with the biography?'

'Of course.' What else, he wondered fleetingly, did she think he'd asked her here for?

'Well, go on.'

'A couple of weeks ago I met someone who knew Harry back in the fifties.'

She sat sipping her beer, waiting for Adam's next words.

'His name is George Meacher. Have you ever heard of him?'

She shook her head. Adam was acutely aware of how artlessly lovely she looked, sitting cross-legged, gazing at him. He wondered if the heart-stopping feeling he experienced was to do with that, or his own immediate anxiety.

'He's a photographer. That is – he was, once. Anyway,

that's not important . . .' Adam took an anguished swallow of his beer. 'Maybe I'm about to tell you something you know already, in which case –'

'Oh, for heaven's sake, get on with it!'

'Right. Right.' Adam took a deep breath. 'According to this man, Harry and Cecile never had any children. He said that . . . you and Charlie were adopted.'

Slowly Bella put down the bottle of beer. The change in her expression, from mild annoyance to one of stark incredulity, told him that she had never heard anything of this in her life before.

'Is that some kind of a joke?' She stared at him. 'I mean, is it?'

Adam looked at her helplessly. 'Look, Meacher shared a flat – a room – with your father after the war. He knew Harry very well. He knew your mother. It's what he told me. I'm really sorry. I thought – I hoped – you might already know. If it weren't for the fact that I'm involved with the biography, I would never dream of –'

'Oh, just shut up! Shut up talking!' She put both hands to her temples, clenching her eyes shut, taking deep breaths. She stood up and walked to the window, then back to the sofa, dashing tears from her cheeks. 'Well, clearly it's a load of lies! I mean – *clearly*! She folded her arms, but he could see she was trembling a little. 'Don't you think my parents would have mentioned something like that? I mean, don't you? You're not a very good journalist, Adam, if you let people con you like that! Who was this man? Someone on the make, probably. Did you pay him for that rubbish?'

'No. Not exactly.'

'Well, what a horrible, *stupid* thing to try and tell me! I know for a fact that it couldn't possibly be true.' He couldn't tell whether she was more agitated than angry. 'I think it is utterly, utterly pathetic of you to repeat that kind of drivel! Do you know what?' He gazed at her blankly, aware only of a physical wish to grab her and stop her, soothe her. 'I think you should just pack this rotten book in right now! If this is the kind of nonsense you're going to peddle, then just forget it! I don't want to know about it, or you! And that goes for our entire family!'

She picked up her bag from the sofa and swung it on to her shoulder, sending the beer bottle flying as she did so. As the flat door slammed shut, Adam sat there, staring at the puddle of lager spreading on the carpet and wondering whether this whole thing was George Meacher's horrible idea of a joke.

Bella paced the pavement until a cab appeared. Back in her flat fifteen minutes later, she sat smoking and thinking. Once or twice she wept. At the end of two and a half hours she rang Adam. Finding him out, she left a message on his answering machine. 'I'm sorry. I should have been a bit calmer. I want to hear it all, properly. Everything this man told you. Ring me.'

Adam had gone out for the evening with Megan and some friends. It was late when they got in. He saw the message light flashing and was unspeakably relieved to hear Bella's voice. He rang straight back.

'It's Adam Downing,' he said, when she picked up the phone. 'Did I wake you?'

'No. No, don't worry, you didn't.' Her voice sounded flat, distracted. 'I'm sorry I got so upset today.'

'I'm the one who should be apologizing.'

'I think we need to talk some more. We can't just leave things as they stand.'

'No. No, I realize that.'

'Do you have any free time tomorrow?'

'As much as you need. You can come here, or we can meet in town.'

'No, that's all right. I don't have rehearsals till after lunch, so I'll come over around half eleven.'

'That's fine.' He paused, hesitating, wanting to say something more, but she had hung up.

'Who were you ringing?' asked Megan, as he came into the bedroom.

'Bella Day.'

'Bit late, isn't it?'

'She left a message. I had to call her. She's very upset.'

'What about?'

'Nothing important. Something to do with Harry. I'll tell you about it another time.' He couldn't tell Megan. He couldn't tell anyone. Until he had sorted out truth from fiction, this was between himself and Bella. He lay awake for a long time after Megan had fallen asleep, remembering the wild misery etched on Bella's face, and how he had wanted to take her and hold her like a child, and make everything better.

The next morning, Adam found it increasingly difficult to concentrate as eleven-thirty drew near. It was almost ten to twelve when Bella rang the bell of his flat and he buzzed her up. Anyone else, he thought, taking in the grubby hipster jeans, trainers, beige denim jacket over a once-white T-shirt, would have looked a mess. But Bella, ethereal with dejection and tiredness, seemed to outshine the clothes she wore. Rather like George Meacher, thought Adam.

He made coffee, and once again she sat on the sofa, shoes kicked off, while he sat opposite.

'Tell me about this man, the one you spoke to. What's he called again?'

'George Meacher. He was a photographer. He worked for *Vogue* back in the sixties and seventies. He was quite well known.' In his research, Adam had been surprised to discover that Meacher had been something of a celebrity, not least because he found it hard to reconcile erstwhile fame with the abject seediness of Meacher's present existence. 'A friend put me in touch with him,' said Adam. 'I saw him in a photo, one of the ones your mother gave me. Hold on a minute, I'll show you.' Adam went through to his study and returned with the photograph. He handed it to Bella and sat down again, watching her intently as she scrutinized the faces. 'That's him at the back, the little guy with the dark hair. Evidently he had known your parents, but your mother skipped over him when I asked her to name everyone in the photo.'

Bella laid the photograph aside. 'Tell me everything he said.'

Adam told her.

Her face was expressionless as she listened, but there was something oddly dislocated about her gaze, as though it was shifting between mental states. Hardly surprising, thought Adam, as he drew to a close. Someone calmly telling you that you're not the person you thought you were. He tried to imagine the incredible jolt, suddenly being set at a remove from everything that had ever bound you to family, blood and being. News that made you a stranger to yourself.

If she believed him.

She sat very quietly, staring at her coffee. Then she shook her head. 'I think you've been had, Adam.'

He nodded. 'Well, possibly.' He felt embarrassed by his own certainty, by having to pretend he thought she might be right.

'I don't blame you for believing it. It's the kind of revelation that helps your book. I mean, if it were true, it wouldn't be anything especially scandalous or startling, but at least it would be something new.'

Again he nodded. He felt rather foolish. He didn't really want to assist her to deceive herself. 'Well, now you know.'

She put down her mug and covered her face with her hands. He thought at first she was crying, but she wasn't. She took her hands away, her face tired. 'The thing is – I don't know, do I? I'm utterly convinced there's not a scrap of truth in it, that he said all this just to stir up mischief. I mean, if it *were* true, wouldn't my birth certificate show a different name? It just seems too far-fetched to bother thinking about. But until I speak to my mother, I won't know. I can't believe she wouldn't have told Charlie and me. I can't believe it. You don't let someone grow up not knowing the truth about themselves, do you?'

Adam shrugged. He remembered what Meacher had said. *You get to a point where it's more of a problem to tell the truth than carry on lying* . . . 'I don't know. I honestly don't know.'

There was a long silence. At last Bella said, 'But you think George Meacher was telling the truth, don't you? Otherwise you would never have said anything to me.'

He hesitated for a few seconds, then met her gaze. 'Yes. I could be completely wrong. Completely. But I do think so.'

'So – I have to speak to my mother. I have to ask her. God.' She picked up the photograph. 'Can I borrow this?'

'Of course. It belongs to your mother, anyway.' He paused. 'I'm sorry. I'm sorry if I've started something that's going to – to cause trouble.' It sounded inadequate.

Bella gave a wan smile. 'That's your job, isn't it?'

'I didn't think my job was going to get this complicated.' He glanced at his watch. 'It's nearly half twelve. Why don't you let me buy you lunch? There's quite a good –'

'No,' interrupted Bella. 'I'm not really in the mood, I'm afraid. I'd better be going.' She stood up and stuffed her feet into her trainers. 'Thanks for coffee. And for your time.'

The more Bella thought about what George Meacher had told Adam, the more ludicrous and unlikely it seemed. Over the next few days, the little seed of uncertainty which had been planted within her almost shrivelled up and died. But not quite. She left rehearsals late one afternoon and went over to Dulwich to see her mother. She did this with the calm certainty that the whole thing was a fiction.

Cecile was busy in her workroom, engaged in the fiddly business of lining the jacket of a suit which she was making for a friend.

'Darling!' She kissed her daughter on both cheeks. 'What a lovely surprise! I'm just busy in the back room. Time I stopped for a break. Come through.'

Bella followed her mother to the kitchen. She was aware of a growing sense of nervousness. This was such a weird and horrible thing to be asking her mother about. But it had to be done.

'Drink or tea?' asked Cecile. She put her hands together and raised her eyebrows in that lovely, smiling way which Bella knew so well. This is my mother, thought Bella. No matter what.

Bella smiled and sat down. 'Drink, please. I really need it. I've had the lousiest day. I hate this play. I wish I wasn't doing it.'

'I never cared too much for Orton.' Cecile fished in the fridge and brought out a half-full bottle of Chardonnay. 'That mixture of silly and sinister.'

'I just have a dud feeling about it. Something tells me nobody's interested in an Orton revival right now.'

'Oh, I know that feeling. The awful instinct that something's a pre-ordained flop. You must inherit it from me. Bad luck. I'm sure it'll begin to feel better closer to the opening.' She handed Bella a glass of wine and sat down opposite her at the kitchen table. She lifted the tape measure draped round her neck and dropped it on the table. In the little silence which ensued, Bella picked it up and began to wind it round her index finger.

'Mother, I've got something to ask you, and I'm going to do it right away so that it's over and done with.'

'My lord,' said Cecile, 'you do sound serious.' Her mind ranged instantly over the possibilities, but did not come close.

Bella put down the tape measure. 'Do you know a man called George Meacher?'

The question so stunned Cecile that it seemed to reverberate, rolling like thunder in her hearing. She let the echoes die away. She took a drink of wine. She became immediately conscious of the very set of her own features, wondered what her expression was. She did not think she had moved a muscle. What had her expression been before the question? Fear took a very hard hold of her, squeezing her insides.

'No, I don't think so.' She essayed a smile.

'A friend of Dad's? Someone he lived with after the war?'

'I didn't know any of your father's friends from around that time, darling.' But the clear, poised features had suddenly begun to soften and tremble.

Bella picked up her canvas shoulder bag from the floor and took out the photo. She gave it to her mother. The effect was distinct and remarkable. Cecile's jaw slackened, her eyes blinked warily. 'Do you see him? There, at the back?' Watching her mother's reaction, Bella's mind faltered. She felt the sudden sick surge of possibility well up within her.

Cecile's words came out with a little gasp. 'Oh, him.

Yes, I remember him vaguely. What did you say his name was?' The effort was supreme.

'George Meacher.'

Cecile nodded. Silence lengthened. 'What about him?'

'He told Adam Downing that Charlie and I were adopted.' At the very words, Bella felt tears pricking at the back of her eyes. The gaze which she kept fastened on her mother's face was almost pleading.

Cecile said nothing for a long, long moment. She felt shaky, sick.

Bella continued to regard her mother, but tears blurred her vision. The sense of certainty that now gripped her was cold and heavy and awful. She put out a hand and grasped her mother's. 'Mother?'

Cecile's strong, handsome face had grown weak and fearful. 'Oh, darling . . . You are my daughter. You are!' She clutched Bella's hand with both her own.

'Is it true?' She had to fight against the awfulness of her mother's distress. She had to know.

Her mother began to sob. 'Yes. Yes, it is.' Her voice was a rasping whisper. In that instant, Bella felt Cecile's tears on her hand, and was shocked by how repulsed she felt at their wetness. This was not her mother. This was Cecile. But she was not her mother, never had been. That thing she had told herself – whatever happens, she is my mother – was suddenly untrue. The shock hit her, and seemed to pass through her mind and body with a shudder. She felt as though she were free-falling. Suddenly cut off and pushed out into a great void.

'Who am I?'

'You're Bella! You're mine!' Cecile dropped Bella's

hand and reached forward, trying clumsily to embrace her. But Bella pulled back.

'How could you never have told us? How could you let our entire lives go by and never have said a thing? Not a thing!' She stood up and walked across the kitchen. She turned and looked at Cecile, who was weeping.

'Who am I? Who's Charlie?'

Cecile drew a hand across her eyes and looked at Bella. Bella was astonished to see anger on her face. 'You're who you always have been! Who do you think you are?' Cecile's expression collapsed pathetically. 'You've both been mine since you were only days old! You've never belonged to anyone else. You're *my* children! I'm your mother . . . Nobody else.'

Bella stared at her. There was a world of incomprehension here, clearly.

Cecile began to cry again, and Bella went to her side, knelt down, and put an arm round her. She had to steel herself to be kind, to contain her own anger. Her voice shook as she spoke. 'Don't you understand, Mum? Don't you know what it is to be told you're not who you thought you were?' Cecile lifted her head and looked at Bella. 'Don't you have any idea?'

Cecile dried her eyes with the end of the long scarf that hung loosely at her neck. 'We would have told you. No – that's not true. I mean, we were going to. But when Harry and I split up, you were quite little, you see. And it didn't seem a good thing to undermine what security you had. We were so anxious to make you both feel that we loved you, despite the divorce, and so on. When you were teenagers – well, I came close to telling you. But I didn't.

I don't know why, but I didn't. It was never discussed between Harry and myself. By the time you were almost grown up, I was too afraid. You and Charlie could be quite hostile creatures a lot of the time, anyway – you know, all those ups and downs, the fights . . . I suppose all families have them, but I was so afraid that if I told you, it might drive you away completely. And then . . . well, there never seemed to be a right time. We'd left it too late. After a while, it didn't seem to matter any more. You were both who you were, you had grown up into such secure, lovely people . . . There didn't seem any need.' She gazed fearfully at Bella.

'Any *need*? When we could have gone on throughout our entire lives, believing something that simply wasn't true?' Bella rose from where she knelt. She pressed her fists hard against her skull, unable to contain the anger and outrage. 'You horrible, horrible, selfish woman . . .'

'No! No, I'm not! I did everything for the best –'

But Bella was now a human storm of tears and emotion. 'You lied to us! Isn't silence a lie? Letting people go through their lives thinking they're something they're not – isn't that a lie? How could you do such a thing? I don't even know who I am, where I come from! I thought everything began with you and Harry, I thought we *were* you. What am I? Where the hell am I from?' She leaned against the sink and wept, while Cecile watched her.

'Oh, darling . . . I never, ever wanted any pain for anyone –'

Bella turned round. 'Don't *say* that! What on earth do you think you've been storing up all these years?' She struck her chest with her fist. 'You let me and Charlie think we're your children, when we're not!'

'But you are!' Cecile's voice was thin with anguish. 'Please, please, sit down. Sit down here. Cry all you like. I'm still your mother – you know that. I'll tell you everything. Sit down.'

Bella shook her head, but she did as Cecile said. She sat down. She wanted to hear. It took her some moments to control her tears. She took a deep breath. 'Go on. Tell me. You owe me that much. Tell me.'

Cecile pressed her trembling lips together, determined not to let herself start crying again. 'Harry and I were married for eight years before we found out we couldn't have children. It was something to do with me, something they couldn't put right. I very badly wanted a family. Very badly. So we decided to adopt. We found out we would have to go through a dreadfully long process, lots of checking and bureaucracy . . . the prospect was a nightmare. I got very depressed, very anxious . . .' Cecile dabbed at her eyes with the end of her scarf, and pushed back strands of loose hair, trying to compose herself. 'While we were still deciding whether or not to go ahead, Harry must have spoken to George Meacher. I hadn't seen him since we were married. I never liked him. He was a horrid little drunk, I always thought, always scrounging money from people and saying vile things behind their backs. Anyway, I don't know what he said, but the next thing I knew, he'd put Harry in touch with a doctor, someone in Deptford, who knew a family . . .'

'A family?' Bella stared at Cecile. The shadowy female

figure which she had begun to imagine – some young girl in trouble, perhaps – instantly vanished.

'Yes.' Cecile met Bella's gaze. 'The woman had one child already, a boy. They had a lot of debt, a lot of problems. The husband was threatening to leave if they had another baby. He was a drinker, gambled a lot, and the woman was the only wage earner . . .'

The man. The woman. My mother and father, thought Bella. How could Cecile tell this story so dispassionately? Maybe to her that was what it had become. Just a story, the ghostly background to the real life she and Harry had given Bella and Charlie. That must be how she saw it.

'We were quite well off back then. Harry was doing very well. The doctor arranged it so that Harry paid for everything – the nursing-home fees, all the expenses, and a few thousand besides. And we got you and Charlie. It wasn't anything illegal, you know. Just private. A private adoption.'

'Did you meet her – my birth mother?'

'Oh, yes. We met them, we checked the family out very thoroughly. Well, as thoroughly as we could.'

'Was she upset? Was she sorry about what she was doing?'

'Darling, I don't know. It was something she had decided she had to do. It was very much a business arrangement.'

A business arrangement. My life, thought Bella. Charlie and me. We have a brother somewhere. I am not who I thought I was. I am . . . Her own identity suddenly failed her. 'What was their name?'

Cecile furrowed her brow in thought. 'Oh, God, I

should know . . . It was a simple name . . .' She closed her eyes. 'Kinley,' she said suddenly, opening them. 'Kinley.'

Bella sat back slowly in her chair. 'But our birth certificates . . . they show our name as Day. How did you – ?'

'You were both ours from the first.' Cecile's eyes filled with tears again. 'I told you, it was all done very privately. It wasn't difficult simply to go to the town hall and register you as our children. Because you *were* our children, you *were* and you *are* . . .' Cecile's voice dissolved into incoherent sobs.

Bella gazed at her with blank incomprehension. 'Oh, God, have you any idea what you've done, keeping this from us?'

Cecile looked up, eyes brimming with tears, and shook her head. 'No, I don't suppose I have. Please don't hate me.'

'It's nothing to do with hating you. But I don't know if I can begin to forgive you . . .'

'Are you going to tell Charlie?'

'How can you *ask* that? How can I not?'

Suddenly the telephone rang, making Cecile jump. She dabbed away her tears and went to answer it. Bella buckled her canvas bag and put on her jacket. Cecile turned and saw she was about to leave. She covered the mouthpiece with her hand.

'Bella . . . wait. Wait!'

Bella shook her head. 'I have to go. You carry on. I'll call you. I have to go.'

6

When Bella showed up for rehearsals the following morning, she felt gritty with lack of sleep, her head aching from an evening spent with too many cigarettes and her own thoughts. The other three cast members were already assembled on stage.

'Sorry I'm late,' said Bella, giving everyone quick air kisses. Jeremy put both hands on her shoulders and studied her features. A tall, sad-eyed man in his early fifties, Jeremy had been big in television drama in the eighties and was looking to this play to bring about a revival in his fortunes. He worked tirelessly on his fading good looks, combing his hair carefully to conceal his bald patch, dyeing it discreetly at the temples. He was unremittingly kind and solicitous of the welfare of all his fellow cast members.

'You look washed out, darling. Are you unwell?' he asked Bella.

'No, I'm fine,' said Bella, and tried to look bright.

'Come on, let's get started!' called Lance, the director. 'I want to sort out this business in Scene Four with the gun and the bottle. It's still very wooden. Bruce, Jeremy . . .'

Bruce, an improbably handsome young man who had been told too often for his own good that he looked like Rufus Sewell, got up from the chair where he had been lounging and prepared to make his entrance. Bella hung her jacket on the back of a chair and picked up a plastic apron from the table. Frank McVeigh, a portly, placid actor in his late fifties, shifted his chair to the side of the stage and carried on reading the sports section of the *Daily Telegraph*. Frank described himself as a character actor, but in fact he made a career out of playing variations of only one character – that of affable British buffer – which he carried about with him from play to play, and from one television drama to another. Since the death of his wife a year ago, he found it increasingly hard to concentrate and learn his lines, and he harboured a deep fear that his career was beginning to falter. He had been desperately relieved to get this role, much as he loathed Orton. He simply couldn't afford not to work.

'OK . . . We'll take it from the point where Caulfield enters. Just Bruce and Bella. And Bella, put a bit of starchy brightness into it. Look like you *want* to give Frank a blanket bath.'

Bella shook out the apron, trying to conjure up a vitality she did not feel. Lance gave a nod, Bruce made his entrance, and Bella, glancing across at him, spoke her line. 'Who are you? What do you want? I'm frightfully busy.'

'Your husband is outside. He's going to murder you.'

'You must be mistaken. We celebrate our wooden wedding in a fortnight.'

Lance interrupted. 'No, no. Come on, Bella – be snappy with that apron. Brisk, middle class – think Prunella Scales, think Briony Nugent.'

Thank you, Lance, thought Bella. Mothers, stepmothers, ghosts of mothers, were the last thing she wanted to conjure up. She delivered her line again, and Jeremy entered stage left, gun in hand, looking suitably distraught.

'You've strayed from the paths of righteousness. I'm going to kill you!'

At that moment, Bella's mobile phone began to warble from the pocket of her jacket hanging on a chair. Lance groaned.

'Sorry, sorry . . . I forgot to switch it off.' She answered it anyway.

'Bella, it's Mummy. I thought you'd be rehearsing. I was going to leave a message.'

'I am. What is it?'

'Please meet me for lunch. I really must talk to you.'

She hesitated. 'All right. There's a pub on the corner near the theatre, The Grapes. I'll see you there at one.'

She switched her phone off and hurried back to her mark.

'Thank you,' said Lance. 'Right. In you come, Jeremy, gun in hand . . .'

Cecile was already in the pub, sitting on her own in a booth, when Bella arrived. She looked very smart in a grey trouser suit, carefully made up, grey hair tied back, sipping a gin and tonic. Bella realized instantly that her mother was trying to retrieve something of the poise and certainty which had fled from her the day before. Her own hollow-eyed scruffiness was a sharp contrast.

'Darling, you look wretched.' Cecile's voice was soft with concern.

'Are you surprised? I had the most hellish night. Let me get myself a drink and a sandwich. D'you want anything?'

Cecile shook her head.

Bella returned with a mineral water and a cheese sandwich.

Cecile waited until Bella had sat down, then spoke carefully. 'I thought, after all the shocks of yesterday, that we should try to deal rationally with what's happened.'

Bella recognized this attempt to regain lost moral ground, even if she didn't entirely sympathize with it. 'I think it was a bigger shock for me than for you, somehow.'

'It's all been –' Cecile sighed, 'such a mess. My fault, I know.'

'And Harry's, probably. But there's no point in finding fault. Things are as they are. Funny, really – I spent a lot of last night wishing I'd never known. Which is what you had intended.'

'No, it was never –'

'The point is, I do know.'

'Have you spoken to Charlie?'

'God, no . . .'

'Good. I'm glad. I'm frightened to think how badly he may take it. In fact . . .'

'Don't. Don't even think it. He has to know.'

'I know.' Cecile opened her handbag. 'I imagine –' She hesitated, drawing out a piece of paper and laying it on the table. She took a hasty sip of her drink. 'I imagine you'll want to try to find her.'

'My birth mother, you mean.'

'Yes.'

'I don't know. I spent a long time last night trying to

make sense of – to work out what I feel. I'm still not sure.'

Cecile nodded. 'After you'd gone, I went through all my papers, and I found a few things. I would never have thrown anything away. I suppose I realized there was always a chance . . . Anyway, these are their names, and the address they were living at in Deptford.' She pushed the paper towards Bella.

'It was nearly thirty years ago, Mummy. I shouldn't think they're still there.'

'No, perhaps not. Anyway, it's a start. If you do intend to do anything, that is.'

'I won't know until I've spoken to Charlie.' She ate one of her sandwiches. 'It did occur to me that perhaps you should be the one to tell him.'

'Bella –'

'Don't worry. I'll tell him. I am his real sister, after all.' Bella caught her mother's swift, unhappy glance. 'You think this can be dealt with rationally. It can't. I feel such incredible anger towards you, such seething bloody *rage* –' She clenched one hand into a fist, then spread the fingers slowly out. 'I don't know how long it's going to take me to get over it. Maybe it'll stay for ever. I spent all yesterday evening thinking about everything, trying to see things from your point of view. I know you've given us the best life possible, that you've done so many things for us and we should be very grateful. But I find it so hard to forgive you for not telling us. I don't think you can begin to understand how entirely it changes the way I feel about myself. All the things I've ever accepted about my identity . . . Little things, being told I take after Grandma . . .' She looked strangely at her mother. 'You've even talked about what a difficult time you had when I was born. How could you do that? How could you go around embroidering this – this fantasy?'

Cecile's eyes filled with tears. Embarrassed, she kept them fixed on her glass. 'Because that's what it was. A fantasy. I wanted to pretend that you were absolutely mine, that I'd given birth to you. It made it seem more real, to hear myself saying things . . . Anyway, it was true. It happened that way – for your mother.'

'But just saying those things made it impossible for you to tell us the truth, ever! You must have known that.'

Cecile said nothing.

'I don't believe the things you said yesterday,' went on Bella. 'I don't think you missed chances, or kept meaning to tell us. You never meant to. You couldn't have. That was such a mistake. You've done damage that may be beyond repair. I don't know. I only know that things are not going to be the same for a long time.'

Still Cecile said nothing.

'I have to be going. I've some things to do before I get back to rehearsals.' Bella drank the remains of her mineral water and stood up.

'Don't leave this.' Cecile pushed the piece of paper across the table.

Bella hesitated, then picked it up. She left Cecile sitting alone, staring at her drink.

That evening, Bella rang Adam. She didn't want to have to tell him that he'd been right all along, but she had to. He deserved to know. She caught him just as he was about to leave to meet Megan and some friends.

'I thought you might like to be kept up to date. I spoke to my mother.'

'Oh?'

There was a pause. 'You were right. George Meacher was right.'

'God. I see. I'm sorry. I mean, I feel like I brought all this about –'

'Don't. I suppose I should be glad I found out. I don't think I ever would have, otherwise. At least I know . . .' She had intended to remain self-contained, controlled, but tears began to break up her voice. 'At least I know . . . oh God, I don't know anything! I feel so empty. I don't know what to do.'

'Look, I can come round, if you want to talk about it.'

She snuffled into a tissue, then said, 'Would you mind? You're the only person I *can* talk to. I haven't spoken to Charlie yet. God knows how I'm going to manage that . . .'

'Give me half an hour,' said Adam.

He called Megan on her mobile. He could only just hear her voice above the Friday-night roar and babble of the wine bar.

'Sorry, I don't know if I can make it. Something's come up.'

'Oh, darling, that's a shame.' She had only begun to call him 'darling' very recently. He found it hard to get used to. 'What is it?'

He hesitated. 'I'll tell you when I see you.'

Adam doubted very much whether he would. So far he hadn't uttered a word of any of this to Megan. He didn't entirely trust her discretion. Like all PR people, she was an insatiable gossip.

'Thanks for coming over.'

Adam followed Bella into her living room and sat down on the sofa. The room smelt of stale smoke.

'Would you like some wine?'

'Thanks.'

She brought through a bottle of white wine and poured out two glasses, then curled up at the other end of the sofa. Her hair was ragged and uncombed, and her face bare of make-up, dark hollows beneath her eyes.

'When did you speak to your mother?'

'Yesterday.' Bella picked up her drink. 'And today. She came over to meet me in my lunch break. I think she was trying to repair the damage done to her dignity the day before, as much as anything else. Yesterday, when I finally got the truth out of her, she just fell apart.'

'Do you blame her?'

'Not really. She'd spent nearly thirty years keeping up a lie. Being found out must have been fairly awful.'

'So what happens now?'

Bella sighed. 'It's a process of rebuilding, I suppose. I start from nothing. I *am* nothing.'

'That's not true. There's more to identity than –'

'Than what? Knowing who your mother and father are? Knowing why they gave you away?' She finished her wine and refilled her glass. Adam had drunk only half of his. 'Though I think I know the answer to that one. Charlie and I were worth more to our real parents in terms of money than as children. Their children.' Her eyes brimmed with tears. 'I thought – well, not that George Meacher said anything . . . I suppose I had the usual stereotypical situation in mind. Some young girl, pregnant by accident – that kind of thing . . .' Bella dashed away her tears. 'Yes, well, guess what? My real parents were married. They already had a son. They just didn't want me, or Charlie. They preferred money instead.' She told Adam, jerkily, everything that Cecile had told her. 'So – all my life I've had another brother, and I didn't know.'

There was a silence. Adam felt totally inadequate, quite unable to find any words that would help Bella in her anchorless, unhappy state. He noticed the cigarette packet lying at the end of the table. He flicked it towards her.

Bella sighed and shook her head. 'I gave up this morning. It's empty.' She picked up the packet and crushed it between both hands. 'Part of the new me. Whoever I am, she doesn't smoke.' She got up to drop the packet in the wastepaper basket.

'What will you do now?'

'Oh, Christ, how do I know?' She moved across to the window. The sky outside was deepening to dusk. She flicked the blind shut. 'I'm sorry. I shouldn't be so angry. Not with you.'

'Oh, I don't know. You have every right. I meddled.'

'Stop apologizing. I've asked myself hundreds of times whether it wouldn't be better if I'd never found out. That's pointless. I have to face the fact that I know, and decide what to do about it.' She came back and sat down. 'My mother gave me the address of the house my parents were living in when Charlie and I were adopted.

Somewhere in Deptford, of all places. That's all I have to go on. Because it was all done privately, it's not as though there's some great DSS file on me. The chances are they moved away long ago.'

'Do you want me to help?'

'How d'you mean?' She rubbed her eyes and poured him some more wine.

'I could go round there, make some inquiries. Good investigative journalism.'

'I could do that myself, you know.'

'True. I just thought it might be harder for you – I mean, you don't know what you're going to find. Or who. If someone else goes, it's at arm's length. You can feel your way.'

'I'd thought of writing. God knows what I'd say. Anyway, writing or going there, the whole thing could well be pointless. It's so long ago.'

'You don't know. It's worth trying. I take it you want to make some kind of contact?'

Bella gave a heavy sigh. 'Yes. Having spent my entire life thinking I was the real daughter of Harry and Cecile . . . Well, having that shot from under you leaves a hell of a hole, I can tell you.'

Adam pondered this. 'It doesn't change the fact of who you are. All the things that have happened to you since the day Harry and Cecile adopted you – they're the really important things. The people who have been there in your life matter more than the ones who weren't.'

'That's so trite, so easy to say! How do I know what I've lost? How can I ever recover what's been taken from me?'

'It's not trite,' said Adam. He gazed down at his glass. 'I lost my mother when I was eight. My father effectively farmed me out to boarding school because he didn't know what else to do with me. I must have seen him all of nine times – the longest was for a whole week – until he died when I was nineteen. So I do know a little of what I'm talking about.'

'God, I'm sorry . . . It's very selfish of me, thinking I'm the only one that's had awful things happen to them.'

'That's just it.' Adam smiled. 'Nothing awful *has* happened to you. Admittedly, finding out you were adopted is one hell of a thing, but when you consider the life you've led this far, you have to ask – couldn't it have been worse?'

'But don't you *see*? I don't know! I don't know how it might have been!'

'I don't know how it might have been if my mother hadn't died,' said Adam. His eyes darkened a little, and he reached out to refill his glass. She watched his face carefully, thinking how little she knew him. 'Nobody knows the things that could have happened, all the imponderables. All we can do is play the hand we've been dealt.'

Bella leaned her head on her hand, gazing at him thoughtfully. 'You're quite a lonely guy, aren't you?'

'I don't know about that. Alone, perhaps. I suppose from an early age I've seen myself as – well, fairly singular. You know . . . Everyone else at boarding school had something stable in their background: a family, parents, brothers, sisters, somewhere they came from. I had my aunt and uncle. Lovely people, but they were very much guardians. They weren't where I came from. They were where I went in the holidays. So I've always been a bit of a loner, self-reliant. But I like being by myself. I like my thoughts, my work.'

There was something touching in the way he spoke, and she gave a small smile and stretched out her hand to his. It was a slight, friendly gesture, lasting no more than a second. Adam wished it didn't have such an electric effect on him. He drank off the remains of his wine, conscious suddenly of an almost imperceptible alteration in the atmosphere between them. Bella spoke, as if to fill the silence. 'I take it that was your girlfriend – the one you were with at Toby's wedding?'

'Yes.'

'Long term?'

'You could say. So far . . . That is – I don't know.' His eyes met hers. 'You know.' Adam wondered how she would react if he said what he really thought. Along the lines of, *It was all going along fine until I met you, sat next to you in church. Since then, I don't know what I think about her, about anything.*

'What's her name?'

'Megan.'

'What does she do?'

'She works in PR. Vosper Barker Finch.'

'I've heard of them. Maybe she'd like to do a bit of PR on this wretched play of ours.' Bella yawned. 'Sorry. I didn't get a lot of sleep last night. So, tell me more about her.'

'Why?'

'I'm interested.'

'Why?'

'I'd just like to know.' Bella sipped her wine and gave Adam a wry smile. 'After all, she was the reason you turned me down.'

'No, she wasn't.'

'I distinctly remember you saying at the time that you didn't want to sleep with me because you had a girlfriend.'

Adam leaned his head back and closed his eyes. He had no idea what to say to this. He had never met anyone so constantly challenging, so intensely provocative and evidently insecure.

Bella shrugged. She lifted the empty bottle and waggled it mournfully. 'I'll get us another.'

'No, look –'

But she'd already gone through to the kitchen. A moment later she reappeared with another bottle and refilled Adam's glass and her own. She snuggled into the cushions in her corner of the sofa, and they sat there and talked about their childhoods, mulling over questions about one's sense of identity, of self. After an hour or so, Bella said, 'This is lovely, getting pissed with you.'

'That wasn't quite the point of this evening.'

'Yes it was. Is. You came round to make me feel better, and I do.'

'I'm not going to be able to drive back, you know. I'll have to get a cab.'

'You don't have to go. Stay. Stay the night.'

Some contemplative seconds passed while Adam put together what he felt he should say. He set down his glass. 'That time – the night you came to my room at your stepmother's house – it wasn't just to do with Megan.

It was because I hardly knew you. We'd only just met. And now you're doing it again.'

'Actually, I'm offering you the spare bed.'

Adam laughed, and then she laughed. They looked at one another for a long time. Adam simply couldn't take his eyes away from hers. It was the kind of moment in which a hundred things happen without anyone doing anything. At its end, at its perfect conclusion, Adam leaned across. She came to him, and he kissed her in a state of utter and close absorption. It was amazing, perfect.

He drew one finger gently down her cheek. 'God, you are beautiful. And a bit drunk. And full of problems. To which casual sex is not the answer.'

'It might help.'

Before he could answer this, the phone trilled from the kitchen. While Bella rose to answer it, Adam sat in a state of dazed arousal, trying to recover his senses. All he had to do was to get up, put on his jacket . . . He could take a chance on driving home. He couldn't be that far over the limit.

Before he could stir himself into any kind of action, Bella came back. 'That was Cecile. She's told Charlie.' She sat down, white-faced.

'But you said –'

'I know, I know. But she seems to have had some kind of crisis of conscience. Said she realized how unfair it would have been to burden me, it was her duty, stuff like that . . .'

'What happened?'

'Charlie went round to see her earlier this evening

after work. She's making the dresses for Claire's stupid bridesmaids, and he was dropping something off. I don't know . . . Anyway, she told him. Where she found the courage, I can't imagine. I know she would be terrified of how Charlie would react.'

'And how did he react?'

'She didn't say. She couldn't, really. She seemed quite . . . overwrought. I suppose it's pretty hellish, going through the same ordeal twice in two days, telling your adult children they're not who they think they are.'

'But out of the blue? At least with you there was some kind of build-up, you already knew there was a possibility.'

'I know. I know.' Bella stared into the distance, head in her hands, and her eyes filled with tears. 'God knows how he is.'

The phone rang again.

'I suspect you're about to find out,' said Adam.

'D'you think?'

He nodded. She brushed away her tears and rose to answer it.

This time Adam got up and put on his jacket. He fished for his car keys and waited for Bella to come back.

She nodded. 'He's coming over. He sounded – he sounded sort of stunned. A bit out of it. Poor Charlie.'

'Poor you. Poor both of you.' He put one hand on her shoulder, touched her face with the other.

'Thanks for coming round.'

'Any time. And I meant what I said. If you need my help, just call.'

'I will. Thanks.'

Adam drove carefully home, trying hard not to think about what had nearly happened between himself and Bella. Failing, he let himself think about it over and over again.

Megan was in when he got home, curled up in short pyjamas on the sofa, watching television.

'What happened? We waited for you till nine, then we went to that Thai place round the corner. It's very good. I tried to call you on your mobile, but you must have had it switched off.'

Adam sank into a chair. 'It was Bella Day. She needed to talk to someone, so I went round to see her.'

Megan gave him a glance. 'She seems to be making quite a few demands on your time. What's her particular problem?'

'It's to do with the biography. I turned up a piece of information that isn't exactly welcome news for the family. She was rather upset.'

'What information?'

'I honestly can't tell you. Not right now. It's still something of a mess.'

'Oh, that's great. You spend all Friday evening with some other girl and you can't even tell me what it's about.'

'Come on, Meg. You know everything to do with the biography has to remain confidential for the moment.'

'So you don't trust me?'

He could tell she was sparring idly, purely for the sake of it, not out of real annoyance. He reached out a hand. 'Come here.'

She rose and came across, sat on his lap, and allowed herself to be cuddled. 'I'm sorry I messed up tonight. We can do something tomorrow.'

'That's all right. You're here now.' She kissed him, and he kissed her back at some length, trying not to remember the touch and feel and scent of Bella just half an hour ago, knowing that the worst part of his betrayal lay not in having kissed Bella, but in wishing he could do it again. And again, and again . . . He had, he realized, some rather confused emotions to deal with.

Charlie spent Friday night at Bella's place. They talked until half three. Bella came into the kitchen the following morning at eleven to find Charlie already up, sitting over coffee in his boxer shorts and unbuttoned shirt, unshaven, still with a stunned, hollowed-out look on his face.

'How did you sleep?' asked Bella.

'Quite well, oddly enough.' His voice was flat, emotionless. He turned to gaze out of the window at the soft, early sunshine. 'I'm just trying to get used to feeling utterly . . . dislocated.'

'I know what you mean.' She sat down opposite him, took one of his hands in hers, and together they went through again, as if for reassurance, their new, disjointed feelings.

'All that thing you take for granted,' said Bella. 'That thing of being part of this larger whole. Like when Grandpa died, that idea of some . . . some past continuity, like his death was part of my story. Our story. And of course, it wasn't at all.'

'It was, in a way. If that's the way we believed it, took it to be.'

'But not really. I mean, there's a shadow life out there. There's something that actually was our real beginning, going on without us. And we've spent all that time somewhere else.'

'I've been telling myself I mustn't look at it that way. Life is real, it's what it is, what it's been for us. You know we've been lucky.'

'Yes, I know that. It's exactly what Mummy said. It's just . . . you know, the might-have-been part of things. To know that you began somewhere else, somewhere you were meant to belong.'

Charlie shook his head. 'I've thought about that. We belong to the past we actually have. After all, there's such a thing as destiny.'

Bella was suddenly reminded of the conversation she had had with Adam the evening before. She felt a little flicker of emptiness. She missed him, or something about him. Probably just because she was tired, and he was the last person to have been kind to her.

'We are who we are because of what happened,' went on Charlie. 'We couldn't have been any different. That's simply not what happened.'

'I know. The point is, nothing in me will feel right until I find out, until I learn who our real family are. If I don't, it'll be like a part of me that doesn't fit, that I can't place. Don't you feel that?'

Charlie shook his head. 'All I feel is . . . anger. Such anger. Such disbelief.'

'Were you horrible to her?'

'To Mother? I was utterly foul. And I don't blame myself. Not at the moment. I just cannot comprehend how she could let us – let us . . .'

'I know. I know all of that.' There was silence. 'What I want to know is – do you want to find them?'

'Jesus, Bell . . . have you any idea what that might be like? Our brother could be an armed robber, a drug addict – the entire family might be a swarming nest of horrible people. Maybe you've got some rosy notion that it will all be wonderful and heart-warming, that –'

'No! I haven't any more idea than you do what they'll be like! Of course I haven't.' She got up wearily and poured some coffee from the pot which Charlie had brewed. She instinctively reached to the shelf where she kept her cigarettes. She remembered, stopped, and sighed. 'But I'd rather know, I'd rather find out, than wander around day after day, week after week, wondering who they are, what they're like. Wouldn't you?'

Charlie stared out of the window, saying nothing.

'I mean, we have a brother. Not a half-brother, but a proper brother, like you are to me. Aren't you curious? Wouldn't you like to meet him? To meet our real mother and father, if you could?'

Charlie thought for a while, and at last he said quietly, 'I don't think so. Not necessarily, no. It could start something we'll both regret for a long time.'

'How can you say that? Surely it's the other way round?'

'Bella, don't you realize who you are? You're a well-known actress. You don't know these people, or what they might be like. They might want to exploit you, us . . .'

'Will you stop talking about them like that? They're our family!'

Charlie looked at Bella, his gaze unsteady. 'Are they?'

Bella said nothing.

At last she shook her head. 'Charlie, if I don't follow this up, I'll go out of my mind.'

'But if you do follow it up – well, then, I haven't really got a choice, have I?'

'Look, the chances are they haven't lived at that address for years. It'll probably come to nothing.' She watched as Charlie rose, slopped the dregs of his coffee into the sink, and poured himself a fresh cup. 'I'm just as scared as you are.'

'No doubt.' He sat down again. 'I think I'm just being more realistic.'

'Adam Downing offered to help.'

'Oh, Adam Downing . . . right. The busybody who stirred up this whole mess.'

'He had no idea. You can't blame him.'

'Don't worry. I know none of it's his fault.' He sipped his coffee. 'So how does he intend to help?'

'Well, if you like, he'll go to the address, find out if they still live there . . .' Bella watched Charlie's face, could tell he was working through the advantages of this proposal. 'That way,' went on Bella, 'we only need to get involved if we want to. If –'

'If what we find isn't too awful, you mean?'

Bella shrugged.

'Put that way, it sounds very cowardly.'

'Yes.'

'It's not the way you'd want to do it, is it?'

'No.'

'But there's no halfway house here. If you find them, then, as I said, I'm left without any choice.' Bella said nothing. 'Oh, God,' said Charlie, rubbing his hands wearily across his face. 'You have to do what you want to do, Bell. Only don't expect things to turn out the way you want them, that's all.'

The next week, Charlie had an important criminal trial in Leeds, and Bella was busy rehearsing for the opening of *Funeral Games*. Bella suspected that Charlie was trying to deafen himself, to defy fate, to obliterate the enormous change in his life by pretending it hadn't happened. She had seen him do the same thing with less momentous issues in the past. She had no real notion of how he was coping, but she knew that this would be his way of trying to stop it affecting his life. If Bella did nothing, Charlie need do nothing.

In the meantime, Cecile was trying tentatively to build bridges. The strategy she adopted was similar to Charlie's, in that she made no reference to the adoption, asked no questions about what steps Bella and Charlie intended to take, but conveyed in every gesture and phone call a sense of apologetic hopefulness. It was very hard to resist. Bella sensed her mother's very real fear of estrangement, and pitied her. To create hostility seemed futile, given the problems which she and Charlie now faced.

Bella knew that, whatever truth she and Charlie were now in possession of, it was a mere fragment of the whole. She pondered Charlie's desire to leave things as they were, and instinctively felt that it would be ultimately destructive to both of them not to find out more. When she found herself copying out the address in Deptford into her address book for fear of losing the piece of paper, even though she knew it off by heart, she knew she had to do something. She rang Charlie in chambers at the end of the week.

'I think we have to do something about finding our real parents. I know you're not keen, but I can't go on like this. I can't stop thinking about it.'

To her surprise, Charlie said, 'I know. There was a chap on the jury in Leeds, and he looked a bit like me, a few years older, and I kept thinking . . .' Charlie stopped. Bella heard him sigh at the other end of the phone. 'To be honest, I wish it would all just go away. It's on my mind all the time. I've even thought about seeing an analyst.'

'That's not the answer. Talk to me, talk to Cecile, talk to Claire –'

'I haven't told her.'

'Why not?'

'I don't know. I'm not sure what I'd be telling her . . . That I'm not who she thinks I am? That she's marrying someone under false pretences?'

'Oh, come on, Charlie. She's marrying you for who you are. Anyway, how can you not tell her something like this? She's meant to be the most important person in your life.'

'Yes, but it's more complex than that. When you marry someone, their family is important . . . Who they are, where they come from. It's not easy, when suddenly every assumption you ever made about yourself is – is –'

'All the more reason why we have to do something. I'm going to ask Adam Downing if he'll help. He said he would, and I don't want to do it on my own. I can understand if you don't want to. But one of us has to find out.'

Charlie sighed. 'All right, all right. You know, Bell –' She could hear his voice break a little, 'this past week has been the purest nightmare for me. I just don't know what's going on any more.'

'Oh, God, I know. Charlie, you should have talked to me.'

She could hear the tears in his voice now. 'You're much stronger than me. You seem to be coping . . .'

'No, Charlie, I'm not. I'm not. I just know that it will help if we can find out more. I truly believe it will. I'll call Adam. And please – talk to Claire. Don't try to handle this on your own.'

'No, OK.' He tried to steady his voice. 'Call me soon.'

When he put the phone down, Charlie sat for a while with his head in his hands. Then he looked up and glanced at the papers on his desk. Everything seemed to be such a struggle at the moment. The last thing he wanted to do was work. A drink. He could use a drink, something to blot out this sense that he was losing himself. Over the past week he had had a recurring dream. He was in court, it was important, he was about to cross-examine a witness, or make a closing speech, and suddenly someone would stand up in the courtroom. He couldn't ever make out clearly who they were, but they would begin to denounce him, strip away his credentials, point him out as an impostor, not a lawyer at all, not Charlie Day . . . And in the dream, with every mocking word uttered, he would feel himself slipping, as though away from his own self. It was horrible, jerking him awake with a sense of debilitation and panic. He knew it was to do with being told, after twenty-nine years, that he wasn't who he had thought he was. That was clear enough. But the dream seemed to have its own ghostly reality by day, filling his waking hours with a sense of personal inadequacy. In the loneliness of his Leeds hotel room he had got drunk night after night to deaden those feelings and make himself numb to the reality of his new isolation. It was easier than trying to address the situation. First thing after work, a few glasses with fellow barristers. Then more. As much as he could stand. He didn't care. He could handle it. It was the other thing, this new thing, that he couldn't handle.

7

Coming into the theatre for rehearsals one morning, Bella found Bruce lying in wait for her in the corridor.

'Bella, sweet, I need to have a word.'

'What?'

'Come in here.' Bruce opened the door of an empty dressing room. He waited till she was inside, then he closed the door and leaned against it. 'I've had the most marvellous idea.'

Bella surveyed the amazing emptiness of his handsome face, with its liquid eyes and sensuous mouth. The notion of Bruce having anything approaching an idea was so unlikely that she was curious to hear what it might be.

'Well?'

'It's this. You know I'm gay, don't you?'

Bella opened her mouth, then closed it. 'No. Yes. That is . . . Well, I did wonder . . .'

He clapped his hands together and rolled his eyes, as though at some marvellous revelation. 'That's it, you see. I'm so amazingly discreet. Can you believe it?' He crossed the little dressing room and put both hands on her shoulders, gazing at her intently. 'Now, what I thought is this. You already have your adoring male public. I have my adoring female public.'

'Do I? Do we?'

'Yes, yes, of course we do. Trust me. Now, what we

have to do is to utilize this play to build that up. Capitalize.'

'I don't follow. Is this meant to be your brilliant idea? It's actually called publicity, Bruce. It's built into the job.'

'No, no. You don't understand. What we do is – we start having a little fling. You and me. A thing. A relationship. We become an item.' He moved round the cramped space, elaborating on his theme with gestures. 'We go here, we go there, we get photographed at clubs, parties, everything on the circuit. We become *the* thing in the gossip columns . . . I mean, we *are* both extraordinarily lovely human beings –'

'You may be, Bruce. I know what I look like first thing in the morning.'

'The point is, we become a real showbiz power couple.' He stopped, glanced at Bella. 'You're not seeing anyone at the moment, are you?'

She shook her head. 'No.'

'Excellent. So that's what we do. It generates great publicity for the play, and for both of us. I mean, just *think* – when I come out eventually, it's going to be the most *outrageously* wonderful thing! I'll be all over the tabloids! Casting directors will be falling over themselves.' He gazed at her with shining, dumb eyes. 'What do you think?'

She looked at Bruce thoughtfully. 'I'm not entirely sure what the pay-off for me is meant to be. Still, it has possibilities.'

'Of course it does! All we have to do is fake it. We do that all the time for a living.'

Bella considered for a few moments. 'What about Jeremy and Frank? What are they going to think?'

'What everyone else thinks. That we've fallen madly in love while working on the same play. Happens all the time.'

Bella considered the suggestion for a few moments. What about Adam Downing? After that night at her flat, that amazing kiss, she was pretty convinced he was hers for the taking. He hadn't been in touch since, admittedly, but it was only a week . . . If she and Bruce were to pull off this stunt, she'd have to put Adam on hold. Then again, maybe it would be no bad thing. Give Adam something to get jealous about. It was only going to be for a few weeks, then she'd get right back in there.

'All right. Why not?' Bella put out her hand, and Bruce shook it, beaming broadly.

'Fantastic. Now, all we have to do is find some interesting places to be seen together.'

In the run-up to the opening of *Funeral Games*, Bella and Bruce began to turn themselves into the subject of speculation. Wherever they went they entwined themselves together, gazing at one another adoringly for the benefit of photographers. It paid off. They became a talked-about couple. To Bella's amazement, there seemed to be no subterranean current of rumour about Bruce's sexuality. Everyone believed them to be a golden item. On top of this, the PR machine for the play chugged manfully away. Bella appeared on the cover of *Time Out*, and there was a feature about her in the *Telegraph* Saturday supplement.

None of it passed Adam by. He read the articles and the gossip-column pieces, saw the photos of Bella and Bruce together. The first time, it gave him a heart-stopping little pang, which he tried to pretend he didn't feel. It was a good thing that Bella seemed to have found someone. Maybe the relationship would give her the security she badly needed, help her make better sense of things. Bruce Redmond, according to Megan and her friends, was the hottest thing since Jude Law. He was a natural choice. Bruce and Bella could have been made for each other. Adam assured himself that he wasn't the slightest bit jealous. He was very happy for both of them.

On the day the play was due to open, Adam faxed Bella a good-luck message, hesitating for a ridiculously long time over how to sign it, and eventually just putting 'best wishes, Adam'. He could easily have got press tickets for the first night, but something held him back. He would have liked to ring her, but as things stood, it probably wasn't a good idea. After he had sent the fax message he sat at his desk thinking, remembering the two times they had kissed. What had all that been about? Best not to dwell on it. He glanced out of the window and saw Megan's car pull up outside. He watched her get out of the car, ducking into the back seat for her belongings. She slammed the door and crossed the road, flicking her hair from one shoulder in that familiar way she had. Did he love her? Of course. Yes. It was deeper and more substantial than any ridiculous infatuation or mere physical attraction. That was all there had been between himself and Bella, and nothing more would ever come of it.

The next morning, Bella lay in bed, reading despondently through the reviews of *Funeral Games*. No one gave it a complete pasting, but there was a distinct lack of enthusiasm. She shouldn't be surprised. She had felt it all along. As an actor, you could feel in your very bones how well a thing was likely to go down. The critic in *The Times* had tried to like it, but such praise as he gave was lacklustre.

FARCE AND FURIOUS, ran the headline, alongside a small picture of Bella holding a cake-stand, and Bruce Redmond looking very hunky in jeans and a vest and wielding a meat cleaver.

This wildly absurd play, originally presented by Yorkshire Television in 1968, demonstrates the mad, circular logic of dementia that Joe Orton understood so well. The bewilderingly complex plot turns on a neat reversal of conventional morality, constituting an ironic comment on the narrative tradition in literature and presumptions of human rationality and spiritual integrity . . .

Bella sighed and skipped ahead.

Lance Welthorpe's direction is not without flaws, and one is left with residual doubt as to whether the play, unlike *Loot* or *What the Butler Saw*, is sturdy enough to hold its own . . . Although the script is at fault for failing to invest the part of Tessa with the appetite and earthiness of most of Orton's female characters, Bella Day's reading of the part is too demure. She fails to convey the hint of matronly menace which the late Vivien Merchant always evoked so well and doubtless brought to the original production . . .

Bella's eye skimmed through the rest of the review, which ended:

Orton's is an impossible world, but one that is painfully close to our own. The patterns are self-destructive, wholly unrelated to any concept of reality or truth. Tellingly, when Tessa announces that 'Truth must win. Otherwise life is impossible,' this is simply a prelude to the blatant lie with which the play ends.

Bella puzzled briefly over this last statement, uncertain whether it was intended to be critical or not. She gave up. On the floor by her bed lay the fax message which Adam had sent the day before. She hadn't seen it till she got in late last night. She reached down, picked it up, and read it through again. *Best wishes.* Well, what did she expect? Presumably Adam, like everyone else on the planet, imagined she had a thing going with Bruce. If only he knew . . . She lay back, thinking about the evening he'd come to her flat, the wine, the talk, the growing sense of understanding between them. And that kiss. Wow. She closed her eyes, letting a little pang of longing subside. She should be realistic about this. He was with someone else. What was he, after all? What did she think she wanted from him? She hadn't a clue. She only knew that she badly wanted to see him. And since Adam had kindly offered to help her get in touch with her original family, she had the perfect excuse to ring him.

She unfolded the fax message, picked up the phone, and punched in his number. Adam, working at his desk, answered almost straightaway.

'Hello, it's me – Bella.'

'Oh, hi . . . How did last night go?'

'So so. I've just been reading the reviews. *The Times* seems to think I'm not womanly enough.'

'Really?' murmured Adam.

'For the part of Tessa. They seem to think someone with rough elbows and a matronly bosom might be more the thing. More Ortonesque.'

'I see. Well, I think you're quite perfect. Whatever. Elbows, anything.'

There was a pause. Bella smiled and rolled over on to her back. 'I thought you might have called before now.'

'I thought you and Charlie needed some space, you know . . . to sort things out between you. How is he?'

'A mess, frankly. He's been away on a big case, so we haven't seen one another since – well, since that evening you were here. But I spoke to him this afternoon, and it's affected him pretty badly. I've told him I think the best thing is to follow up the address Mother gave me.'

'I see.'

'Did you mean it when you said you would help, if you could?'

'Of course I did.'

'It's just that Charlie's not in any state to face up to things at the moment, and I'm not sure I can do this on my own . . .'

'I can do it for you, if you want. Report back.'

Bella thought for a long moment. 'No. I want to go, but I'd like it if you'd come with me. I want to see – I want to know . . . Even if they left there long ago, I still want to see where they lived. Isn't that stupid, wanting to see a house? I mean, what difference can it make, seeing a house? So stupid . . .'

'It's not stupid. It's not stupid at all. When do you want to go?'

'I don't know . . . Maybe this weekend?'

'There's more chance that someone might be around,' Adam agreed. 'How about Saturday?'

'Fine.' Fear at the prospect made her voice tentative.

'What time do you want me to pick you up?'

'No, please, let's take my car. You've done enough for me already.'

'I've done nothing. Quite the opposite, some might say.'

'Well, anyway . . . I'll come round at ten.'

Adam put the phone down and sat there for a long while, doing nothing. Then he realized he was already missing the sound of her voice.

Bella arrived punctually on Saturday, wearing a pale lemon crop-top and skin-tight white jeans.

'You've had your hair cut,' observed Adam, as he let her in.

She ruffled her skimpy blonde locks with one hand, making the multitude of thin, silver bracelets on her arm tinkle. 'It was getting too long for hot weather.' She gave him a doubtful glance. 'Don't you like it?'

He smiled. 'Yes, I like it. Come in for a moment while I get my things.' Adam disappeared into the bedroom to fetch his jacket.

Bella wandered through to the kitchen. There was Megan, splashing water over crockery in the sink.

'Hello,' said Megan, surprised to see Bella. Adam had said he was going out for a few hours, that it was to do with the Harry Day biography, but he hadn't mentioned anything about Bella. She looked fantastic in that top. Megan wished she could wear something like that without a bra.

'Hi,' said Bella.

'Right,' said Adam, appearing in the doorway. 'Let's get going.'

'What time will you be back, darling?' Megan asked.

'No idea. Two or three hours, perhaps. You get going and do whatever . . .'

'I'll do some shopping. We seem to be running short of a few things.'

He was too far away from Megan for her to kiss him fondly on the cheek, but Bella suspected she would have done, if she could. Proprietorial gestures. She liked that. She liked a bit of a challenge.

'Bye,' she said to Megan.

Megan gave her a cool smile. 'Bye.'

'Next time,' said Bella, as they went downstairs to her car, 'you really must introduce us.'

Adam was startled. 'God, I'm sorry. Didn't you meet at the wedding?'

'Don't worry. Each of us knows who the other is.'

'So, how have you been lately?' asked Adam conversationally, as they walked to the car. 'I saw a picture of you in the paper last week at that film premiere.'

'Mmm. I went with Bruce.'

Adam nodded. 'Right.'

Adam assumed the tone of his voice as he spoke this one word to be entirely neutral, but Bella picked it up instantly. He cared. He was jealous. She could tell. It was unmistakable. Perfect.

She smiled disingenuously at Adam. 'Bruce is such an amazing man. I'm very lucky.'

Adam said nothing.

Bella unlocked the car, and they got in. 'God, five minutes and it's already blistering in here. I'll turn on the air conditioning.'

She ran the fan for a few minutes until the car had cooled, and they set off.

Adam allowed a few moments for his resentment of Bruce Redmond to dissipate, then glanced at Bella's profile. She looked inscrutable behind her sunglasses. His mind shifted to the purpose of their journey.

'Are you scared?'

'Terrified.' She grimaced. 'I've got a thousand and one possible scenarios in my head, and each time I play one of them through, I haven't a clue what I might say or do, really.'

'Don't worry.'

'Fish the *A–Z* out of the side pocket and tell me where I'm meant to be going,' said Bella.

'How's the biography coming along?' she asked, as they headed towards Battersea Bridge.

'Fine. Though I'm concerned that the business about the adoption should be handled the right way. I don't want to upset your family.' He glanced at her. 'How will you feel about that coming out?'

'I don't know. I don't suppose it will matter. Cecile's the one you should worry about, if anyone. Charlie and I just have to come to terms with it.'

'The rest of it should be coming together, but it all takes much longer than I expected. I've spoken to one or two new people over the past few weeks, the ones I met that night at your stepmother's. Everyone comes up with another couple of names of people I should talk to. It's a sort of self-generating process. For instance, Joyce Cole, your father's old editor at Barrie and Jenkins when he first published *Pale Journey*, was very insistent that I should get in touch with someone called Richard Compton-King. Do you know the name?'

'Nope. Who is he?'

'According to Joyce Cole, he was quite close to Harry during the sixties.'

'Are you going to speak to him?'

'If I can track him down. He's in the music business. Old, but still a player, apparently.' He smiled at her. 'I'll let you know what fascinating insights he has, if any.'

For the next forty minutes, Adam guided them through the dense Saturday-morning traffic of south-east London. Eventually they came to Deptford, and after five minutes they found Duffy Road. It was an unremarkable street of tatty terraced houses with a row of shops at one end – a newsagent, barber, kebab takeaway, and a dilapidated minimart. It was lined from end to end with parked cars. The rattle of Connex South East trains could be heard from the station two streets away.

'What number?' asked Adam.

'Forty-four,' said Bella. 'God, I'm so nervous. *So* nervous . . .'

'I know. Don't worry. Thirty-six, thirty-eight . . . It's this side. Look, park over there, outside the pub.'

Bella pulled up. The Southbrook. *Beers, spirits, fine*

wines. Family beer garden. Sky sports, big screen, all top sporting events.

Adam twisted round in his seat and looked back up the road. 'It's the one with the yellow door. There's a sort of alley next to it.'

Bella stared straight ahead of her, hands clasped in her lap. 'I'm shaking. This is pathetic.'

Adam looked at her. 'Why don't you wait here? I'll go.'

She took off her sunglasses, nodded. 'I don't think I can move.'

When Adam had set off she got out of the car and stood leaning against it, staring at the house with the yellow door. There was the house where she might have spent her childhood. Where she was probably conceived. Where lives had been lived that had not included hers. Should have. Still no feeling came. No sentiment. She found herself thinking disloyally of the house where she and Charlie had grown up, the two-acre garden, and of Montresor, holidays with her father.

Adam walked along the pavement. He stood outside number forty-four for a few seconds, then took a few paces to the side of the house and glanced up the alleyway between it and the house next door. A painted board leaning against the brickwork read 'Crash repairs. Free estimates.' Adam walked slowly up the alleyway and round to the back of the house, into a large yard with three cars parked in it. He looked up at the silent windows at the rear of the house.

'Can I help you, mate?'

The voice startled him, and he swung round to see a figure squirming its way out, face-up, from beneath one of the cars, spanner in hand. A lanky, dark-haired youth, wearing oil-stained overalls, got up. He wiped his hands and came over to Adam.

'I'm looking for a family called Kinley,' said Adam. 'Mr and Mrs Kinley. Do they still live here?'

The boy looked uncertain. 'You mean Derek and his mum?'

'Is their name Kinley?'

The youth nodded. Only at that moment did Adam become aware of the incredible tension which had gathered in him. He felt a dizzy mixture of elation and relief – and had no idea what to do or say next.

He nodded. 'Right. Thank you.' He turned and walked back down the alleyway. The youth stood looking after him. Then after a few seconds he went to the back door and called inside.

Adam went back to the car. Bella was leaning against the door. Her eyes looked enormous, tragic, as she stared at him, trying to prepare herself. All he had to do was nod, and watch her expression, the anxiety disintegrating into wild and astonished disbelief.

'God, they're still there?' She clasped her hands to her mouth.

'There was a boy working on a car out the back. I don't think he's anything to do with you, but he confirmed that there's a Kinley family living at forty-four. He mentioned someone called Derek, and his mother.'

Bella clutched tightly at his sleeve. 'Adam, that must be my brother. My brother, and my mother . . . Oh God, oh God . . .' She leaned against Adam for a brief moment.

'What do you want to do?'

'I don't know. Do you think they're there?'

'No idea. Do you want me to wait here?'

Bella shook her head. 'I'm so scared. Would you come with me?'

'Of course.'

As they approached the house, a figure appeared at the end of the alleyway, a tall, muscular man, middle-aged, with scant blond hair, close-cropped. 'You the fella that was asking about me a minute ago?' He had a heavy south-London accent.

Bella looked at him in astonishment. Christ, thought Adam, he looks just like Charlie. Charlie, ten years older, with suntanned biceps, tattoos, wearing a T-shirt and jeans.

'Are you Derek Kinley?' asked Bella. Her voice was weak with nerves.

The big man nodded.

Adam saw the whiteness of Bella's knuckles as she clasped her hands hard together. 'Look, I know this must seem like an awful intrusion, but I have to find out . . . About thirty years ago, a woman who lived at this address, at number forty-four, called Kinley, had twin babies. She gave them up for adoption. I was one of them. Do you know anything about it?' Her eyes searched his face anxiously.

Seconds passed like an eternity. It seemed to Adam that a whole world of improbability and conjecture made its slow revolve as Derek Kinley attempted to make sense of what Bella had said. How much did Derek recall of the time just before Bella and Charlie had been born? He would have been ten, according to everything Cecile had told Bella and Charlie, so he must remember something. Perhaps he had obliterated or buried that childhood recollection. The silence lengthened.

'Sorry? What are you on about?' The man seemed on the verge of becoming truculent. God, thought Adam, he was like Charlie.

'Look, do you think we could go somewhere else to talk? It's not easy, here in the street . . .'

Derek glanced from Adam to Bella, then said, 'You'd better come indoors.'

They went up the alley and past the repair yard, and followed Derek through the back door. They sat in the front room, on the three-piece suite. Adam glanced round, taking in the cheap furniture, the standard lamp, the budgerigar cage on its stand, the nets at the windows, the ornaments on the mantelpiece. The television in the corner was large, too big for the room, with speakers either side. Bella and Derek stared at one another.

'Right,' said Derek. 'You'd better give us this again.'

Bella swallowed. 'There was a family at this address, by the name of Kinley, who gave up twin babies for adoption.' She gazed intently at Derek. 'If that's your name, then I know I've come to the right place.' Bella's voice grew weak with nervousness. 'I think . . . I'm your sister.'

Derek Kinley smiled an unamused smile. 'I think someone's been having a laugh with you, love. I haven't got no brothers or sisters.'

Bella nodded. 'If the woman I'm talking about, Doreen Kinley, is your mother, then I'm your sister.'

Adam watched in fascination as something touched a

nerve, a buried recollection. 'Jesus,' said the man at last. 'That can't be right. No.' He seemed dazed by the effort of making sense of the past. 'My mother never had any more kids. She lost a baby, that was all.'

Bella's eyes were huge, bright with the effort of concentration, or with tears, Adam didn't know which. 'Oh, look, I don't know what you were told, I don't want to cause any pain, but . . . if you remember her being pregnant . . . How old were you then?'

'Nine? Ten?' Adam saw that Derek Kinley was now actually looking properly at Bella, taking her in, on the verge of the connection Bella so desperately sought.

'She didn't lose the baby. Babies. My parents adopted them. The parents were called Kinley, and they lived at this address. They had one child, a boy.' Bella nodded, swallowed. 'Our brother.' Bella's eyes swam with tears. 'I can't believe I've found you.' She glanced at Adam. 'This is my friend, Adam Downing. He helped me to find you. I only found out a few weeks ago that I was adopted, you see.'

Adam could sense the man's panic and uncertainty.

'I'm sorry if this has been a shock for you,' said Bella.

Derek said nothing. He seemed baffled, as though someone had put one over on him when he wasn't looking.

'Didn't you know anything?' asked Bella.

Derek shook his head slowly. 'Nothing. I'd forgotten the whole thing. It was that long ago. She was expecting, and then she . . . Everyone said she lost it.'

Adam, watching his face, wondered what Derek's feelings towards his mother were at this moment.

Derek stared at Bella, long and searchingly. At last he put his head in his hands. 'Bloody hell.' There was silence for a few seconds, then he looked up again. 'Twins? You said there was you and your brother?'

'His name's Charlie.' Adam could hear tears choking her voice. 'I don't know the details of what happened, but the adoption was done privately and arranged very carefully. I think it cost our parents a good deal of money.'

'Knowing my dad, I'll bet it did.' Derek Kinley nodded slowly. Adam detected no bitterness in his voice, merely understanding.

'Shall I make some tea?' Adam asked. No one said anything, so he got up and went to the kitchen at the end of the narrow hallway. The kitchen was very small, with just a cooker, a fridge, a sink, and some cupboards. Like the front room, it had a timeless quality about it. Adam filled the kettle and found a teapot and some tea in a tin caddy. He got some mugs and a milk jug from a cupboard. He brewed the tea, and poured some milk into the jug from a half-full bottle in the fridge. He noticed a hand-knitted woollen tea cosy on top of the fridge. He hesitated, then put it over the teapot. He put everything on a tray and took it through to the front room.

'Thanks,' said Derek, as Adam poured out some tea and handed it to him. He gave some to Bella. She hardly glanced at him, utterly absorbed in her cross-examination of Derek. He gave his answers to her questions with a reluctance that concealed itself as an effort of memory.

'What do you remember about that time?'

'I dunno. I haven't thought about it in a long while.' He pondered. 'I remember I knew about the baby coming.

But no one bought anything for it. Then Mum said she lost it. I remember we got a new car. We went to Butlin's that summer, down in Walton. We was well off for a bit, that much I know. Well, by our lights.' He looked at Bella, shook his head again in disbelief. 'This has done my head in, you know that?'

'Are my – our parents still alive?' asked Bella. Her voice was faint.

'Mum is. Dad passed on a while back. You didn't miss nothing there.'

Adam saw a flicker of emotion tremble on Bella's face. A long moment passed. 'Is she here?'

Derek shook his head. 'Mum? She's up the shops. Lil took her. She doesn't get about too well.' He fell silent again. Just as the pause was growing awkward, Derek gave Bella a searching glance, almost as if he didn't want to, and said, 'I don't reckon she would know you.'

'I wouldn't expect her to. Why should she?'

'No, I mean, she doesn't know who anyone is half the time. She's lost her marbles a bit.' He sipped his tea. Silence fell again, lengthened.

'Don't you want to know my name?'

'Sorry, yes. Go ahead.'

'It's Bella.'

Derek Kinley nodded. 'You look a bit like that actress that was in that film – that drug thing, with the bald guy who had the three-legged dog.'

She nodded. 'That's me. My name's Bella Day.'

Derek gaped. 'Right. Right.' It was all too much for him. Adam sensed that Derek wished his Saturday morning hadn't gone this way. The enthusiasm, the hope, the need which radiated from Bella was not reflected by this stolid, puzzled man.

'Do you want to know about Charlie?' said Bella.

Derek nodded with an air of interest which Adam guessed he did not feel. Perhaps it wasn't interest that he lacked, exactly – more that he felt apprehension, that things were rolling towards him which he didn't know how to handle. Adam thought he could understand that. Bella, rendered oblivious to any of this by the adrenalin rush of meeting her new-found brother, told Derek all about Charlie.

'A brief, eh?' Derek gave a sad laugh. 'There was a few times we could've done with one of those in the family.'

Another long moment passed. Adam could tell from Bella's eyes that it was dawning on her that the elation of this reunion was somewhat one-sided. It was painful.

'Look,' said Derek, putting down his mug of tea, 'Mum's gonna be back in ten minutes or so. I'm not being funny or nothing, but I think it would be best if you wasn't here.' Adam noticed for the first time that the slow, dejected way in which Derek had answered Bella's questions was his normal manner of speaking.

Bella looked bewildered. 'Not meet her? After everything . . . I *have* to see her! She's my mother.'

Derek regarded her frankly, thoughtfully. After a space of some seconds he asked, 'What kind of a life have you had, then? Being adopted? They must have been pretty well off, your folks, given you a good education, a decent start in life.'

'Yes, I suppose so.' Bella gave Adam a brief, baffled glance.

'Right.' Derek nodded. 'So you've got a good life, done all right for yourself, actress and all that. Brother's a lawyer . . . Point I'm trying to make here is – when Mum gave you up, that must have been a hard thing for her to do. Now I look back, I can guess why she did it.' But Adam sensed that this was not entirely true, that there was unsolved anger and pain. 'She did it to see us better off, to stop Dad leaving, keep money coming into the house. She's not had a great time of it, Mum. And now she's not too well. Like I said, she might not know you after thirty years. But she might. And if you look at it from her point of view, maybe she doesn't want to be reminded of you, and what happened back then. I know it sounds hard, but she needs looking after.'

'Believe me,' said Bella earnestly, 'I can see that it might be a shock for her. But you don't understand what it would mean to me, how badly I need to –'

'Yeah, well, that's what I'm getting at. It's not just a question of what you need. Like, you come here, you're my sister and all that. But in a way, you're not. We're not really anything to do with each other. I'm sorry if it sounds hard and all, but I'm thinking about Mum here.'

'She's my mother,' said Bella, somewhat dazed by this. 'Don't you think she's thought about me all this time, wondering what I'm like, what Charlie's like? Why would you want to stop her meeting me again? Don't you think it might be as important to her as it is to me?'

Derek stared down at his hands. They were heavy, freckled and furry with blond hairs. He twisted a chunky gold ring on one of his little fingers. 'I'll tell you a bit about Mum. She's seventy. Since she left school she's always worked. She worked in a baker's, then in a bookie's, she did twelve years in the laundry on the council estate, she worked another fifteen years down the rope factory in Woolwich. She's had two hip operations, and needs a stick to get about. She's had a lot of worry one way or another, what with my dad, and not having much money. I'm divorced, with two little girls. They live with their mum. I've lived here for the past four years, looking after things, running the business out the back. The last year or so, she's begun losing it. They reckon it could be the beginning of Alzheimer's, I dunno. She goes up the day centre on weekdays, has her lunch there, talks to all the other old dears, comes home teatime. Weekends, like today, she goes up the shops with Lil, sometimes she goes to the bingo in the evening. She watches telly, likes her soaps. Sometimes she thinks I'm her dad, or her brother that died in the War. She can manage things for herself, but she gets confused.' He shook his head. 'That's Mum. That's what the last thirty years have been for her. I don't know what you think it's going to do for her now, meeting you.'

'I'm her only daughter! If I had had a daughter and given her away, I'd spend my whole life hoping she'd find me!' Adam felt for Bella as she struggled to bridge the gap between her expectations and the reality which lay within this cramped little front room, filled with the mementos of a life unshared by her, unknown to her. She stared uncomprehendingly at the stranger who sat opposite her.

A sound from outside made Derek look up. He went to the window. 'Christ, that's Mum now.'

For some reason, Adam and Bella got to their feet as well. From where he stood, Adam could see two old women alighting from a Dial-A-Ride bus, one slightly stooped and the other more erect, a protective arm around her companion.

There was the sound of a key in the front door. 'Coo-ee! Derek! We're back!'

Derek went out into the hallway. Coats were being taken off, bags put down. Adam glanced at Bella. Her face looked stricken, pale. She met Adam's eye.

'I have to see her. I just have to.'

Given the geography of the house, Adam didn't see how an encounter between Bella and Mrs Kinley could be avoided. Even so, as Bella stepped towards the hall, he couldn't help putting out a hand, as if to stop her, or protect her. The gesture got no more than halfway; he let his arm drop to his side. He watched from the doorway. The woman who was evidently Lil, Mrs Kinley's friend, glanced at Bella and Adam.

'Oh, I never saw you had visitors, Derek.' Lil looked brightly and expectantly from face to face. Mrs Kinley's stooped figure turned slowly, with difficulty, to face Adam and Bella. She was of slight build, like Bella, sweet-faced with confusion and age. Adam wondered what Bella had been expecting, whether she saw something, someone there that he did not. Bella's mother might have been any other little old lady, dressed in a dingy blue raincoat, with her ragged halo of permed white hair, her bemused expression. It was impossible to tell, from the drooped and pouched features, whether she had ever looked anything like Bella.

Derek gave Bella a rapid, unfathomable glance, and said to his mother, 'Just someone come about their car.'

'About their car?' Mrs Kinley's voice was high, a little lost. She looked at Bella. 'I thought I knew you. You look like Beryl, that used to work down the rope factory. Doesn't she look like Beryl, Lil?'

Lil gave Bella a smile. 'She does rather. Come on now, Doreen, let's get you a nice cup of tea.' Lil steered Bella's mother towards the kitchen.

Derek knew the moment was Bella's. He said nothing, did nothing. But Bella, with eyes that seemed to Adam to be filled with either longing or hopelessness, made no move towards the slight figure shuffling in the direction of the kitchen. Lil and Mrs Kinley went into the kitchen, and the door closed.

'I don't want to hurt her.' She shook her head, looked at Derek. 'I didn't come here to hurt anyone.'

He nodded. 'I know.' In an awkward gesture, an attempt to recognize what they were to one another, he touched Bella's shoulder. 'What I said back there – I can't stop you if you want to tell her. It's up to you. I mean, like, you've every right, as such. I just think – maybe not today. Today's not a good day.' It was unspoken – no day would be a good day.

'No,' said Bella. 'Maybe not. I wouldn't like to upset her. I think it would, wouldn't it?'

Derek said nothing. From the kitchen the murmuring sound of voices, the opening and closing of a cupboard and the rattle of teacups seemed to suggest a closed world, one in which Bella could only be an intruder.

At last she said, 'I'd like to know what she was like

when she was younger. And my father. Do you have any photographs?'

'Yeah,' said Derek. He looked a little surprised, like someone just woken up. 'I'd have to look them out, like.' He paused, raised his eyebrows and sighed in a manner that reminded Adam again of Charlie. 'This has all been a bit weird. I don't want you to think –' He stopped. 'Like I said, I'll have to look them out. Maybe I could send them to you.'

Bella already had her address and telephone number written out on a piece of paper. She took it from her bag and gave it to Derek. 'I'm sorry if I've upset things by coming here.' Derek shook his head, yet another in a long line of gestures that seemed to mean something else entirely. 'I suppose I hadn't really worked out in my head how – well, how much of a shock it would be. I've been thinking about nothing else for weeks, you see. But for you, it's straight out of the blue . . .' She paused. 'Are you sorry I came?'

Derek gave this some thought. 'I dunno.' His expression was frank, apologetic. 'No, I reckon not. I mean, a sister, and that . . .'

'And another brother.'

'Yeah, right.' Derek glanced at the piece of paper. Then he looked up at Bella. 'I just need time to get things straightened out in my head.'

Bella and Adam walked down the street to the car. Bella unlocked it, took her sunglasses from her bag, and got in. Adam got in next to her. They sat in silence for a few seconds.

'I thought it would be quite different,' said Bella at last.

'I don't know *what* I thought it would be . . . Just different.' Her voice sounded frail, detached. Adam suspected this wasn't a good defence, as defences went.

'Take off your sunglasses,' he said.

She took them off and let the first tears trickle down her cheeks. Adam tugged a wad of tissues from the box in the glove compartment.

When Bella had eventually finished crying, she wiped her nose. 'Thirty-five minutes. Just thirty-five minutes. I can't believe it was so much, and so little.' She sniffed. 'He looked a lot like Charlie. Didn't he look like him?'

Adam nodded, uncertain what to say. Already he could sense her building connections, trying to establish links between the mystery of Derek and the long-established actuality of Charlie. Brothers. Hope was regenerating. She desperately wanted to put behind her any sense of anti-climax.

'What do you think will happen now?' she asked, as though she genuinely thought Adam knew the answer.

'Wait and see what happens.'

'I wish now I'd said something. To her.'

'Doreen.'

'Yes.'

'Maybe Derek had a point.'

She put her hands over her face, a childish, blind gesture. 'I don't want to hear that.'

'No, I know,' said Adam. 'Come on, let's get going.'

When Bella dropped Adam off in Baron's Court, he asked, 'Will you be all right?'

'Of course.' She nodded. 'I'm glad I've done this much. At least I've stopped shaking now. I was so cowardly, though . . . I should have spoken to her, said something. She is my mother, after all.'

'There wasn't much you could do. In the circumstances.'

'Do you know what was the worst thing? I looked at her and felt so little. So little. I thought there would be some kind of . . . recognition. Some – some – oh, shit, I don't know. Empathy? Perhaps Derek was right. Perhaps it would be better for her, easier for her, if she was never to know me . . . Anyway, so much for my fantasy. Nothing like that Mike Leigh film at all, no tears and laughter.'

'That's a lot to expect. You didn't even know if your family would still be living there.'

She shrugged. 'I'm allowed my fantasies. I just didn't expect – well, strangers.'

'Derek?'

'I don't know . . . I think he was glad when I left. I don't think he'd care if I never went near them again.' She nodded. 'That's the honest truth.'

'Don't be too sure about that. You're very different people. You've had very different upbringings. You can't expect to connect just like that.'

'Don't give me that class thing. That's bollocks. If he's my brother, he's my brother. I don't care about that.' She chewed a nail reflectively. 'Charlie will. Charlie won't like having a brother who's a car mechanic and probable Millwall supporter.'

'When are you going to tell him?'

'I don't know. He's at Claire's parents' place for the weekend. He probably won't want to know, anyway.

Charlie's way of dealing with it is to pretend nothing's happened.'

Adam opened the car door. 'Let me know if you need me.'

Because he sounded as though he meant it, Bella paused, one hand on the ignition key. Why couldn't she just tell him that the thing with Bruce was a sham, that she had never felt so lonely and uncertain in her life, and ask him to make everything all right? She knew why. He couldn't give her what she wanted. He had someone else. He was just being kind. And kindness wasn't enough. No, let him carry on thinking she was in love, whatever, with Bruce. It was probably the safest thing.

'Thanks. And thanks for coming with me today. It meant a lot.'

Adam stood on the pavement and watched her drive away. When this episode was over, the biography concluded, he would have no real reason to see her any more. In theory, that was a good thing. In theory.

8

The next morning, Bella woke around eleven and lay in bed, thinking about yesterday's events in Deptford. Apart from finding out that her brother was a car mechanic, and that her birth mother was gently losing life's plot, the only real discovery she had made was that she hadn't been wanted – not then, not now. She could see now that her arrival, plummeting into their lives like someone in emotional free-fall, had not been welcome, not from Derek's point of view. He seemed like a decent bloke – not a fool, by any means. Was she right in thinking that he would have wished her out of existence, if he could? Well, that was something he and Charlie shared, that narrow focus. That hope that things would go away, if you just let them alone.

Was she going to let it alone? If that was what the Kinleys wanted, maybe she should just fade quietly away. She found herself weeping again, inevitably, miserably. Everything she did, every step she took in an attempt to make everything clearer, only left her more confused. She found herself wanting very much to talk to her mother, to Cecile. It was a genuine need, one she would be stupid to ignore.

Bella lay until her tears were finished, then got up, showered, and rang her mother to arrange lunch early in the week. Then she left a message on Charlie's answerphone, asking him to come round that evening for a drink some time after eight. The realization that Cecile and Charlie were the two people she most urgently wanted to talk to gave her pause. This was reality, this was family – why cast around trying to piece together non-existent relationships with people who had put her out of their lives long ago? Yet she couldn't help hoping that Derek would be as good as his word, that he would be in touch.

When Charlie arrived that evening, he poured himself a very large Scotch and slumped into an armchair.

'How was the weekend?' asked Bella.

'Endless. Non-stop stuff about the wedding.'

'It is your wedding too, you know.'

'Oh, really? I get the feeling I'm playing something of a minor role, compared to Claire and her family. Jesus, they went on and on about seating plans, asking my opinion about people I've never even met, whether Florence should sit at the same table as her ex-husband . . .' Charlie took a large swallow of his drink. 'Claire's mother even had the cheek to ask me to make sure my best man didn't touch on certain topics, because there are sensitive areas with some of the bloody relatives.'

Bella giggled. 'Such as?'

'No gay jokes, no Muslim jokes, no Irish jokes . . . As though that were likely.' Charlie knocked back the remains of his Scotch. 'Mind if I have another?'

'Help yourself.' Bella was putting little wads of cotton wool carefully between her toes in preparation for painting her toenails.

'So, what kind of a weekend have you had?'

Bella said nothing for several seconds. She picked up the bottle of nail varnish, about to unscrew it. Then she stopped suddenly, set it down, and clasped her hands between her knees.

'I went to the address in Deptford.'

Charlie sat down with his second drink, a knot of apprehension forming in his stomach. Bella watched his face closely as she went on.

'I met someone called Derek Kinley, who's our brother. And I saw, but didn't actually speak to, our mother.'

She watched Charlie swallow some of his whisky.

'You're saying nothing. Aren't you curious?'

Charlie turned his gaze to hers, his face expressionless. 'What was he like?'

'You. Tall, blond, well-built. He's sort of –' she reflected, '*heavy*. No, not in the way that sounds. Ponderous.'

'What does he do?'

'He runs a car-repair business from a yard at the back of his house.' Bella picked up the bottle of nail varnish. 'You haven't asked about our mother.'

'I know who my mother is.' Charlie spoke with finality, the voice of someone who didn't care to hear any more.

'Her name is Doreen. She's seventy. She looked at me and hadn't a clue who I was. Derek didn't want me to tell her. So I didn't.' Bella unscrewed the cap slowly. Her expression grew strained, sad. 'Anyway, the situation was so odd that I don't think I could have.'

Silence, pregnant with conjecture, with unasked questions, lengthened. Bella painted her toenails, one by one, as Charlie watched.

'Is that it?'

'I have no idea. I asked Derek to send me some family photographs. Of our father and mother, of everyone.'

'I wish you'd stop calling them that. It's unreal. I don't know what you're trying to create here.'

'It doesn't help to ignore it, Charlie. The past isn't just going to run away because you want it to.'

'Yes, well, if you'd left it alone, it wouldn't be troubling me. That fuckwit Downing is to blame.'

'No, he's not. Harry and Cecile are, if anyone is.'

'Fine, fine. I'm having trouble enough dealing with – with a load of things at the moment. I don't want you adding to it by dredging up some run-down bunch in south-east London and expecting me to make a connection with them.'

'Don't you know how strange that sounds? How else are you going to sort it out in your mind if you don't get to know your real family?'

'Because it's not going to help! I just know it's not! So what if I go to Deptford and meet this woman and say, "Hi, I'm the son you gave away, can we talk about it?"'

'Don't cry.'

'I'm not! I'm – I'm just saying I wish you hadn't done this. It's helped no one . . .'

'You probably wouldn't get very far talking to her, anyway. Derek thinks she's suffering from early Alzheimer's. She's a bit wandered.'

It took a few seconds for Charlie to steady his voice. 'Well, fine. I don't want to go anywhere near this, frankly. I've decided I have to try to accept who I am, as I am, by reference to all the things I've ever known and the people who brought me up, and that's the end of it. Nothing else is going to help me.'

'You keep talking about help.'

'No, I don't.'

'You've said the word a few times. It must mean something.'

'Don't do your analytical number on me, Bell. Stick to your own agenda. I want nothing to do with this.'

'If Derek sends me photographs, you'll want to see them. You wouldn't be human otherwise.'

'You don't get it, do you? I don't care! I mean, this person Derek – is he supposed suddenly to mean more to me than, say, a friend like Toby, or Colin, people I've known for years? Is he in any way important to me?'

'Maybe you would be important to him. He lost something too, you know.'

One by one, Bella pulled the little plugs of cotton wool from between her toes. She brushed away slight tears with the back of her hand. Charlie, sipping his second Scotch, noticed.

'I'm sorry, Bell,' he said gently. 'I'm sorry if I can't feel about this the way you do. Maybe it's some form of self-protection.'

'Cowardice.'

'Very possibly. There is only so much I can handle, you know.'

'Oh, leave it. Just leave it. We'll talk about something else. Anything else. I don't care.'

After a short silence, Charlie said, 'OK.' He took a deep breath. 'Let's talk about the house in France. Claire and I are serious about buying this place in Sussex. We need the money.'

Bella screwed the cap on the nail-polish bottle. 'Then there's not a lot I can do, is there? You're effectively forcing my hand. I haven't got the money to buy you out.'

'Oh, come on, Bell. Look at it from the other perspective. If I say, OK, forget it, we keep the house, then you're effectively forcing *my* hand.'

'Please, let's not have this argument again.' A month or two ago, she knew, she would have fought tooth and nail with Charlie to stop Montresor being sold. But recent events had sapped her spirit, drained her strength of purpose. It was a place from her past, a past that had recently taken on an illusory quality. What possible argument could she use to make him keep it? She shrugged and said wearily, 'If you want to sell it, then I suppose we have to. The upkeep was going to be horrendous, anyway. It's just . . . parting with the place, after all the lovely times we've had there . . .'

'I know.'

'Well, if we do sell it, can we leave it for a few weeks? I was going to take a holiday when this play is finished, and it would be lovely to go to Montresor one last time. I can arrange to put it on the market when I'm out there. It'll sell really quickly, you know it will.'

Charlie gave a small smile. 'Funny you should say that. I'd been thinking along the same lines. Take Claire there for a week or two, enjoy it while we've still got it.'

Bella didn't much relish the idea of a holiday with Claire in attendance, but she would like it if she and Charlie went to Montresor for the last time together.

'Right. We can all go. I may invite some people from the play, make up a proper house-party. Yes, let's do that.'

'OK.' Charlie nodded, then tipped back the remains of his Scotch. 'Look, I'm sorry this has to be a flying visit. It's already late, and I've got to be in court in Uxbridge tomorrow morning. I'd better be off.'

Bella got up and walked Charlie to the front door. 'If I do hear anything from Derek –' She paused.

'Derek?'

'In Deptford. Our brother.'

'Oh, him.'

'If I do hear from him, I'll let you know.'

'You don't have to. I'm fine as I am.' He looked at her. 'Not that that's going to stop you, is it? You're determined to make me part of this.'

'You already are a part. Flesh and blood. Family.'

He shook his head, whether in negation or despair, Bella couldn't tell.

'Goodnight.' He kissed her.

'Goodnight, Charlie.' She watched fondly as he loped downstairs to his car, and wondered if she could ever feel about Derek the way she felt about Charlie. Not possible. Not remotely possible. Perhaps that small truth needed close examination.

In tracking down Richard Compton-King, Adam once again enlisted the help of Giles Hamblin. There seemed to be very few people of any note in London whom Giles did not know, or know of.

'One of Harry's editors from way back mentioned his name,' Adam told Giles. 'I've checked through all Harry's articles and interviews and the name doesn't crop up anywhere. All I know is that he used to work in the music business – pop, that is – and that he was close to Harry in the sixties.'

'Compton-King, Compton-King . . . Rings a bell . . . Leave it with me. I know a fellow at Sony who might be able to help.'

Later that afternoon, just as Adam was putting the finishing touches to a review, Giles rang back.

'OK, this is your man. Richard Compton-King, now in his late fifties, started out working for Don Arden in the early sixties, became manager of the Cupids, Tight Finger, Bod Jeffries, and latterly the Keith Harvey Kickband.'

'Good grief.'

'Went on to form RTO, a glam-rock independent record company, then hit the big time in the eighties with a band called Domain. Remember them?'

'Vaguely.'

'Very big in Japan. Opened up the market there, you could say. Oh, and he also wrote a biography of Peter Noone.'

'Who?'

'Herman. Of Herman's Hermits. Don't worry about it. Anyway, Compton-King's still in the business, but only just. His record company folded in the mid-nineties, left him with a lot of debts. I gather his star is somewhat on the wane. He gets by managing various maverick bands that the big boys won't handle. Lives in St John's Wood.'

'Have you got an address and phone number?'

'I have. Ready?'

Adam took down the details. 'I'll give him a ring.'

'Should prove interesting. Then again, possibly not,' said Giles. 'Let me know how you get on.'

When Adam rang Richard Compton-King and explained about the biography, Compton-King's response was enthusiastic.

'Fabulous. Love to talk about the old days, and about Harry.' There followed background sounds, and an extraneous exchange between Compton-King and a woman about something they appeared to have lost. His attention to Adam didn't re-engage for several seconds, and when it did, he sounded distracted. 'Look, why don't you come to lunch?' His voice faded off-receiver again. 'No, I didn't put it there. Why would I put it there?' Back he came. 'Sorry, Alan –'

'Adam.'

'Of course. Where were we? Yes, let's do lunch . . .'

Suspecting that Compton-King's attention was about to fade again, Adam said quickly, 'I'm free any day this week.'

'Are you? Well, that's terrific . . .' There was the sound of the phone being laid down, then papers being moved, and then a long period of nothing happening at all. Adam could hear feet crossing a room. Time lengthened. Adam was about to hang up, convinced he'd been forgotten, when suddenly Compton-King's voice came back on the line. 'OK. OK, here we are. Friday. How does Friday sound?'

'Yes, Friday is great.'

'Right – say, twelve-thirty. Listen, lovely chatting to you. Have to go. Ciao.'

The phone call didn't inspire Adam with confidence. As he parked his car in the leafy St John's Wood road that Friday just before noon, he half-expected to find no one at home. He made his way up the large front garden to the Compton-King residence – a large, double-fronted detached house of some grandeur, but in need of a coat of paint – and rang the bell. As its echoes died away, only the sounds of summer, of susurrating leaves and idle birdsong, filled the silence. The July day was languorously warm. Adam waited. He rang the bell again. Somewhere a dog barked. Dispirited, but not surprised, Adam turned and walked back down the path. He was halfway to the gate when he heard the sound of a door opening, and turned to see a very tall man dressed in baggy striped shorts and a dressing-gown. He called out, and Adam went back up the path.

They shook hands.

'Sorry. I was out back at the pool. Didn't hear you. Shona usually answers. Don't know where she's got to. Come in, come in . . .'

Richard Compton-King was not quite what Adam had expected. He looked younger than his years, marvellously handsome, with a leathery, tanned face and a wide, charming smile. He was well over six feet tall, and wore his long, greying blond hair tied back in a ponytail. Only the incipient sinewiness of his long legs gave his age away, but he seemed to Adam to be in pretty good condition for someone in his late fifties.

Compton-King, towelling robe flapping, led Adam through the house and out into a large, sunlit garden, in whose foreground sparkled the synthetic blue waters of a swimming pool of rather small proportions.

Compton-King squatted down beside a small drain at one end of the pool and fiddled about briefly with something in its interior.

'Bloody pump needs looking at . . .' He rose, strode to the open patio doors and roared 'Shona!' He came back to Adam, smiling his fabulous smile. 'Sorry about this. Won't take a moment . . .'

A girl in her twenties came through the patio doors, dressed in cropped trousers and a T-shirt. 'What?' she asked crossly. She didn't even look at Adam.

There followed a confabulation about the faulty pool pump, and the girl was dispatched to phone someone up about it.

'Shona's my PA,' said Compton-King, as she disappeared back into the house, 'my right-hand woman, my amanuensis . . . Can't run a thing without her. Used to have a complete entourage, but times are tough . . .' He picked up a pair of sunglasses from a table and settled into one of the poolside chairs, gesturing Adam to another.

'OK, Adam, I'm all yours.' He smiled, shifted the sunglasses a little up the bridge of his aquiline nose. Adam, pleased at the businesslike approach, murmured his usual thing about recording their conversation, set up his tape on the table and was about to launch into his first question, when Compton-King said expansively, 'Isn't this fantastic weather?' Adam agreed that it was.

'Had the pool put in last year – been just amazing – have a swim every morning before getting down to work. Day didn't dawn till around eleven for me today, mind you – out rather late last night. This new band I'm managing . . . well, not so much a band as DJs turned music-makers – Mule Skinners. Have you heard of them?' Adam confessed he hadn't. Compton-King looked at him doubtfully. 'Really? Going to be very big – sort of garage disco sound, with a hint of ska, but with really solid four-four rubric. Fantastic . . . Look, we need some lunch, and something to drink. Hold on a moment.' He padded off to the kitchen, and Adam sat back, sighing, and switched off his tape recorder.

After a few moments Adam became aware of the sounds of a muted altercation coming from the direction of the kitchen. Compton-King strode back to the poolside, and Adam thought he heard the words 'fucking woman' muttered *sotto voce*. Compton-King had a bottle of champagne in one hand and two glasses in the other. He gave Adam a regretful-host smile.

'Shona's just putting a few things together. Afraid it won't be much of a lunch. Still, shouldn't be long.' He set down the bottle and the glasses on the table. 'This'll do to be going on with.'

He popped the champagne, poured a glass and handed it to Adam, then settled into his chair, sunglasses on nose, and crossed his long legs. 'I first met Harry,' he announced, 'at a party. God knows whose. Don't ask me. It was back in the sixties. I remember I was really interested in meeting him, because I thought he might be useful in some way. I was twenty, desperate – my sole ambition in life was to make it big. Everyone wanted to make it big. You operated on the basis that anyone who was vaguely well known might turn out to be useful. Connections. All about who you knew. Anyway, I was working for Dick Leahy at Philips Records – sort of a glorified errand boy. The music business wasn't turning out to be the goldmine I'd imagined, and I had this idea that maybe theatre was the place to be. So I introduced myself to Harry, had a chat, got his number, then I met him again a couple of weeks after that at a place called the Ad Lib Club. Now this was a seriously trendy club back in the sixties, I mean absolutely *everybody* hung out there. You had to get to it by a lift, and the walls were lined with fur, as I recall. There was this tank of piranha fish, and a mirrored dance floor . . .'

'Sounds like something out of Austin Powers.'

'Very hip in those days, I can assure you, full of trendy people, people in the music business, the arts, television . . . Anyway, there was Harry having a drink with Joe Orton, as I recall.'

'Really?' asked Adam with interest, thinking of Bella. 'Oddly enough, Harry's daughter is appearing in an Orton play at the moment, in the West End. What was he like?'

'Orton? Dark, schoolboy-like, quiet at first, till you got to know him. I don't think he can have been all that well known back then, the first time I met him. It was around '64, I think . . . I remember him wearing a sort of corduroy cap – a John Lennon cap, as it was called – and he had a wig in a box, which he wouldn't check at the cloakroom – insisted on keeping it with him at the table. Harry kept joking about it. Anyway, I suppose I saw a good deal of him over the next three years, generally with Harry. Orton rarely had a decent word to say about anyone, but he was rather admiring of Harry. Perhaps fascinated is a better word. Ah, here we are . . .' Shona had appeared with a large tray bearing lunch, which apparently hadn't required a great deal of preparation, consisting mainly of French bread, cheese and pâté. Richard busied himself putting up a wayward patio umbrella to shade the table. Eventually, when everything was arranged to Richard Compton-King's satisfaction, they began lunch.

'So, why was Orton so fascinated by Harry?'

Compton-King helped himself to a slab of pâté and tore off a chunk of bread. He chewed reflectively for some seconds. 'Complex, Adam. Very complex. I mean, on the one hand, he thought Harry was a frightful hypocrite, proselytizing on behalf of the working classes when he knew his audience were middle-class, theatre-going intellectuals – the kind who liked to look down on the likes of Jimmy Porter in the same way that they'd looked up to the upper-class inhabitants of the worlds of Rattigan and Coward . . . Here, help yourself to some of this aubergine stuff. Very good. Have you got enough shade? Because we can move the chairs round if you haven't –'

'No, no, I'm fine. Go on.'

'Yes, well . . . on the other hand, he admired the things Harry said in his plays. Both driving at the same kind of subversion, you see. Sexually, it was the same thing, only they worked from different angles.'

'I don't follow.'

'Joe envied Harry. It tickled him enormously to think that Harry should have built such a façade to conceal his true nature, but he hated the fact that Harry thought he had to do any of those things. Set up smokescreens, deceive the world. All very interesting, really.'

'I don't understand. What smokescreens? What d'you mean?'

Richard Compton-King gave a long, considering look. His breezy, charming manner had given way to something more serious and thoughtful. 'Come on, you're his biographer, surely you know.'

Adam shook his head.

'Astonishing.' Compton-King paused contemplatively, turning his champagne glass slowly with long fingers. 'It always surprised me it never came up before. You know, profiles of Harry, stuff written about him when he was up for those big prizes. I knew. Plenty of people knew. Maybe it was because they were all part of that strange charmed circle. People were far kinder back then, you know. Discreet, tactful. Understanding.' He drank off his champagne and poured them both some more.

For a few seconds Adam was too astonished to say anything. He picked up his glass and took a couple of steadying gulps. 'You're saying Harry was *gay*?' This, if true, was going to make something very big of the biography. He felt momentarily dizzy.

Compton-King lifted his chin and looked at Adam pensively. 'Yes – though not entirely. Lots of people like that back then. I don't know whether he and Cecile strictly had what you would call *un mariage blanc* . . . but I think it was a form of protection. That's what really got Joe – he hated the social taboos that forced people into those corners. Couldn't decide whether Harry was giving in to conventionality, or cocking a snook at it. He and Harry argued about it a good deal. In a friendly kind of way. Joe didn't see why homosexuality had to be regarded as outcast and criminal, thought everything Harry did reinforced that. Of course, that was why Joe behaved as he did, all that cottaging, that promiscuity. Said that it was a way of rejecting prescribed patterns of sex. "Sex is the only way to infuriate them," he used to say. Hated the idea of the well-adjusted homosexual, saw tolerance as a repressive concept.'

Adam was working to keep up with this. Compton-King was more than just an old pop-group manager and hustler, clearly. Behind the lazy, lightweight façade lay a busy intellect. Maybe it was the alcohol. Maybe it had a perverse effect on him, making him serious, instead of the other way round. Whatever, Compton-King was turning out to be the best thing that had happened to Adam since George Meacher. If any fleeting misgivings struck him concerning the rest of the Day family, Adam stifled them for the time being, preoccupied with the significance of what he was hearing.

'Joe would go on at Harry about his hypocrisy – Harry would simply point to Joe's relationship with Halliwell and tell Joe he was trapped in his own homosexual marriage, but without any of the tax benefits.' Compton-King grinned. 'Give him his due, Joe was generous enough to accept the truth of that. Which was why he envied the way Harry had arranged his life. Joe saw Harry as having class. It was something Harry tried to disguise, or at any rate downplay in the old quest to be a social dramatist, but it shone through, and Joe liked that. He wanted to move easily through the social milieu like Harry. Harry was quite content to manipulate the truth of his own life, accept conventions and work within them. He wasn't angry, like Joe. For all the social realism of his plays, he wasn't setting out to change the world. It was Joe who remained true to himself – the ultimate bedsitter playwright.'

'But you said yourself that Harry's plays were subversive. He was one of the great social realists. He was ground-breaking, surely.'

'No. He was simply doing what a great many people, including myself, did in the sixties.' Compton-King gave Adam a kind smile. 'He was cashing in.' He emptied the dregs of the first bottle into Adam's glass and popped the second. Adam allowed his glass to be refilled without demur. He was feeling very good indeed.

'Mind if I have some more of this cheese?' he asked.

'Go ahead. I'll get Shona to bring out those strawberries.' He hauled his lanky frame from the chair and flapped off into the house.

Adam put his recorder on pause and sat in a state of incredulity. Unlike with the Meacher situation, he didn't doubt one word of what Compton-King had told him. But how was it that, over all the years, not so much as a hint of any sexual scandal concerning Harry had ever surfaced? How had he managed to conduct himself as a very public personality without scraps of truth emerging, former lovers cashing in, some resourceful journalist getting wind of something?

He asked Compton-King this when he returned. Compton-King, who had brought out a second bottle of champagne, filled Adam's glass, despite his protests, and settled himself back in his chair. Adam flicked on his tape recorder.

'Well, now, to answer that one, you have to understand the way things were back then. Homosexuality? Utterly beyond the pale. Till they changed the law in the late sixties, if you were queer you could be sent to prison for life. Utterly appalling, wrecked people's lives and careers . . .' Shona appeared with a bowl of strawberries and set them down. Compton-King stretched out a large hand and picked up a few, and began to bite them off at the base of their stalks with leonine teeth. Adam helped himself to a handful, and found himself wondering whether Compton-King himself was gay. It was hard to tell.

Compton-King chucked the spent hulls of his strawberries on to a plate and wiped his hands together. 'So –' He picked up the bottle and poured out yet more champagne. '– put Harry in that environment. Think of him – young man in Soho in the late fifties. Hangs around certain kinds of bars and clubs. Plenty of them in Soho. Gets drawn into the homosexual scene, as can happen. Few years later, turns into an established playwright, with a reputation to protect.' Compton-King shrugged. 'As I recall, Harry had girlfriends as well, but no matter how half-hearted a homosexual you might be in those days, you stood to lose everything – career, reputation, family, liberty – if you got caught. Harry was probably just one of any number who got married and kept up an appearance of respectability. Can't say I ever blamed him, even if Joe did.'

'But d'you think Cecile realized? I mean, do you think when they got married that she knew?' asked Adam wonderingly.

'I'm pretty sure she did.' Compton-King stretched out his legs, rose and cast aside his towelling robe. 'Time for a swim.'

He strolled to the edge of the pool, contemplated the water, and then hurled himself in with a tremendous, splashing dive. Adam wiped drops of water from his face and knocked back the remains of his champagne. Through a mild haze of drunkenness crept a realization of the problems which these momentous revelations raised. This would all require careful investigation, and further conversation with Compton-King. This was something no one had ever known about Harry Day, and if they had, it had certainly never been made public before. The main problem lay with Cecile. It wasn't the kind of thing one could just go ahead and publish, without consulting her. Good manners forbade it, and besides, Bella might never speak to him again. Bella . . . There lay problem number two . . . But how could he raise the subject with Cecile? What if she had never known?

'Come on, have a dip,' called Compton-King, surfacing at the side, his long hair streaming down his back.

'I haven't got anything. Trunks, I mean,' said Adam uncertainly.

'Oh God, you're not at your local swimming pool, you know. Come in with nothing on, as far as I'm concerned.' He plunged back into the water. Again, Adam wondered uneasily if Compton-King *was* gay. But, God, it was hot, and a swim felt like just the thing to clear the champagne muzziness from his head. How could he have let himself sit here and drink an entire bottle of champagne in under an hour? Chances were he'd be incapable of swimming. Still . . . He got up and divested himself of socks, shoes, trousers and shirt, leaving on his boxer shorts. Taking a deep breath, he dived in.

Adam woke up on the long leather sofa in Richard Compton-King's office three hours later. He recalled lying down there, a towel wrapped round his waist, but he had no recollection of falling asleep. He must have closed his eyes while Compton-King had been cataloguing his successes and failures in the music business by reference to the various gold and platinum discs which hung on his office walls, and the champagne and sun and swimming pool had done the rest. He passed a hand over his face. His head ached faintly, and his mouth tasted unpleasantly of stale wine. He glanced at his watch, alarmed to see how much time had passed. He got up, the towel and boxer shorts unpleasantly clammy against his thighs. He went to the door, shivering, and looked uncertainly up and down the passage which ran past the office, then made his way out to the sunlit silence of the swimming pool. His clothes still lay on the chair where he had dropped them. On the table the shambles of the champagne lunch remained untouched.

As he finished dressing, Richard Compton-King came out, now fully clad in pressed chinos and a blue open-necked shirt. He looked remarkably fresh and sober for someone who had drunk as much as he had. Maybe that was an average lunch for Compton-King.

'Feel better for your nap?'

'I'm really sorry – it must have been the sun. You should have woken me up.'

'Nonsense. At least now you're more or less fit to drive. Coffee before you go? I'm on my way out, but Shona will make you some.'

'No, thanks all the same.' Adam picked up his tape machine from the table and put it in his pocket. 'I'd best be getting back. Look –' He paused uncertainly. 'When I came here today, I hadn't expected any of what you told me. As you can imagine, it's very important for my book. Would you be prepared to talk to me again, elaborate on things?'

'Of course. Don't know how reliable my memory is for detail, mind you.'

Adam stretched out his hand and Compton-King shook it. 'Thanks for lunch. I'll give you a call in the next few days.'

Compton-King kept hold of Adam's hand for a few seconds, the pressure firm and warm. 'Do that. I would actually love to see you again.'

By the time Adam got back to Baron's Court it was nearly half five, and he would have given anything for an evening of peace and solitude in which to shake off his hangover, listen to the tape, and consider carefully where he went from here. He hoped that Megan had gone off for a drink with friends after work, as she occasionally did, and he would have the flat to himself. But no – there was Megan's VW parked across the road under the plane trees.

In the kitchen, Megan was unpacking bags of groceries. 'I'm going to make us a fabulous supper,' she said cheerfully. She'd been watching Jamie Oliver every week on television for the past month. 'I hope you're hungry.'

Feeling quite unreasonably irritated, Adam replied, 'I'm not, to be honest.' It was true. He had no wish to eat anything at all. The sun and champagne had left him with a feeling of malaise. Never before had he wanted so badly to have the place to himself.

Megan looked at him. 'But I've bought all this stuff . . .'

'I've had a heavy day.' He was aware that his tone was unfriendly, and Megan caught this.

'Heavy lunch, more like. Been out boozing with Giles?' Megan started to slam things into the fridge.

'Oh, get off my case! I've been working, as it happens. And I'm going to spend the rest of the evening doing the same. I'd be grateful if you didn't disturb me.'

He went into the bedroom and flung up the sash window. The air in the room was stale, touched with the cloying note of some perfume of Megan's, which fiercely and unaccountably enraged him. He took his tape machine from his pocket and went into his study, closing the door behind him.

An hour and a half later, he emerged to ask Megan to turn down the hi-fi. This escalated into a blazing row, which ended with Megan in tears, and Adam expressing a contrition he did not feel. When he came to bed around midnight, Megan was asleep, for which he was grateful. He crept beneath the duvet, pondering the events of the day. He had listened twice to the tape of his conversation with Compton-King, typing it up on the computer. He lay in the dark for a long time, thinking, and the last thing he decided before he fell asleep was that, before doing anything else, he would have to speak to Cecile.

9

Despite his resolve, Adam felt some trepidation when he rang Cecile the next morning. Her manner on the telephone was formal, restrained, and almost a little fearful. She could, he knew, have resisted any further intrusion entirely, but she agreed to see him – indeed, she suggested he come round that very afternoon. So after lunch he drove to Dulwich.

'How are you?' asked Adam, as she led him through to the same room where they had talked before.

'Oh, quite well, thank you. I've been recording *A Book at Bedtime* for the BBC, and what with making the bridesmaids' dresses for the wedding, and so on, I've really been very busy . . .'

She closed the door and turned to face him. Adam realized that he couldn't allow politeness to escalate to further, dizzying heights of unreality. 'Look,' he said, 'I feel I owe you some kind of apology. I want you to know that I had no intention of hurting anyone in your family. I simply found certain things out, and the rest took its course.'

'Yes, well . . . Perhaps it was only to be expected.' Cecile gestured for him to sit down. Her manner was still courteous and controlled. 'I suppose in some strange way I'm rather grateful to you for what has happened. I had thought, at first, that it was all going to be quite cataclysmic, the end of everything good between Bella and Charlie and myself. Of course, I'm still not sure quite how they will feel in the long run . . .' Her eyes moistened with quick tears.

'They both love you very much. Nothing that has happened will change that.'

She nodded swiftly. 'No, I realize that. I'm just not sure if the worst has passed yet. I don't know how long it takes to work these things out. It's my fault for not telling them a long time ago. I know that.' She sat down in a chair opposite Adam. 'You know that Bella went to see the Kinleys?'

'Yes. I went with her.'

'Oh?' Cecile looked surprised. 'She didn't mention that.'

'I think she wanted – well, some kind of moral support.'

'I see.' Cecile nodded. 'She told me afterwards that she felt utterly no connection between herself and her mother. I was so relieved . . . it made me feel quite ashamed.'

Adam said nothing. It wasn't up to him to tell Cecile that Bella and Doreen Kinley had done nothing more than look at one another, without Mrs Kinley having any idea of who Bella was. Then again, he began to wonder what *was* up to him. Hadn't he come here to unlock another family closet and bring forth the skeleton?

'Would you like some tea?' asked Cecile.

'Please, don't go to any trouble.'

'I'm always grateful for an excuse to make tea.' Cecile rose. 'I'll only be a few minutes.'

Damn, thought Adam. Back came the politeness, the

fragile decorum. When she came back, he'd have to start all over again. Best not to beat around the bush.

Five minutes later, as she set down the tea tray, Adam said, 'I'm surprised you agreed to see me, to be honest. After what's happened, I thought you might no longer be particularly keen on helping with the biography.'

She looked directly at him. 'I don't really care about events in the past being broadcast to the whole world. That's what you journalists do, after all.' She poured his tea and handed it to him. 'No, my concern is only for the integrity of my family, to keep us close, to ride things out . . . Facts are as they are. I suppose we're all stupid to try to conceal them. If I turned my back on this book, and on you, it wouldn't do any good.'

There was a silence. Adam stirred his tea. She sounded so resolute, almost as though she knew, or suspected, that he was going to broach some further hidden aspect of Harry's life. He decided to be as direct as possible, whatever the risk of offence. 'In that case,' he said, 'I'll be frank with you. I have found a certain source, a man who was a friend of Harry's back in the sixties, who says that at the time he knew Harry, he was having a number of affairs. With men.'

Adam had no idea what her reaction might be. That was the worst of it. Either she knew or she didn't. If she didn't, then the enormity of what he had said . . . He waited, watched.

Cecile merely dipped her head to sip her tea, then said quietly, 'That's quite true. I knew. I knew at the time.' The gaze she fastened on Adam was a little defiant. 'I didn't mind. It wasn't as though he were seeing other women, or having love affairs. I never felt threatened. They were just casual pick-ups, young men, so it was quite unimportant. It was only a sexual thing, you see. There was no . . . emotion involved. He didn't care for any one of them. It's not as though Harry was actually queer, you know. It was simply a habit he had picked up, a vice he had learned during the time he lived in Soho. These things can be learned, you know. I don't care what the modern cant is about men being born that way. Perfectly normal young men can easily be corrupted. It happened to Harry. It was something he had to rid himself of. But it took time. I was a correcting influence, eventually.'

Adam nodded wonderingly. Was she being embarrassingly naive, or had it perhaps really been like that? He remembered what Compton-King had said about the moral atmosphere of forty, fifty years ago, and realized he had simply no way of knowing how people conducted themselves then, or how things were. He put his hand in his pocket and drew out his tape recorder. Cecile eyed it. 'Are you happy for me to tape our conversation?' asked Adam.

Cecile hesitated. 'I suppose so.'

He set the tape down on the table and switched it on. 'Did you know any of them? Harry's –' He hesitated momentarily, floundering for the right word.

'Boyfriends? God, no.' Her voice was sharp with disgust.

'Did you . . . did you and Harry ever discuss what he was doing?'

'No. It was . . . well, I suppose "acknowledged" is the

correct word. He had told me earlier on, before we were married, about himself.'

'How did you feel when he first told you?'

'Pretty appalled. In those days people didn't talk about such things, not openly. Being in the theatre . . . well, one knew any number of homosexuals, but I suppose I wasn't prepared . . . We had vowed to tell each other everything, the way people do – not keep anything back. It was very upsetting when he told me about his past, things he had done. But I was very much in love with him. He told me it was over and done with. I believed him. I wouldn't have married him otherwise. When you're in love, you do want to believe in the other person . . .'

Her manner was still entirely composed, but something about the expression in her eyes made Adam hesitate before continuing.

'And later . . . how did you find out that it was still carrying on?'

'Oh, I just guessed. The people he knew, some of the types he hung around with. He was very friendly with Joe Orton and that companion of his, Halliwell. There were evenings when he didn't come home, and he said he was at such and such a place, and I found out later that he hadn't been.' She shrugged. 'Little things. Little lies.'

'Did you confront Harry about it?'

She hesitated, then said, 'It came up. We talked. I'd really rather not discuss it in great detail.'

'It must have been something of a shock.'

'Yes. But I overcame it. I was determined that it shouldn't be a threat to our marriage. Harry didn't want it to be. He saw it as an aberration, a kind of backsliding.

It really was very difficult for him. As I said, it was a habit he had to break. And he did, in the end.'

'Can I ask . . . forgive me if this is difficult . . . Did Harry's bisexuality –'

'I'd rather you didn't call it that. It was nothing of the kind.'

'Fine. I'm merely trying to understand . . . Did his behaviour – I mean, did it have any bearing on the fact that you couldn't have children?' *I don't think I'm cut out for this kind of work*, thought Adam.

The question brought spots of angry colour to Cecile's withered cheeks. 'Our marriage was perfectly normal, in the physical sense, if that's what you're implying. I have told you twice already that Harry dealt with his problem, overcame it. It had no relevance to the fact that we couldn't have a family. The problem there lay with me.'

Adam nodded. 'This is a difficult conversation for both of us. I apologize if –'

'I quite understand that you don't mean to be offensive.'

'It's just that the truth often is just that. Offensive.'

She gazed at him implacably. 'Would you like some more tea?'

'Thank you.'

She refilled his cup. 'May I ask you – who was the third party who told you about this?'

Adam hesitated. 'Someone called Richard Compton-King.' He watched and waited.

'Ah, yes . . .' Her face gave nothing away.

'You know him?'

'I haven't seen him in – what? Nearly thirty years? But, yes, I remember him.'

A thought occurred to Adam for the first time, and he wondered why it hadn't struck him before. 'Was he one of Harry's lovers?'

Cecile looked at him in astonishment and burst into a peal of genuine laughter. 'Oh no – heavens, no!'

Her evident amusement at this made Adam smile. The momentary change of mood was a mild relief. 'Why is that so funny?'

'Well . . .' She smiled reflectively. 'I think I would have known if that was the case. And I can assure you it was not. Anyway –' Her smile faded as she set down her cup, 'as I told you, the men involved were mere pick-ups. Quite faceless. I shouldn't think he knew their names, ever.' There was a pause of several seconds. 'So you see, whatever you intend to make of this in your book, I'm afraid there are no personalities involved. No names. I imagine that is disappointing.'

Cecile's slant on things was quite different from Compton-King's in more ways than one. Not the remotest suggestion that her marriage to Harry had been one of mere convenience. Far from it. Not that Adam had any intention of telling Cecile. He shrugged. 'It's another aspect of Harry's life. That's where my interest lies. Everything else that follows is incidental. This biography isn't intended to be –' He paused.

'A muck-raking exercise?'

'Just the truth,' said Adam. 'That's all I'm after.' He reached across and switched off his tape recorder. He had the impression this couldn't be pursued much further

– not with Cecile, at any rate. 'Thank you for being so frank.'

'Not at all. I really think the whole thing is quite trivial, actually. It lasted only a couple of years into our marriage. It was all well over by the time the twins arrived. Not really worth making much of a fuss about in your book, I wouldn't have thought.'

Adam made no response to this. Instead he asked, 'I wonder – not that there's any reason why you should know the answer – but do you suppose Briony knows anything about this?'

'Briony? I'm sure I have no idea.' The look she gave Adam was cold and defensive. 'Harry may have told her. Or he may have regarded it all as too trivial, too far in the past. You'd have to ask her.'

Adam nodded thoughtfully. He'd taken this as far as he could. It had plainly been difficult for her, and for that he was sorry. But the task he had undertaken was a serious one, and he had to pursue it in a professional manner. Would he have undertaken it, if he had known at the outset how much pain might be involved? He had no idea. He put his tape recorder back into his pocket and, in an attempt to relax the atmosphere between them, said, 'I take it you've been to see Bella's play?'

'Of course.' Cecile's eyes brightened at the thought of Bella. 'I went on the opening night. It's hard to say whether it will be any kind of a success. I don't think the play has ever been staged before, so it's something of a leap in the dark. They televised it back in the sixties, but I didn't see it. Orton is difficult, I always think . . . How can one tell when the time is right for a revival?'

'Perhaps we'll be seeing some of Harry's plays in the West End soon.'

'Not soon,' said Cecile. 'There's always a decent interval of obscurity after a writer dies. Maybe in fifteen or twenty years. We shall see – or at any rate, *you* shall . . . But I hope, for Bella's sake, that *Funeral Games* does better than the critics have suggested. Have you seen it?'

'I'm planning to go next week.'

Adam rose, and Cecile went with him to the front door. They stood together for a hesitant moment, and then Cecile said, 'You know, it might be a kindness to everyone involved if your book didn't touch on this part of Harry's life.'

'That's asking a lot.'

'I know. Of course, I could have simply denied that any of it ever happened, and tried to conceal it that way. But you already knew, so that would have been pointless. So I'm appealing to – to your better nature, if you like. I don't see what good it will do anyone for these things to be brought out.'

Adam didn't know what to say. 'I intend to be no more than truthful. But no less. I can't –'

'You can. You have a conscience.' Her voice rose, trembling a little. 'Don't you think you've already unearthed enough things that Harry might have wished left alone?'

Adam turned and walked down the path to the garden gate. 'I'll be in touch. I won't do anything without speaking to you again. I promise.'

Driving back across London, Adam reflected on Cecile's attempt to appeal to his conscience in the matter of Harry's youthful indiscretions. This was surely just the beginning. Once the rest of the family knew, the pressure not to publish would grow, and would inevitably be less gentle than Cecile's dignified supplication. If it were a matter of conscience, as Cecile had suggested, he didn't see how he could be selective with the truth. Presumably Cecile didn't want any mention made of it because, by the standards of her generation, the revelations were to Harry's discredit. But were they? Adam couldn't decide. By today's standards, one would say not, but Adam knew in his bones that there was a wider moral perspective to this. It was more a question of hypocrisy, of concealment. Smokescreens, as Compton-King had put it. And, if he were honest with himself, this aspect added the touch of sensationalism which the book badly needed. No – he would not be baulked by Harry's family. As he formed this resolution, Adam was dimly aware that a streak of ruthlessness had entered his soul.

When Adam had gone, Cecile began to clear away the teacups. She moved slowly, her mind still working on the conversation which had just taken place. Whatever Briony and Harry had assumed about that young man, they were guilty of a serious underestimation. Or complacency, at the very least. Adam Downing had certainly done his homework . . . unearthing Richard Compton-King, of all people. What a charmer he had been. She paused by the sink, staring across the garden, across the years. Afternoons in that cramped little flat of his in Greek Street. Rain on the windows.

After a few moments she turned and went to the

telephone. There were several seconds of tiresome negotiation with Briony's PA, Peter, before she managed to get through to Briony herself. Really, the woman behaved as though she were Elizabeth Taylor . . .

'Briony? It's Cecile. I thought you should know that Adam Downing came to see me again today. He's dug up an old friend of Harry's – and mine. Someone with a nice, long memory who isn't at all interested in protecting anyone's reputation, much.'

'Who?' Briony's voice at the other end was sharp, anxious.

'His name is Richard Compton-King.'

'I've never heard of him.'

'Well, that's neither here nor there, dear. He knew both of us very well at one time. Mr Downing has just been plaguing me with questions – quite tactful questions, naturally – about young men that Harry was cavorting with back in the days when we were married.' Cecile's tone was dry and light, in contrast to Briony's anxiety.

'And you said?'

'Well, I was as honest as I could be. Given the extent of his knowledge, there seemed little point in lying. But I think I managed to convey the impression that it was all a youthful aberration, nothing of any consequence or duration. He did ask whether you knew. Of course I said I had no idea, that he would have to ask you.'

'Oh, wonderful! That's the last thing I need.'

'You needn't sound so cross with me. It's not my job to throw shadows and protect you from scrutiny. Or the things you get up to on the quiet. I had a lifetime of equivocation when I was married to Harry. It's up to you to look after yourself. I'm quite sure you can deal with Adam Downing. Besides,' added Cecile reflectively, 'I don't actually think he's looking for trouble, you know.'

'If Adam Downing wants my continued cooperation,' said Briony evenly, 'he'll have to be very careful not to stray into areas where his intrusion is unwelcome.'

'Well, now, if I were a journalist,' said Cecile, 'I think that kind of attitude would rather whet my appetite – don't you think? Good luck fending him off, at any rate, dear. Who knows? He may not think it worth asking you about.'

Briony sincerely doubted that, and she was right. Adam rang the very next day.

'I'm afraid I'm very busy, Adam,' said Briony when she came on the line. 'I can't talk to you for long.' She had hesitated before letting Peter put the call through, but had decided there was no point in putting Adam off. She might as well dispose of the problem sooner rather than later.

'It's not something I really want to discuss over the phone,' said Adam. 'I wondered if there was some time we could meet.'

He heard Briony sigh impatiently at the other end. 'I have to come up to town on Wednesday to see my agent. I suppose I can spare you half an hour.'

Distinctly offhand, thought Adam. Had Cecile tipped her off? He recalled very clearly the way the two women had stood together outside the church after Harry's memorial service, their shared composure. Guarding something. Guarding Harry? Guarding themselves?

'That's kind of you. Where do you suggest?'

She thought for a moment. 'The American Bar at the Ritz is as good a place as any. I'll be there around six.'

Adam hesitated. It was very public, but he couldn't think of anywhere else more suitable. 'Fine,' he said. 'I'll see you there.'

He hung up, reflecting on the contribution made thus far to the biography by Briony Nugent, forty-something spun sugar, bright with daytime-television glamour and elfin charm, and hard as nails. She had been at pains to present Harry and herself as a devoted couple, with a loving and idyllic marriage, he in the autumn of his years, living quietly with his young (youngish) wife in their country home, at peace with his poetry, she devoted and attentive, dividing her busy time between TV commitments and caring for Harry during his final illness. A lot of *OK!* magazine tosh, a PR exercise in the furtherance of Briony Nugent's public image. Still, even Briony's version of events must possess its own strange veracity. It was just that Adam suspected there might be something more to it than that.

Adam sat in the Ritz for half an hour on Wednesday evening, waiting for Briony, spinning out an extremely expensive dry martini and trying to work out the best way to broach his subject. He had deliberately chosen a table tucked away in the corner, which seemed private enough. Only a handful of people were in the bar.

When she appeared at last, Briony crossed the room quickly, as if to draw minimum attention to herself. She looked as immaculate as ever, but her eyes were tired, and her expression as she greeted Adam lacked any warmth. She ordered a whisky cocktail, and offered Adam no apology for her lateness.

'I imagine this has to do with the biography?' she asked. 'I must say I was surprised you wanted to see me. I think by now you know all I have to tell you.'

'Something new has come up,' said Adam. 'It's to do with a part of Harry's life that nobody has touched on. Ever. Not even Harry himself.'

Was there the smallest flicker around the pretty eyes, the tiniest change of expression? She said nothing, so Adam went on. 'Since we don't have long, I'll come straight to the point. I've run down an interesting source, a man who was friendly with Harry back in the sixties. Not someone on Harry's accredited list of friends and relations.' Briony's drink arrived. She picked it up and took a sip. 'His story is that Harry's sexual proclivities around that time included young men. It was something I had to put to Cecile, naturally, and she confirmed it.'

Nothing tactful or apologetic here, thought Briony. She had given some thought as to how she was going to play this, but she paused for a moment before replying. She gazed at Adam reflectively. Where had the nice, deferential young man of last summer gone? Or could it be that Harry had been deceived by something as trivial as good manners? Wearing an expression of mild surprise, she said, 'I don't quite understand why you see the need to talk to me about it.'

'I wondered if it was something Harry ever discussed with you.' He could tell from the coolness of her reaction that he hadn't shocked her, that it was something she'd already known about. From whom? Harry, or Cecile?

'No.'

'But you knew about it?'

Again Briony paused for some seconds before replying. 'It was long in the past. Call it a youthful indiscretion, if you like. I imagine it's not that unusual.'

'It's just that . . . well, a tendency like that doesn't generally just fade away.' Adam was making an effort to keep his tone light, appeasing.

'Meaning?'

'Meaning that it may have been an enduring part of Harry's life. I wondered to what lengths someone might go to conceal certain things. Especially someone who grew up in an era when to be a known homosexual could spell certain disaster.'

'How ridiculous.' Briony's tone was cool and dismissive. 'No person could keep up such a pretence for an entire lifetime.'

'People have. Any number.'

'I think I would have known, don't you?'

'You pre-empted me. I was just about to add that it might call for a certain amount of collusion on the part of friends and family.'

Briony drank the remains of her cocktail. 'I've been very polite to you so far, Adam. What you are suggesting is both offensive and potentially libellous. I suggest you limit the scope of your book to the areas defined by my husband while he was alive.' Her eyes were suddenly bright with indignant tears, and she reached into her bag for a tissue. 'I don't know how you can embark on such crude speculation concerning someone who befriended and trusted you in the months before he died.'

Adam, reminding himself that Briony was a consummate actress, endeavoured to remain unmoved. 'I've no wish to upset you or your family. But we know now that Harry was capable of deceiving those close to him.'

'We were all shocked by the business of the adoption. There were mistakes made, and reasons for those mistakes, I'm sure. You say you have no wish to upset the family, but don't you think you've done enough in that direction?'

'I'm writing a biography, Briony.'

'Of an admired and cherished writer, I would remind you. If Harry made a few excusable mistakes in his youth, you'd serve his memory better by ignoring them, instead of trying to fabricate this kind of sensationalist rubbish just to sell your book.'

'I'm merely trying to establish the truth.'

'The truth is that Harry was a wonderful man, a wonderful husband, a wonderful writer, and a wonderful father!' Briony leaned forward, her words clear and icy. 'Your role is no more than that of a parasite, Adam. If you try to discredit his memory, I will sue you.' She gathered her possessions together and stood up. 'I'm beginning to wish he'd never employed you to write his biography.'

I'll bet you are, thought Adam, watching as she left the bar, wondering just what it was that she was so anxious to protect. Despite what she said, he suspected it wasn't Harry's reputation, but something rather closer to home.

In a West End already struggling against the beginnings of recession, *Funeral Games* was not going as well as its producers had hoped. A fortnight after its opening, when Adam went to see it, the audience numbered just thirty-six. He had chosen to go on an evening when Megan was working. For some reason, he wanted to go alone. The play turned out to be better and far more amusing than he had expected, and Bella, it seemed to him, was very good. It afforded him particular pleasure, of an infatuated kind, to watch her perform. Everything she did seemed charged with erotic, faintly dangerous undertones, though he could see that she was probably too young and lovely for the part, and not earthy enough. For which he gave thanks.

He went to the stage door when the play was over and asked to see her, giving the doorman his name. He was admitted backstage, and found Bella in her cramped dressing room, taking off her make-up.

'Did you like it?' she asked, glancing in the mirror at his face.

'I did. Very much. You were very good.'

She sighed. 'I like doing it. The play's fun. But what a lousy house.'

'I thought Wednesdays tended to be quiet nights.'

'Not this quiet. Last night and Monday night were hardly any better.' She chucked a used ball of cotton wool into the bin and rubbed her face with a towel. 'Anyway, thanks for coming.'

'I wanted to. I wanted to see you. The play, I mean.'

She smiled. 'You didn't bring the girlfriend. Wasn't she keen?'

'She's at a Botox party.'

'A *what*?' Bella laughed.

'I know,' sighed Adam. 'It's the work she does, she's into all that stuff. She actually came home from work the other day with a pair of pre-laddered tights. Some promotional thing that a fashion house sent to her office. She thought they were fantastic.'

Bella laughed, and gave him a glance in the mirror. 'How's the biography going?'

'So-so. It's coming along. The trouble is – or rather, it shouldn't be trouble, it should be excellent, really . . . from my point of view, I mean, though not necessarily from other people's –'

'What? You're beginning to ramble.'

Adam leaned against the edge of the dressing table and folded his arms. Bella had a sudden urge, which she resisted, to stretch out her hand and run it the length of his thigh. 'I keep turning up unexpected pieces of information, things no one appears to have discovered about your father before.'

'As in . . . ?'

'As in –' He stopped and glanced at her. 'I actually meant to take you for a drink after you'd finished tonight and talk to you about it.'

She examined her nails. 'You should have rung. I might be busy. I might be too tired.'

'Are you? Either of those things?'

'Busy – no. Tired – yes. But not too tired. Wait at the stage door while I get changed.'

They went to a quiet downstairs wine bar near the theatre, and Adam bought a couple of glasses of Chablis. Bella leaned back against the wall, propped her feet against the rung of the chair next to her, and took a sip of her wine. Adam sat opposite, thinking how childlike her oval face looked, bereft of any trace of make-up, still a little shiny from being creamed and towelled. He liked the fact that she had to make no effort at all to look lovely.

'Please don't think me rude, but I don't want this to last too long,' she said. 'I'm really bushed.'

'Don't worry,' said Adam. 'It's not much to tell. I've already spoken to Cecile about it.'

'Go on.'

'Well –' Adam paused, trying to find the right words. 'It seems that your father had quite a colourful sexual career before he met your mother. That is to say, apparently he liked boys as well as girls.' Christ, thought Adam, how twee did *that* sound?

'Gay? My father?' Bella regarded him with astonished eyes, then said firmly, 'He was not gay.'

'No, I don't mean that. Not quite. From what I can gather . . . Well, look, Cecile's line is that he got caught up in the gay scene while he was living in Soho, but that she managed to straighten him out.'

'I mean,' went on Bella, as though she hadn't heard him, 'I'm not saying it would matter if he had been. Fine. I don't care. I have absolutely nothing against anyone being gay. Nothing at all. It's perfectly fine. I'm just saying that my father wasn't, that's all.' She took a long drink of her wine.

Adam nodded. 'No, I understand that. What I –'

Adam's previous words seemed suddenly to have registered with her. 'Who said he was caught up in the gay scene? My *mother* said that?'

'She – she corroborated it. It was someone else who told me. A man called Richard Compton-King. Do you know him?'

Bella shook her head. 'Never even heard the name.'

'No, well . . . He knew Harry very well back in the sixties. When I put it to Cecile, she didn't go off the rails, or anything. She was very good about it. Said she'd known about it before she and Harry married. I think it was something she came to terms with, and from what she says, it eventually stopped. Or so she says.' He regarded Bella anxiously, afraid this was more problematic for her than he had anticipated. Since they both came from a supposedly enlightened generation, he had imagined she would accept news of Harry's brief foray into bisexuality with equanimity. Whatever she was thinking, she was murdering her wine. Her glass was nearly empty.

But Bella's agitation seemed to be levelling out. She sat thinking, frowning, for a while. 'Are you going to put this in the book?'

Adam considered this for a few seconds. 'Your mother asked me not to. But I don't see how I can leave it out.'

'I see. Well, you have to do what you think is right.' She made a wry face. 'At least Charlie won't have to go into agonies over it.'

'What d'you mean?'

'I mean that when he finds out about this, Charlie will probably be relieved by the fact that Harry wasn't our real father. Otherwise he'd be convinced it was something genetic, and that he must be like that. I'm not saying,' added Bella quickly, 'that Charlie is bothered about anyone being gay –'

'Just himself. No, I understand. I'm sure he's as enlightened as the next person.'

Bella scrutinized Adam's face, wondering if she detected mild irony in his tone. But no, she didn't think so.

She rested one elbow on the table and propped her head up wearily. 'I don't know why I should feel surprised. People do get up to the strangest things. Even one's parents. I don't suppose it matters. It's all gone now.'

'Anyway, I thought I should tell you.'

'It's just . . . well, things one would rather not have known . . .' She looked at him appealingly. 'Do you *have* to put it in?'

He decided to duck the issue for the moment. 'Much depends on the detail.' He still had no idea what names Compton-King might come up with, if any. He gestured to her almost-empty glass. 'Another drink?'

Bella shook her head. 'I have to go.' She paused. 'Adam, I really hope you will think twice about putting it in the book. It could be pretty upsetting for a lot of people.'

'We'll see,' he said. That was a lie, but he didn't want to argue about it right now.

She sighed and rose, picking up her canvas shoulder bag from the chair. 'By the way, while you're here –' She delved into the bag and handed him an envelope, '– have a look at this.'

Adam pulled out two handwritten pages and read them.

Dear Bella Day,

I am writing to you as Doreen Kinley's sister in the hope that I can be of help. Derek has told me you came to see him in hopes of finding your 'real' family. It was a great shock to Derek to find out what happened all those years ago, though of course you had no way of knowing it would be. We have not told Doreen of your visit and who you are, it would be a tremendous upset and as you saw that day she is not a well woman. As your aunt I would like to meet you if possible and explain a few things that I am sure you are anxious to know. You can contact me at the above address or phone number, evenings are best.

Yours sincerely,

Joyce Barrow (Mrs)

Adam folded the letter up and put it back in the envelope. 'Have you talked to her?'

'Not yet. It only came this morning.'

'Well, I imagine it will help to talk to someone who knows what went on.'

'I suppose.' She glanced at her watch. 'I should be going. Give me a ring some time.'

When she had gone, Adam sat with the remains of his wine, thinking. She hadn't said a great deal, hadn't really had time to absorb the full implications of what he'd told her tonight, but her instinctive reaction had been to ask him not to publish what he had found out. A mild request, just like Cecile's, an appeal to his better nature. He wondered how long it would take before these gentle appeals turned into fully formed resistance from the entire family. Then he really would have a problem on his hands.

A few days later, just before she left for the theatre, Bella rang Joyce Barrow.

'Hello?' The voice that answered was soft, and a little breathless.

'Hello – is that Joyce Barrow?'

'Speaking.'

'This is Bella Day.'

'Oh. Goodness.' There was a pause. 'How are you? I'm sorry if I sound a bit surprised. I was expecting you to call, but I'm just a bit . . .'

'Don't worry,' said Bella. 'It's strange for both of us.'

'Yes.'

'You said you'd be happy to talk to me.'

'Yes.'

The woman was so unforthcoming, Bella wondered whether she had begun to have misgivings.

'Can we meet?'

'Yes. All right. Just a moment . . .' There was the sound of a phone being put down. After a few seconds, Joyce Barrow came back on the line. 'I work Tuesdays and Thursdays . . . What about tomorrow? Would you like to come here?'

'If it's not inconvenient.'

'Oh no, it's not a problem.' Her voice sounded a little more cheerful. She gave Bella the address, which was in New Cross, not far from where Derek and Doreen Kinley lived. 'Shall we say around eleven?'

'Fine. I'll see you then.'

She put the phone down. How extraordinary, to think that that was her aunt. Her aunt, by blood, by birth. Yet she had been speaking to a complete stranger. How odd this entire process of discovery was. That the deeply personal should be so utterly impersonal, that near relations should be at such a remove. It made her wonder what kind of truth she hoped to find out in the end, whether it would be of substance, or quite illusory.

She put her things together and set off for the theatre.

On her way to her dressing room she met Bruce, looking despondent. 'Lance and Brian want to speak to everyone on stage in five minutes.'

The little cast assembled on the set. Brian, the production manager, spoke.

'This isn't a happy thing for me to do. Everybody has worked tremendously hard, you've all put a lot into this play, but the fact is, attendances haven't been good, and we have decided to end the run early.'

'How early?' demanded Bruce.

'Next Friday. You're all on a week's notice. Sorry, everyone.'

There was a collective groan. Not that it was entirely unexpected. As things stood, audiences were unlikely to pick up. Even though the play had only been scheduled for an eight-week run, news of the early closure hit everyone's morale. At the end of that evening's performance, the four cast members went to the pub on the corner for a drink.

'Bloody marvellous,' said Jeremy gloomily. 'You come in Thursday and get told you're finishing a week Friday.'

'Only another week's money,' said Bruce.

'And I can't see any new work coming up in the near future,' said Frank. 'Not with the way things are.'

'I've got some voice-over work coming up in August,' remarked Bruce.

'Lucky you.'

They grumbled into their drinks for a few minutes, and then Bella, who had been silent, suddenly said, 'Why don't you all come on holiday with me?'

Everyone stared.

'It won't cost anyone a thing,' said Bella. 'Well, just the air fare to Bordeaux. My brother and I have a house down there, and we have to sell it. I promised myself one last holiday before it goes on the market. I'm inviting you all to come with me.'

Bruce lifted his glass. 'Fantastic. Count me in.'

'Southern France,' said Frank. 'I haven't been there for years. Jenny and I used to go camping there, when we were younger.' He debated. A holiday would be just the thing to lift his spirits. He smiled, raised his glass and chimed it against Bruce's. 'Bella, darling, I should love to come.'

She looked at Jeremy, whose expression was wistful. 'Afraid not, darling. I can't leave the dogs. Besides, my agent's lined up an audition for some murder-mystery two-parter in a couple of weeks. I can't afford to turn work down.'

'That's such a shame.'

'I know. I'm sure I would have loved it.' Jeremy sighed. He glanced at his watch. 'I must love you and leave you all, or I'll miss my train.'

'Hang on – I'll walk down to Charing Cross with you,' said Frank, and knocked back the remains of his drink. He gave Bella a kiss. 'You've given me something to look forward to. Thank you.'

When they had gone, Bruce said to Bella, 'I suppose

we don't have to keep up our passionate romance any more, do we? Not much point.'

'No,' agreed Bella. 'It was fun while it lasted.'

'Would you like to stage a blazing public row, end it that way?'

Bella sighed. 'I don't think I could summon up the energy.'

'Maybe you should just find someone else.'

Bella thought of Adam. 'If only it were that simple.'

10

Joyce Barrow's home in New Cross was a fifth-floor flat on a run-down council estate. Bella, rather than take the rancid-smelling lift, trudged up the dank stairwell to a walkway of front doors, overlooking a green where washing hung in rows.

She knocked, and a few moments later a small, elderly woman in carpet slippers came to the door. Like her sister, Joyce Barrow had a sweet, delicate face, but her white hair was cut short, unpermed. *My aunt*, thought Bella. They smiled uncertainly, searchingly at one another. Bella put out a tentative hand and Joyce Barrow shook it.

'Come in,' she said, padding down the hallway ahead of Bella and into a small, stuffy sitting room, its windows closed despite the heat of the day. An old, very thin man sat in a large armchair in one corner of the room, opposite the television, a copy of the *Daily Mirror* on his lap. He had about him an air of distinct permanence, as though he did not move much from that spot.

'This is my husband, Arthur,' said Joyce. 'I won't introduce you, because he's very deaf. He knows who you are, though.'

Bella nodded and smiled at Arthur, who nodded back and scrutinized her carefully, before turning his attention back to the newspaper once again.

'Sit down, do.'

Bella sat at one end of the small sofa, and Joyce Barrow sat at the other, hands folded in her lap, inspecting Bella. Bella allowed herself to be looked at. Joyce Barrow shook her head, and Bella saw tears spring into her eyes. 'This is such a lovely surprise. I never thought it would happen. Can I give you a hug, dear?'

Bella and Joyce Barrow embraced briefly, awkwardly. The old lady smelled faintly of onions and furniture polish.

'This is all very strange for me,' said Bella. 'I only found out recently that I was adopted. That my brother and I were. You said in your letter that Derek was a little shocked when I showed up on his doorstep, and I am sorry about that. I was rather working in the dark, you see, and I had no idea who knew . . .'

'Don't worry.' Joyce Barrow put out a hand and patted Bella's. She made the gesture hesitantly, feeling somewhat awed by this very beautiful young woman, by the way she spoke and looked. She could see some resemblance to Doreen, even to their own mother, who'd been something of a beauty, but she felt no instant affiliation, no sense that this girl was part of their family. She seemed too remote, almost too exotic, to be connected to their life and world. But she had to be. There could be no doubt, from all that Derek had told her, that this was Doreen's daughter.

There was an awkward pause, and Bella said, 'If you could tell me more about what happened when I was born, I'd be very grateful. I still don't know much beyond what my mother – my adoptive mother – told me. I mean, I know why my mother and father adopted Charlie and me, and they've been wonderful parents, the most wonderful, but I have to know . . . I have to know why our real parents –' Bella, who had resolved not to become emotional, felt helpless tears welling up, '– why they gave us up. It's something I have to understand.' She searched in the pocket of her denim jacket for a tissue and wiped her eyes quickly.

Joyce Barrow shook her head sadly. 'I'm very glad you've had a good father in your life, dear, because I have to say – and I don't say this to upset you – your real father was not someone I ever liked. Nor Arthur.' She glanced at Arthur for some kind of mute corroboration, and shook her head again. 'Len was very much a bad sort, I'm sorry to say. I remember during the war, when he was in the army, he was always getting into trouble for being drunk, he'd come home on leave and not go back, and the military police had to come and fetch him. He was shiftless, could never hold down a job, would spend his money on drink and the horses before he'd see to his family.' She paused, raising her eyebrows. 'Not that he wasn't a charmer, though. Very attractive, I'll give you that. Doreen wouldn't hear a word against him, even though it was she who had to go out to work to keep bread on the table.'

Bella tried to make sense of what she felt at this information. It was oddly difficult, because it was like listening to an account of a stranger, not someone who was in any way connected to her. The word 'father' continued to conjure up images of Harry, of a warm past, a safe place, another person. Not this man.

'I'm not saying he wasn't a good father to Derek, in his

fashion,' went on Joyce, 'but when Doreen fell pregnant again, quite unexpected . . . well, it was another story. He wouldn't hear of her having another baby. He said if she had it, he would leave, and your mother believed him. Whatever the rest of the family might have thought of Len, he was the world to Doreen. I hate to think how she would have been if he had left.'

'Couldn't she – well, didn't she think of having a termination?' Even talking about the putative extinction of her own self, Bella felt only the dispassionate curiosity of an outsider. It added to the sense of unreality she felt about her immediate situation here, in this flat, with her aunt and uncle.

'Oh, no, never!' Joyce regarded Bella with dismay. 'Can I ask you, dear – were you brought up a Catholic?'

'I wasn't brought up as anything much,' said Bella. 'C of E, I suppose, but not in a bothering kind of way.'

'No, well, our family is Catholic, you see. Devout. No, Doreen would never have considered that.'

Another small gulf . . . 'How did the idea of adoption come about? Was it Doreen's?'

'No. That was Len's idea at first. He found out about this doctor, you see, who would arrange things for girls in trouble, have babies adopted by well-off people, in exchange for money paid under the table, so to speak. It must have seemed like a dream come true to Len,' added Joyce witheringly. 'A way of getting rid of unwelcome responsibilities and lining his pocket at the same time.'

'But Doreen can't have wanted to, surely?'

'I have to say, dear, that I'm not sure exactly what Doreen wanted at that time. When she told me about

Len's idea, we had an argument, and I wasn't so much in contact with her after that. Not for a long time. But my guess is that Len persuaded her to do it, that once the bandwagon started rolling and your parents – you know, the people who brought you up – once they were involved, she wouldn't know what to do to stop it.'

'But what about the neighbours, other people in the family? Didn't they wonder what had happened? It must have been obvious she was pregnant.'

'As far as we knew, everyone was told she'd had a baby, but that it had been stillborn.' She shrugged. 'Like I say, we weren't speaking at that point. I didn't hold with any of what was going on. But Len would find a way to still wagging tongues. Len would think of what to tell people, and Doreen would have to say it. She was a lovely girl, Doreen,' Joyce shook her head, 'but she was ruled by Len. She would do most things he wanted.'

'Even give up her own children.'

The note in Bella's voice must have touched Joyce, for she put her hand out once again to Bella's. 'I don't blame you for thinking badly of her. I know I did, I thought it was dreadful. But it couldn't have been easy for her. When we made up eventually, we only ever mentioned it once, and I know from the way she talked it was something she never got over. Not ever. But –' Joyce drew a long breath, 'you have to look at it this way. What happened, happened. Right or wrong. You were brought up by loving people, for which I am more glad than you can know, and you seem like a nice, happy girl.' She gave a little laugh and added, as though to a child, 'I'm very proud to have such a pretty girl for my niece.'

Bella sat saying nothing for some moments, trying to construct a situation where there was so much love and fear and desperation that children could be bought and sold, futures handed over, lives closed. It lay beyond her own experience, her sphere of understanding. At last she said, 'It's just so strange and sad . . . I don't blame anyone. As you say, it's what happened. But don't you think –' She raised her eyes hopefully to Joyce, 'don't you think it might do her good to know that Charlie and I are – well, all right? To see us, know about us? If I were her, I think I would want that.'

There was a long pause before Joyce spoke. 'I'm not sure it wouldn't do more harm than good, dear. Who knows what she's felt all these years? As I say, we didn't talk about it. It's one thing to tell yourself that it will make her feel better, that she'll be glad to see you. But I don't know. It might just bring back a tremendous lot of guilt. And you know, she's not herself these days. She hasn't been well these past weeks, and I don't know that she'd be up to such a shock.'

'I didn't know she was unwell.'

'Poorly, let's say. It's hard for Derek, coping.' She gazed sympathetically at Bella. 'It can't be easy for you and your brother, any of this. I think it's a shame your adoptive parents never told you the truth. A real shame. But I hope you understand the circumstances a bit better now.'

'Yes, yes, I do. Thank you.' Bella decided that the question of meeting her mother properly was best left alone for the moment. 'I was just wondering . . .'

'Yes?'

'Do you have any pictures? Of the family, I mean – of my mother and father when they were younger? Derek said he would send me some, but he hasn't been in touch.'

'I thought you might ask that,' said Joyce, rising from the sofa and going across to a little bureau, from which she took a bulging photo album. Bringing it back to the sofa, she sat down, laid it on her knee and opened it. Bella drew nearer to look.

There, as her aunt turned page after page, Bella saw captured the various images of the family she had not known. Black and white at first, very small prints of Joyce and Doreen as girls. Bella, making no connection with the old woman she had met, stared long and hard at her mother, at the pretty, fair-haired fifteen-year-old with the grave, reserved expression. At the turn of a page, years moved by and Len appeared. Bella studied the pictures of him closely. Len. Her father. Tall, fair, well-built, laughing or smiling in every picture. She searched his features for traces of weakness and unkindness, but could see none. She marvelled at how like Charlie he was. There was a photo of Joyce and Doreen sitting on a sea wall, skirts blowing about, Len and Arthur leaning by their sides, squinting into the sun. 'We were a great foursome before the war,' said Joyce. 'Len wasn't too bad then. Just a bit wild. We had some great times.'

Then there came baby photos, Christmases, beach picnics, birthdays, outings. There were school portraits of Derek in blazer and tie, hair combed, face shining, smiling. In his young face she recognized her own eyes from childhood portraits, wide and guileless. She went slowly and carefully through this era of photographs, trying to find blanks, places where she and Charlie might have fitted. But theirs was not even a ghostly absence in the frozen, camera-fixed moment. They simply hadn't existed. This was another world, and they were not in it. Merely of it. And that, only long ago.

At the end of her visit, Joyce told Bella to choose a handful of photographs of Doreen and Len and Derek, to show to Charlie.

'I'll make sure you get them back,' said Bella.

'Don't trouble, dear,' said Joyce. 'You keep them. They're your family, after all.'

When she left the flat and went back down the stairwell, Bella felt almost giddy with the sensation of being transported back to a lost time, immersed in another world. She got into her car and sat there for a while, thinking about it all. She took the photos which Joyce had given her from her bag and studied them again, trying to work out where these people fitted in; what, if anything, they had to do with her life. It seemed that the deeper she probed, the closer she got, the more tenuous the connections became. She put the pictures away and drove home through the slow lunchtime traffic.

Adam and Giles Hamblin were sitting in the beer garden of Adam's local, discussing, among other things, the progress of the biography.

'The whole thing is largely there to be written. It's just that there are certain areas where I feel I'm groping in the dark, or rather, not getting the full picture.'

'I take it you're talking about wife number one?'

'She's part of it. I don't know what to make of what

she tells me. If I hadn't found out about the adoption by accident –'

'Good journalism, I'd say.' Giles took an approving swig of his whisky.

'Thank you. I thought so myself. But if I hadn't sleuthed about, she'd never have told me. I suppose I should be glad she's still prepared to talk to me, all things considered, but I don't know if she's making stuff up, or concealing it.' Adam finished his beer. 'She's such a valuable source, but she's got her own agenda. They all have, the entire family. It's only natural.'

'So you think maybe she's not being entirely honest about old Harry's sexual proclivities?'

'Well, she's telling it her way. As far as she was concerned it only amounted to a little bit of cottaging, a few casual flings with inconsequential nobodies. Something he grew out of. She tried to persuade me to leave it out of the book.'

'Harry's gay days? You can't. It's too good.'

'I agree. I foresee a certain amount of conflict with the rest of the family. Bella wants me to leave it alone. Briony took the same line as Cecile to begin with – that it was trivial, a "youthful indiscretion", as she put it – but she got quite poisonous when I ventured to suggest, as tactfully as I could, that it might have amounted to more than that, that Harry was homosexual and tried to conceal it throughout his life.'

'What? That he was queer and she knew about it? You'll have your work cut out to establish that. And there's no room for speculation, not where lawyers are concerned.'

Adam sighed. 'I know. It's just that I'm sure there's something there. The way Briony behaves about it all. She's always been so keen to paint the right picture of herself and Harry, idyllic marriage and all that. There were times, talking to them both, when it all seemed too good to be true. Still –' Adam took a swig of his beer, 'she made it pretty clear that I risk losing her cooperation if I do write about that aspect of Harry's past.'

'But you're prepared to?'

'Yes.' Adam nodded. 'If it comes down to it, telling the truth is more important than maintaining good relations with Harry's family.' He thought fleetingly of Bella as he said this, and hoped it never need come to that choice with her.

Giles gazed idly at Adam's face, thinking that he detected an imperceptible hardening of Adam's attitude – indeed, his very personality – since taking on this commission. He pointed to Adam's glass. 'Another?'

'My round.'

Adam returned with the drinks and sat down. 'Anyway, before I do anything else, I'm going to have another talk with Richard Compton-King.'

'What's he like?'

'Interesting. Fascinating, in the true sense of the word. He talks, you listen. Lots of insight. I don't know what he's doing managing pop groups. Seems too bright for that.'

'I wouldn't underestimate the power of intellect required to do that particular job, and do it successfully.'

'I get the impression he's not as successful as he used to be. From what he says, he's still out there, hustling and pitching, but I think his glory days are well in the past.' Adam took a drink of his beer. 'Anyway, after I've done that, I intend to go to France with Megan for a couple of weeks.'

'Lie in the sun and drink lots of wine?'

If I get the chance. It's actually research for an article. The commissioning editor rang yesterday and said he wants the copy by the end of August, latest. At least it's an excuse to down tools on the biography for a while.'

'Should be a nice jaunt.'

'Hmm. To be honest, I think it'll do us both good to get away. Life in the flat is getting a bit claustrophobic. I do like my privacy, and Megan isn't very understanding if I'd rather work than spend cosy evenings on the sofa in front of the television.'

An hour later, mellow with sun and beer, Adam went home and rang Richard Compton-King, and asked if they could meet up to discuss Harry a little further. Compton-King was happy to see Adam again.

'How about the Groucho at twelve-thirty on Friday? I've got a meeting in Dean Street that morning, and you'll be the perfect excuse to get away.'

Adam, scarcely flattered, said this would be fine.

That Friday, he waited for thirty-five minutes in the bar of the Groucho Club, spinning out a white-wine spritzer. At five past one, Compton-King's tall, unmistakable figure strode into the lobby from the street. The girls at reception seemed inordinately pleased to see him, and he paused for a few chatty moments to bathe in the warm glow of their appreciation before sauntering into the bar to meet Adam.

'Sorry I'm late. Bloody meeting went on for ever. For some reason the members of my new band insist on going through every line of their recording contract with the lawyers. I wish pop stars would just stick to things they know about, like drugs, and trashing hotel rooms.' He glanced at his watch. 'Shall we go straight in?'

They went into the dining room, and Adam listened to a twenty-minute Compton-King discourse on copyright exploitation before he could get round to the subject of Harry. Lunch came quickly, and Compton-King was such a prodigiously fast eater that Adam was worried that the meal might be over, and Compton-King off to his next meeting, before he had had time to get answers to his questions.

'It's the main focus of the major record companies now,' Compton-King was explaining. 'The multinationals don't want a volatile asset, they don't want a rock star who gets stoned in the middle of the night and rings up to say he's going to become a Buddhist monk. They want their pop stars to be anodyne, safe. It's all about money-making. Not that I'm knocking that, but where's the creativity, where's the danger?' Compton-King was halfway through a plate of seared scallops with spinach mash, and three-quarters of the way through a bottle of Sancerre, of which Adam had had only half a glassful. He knew now the pitfalls of trying to keep up with Richard Compton-King in the matter of lunchtime drinking.

As Compton-King ladled in another forkful, Adam said diffidently, 'Listen, I know we probably don't have long, so do you mind if I take up where we left off last time?'

'About Harry? Sorry, Adam. Fire away.'

'Thinking back to our conversation –'

'Before you fell asleep.'

Adam smiled weakly. 'Quite. Anyway, you suggested that Harry's marriage to Cecile was a sham, that it was just a façade to enable him to live as he pleased.' Compton-King nodded. 'But when I spoke to Cecile a couple of weeks ago, she painted a rather different picture. As far as she was concerned, she and Harry married for love. She knew about homosexual connections he'd had in the past, but he told her it was over and done with. The way she tells it, any gay relationships he may have had after they were married were merely in the nature of backsliding. She reckons she cured him of all that.'

Compton-King, his food finished, sat back in his chair with a smile. 'Dear Cecile. Always had a blind spot where Harry was concerned. Or perhaps the blind spot was about herself. You have to remember that Cecile in those days had a reputation as a very beautiful, sexy actress. Believed her own publicity. The idea that Harry might have preferred some boy to her can't have been very appealing. Probably still isn't. She always had to believe in the power of her own charms.'

Again Adam found himself wondering if Richard Compton-King's certainty about Harry stemmed from some affair between the two of them. It seemed the most likely explanation. Still attractive now, Richard must have been a beautiful young man back in those days. But Cecile had found the idea laughable . . . He was pondering how to broach this matter tactfully, when Compton-King added, 'Probably why she had so many affairs – took the edge off the fact that Harry was playing away, so to speak

– and with boys at that. Helped to reassure her of her own attractiveness.'

Adam was intrigued. Cecile, in their conversations, had painted herself as an ever-faithful wife. 'Is that supposition?'

'Hardly. I was shagging her senseless myself for nearly a year.' Compton-King signalled to the waiter and asked for coffee. He glanced at Adam. 'Don't look so astonished. She was pretty gorgeous back then. I was twenty, randy as hell – thoroughly enjoyed it while it lasted.'

Adam remembered Cecile's sudden and unexpected burst of laughter when he'd asked her if she thought Compton-King was gay. Now he understood. It bemused Adam that he'd misread the situation so utterly. 'But when we first spoke, you suggested that it was a marriage of convenience. Now you're saying that the whole thing devastated Cecile, and that she tried to compensate for what Harry was doing.'

'You misunderstood me. It was *Harry*'s convenience I was talking about. I think he married Cecile to create a smokescreen. You could say that Cecile went her own sweet way, with me and plenty of other guys, but she was always trying to get Harry's attention. Only he wasn't looking.'

'D'you think that's what finished the marriage off?'

Compton-King shrugged. 'As I recall, they were divorced on the grounds of Harry's adultery with some model. Penelope something. Possibly another smokescreen. Having said that, Harry did swing both ways. Maybe that was what really got Cecile. Anyone and everyone, except her.'

Adam pondered this. 'Do you remember any – well, any particular relationships that Harry had with men?'

'Special boyfriends, you mean? Been thinking about that since we last spoke and I'm afraid I can't, no. Very bad memory for detail – those days are a bit of a haze, what with one thing and another.' Compton-King grinned. 'Which is probably just as well. Do I sense a loss of nerve?'

'Far from it,' said Adam. 'Merely a lack of clarity.'

Compton-King asked a passing waitress for the bill. 'Sorry I can't make this longer. My fault for being late in the first place.'

'It doesn't matter,' said Adam. 'I've got a bit of thinking to do. I'll get back to you, if I may.'

'Fine.' Compton-King finished his wine. 'By the way, I see Bella Day's play is closing early. Shame I didn't get round to seeing it. Mind you – liked Joe and all that – never found his plays very funny.'

'I didn't know it was closing,' said Adam. Poor Bella. He would ring her. Merely friendly commiseration.

'So,' asked Compton-King, 'what are you working on when you're not doing this biography?'

'Bits and pieces. I'm off to France in a week to research an article.'

'Nice work. Whereabouts?'

'Lot-et-Garonne. Do you know the region? I've never been there before.'

'Absolutely stupendous. Love it,' said Compton-King, with an enthusiasm that surprised Adam. 'I adore France, especially that part. Has a medieval quality. Haven't been down there for years.'

'You should come,' said Adam, uncertain where this impulse came from.

'No, no – two's company.' But Adam could tell from Compton-King's smile that he was pleased to have been asked. 'Saying that, I could do with a holiday . . .' At that moment the bill came, which Compton-King insisted on paying.

'You should let me,' said Adam. 'This is part of my research.'

'Have this one on the Mule Skinners. Little buggers are earning me enough.'

Compton-King got up, reached out his hand and shook Adam's. 'Give me a call, we'll talk again. Sorry this had to be so short.'

'I will. Thanks.' As he sat over the remains of his coffee, Adam remembered the last time they had shaken hands, his misreading of the firm, warm handclasp. It hadn't been what he'd thought at all. The guy simply liked him. And he liked Compton-King. How could anyone help it? And he had to assume, for the present, that his version of certain events in the life of Harry Day was more honest than Cecile's.

He rang Bella late that afternoon.

'Someone told me your play's closing.'

'Next Friday. Not doing enough business, I'm afraid.'

'I'm sorry. I thought it was very good.'

'Oh well, theatre's not in great shape at the moment. I'm not going to mope about it. I'm off to France on holiday.'

'That's a coincidence. Megan and I are going to France.

Next week, as a matter of fact. I'm doing research for an article. Whereabouts are you staying?'

'Near Montauban, down in the south-west. It was my father's house, and he left it to Charlie and me when he died. It's a fantastic place, I really love it, but it looks like this is the last visit I'll make there. We've got to sell it so that Charlie can raise the capital to buy Claire some mansion in Surrey. I've invited the other members of the cast along, to cheer them up. Should be quite a jolly little house party. Charlie and Claire may be going down as well. I haven't spoken to him for a week or so.'

Of course . . . *Bruce Redmond and Bella Day, holidaying together in her French home.* A miracle *Hello!* magazine hadn't been invited along as well . . .

'What about you and Megan? Whereabouts are you headed?' asked Bella.

'Roughly the same part of the world. I'm going to interview a couple of Yorkshire farmers who upped sticks a few years ago and moved there to farm. I haven't booked anything yet. We'll probably just stay locally.'

'Why don't I fax you details of how to find our house? It's called Montresor. If you're in the area, you can both come over for the day, have lunch and a swim.'

'Thanks.' Adam didn't think he had any wish to witness the holiday idyll of Bruce and Bella. 'By the way, how did it go with your aunt, the one who wrote to you? I've forgotten her name.'

'Joyce Barrow.' Bella sighed. 'Auntie Joyce. She was very sweet, quite moved to meet me and so forth, showed me lots of photographs, told me what a bastard my real father was and how he engineered the adoption. It was odd. I think she wanted to feel close to me, bring me into the family, but there was a kind of remoteness about it all. Like it was too long ago to heal, or make things different.'

'She must want to meet Charlie. Have you told him?'

'Not yet. Besides, I'm not sure he'd want to hear. But yes, Joyce says it would mean a lot to her to meet him. I can't see it happening, somehow. You know how Charlie feels about all this, anyway, and I can't see him hitting it off with Joyce and Arthur. That's her husband. I've been the one who's been telling him it'll make him feel better about the whole business if he meets his real family, gets to know them and finds out more about himself, but I'm not so sure . . .'

'Did it make you feel better?'

'Not much, to be honest. If anything, meeting Derek, and then Joyce, seeing all the photos . . . the whole thing makes me feel lonely. I realize I don't belong, I lost the chance. Is that stupid?'

'I think I understand. But, you know . . . maybe it's a way of making you see that it's your real past, the people you've grown up with, that count.'

'But I lost something, and I want to try to get it back . . .' She sighed. 'I know what you mean, though. I've been ringing Mummy up a lot, needing to talk to her. I haven't had the nerve to ask her about – you know, what you told me about Harry before they got married.'

Before, during and after, thought Adam, if Richard Compton-King was to be believed. Not that he was going to tell Bella. Not at this particular juncture.

'No, well, I can see that would be difficult.'

'Have you decided yet?'

'Decided what?'

'Whether or not to include it in the book? I so hope you won't. I mean, honestly, Adam, you have to ask yourself what good it's going to do.'

'What good it's going to do?' Adam was perplexed. 'Look, this is a biography. It's a portrait of a human being.'

She sighed. 'Oh God . . . integrity.'

'Yes, if you like. I know it's difficult for the family, but how can I compromise? It's just not possible.'

'Do you think it's what my father would have wanted?'

'When I started this biography, it was with your father's cooperation, and – to a certain extent – control.' He paused. 'But it's under my control now. I have to do what I think is right.' She said nothing. 'Bella, I don't want to cause any friction. I badly need your cooperation. I'll need to talk to you and Charlie when I get back from France. And Briony.'

'I know you feel you have to be completely honest. I respect that. It's the truth that's important, I suppose.'

He sighed. 'Thank you. Though as I've been discovering, there's no whole and complete truth about anyone. Every individual is so many different things to so many people.'

'Well, don't expect any exciting revelations when you talk to me. He was just my father.'

Both paused, and Adam wondered if she was as aware as he was of the sense of intimate closeness he felt in their conversation. Perhaps not, he decided, because suddenly she said with a yawn, 'Anyway, thanks for ringing. As I said, do look us up when you're in France, if you get the chance.'

'OK. Thanks.'

She put the phone down. She meant what she said. She hoped he would come to Montresor.

Three days before the play was due to close, Joyce Barrow rang Bella.

'I felt I had to let you know –' Bella could tell from the rapid, hushed tone of her voice that it was something serious, 'Doreen's been taken into hospital. She's had a heart attack.'

'How bad is she?' News of a stranger, yet the danger that her most intimate connection might be severed for ever without having been properly made galvanized Bella.

'Well, she's serious, dear.'

'Should I – can I go and see her?'

'Well –'

'I don't want to do anything to make her worse –' Bella suddenly realized she had begun to cry, and brushed tears away.

'She's unconscious. For the moment, anyway. Even if she wasn't, I don't think she would recognize you, not the way she's been recently. She hasn't known me, half the time. Only Derek.'

'Where is she?'

'Lewisham hospital. Carpenter Ward. Derek's there. He's been there since they took her in.'

Bella glanced at her watch. Ten past five. Could she possibly get all the way over there and still make it back to the theatre on time? It didn't matter. She had to go.

This was her mother. It might be the last chance that Doreen ever got to look at her daughter. To Bella, that seemed the most important thing of all.

The taxi across London took an hour. By the time Bella had negotiated the corridors and staircases of the hospital and found the nurse's station on Carpenter Ward, it was nearly six-thirty.

'I'm inquiring about a Doreen Kinley,' Bella told the nurse on duty. 'I believe she's a patient on your ward.'

The nurse hesitated, then asked, 'Are you a member of the family?'

For a few long seconds, Bella struggled for an answer. 'I'm – I'm a family friend. Mrs Kinley's sister rang me.'

'And your name is . . . ?' Bella gave her name. 'Just a moment.' The nurse went down the corridor and through a door. After a moment she came out and beckoned to Bella. Bella went into a small room and found Derek sitting there on his own by the window. The room was furnished with blue carpet tiles, functional, mock-leather chairs, and a low table. It spoke of waiting, of emptiness, of dead hours.

'Hi,' said Derek.

'Hello,' replied Bella. The nurse closed the door and left them alone. 'How is she?'

'She's gone,' said Derek. 'She died ten minutes ago. I'm waiting for Joyce to get here.'

'Oh, God.' Bella put her hand to her mouth.

Derek just sat there, folding his knuckles together, twisting the gold ring on his little finger. He seemed uninterested in Bella's presence, or her reaction to the news.

Bella sat down. 'I'm sorry,' she said softly. 'I'm terribly sorry.' She put out a hand to his, and to her surprise he gripped it, pressed it. He began to weep, his broad shoulders shaking. Bella had no words to say. She was simply grateful for the fact that he held her hand, for without that she would have felt like the merest intruder. It was Derek's mother who had died, not hers. His grief was for the sum of countless childhood days, the loss of a love which had begun at birth and gradually transformed and reversed itself, so that in the end he had cared for her, in a slow revolve of mutual feeling and dependency, son and mother, mother and son. Whatever loss she imagined she felt, it was not the same.

After a few moments, Derek wiped his eyes, shaking his head slowly as if to clear it of unhappiness. He relinquished Bella's hand.

'I'm just sorry I didn't know her,' said Bella.

'That wasn't her fault.'

'I know that.'

'After you came that day –' Derek swallowed, composing himself, 'I was really angry. Angry with you for coming. Angry with Mum for never telling me. Then I saw that it was pointless, being angry. I decided it was best just left alone. That's why I never wrote, never sent you any photos.'

'I remember thinking that you looked at me like you wished I'd never happened.'

'Nah, I didn't mean that.' Derek shook his head again, as though inexpressibly weary. 'The more I thought about it, I began to think it would be nice to get to know you. But it's too late, don't you reckon? I mean, too long a time.'

'I don't think so. But I don't understand why you told Joyce. If you wanted to keep me at a distance, you need never have said anything to anyone.'

'I told Joyce because I wanted to know what really happened back then, the adoption and all that. I reckoned she would have known all about it, if anyone did. I wanted to understand.'

'That's just the way I've been feeling.'

Their gazes met. Derek managed a small smile. 'You had a bigger right than me to feel angry, I reckon.'

'Oh, I think it's just about even. But like you said, anger's pointless.'

The door opened. Both looked up to see Joyce come in.

'Oh, Derek, love – I'm so sorry,' said Joyce, her voice wavering. Derek rose and hugged her. Bella sat for an uncertain moment, then she rose too, and exchanged a tentative embrace with her aunt. Joyce's eyes looked searchingly, anxiously into Bella's.

'Don't worry,' said Bella. 'Nothing happened. She didn't see me. She died before I got here.' Bella knew that even if she had got here in time, she wouldn't have asked to see her mother. She wouldn't, couldn't have let anything happen to disturb those fragile last moments, whatever intentions she might have had when she left the flat.

'I'm sorry,' said Joyce. She stood close to Derek, who had placed a large, comforting arm round his aunt's shoulders. 'I'm sorry you never got to know one another. But I think it was for the best.'

Bella had nothing to say to this. The words, the way in which Derek and Joyce stood together, part of something to which she did not properly belong, made her feel like an interloper. 'I'll leave you two together,' she said awkwardly. 'I have to get to the theatre.' Derek and Joyce both nodded. 'Will you let me know when the funeral is? I might want to come.' She hesitated. 'I don't know about Charlie –'

'Don't worry,' said Joyce. 'We'll understand.'

Outside, Bella walked slowly to the nurse's station. The same nurse looked up from notes she was writing. 'About Mrs Kinley,' said Bella, 'I said before that I was a family friend. Actually, I'm her daughter. Was her daughter. *Am* . . .' She stopped in confusion. 'Could I see her, d'you think? It would mean a great deal to me.'

The nurse gazed at her for a few seconds, then nodded. She led Bella up the corridor and into a small side room. Bella entered. The nurse stood in the doorway, hesitated, then left, closing the door gently. Bella stood at the side of the bed and looked down at the frail shell of humanity lying there. She seemed so small, shrunken, nondescript. Any old woman, really. Just the way she'd looked when Bella had first met her at the house in Duffy Road. The house where she would have lived, had things been otherwise. She stared for a while at the wispy, white hair, the delicate features, waxy and slack in death, and tried to make the connection, feel the reality of her own mother lying beneath those sheets. But it refused to happen. All she could think was that she could have passed Doreen Kinley a hundred times in the street and never known her. Would Doreen have known her, in any of the thirty years that had passed? She would never know.

Bella left the room a few moments later and walked

quickly down the corridor to the lift. She knew now that whatever sense of loss or emptiness she felt, it was only for something that had never been. She suddenly found she could hardly wait to be out of the hospital building so that she could take out her mobile and ring Cecile. She felt an urgent need to talk to her mother, tell her everything.

She reached the theatre with only minutes to spare, not enough time to call Charlie. When the performance was over, she rang him at home from her dressing room.

'Can I pop in and see you on the way home?'

'Of course. What's up?'

She hesitated. No, not on the phone. 'I just want to talk. Not a marathon session. I know you've got work in the morning.'

'That's OK.'

'Will Claire be there?'

'No. She's in Amsterdam all this week.'

'I'll see you in a little while.'

When she got to Charlie's flat, Bella could tell from his flushed face that he'd been hitting the whisky most of the evening.

'You shouldn't drink on your own, you know,' said Bella. She slung her bag on a chair.

Charlie gave a sloppy shrug. 'I've been celebrating. I settled a case today. Very favourably. So Claire and I will be able to get down to France for a couple of weeks after all.'

'You still shouldn't drink so much. Anyway, pour me a small one. I'm wiped out.'

She went to the window, wide open to the summer night air, and leaned out. A faint thump of music came from a nearby garden. Someone was having a party.

'Here you go.' Charlie handed her a glass of Scotch with ice. Bella noticed he'd topped his own glass up.

They sat down together on the sofa.

'So, what's up? How are you?'

Bella took a sip of her drink. 'Sort of OK.'

'No, you're not. I can tell from your face.' Charlie put his glass down on the coffee table. 'Tell me what's wrong.'

Bella hesitated for a few seconds, then decided it was best to come straight out with it. 'Doreen died today.'

'God. I see . . . Oh, Christ.' Charlie leaned forward, head in his hands. Bella thought for one second he was about to be sick. She bent down next to him in alarm, hand on his shoulder.

'Charlie, are you all right?'

Charlie didn't move, just remained there, hunched forward. As she sat next to him, holding him, Bella suddenly became aware of the similarity of the situation with Derek a few hours earlier. Nothing so far had brought home to her so clearly, so forcefully, the fact that they were brothers. And yet, how different. Why was it, then, that she had understood completely the nature of Derek's grief this afternoon, when she had no idea of what was passing through Charlie's mind at this moment?

She waited. Eventually Charlie shook his head, lowered his hands and leaned back. His face was white.

'I'm so, so sorry.' Bella stroked his shoulder anxiously, gazing intently at his face. 'I didn't mean to shock you. I didn't know how to say it.'

'It doesn't matter. Oh, bloody hell . . .' He reached for his drink, and Bella put a hand on his arm.

'No, don't have any more to drink. It doesn't do any good. Better to tell me what you're thinking.'

Charlie took a couple of long, deep breaths and shook his head again. 'It shouldn't matter. It's not even as though she figured in my life. I can't . . . I've been going around hating this – this faceless person. This woman. For doing what she did. And you know what?' He turned his gaze intently on Bella's.

'What?'

'I'm glad she's dead. When you said it, I wasn't sure who you were talking about for a second. Then it was like having it brought home to me. Like she'd done it again. I never even knew her, and she'd done it again. Cut me out, kept me from her. And then I thought – good. You can't do anything else to me.' Charlie's eyes were bright with rage and unhappiness.

'I didn't think you cared.' Bella wiped away her own tears. 'You told me she didn't matter to you.'

'She didn't. She didn't. How could she? She gave me away. She gave *us* away.'

There was a pause of several seconds, then Bella said, 'I haven't told you this, because you've been away, but her sister got in touch with me. Her name is Joyce – Joyce Barrow. I went to see her. She lives in a flat in New Cross. We had a long talk.' And Bella told Charlie everything that Joyce had told her about their parents, and about Len in particular. 'She gave me some photographs of them. I've got them here.'

'I don't want to see them.'

'You do. I know you do.' Bella got up and fetched her bag from the chair. She unzipped it and pulled out a brown envelope. She took out the photos and handed them to Charlie, who took them without protest. 'I know it sounds strange, but it helped me to understand things a bit better, just to see their faces.'

Charlie looked at the photos one by one, not saying a word.

Bella sat next to him on the sofa, chin resting on one hand. 'It's like looking at a little piece of yourself . . .'

Charlie stared long and hard at a photo of Len in shirtsleeves, arms folded, blond hair combed back, leaning against the bonnet of a car. 'I thought I didn't ever want to know what they were like,' he said slowly. 'I thought that if I saw them, saw that they actually existed, then it would somehow make Mum and Dad, and everything about the life I've had, become less real. That it might take it away.'

'But it hasn't.'

'No. They're just people. She looks a lot like you.'

'Mmm. You should meet Derek. You're so alike.'

Charlie shuffled the photos together and put them back in the envelope. 'I don't want to meet Derek. This is as far as I want to go. I meant it when I said I'm glad she's dead.'

'It's a horrible thing to say.'

'I don't mean for her, or the people who loved her. I mean, I'm glad I don't have to think about her, or wonder if I should meet her, or any of that crap. No extra family. Just what I have. I don't need a brother. I don't *have* a brother.' He gave the photos back to Bella. 'If you go on trying to get somewhere with this lot, it'll just turn into a big mess. You're not going to get what you want. You're not going to get some magical love you think you missed out on. It was never there.'

She put the photos back in her bag. 'Maybe you're right. I don't know. I take it you don't want to go to the funeral?'

'Too bloody right.' Charlie picked up his glass and emptied it in one swallow.

'Well, anyway . . . That was all I came to talk about.' She stood up. 'Oh, by the way, I've invited Bruce and Frank down to Montresor for a couple of weeks. To cheer them up because of the play closing early. You don't mind, do you?'

'Course not. The more the merrier. God knows, the house is big enough. When are you going down?'

'At the beginning of next week. Tomorrow night's our last night. We're going to fly to Bordeaux and hire a car.'

'Claire and I will probably get down around the end of next week.'

Bella picked up the envelope containing the photographs from the coffee table. 'Shall I leave these? Perhaps you'd like to look at them again.'

Charlie shook his head. 'No, thanks. That chapter's closed. Finito.'

'OK.'

Charlie followed Bella out to the front door, still holding his empty glass. As she was about to leave, she glanced at it. 'Don't drink any more tonight, Charlie.'

'Don't worry.'

When she was gone, Charlie went back into the living room and poured himself another drink, then sat down on the sofa. He sat there for a long time, drinking, thinking, staring at nothing.

Joyce rang Bella to tell her the funeral would be on Friday. Bella couldn't tell from her voice whether Joyce hoped she would come or stay away. In the event, she went. The day was warm and close, the summer sky leaden with the threat of rain. The service in Doreen's local Catholic church seemed to Bella to go on for ever. She looked at as many faces as she could from her vantage point at the back, and found none of them interested her, whether they were family or not. Family. She felt these people were nothing to do with her. Even Derek's broad back, his blond head, stirred nothing in her, no sisterly feeling. The very service, the dingy, lofty spaces of the large and unfamiliar church, increased her sense of alienation. She wondered what on earth she was doing there. As the coffin was borne to the front of the church, she stared hard at it, as if to penetrate the mystery of the death of the woman who had given her life. But all she could think was that the thing must surely be empty. There could be nothing there.

At one point, towards the end, her mind slipping into her own thoughts and concerns, she felt herself give way to tears. She knew that they had nothing to do with anything happening today. She was simply depressed. Depressed because the play was closing. Depressed because she found herself thinking about Adam Downing too much for her own good, considering he was living with someone else. Depressed because, ever since the day she had found out who she really was, she had been travelling hopefully along a road that seemed to be going nowhere. The discoveries she had made had not given her any sense of completion, or revelation. All she had encountered were uncertain strangers, like Joyce and Derek, who wanted nothing from her, and who had nothing much to give.

She had decided not to go to the crematorium. Already she was longing to find a taxi to take her back to west London and reality. As she stepped from the gloom of the church into daylight, she felt a hand touch her sleeve. She turned to see a girl, thirteen or fourteen years old, her long blonde hair tied back, dressed in a dark-blue school sweatshirt and jogging pants, an approximation of mourning.

''Scuse me, are you Bella Day?' asked the girl. Her blue eyes were large and round.

Bella nodded and smiled. 'Yes.' She hadn't expected anyone here to recognize her.

'You were in that film, *A Man, a Dog and a Gun.*'

'That's right, I was. I'm sure you can't have seen it, though. It's an eighteen certificate.'

The girl grinned and shrugged. 'My dad let us see it on video. Me and my sister. Language doesn't bother us. I thought it was wicked.'

'Thanks.'

'Can I have your autograph?'

'Of course. Have you got a pen and paper?'

'Nope.'

Bella rummaged in her bag, and as she did so, Derek

came across at some speed and said to the girl, 'Leanne, we're waiting for you. Don't bother this lady.'

'I know who she is,' said the girl. Derek's eyes darted anxiously from Bella to his daughter. 'She's an actress. She's Bella Day. She's going to let me have her autograph.'

'And now I know who you are,' said Bella, signing her name on the back of a Peter Jones receipt. 'You're Leanne. Here you go.' She handed the autograph to the girl.

'Thanks.'

'On you go, love. I'll be with you in a minute.' Derek shooed his daughter in the direction of the cars waiting to take the mourners away. When she was out of earshot, he said to Bella, 'I haven't told the girls about you and Charlie. Not that I don't want to. It's just a hard thing to explain.'

Bella watched Leanne join her younger sister. Both girls turned to glance at her and Derek, then turned away, giggling. 'Perhaps you were waiting to see whether there would be any need.' She met Derek's gaze. 'If you'd rather I left it alone, stayed out of your life, I'll understand. As you said, maybe it's a bit late to get to know one another.'

'No,' he said quickly, and shook his head. 'I don't think that at all. I just – like, I don't know where to start.'

'Come on, Del!' called a man standing by one of the cars.

'Don't worry,' said Bella.

'Look . . .' Derek hesitated, about to go. 'Stay in touch.'

Bella nodded, and watched as Derek got into one of the funeral cars with his daughters.

11

Adam was sitting in his study, putting the finishing touches to an article, when the phone rang. He picked it up and recognized instantly the deep, public-school drawl.

'Adam, RC-K here.'

'Richard –'

'Look, this trip you're making to France –'

'Yes?'

'I don't want to muscle in on your holiday, but you've given me the idea that I could do with a change of scene. God knows I need a break from these bloody record people. Why don't you let me drive you and the girlfriend down to France in my Bentley? It needs a spin, hasn't been out on the road for ages. You can go off and do your own thing once we're down there.'

Adam had to admit the idea was an attractive one. Driving to France with Compton-King would be much more fun than just himself and Megan in the Fiat, which had been acting up a bit lately. 'Well – it's a nice idea . . . I mean, thanks very much for the offer. I need to be mobile, but I suppose I could always hire a car at the other end. I booked us a gite near Cahors. Very much last-minute, but it sounds all right. Where will you be staying?'

'Oh, I'll find some hotel in the neighbourhood. I'll be moving around a bit, I imagine. Touring the vineyards, that kind of thing.'

'Well, look, if you're sure –'

'I knew you'd like it. Suggest we set off on Sunday. Give me your address, I'll pop round and pick you both up mid-morning. I'll book the old Shuttle for some time in the afternoon.'

'I can't let you pay for us –'

'No intention. You pay me back when you come to sort out your expenses. Ciao.'

Smiling, Adam shut down his laptop and went through to the kitchen. Megan had nearly finished cooking supper, and Adam began to lay the table.

'Richard Compton-King was on the phone a moment ago.'

'Who?' Megan glanced at Adam through a haze of steam from the drained beans.

'The chap I told you about who manages bands. He's just offered to drive us down to France in his Bentley.'

'Why?'

'Why? Because he wants a break and feels like company. Don't worry, you'll like him.'

'You said yes?'

Adam took some wine from the fridge. 'Yes, why not? He's a very amusing guy. It'll be fun.'

'Thanks.' Megan put the dishes on the table and sat down.

'What d'you mean?'

'Sorry my company's not good enough. I was looking forward to it being just the two of us.'

'It will be just the two of us, once we get there. Anyway, don't you think we get quite enough of that at the moment?'

'What a bloody thing to say.'

Adam sighed, exasperated. 'Is this PMS or something? I just mean that we spend quite a lot of time together, and I like seeing other people. He's a great guy.'

'So you keep saying. Well, if you've said we'll go with him, there's not much I can do about it, is there?'

'Fine. If that's how you feel, why don't you stay in London? You don't have to come, you know.'

Megan stared at him across the table, eyes bright with quick tears. 'Why are you being so horrible? You come and tell me we're going to France in a threesome with someone I don't even know, after I've spent all bloody evening cooking your rotten supper –'

'I don't necessarily want supper cooked for me! I didn't ask!'

The row that ensued took its predictable course. Megan left the kitchen in tears; Adam sulked briefly, then placated her; they ate a lukewarm supper while tentatively negotiating their way back to affection, and made it up properly, and quite passionately, in bed an hour later.

On the morning after *Funeral Games* closed, Bella woke up to find her senses still clouded by the melancholy which had settled upon her at the funeral the day before. She lay in bed for a long time, burrowing in the comfort of her duvet, ignoring the reproach of the sunny day beyond her window, trying to locate the source of her feelings. Everything came back to the day when she and Adam had gone to Deptford in search of her family, the suffocating sense of excitement and fear she had felt on meeting Derek, the moment when she had turned and seen him, seen someone who was part of her, yet an utter stranger. Such high hopes, such nebulous expectations. Her lost family. Since that day, nothing had been as she had hoped it would be. Her existence was not of theirs. She could look into her aunt Joyce's eyes and see something of herself, but the connections which blood and genes had established had been severed by time, and upbringing, and the different quality of her experience and expectations. She couldn't just become part of a world of which she knew nothing, and in which she had never figured. She tried to imagine the effort of maintaining a connection with Joyce, visits and phone calls, and knew how barren it would ultimately be.

And Derek. She thought of their encounter outside the church. Was he so reluctant to acknowledge her, or was he just unnerved by the complexities of admitting a sister into his life? She thought back over their few brief conversations, particularly the one in the impersonal waiting room at the hospital. Too late to get to know her, he'd said, though he wanted to. Maybe it was true. She had come this far, hoping for so much, finding only disappointment, shadows, family photos with no spaces where she and Charlie should have been. Charlie himself had never wanted to pursue this, was happy enough with the reality which time and fate had constructed. Perhaps his instincts had been right.

She uncurled herself from her duvet and pillows and rolled over, blinking against the late-morning light filtering through the blind. She had reached a turning point, she realized. Either she stopped now, never got in touch with Derek again, let everything slide away back into the shadows – or she did something positive.

She lay inert for a few moments, decisions forming in her mind. Then she got out of bed, showered and dressed, and drove to Deptford, the *A–Z* open on the passenger seat beside her.

Bella parked outside the pub and walked slowly towards the alleyway entrance where the crash-repair sign leaned against the wall. She thought she had conquered her feelings where number forty-four Duffy Road was concerned, but the sight of the house filled her again with a vivid feeling of loss and dislocation. The unknowable, the might-have-been. She walked up the alleyway, and there was Derek, dressed in an oily blue boiler suit unbuttoned to the waist, sleeves rolled up over bulky, tattooed biceps, bent under the bonnet of a Ford Mondeo. He straightened up and shouted something to the other mechanic working in the yard, and then saw Bella. He paused, spanner in hand, and nodded to her. She couldn't tell from his eyes whether he was pleased to see her or not. A closed book, just like Charlie.

As she strolled into the centre of the yard, he put down his tools and came towards her, wiping his hands on his thighs.

'You should have rung.'

'Sorry, I came on impulse. I wanted to talk to you.'

'Right.' Derek glanced towards the kitchen door, which stood ajar. 'Go on in. I'll be in in a minute. I'll just clean up.'

Bella went into the kitchen. A batch of dirty tea mugs cluttered the sink. A packet of sugar and half-empty bottle of milk stood on the side. She leaned against the sink and waited. After a few seconds, she heard children's voices from a neighbouring room, and out of curiosity she went down the hall and looked into the sitting room.

Two girls were sitting on the floor, the ones she had seen at the funeral, Playstation controls in hand, staring intently at the television screen. The elder, Leanne, glanced up. She recognized Bella instantly, astonished.

'Hello,' said Bella. The younger girl looked up, too. She looked about nine or ten.

'Hello,' they chorused, uncertain what to make of the situation. There was a long pause.

'Have you come to see Dad?' asked Leanne.

'Yes.'

The girls looked at one another. 'He's out the back.'

'I know. I was waiting for him in the kitchen, and I heard you two.'

Derek came down the hall behind her. Bella turned to him. 'I was just saying hello to the girls.'

'Yeah, right . . .' He glanced at his daughters. 'They should be outside, by rights, day like this. Go on, take your bikes down the park.'

'Da-ad!'

'Come on. Turn that thing off. Get some fresh air for a change.'

They switched off the Playstation and trooped off, giving Bella curious glances as they went.

'Have they asked how you know me?' said Bella, when the girls had gone.

'I said you were a friend.'

'I think they think I'm a girlfriend, or something like that,' said Bella with a grin.

'Yeah?' Derek returned the grin. 'I'll have to knock that idea on the head.'

'You mean, tell them who I really am?'

Derek nodded reluctantly. 'I suppose. I'm going to have to do it sometime, aren't I?'

Bella's heart leapt a little. 'I hope so. How long are they staying with you?'

'I've got them for three weeks. Their mum's off in Spain, on holiday with her boyfriend. It's difficult, with them not knowing the kids round here. Not much for them to do.' There was a short, awkward silence. 'Like a cup of tea, or something?'

'No, thanks.' Bella shook her head. 'As I say, I just wanted to talk.'

'Right. Have a seat.'

Bella sat down. Derek paced across the room and leaned against the mantelpiece, arms folded. He looked a little intimidating, just as Charlie did on the occasions when she had seen him in court, standing just like that, cross-examining a witness. Derek's expression, however, was benign and patient.

'I realized today that we have to make a choice,' said Bella. 'You and I. About what we are to one another.' The words, which she had rehearsed in the car on the way, sounded to Bella's ear stilted and unnatural, but Derek simply absorbed them, his eyes fixed on hers. 'Charlie has a lot of problems about this whole thing. I was the one who did everything, who came and found you – and Doreen. I didn't stop to ask myself why I was doing it. I suppose I had some stupid expectations. But the thing is, now I've found you, I do want to get to know you. I know you think it's too late, but I really don't think that's true. I can't just go through life pretending you don't exist. You're my brother.'

Derek paced around the room for some seconds, arms still folded. 'That's nice, and all, but I just don't see how we do it.' He turned to look at her. 'I've thought about this, don't think I haven't. I've hated Mum and Dad for giving you away, for never letting me get to know you, and my brother. But here we are. You're you, I'm me. What happens?'

'God, you sound so matter-of-fact –'

'No, listen, I'm being practical. That's what I am, see. That's what I've got to be. When you let people in . . . you have to be sure it's for your own good. What I'm trying to say is –' Derek broke off, baffled, '– you can't just invent relationships.'

'I'm your sister.'

'I know. I love that. You don't know how much I wish I'd had that. But *now* . . . Well, it seems weird. What do we do? Meet up once a month? Ring each other up and talk about things we haven't got in common? You're an actress, I'm a bloody car mechanic!'

'We *make* it happen! If we decide that we want to get to know one another badly enough, then we'll just do it! Of course we don't have things in common – that's what this is all about! That's something we achieve between us, by getting to know one another, doing things together now and then. I want us to become friends, to become –'

'Oh, right, right –' Derek paced round the room, agitated. 'So I can take you to Catford Dogs and you'll be fine with that, will you?'

'Yes! Why not? At least we've got a basis, at least we can start from somewhere! And don't be so bloody patronizing – I have been greyhound racing before, you know.'

'Have you? Where?'

'Wimbledon.'

'Oh . . . yeah. Nice stadium.'

Each glanced at the other, enjoying the astringent warmth of their exchange, surprised by the ease of it.

'The point is,' said Bella, 'we have to start somewhere.'

'Exactly. Just what I was saying in the first place. It isn't that easy.'

'It could be. I've got a proposal.' She took a deep breath. 'I have a house in France. It belongs to Charlie and me. It's a big place, and we're going to have to sell it soon. Anyway, the point is, I'm going there on holiday with some friends next week. I'd like to invite you and the girls to come along as well.'

Derek frowned. 'France?'

'Yes.' She clasped her hands on her knees. 'Please, please, *please* say you'll come. It would be the perfect chance to get to know one another. The girls would have a lovely time. There's a swimming pool and lots to do.' She gazed at him hopefully.

'I can't speak French,' said Derek, looking a little dazed.

'It doesn't matter! The point is, we could actually share something – no pretence, no artificiality. Just some time.'

'I wouldn't get on with your friends.'

'Derek . . .'

He shook his head. 'Thanks, but it's not on.'

'Why?'

‘I don’t know.’

‘Wouldn’t the girls like it? Have they ever been on holiday abroad with you?’

‘No.’

‘Wouldn’t it be better for them than being cooped up here for the next two weeks?’

This gave him pause. ‘Yes, but –’

‘Then just do it!’

‘I don’t know if I could get away. I can’t just close up the yard.’ Nearly there, thought Bella. She held her breath. Derek suddenly shook his head. ‘No, I don’t see how it would work, me and the girls and your friends. Sorry.’

‘What? How can you throw away a chance like this? Charlie will be there. It could make all the difference in the world to all three of us . . .’ She was near to tears with frustration.

Suddenly Leanne put her head round the door. ‘Dad, Emma’s chain’s come off and I can’t fix it.’

‘Go and ask Paul or –’

‘Leanne,’ said Bella quickly, ‘would you like to come on holiday to France? To a house I have there? You, your dad and your sister. To stay with me and some friends of mine.’

Leanne looked at her father, mouth open. Derek, not even looking at Bella, said, ‘Go on. Hop it. Get Paul or Terry to fix the chain.’

Leanne switched her glance to Bella. ‘Why are you asking us to go to France with you?’

‘Because,’ said Bella, ‘I’m your aunt. Your dad’s my brother.’

‘That’s it,’ said Derek. ‘Go. I mean it. I’ll talk to you

later. You and your sister get to the park.' He closed the door firmly, waiting for the sound of the child's steps fading towards the kitchen, then turned to Bella in a fury. 'What the bloody hell did you do that for?'

'Because it's true.'

'It's up to me to tell them!'

'Why?'

Derek didn't know what to say. He paced around in agitation, trying to calm himself. 'Look, you can't go treating us like some ready-made family. We don't just slot into your life because you feel like it!'

'You won't even think about it. You don't want to know me, or Charlie.'

He rounded on her. 'Don't say that! You have no idea what this has done to me! Don't you think I'd have liked a brother and sister? I feel like someone's robbed me! Even when she was dying, I could hardly bring myself to forgive my mother for what she did! Do you know what that's like?'

Bella stared into his angry, stricken eyes, a little taken aback. 'Yes,' she said at last, 'I do. I still find it hard to forgive my mother for not telling me that I was adopted. If she had, I could have found you years ago. I could have known Doreen, and she could have seen me and Charlie and maybe been happier for it. But here we are, and we have to make the best of it. That's why I'm asking you to come to France with me. Just to take the chance.'

Derek shook his head slowly. 'That's your world. I don't think it's a very good idea. Sorry.'

'Say you'll think about it.'

Derek scratched the back of his neck with oil-stained fingers. 'If you want,' he sighed, 'I'll think about it.'

Bella got up, thrusting her hands into her jacket pockets. 'I'll let you get back to work.'

He nodded. 'Sorry if I was a bit . . .'

'Don't worry. I'll see myself out.'

Driving back, Bella went over their conversation. Just like Charlie. Stubborn, and bloody impenetrable. Well, at least she'd tried. At least it didn't stop here.

Bella spent the afternoon clothes shopping, which she knew would have a pleasantly palliative effect on her melancholia, and met up with some girlfriends at the Manor Bar in Notting Hill. She rapidly realized, however, that she wasn't in the mood for drinking and gossiping, and left after half an hour.

When she got in, the message light on her phone was flashing. She pressed the playback button, hoping illogically that Adam Downing might have called – why would he? But it was Derek's voice, saying nothing more than his name and that he would speak to her later. Quickly she rang back.

'Derek, it's Bella. You called when I was out.'

'Yeah. Hold on while I turn the telly down.' She heard voices, a door closing, and he came back on the line. 'I've been having a long talk with the girls. I explained everything to them. I thought you'd like to know.'

'I see. What did they say?'

'Oh, at first they thought I was having them on, that kind of thing. You know kids. But they understand. Sort of. They asked stuff like why did Nana give you away, and so on . . . I didn't really have an answer. I think they're kind of fascinated by it all – if that's the right word.'

'I can imagine.'

'Anyway, because you said what you said to Leanne, they've been banging on and on about you inviting them on holiday.'

'And?'

'In the end, I said yes. Paul can open up the yard while I'm away, we're a bit light on work with people being on holiday and stuff . . .'

Bella felt exultant. 'Derek, that's fantastic!'

'Yeah, well . . .'

'Come on – try to sound more enthusiastic. It'll be good for us to spend some time together. It's a marvellous place – you'll love it.'

'If you say so. I haven't had a holiday for four years, to be honest.'

'I'll check on flights straight away. Oh, I'm so thrilled!'

'I'll square this up with you. I've got a bit put by.'

'We'll worry about that later. I'm just so pleased you're going to come.'

Bella rang the airline and managed to book three more seats for the Monday flight. Her next instinct, when she'd put the phone down, was to pick it up again straight away and call Charlie, to tell him. But she hesitated. Knowing Charlie, if she said that Derek and his daughters would be in residence at Montresor when he got there at the end of the week, he'd run a mile. Anything rather than face up to the reality of his past, in the shape of a brother he'd never met. Perhaps the best thing to do would be to say nothing, let matters take their course. Charlie couldn't run away from his beginnings for ever.

Always a late packer, Adam was still in the middle of throwing clothes into a bag on Sunday morning when he was startled by three deep blasts of a car horn from the street below. He went to the window and looked out. There next to the kerb stood an enormous silver-grey Bentley. He pushed up the sash window and at the same time Richard Compton-King leaned out of the car window and looked up. He raised a hand in salute.

'Down in a minute!' called Adam. He zipped up his bag, picked up his laptop and a canvas bag holding his notes for the article, and went through to the living room, where Megan was riffling through her handbag.

'Got everything? Compton-King's downstairs.'

'Yes, OK.' Megan closed her bag and picked up her holdall.

As he locked up the flat and followed Megan downstairs, Adam felt in excellent spirits. He pushed to the back of his mind the problematic knowledge that this was far preferable to going alone with Megan. For the moment, he just wanted to enjoy the adventure.

Richard Compton-King was lounging behind the wheel of his Bentley, a battered but very becoming Panama tilted on the back of his head, the engine gently thrumming. 'Good morning,' he called. 'Sling your things in the boot.'

Adam put his bag and Megan's in the boot of the car, inhaling the delicious, evocative scent of old leather and petrol. When he walked around to the front of the car, he saw a figure slumped in the passenger seat next to Compton-King with its head resting on the door sill. It was a young man, unshaven, his dark-blond hair in messy dreadlocks, dressed in jeans and an unseasonably bulky sheepskin coat, and apparently fast asleep. 'Hop in the back,' said Compton-King. 'My young friend is just sleeping off the excesses of last night.' He shot a dazzling smile at Megan and extended a large hand. 'Richard Compton-King. Hi.'

'Megan Philips.' She shook his hand. Adam could tell by the way she returned the smile that the Compton-King magic was destined to have its potent effect, and felt relieved. They settled themselves into the comfort of the squashy leather seats, Compton-King shifted the car into gear, and they set off down the road at a stately trundle.

'What an amazing car,' said Adam.

'Had the whole thing customized,' replied Compton-King. 'Nineteen fifties' workmanship, plus some twenty-first-century technology. Best of both worlds.'

'It's fantastic,' murmured Adam, glancing round the capacious interior, noting the little silver vases mounted next to both rear windows, the inlaid-walnut drinks compartment, the DVD screens in the back of the front seats.

Suddenly the young man in the front seat gave a groan and lifted his head. Without opening his eyes, he repositioned himself, burrowing his head down into the collar of his coat.

'This is Bruno,' said Compton-King, nodding in the direction of the sleeping form. 'Bruno Skeffington-Ancram. Known to close friends as Skank, for obvious reasons. Lead singer of the Mule Skinners.'

'Really?' The name of the band evidently rang a clearer bell with Megan than it had with Adam. She leaned forward from her seat and peered with interest at what could be seen of young Mr Skeffington-Ancram above the collar of his coat.

'Is he coming with us?' asked Adam.

'Unless he wakes up before the Channel Tunnel and demands to be let out. I decided he's in need of a rest-cure. France is just the thing. Not that he knows he's going.' Compton-King glanced again at his inert companion. 'Not that he knows much at any time. Excessive abuse of substances. Lack of sleep. Emotional difficulties. Could see we were heading for one of those immortal rift-within-the-band scenarios. Entirely against my interests, naturally, so decided to bring him along and let time the great healer take a hand for a couple of weeks. Some sunshine, decent food, sleep and basic lack of amphetamines should do the trick.'

'So, what's the itinerary?' asked Adam.

Compton-King glanced at his watch. 'Shuttle's booked for three, so I suggest we head in a Doverly direction, stop for lunch somewhere along the way, then once we hit the other side we can probably get as far as Orléans before stopping for the night. I've got the numbers of a few hotels there.'

'You know, we'll really have to settle up with you for the cost of this trip.'

Compton-King waved an airy hand. 'I only pay for the car on the Shuttle, so thus far it's on me. Don't worry, you can make a petrol contribution at some point. Now, music for the journey.' He leaned forward and pressed a button, and the sounds of John Lee Hooker filled the car. Bruno lifted his head briefly, gave another groan, and burrowed back into his coat.

Bella had arranged, with some difficulty, to pick up a people carrier at Bordeaux airport.

'The journey only takes a couple of hours,' said Bella, as she settled herself behind the wheel, Derek next to her, Bruce and Frank behind, and the girls in the back. She glanced in the rear-view mirror. Leanne and Emma, as soon as they'd buckled their seat belts, were instantly absorbed in their Gameboys, as they had been throughout the flight to Bordeaux. They really seemed to be quite dull little creatures. It irked her that they were probably going to spend the entire car journey hunched over those machines, instead of taking in the glories of the French countryside. So far she had hardly exchanged one word with them. Well, time enough to get to know them over the next two weeks. She was happy enough to have Derek to talk to all the way to Montresor. They had sat next to one another on the plane, and had already begun the absorbing process of unravelling one another's past. Derek had come a long way from that first wary encounter, and now seemed easy in her company, even to the point of teasing her gently about her French at the car-hire desk. Bella felt quietly confident that these two weeks together would give them both back a little of what had been missing in their lives. She just hoped Charlie could see it that way, too.

Further north, the trip in the Bentley had begun delightfully well. After an excellent lunch at a pub near Ashford (throughout which Bruno remained in the car fast asleep), they sped to Dover and on to the Shuttle without any delays, then on down the autoroute from Calais in brilliant sunshine. Compton-King beguiled them on the journey with a wide-ranging selection of music and scandalously amusing anecdotes from his many years in the music industry, which Megan enjoyed immensely, seeking occasional breathless elaboration of details. Bruno roused himself in the late afternoon, divested himself of his coat, and sat blinking inertly as they headed southwards, saying nothing at all.

It was around eight in the evening when the air conditioning broke down. Compton-King, after an irate and futile investigation of the problem at a motorway service station, rolled all the windows down, and the rest of the journey proceeded in silence, as the rush of tepid air drowned all possibility of music or conversation. Compton-King and Bruno managed a brief exchange of words, which Adam was unable to overhear, culminating in the production from the glove compartment of two fruit cereal bars, which Bruno ate.

Despite the slight mechanical setback, everyone was in good spirits when they stopped for the night at the hotel, booked ahead by Adam on his mobile phone during their last motorway stop. Adam and Megan were sharing one room, Compton-King and Bruno another. When shown to his room, Bruno sank immediately on to a bed and rolled himself up in his coat, clearly intending to stay there.

Adam, Megan and Compton-King went downstairs to the little terraced bar which served late-evening snacks, and sat outside in the balmy night air, drinking and talking, before turning in a little after midnight. They had agreed to be up early the next day to complete their journey, which, according to Compton-King, would take no more than six or seven hours, even throwing in a leisurely lunch in Limoges. By the time he fell asleep that night, pleasantly exhausted by the journey and late-night cognac, Adam congratulated himself that thus far the trip with Compton-King seemed to be going pretty well.

Bella and her party reached Montresor late on Monday afternoon. They turned off the narrow road just past Sainte Levroux, and drove up a sloping lane winding past sunflower fields and into the shade of distant trees.

'It's a long way off the beaten track,' said Derek.

'Which is how I like it,' said Bella. 'No one and nothing to disturb us. Just the village back there, and our neighbours over on the other side of that melon field.'

The girls had given up their Gameboys some time ago, and, to Bella's satisfaction, were taking an interest in their surroundings, exclaiming at the rows of sunflowers.

They rounded the bend, emerging from the shade of the trees, and pulled into a broad, sunlit area by the house. 'Wow!' said Emma. 'Is that it?'

'That's it.' Bella parked the car in the shade of a wall.

'It's fantastic,' said Leanne, as she and Emma got out of the car.

The house had once been a big, stone farmhouse, and in restoring it, Harry had incorporated two large barns to the rear of the house, so that the whole was now a large L-shape, with two storeys where the barns had been, three in the main part of the house. The white window shutters looked very pretty against the worn grey stone, and the surrounding garden was filled with colour and scent from geraniums and roses.

'It should be open,' said Bella, as Derek took bags from the boot. 'Marianne should have done the shopping and made up the beds. Go on in,' she said to the girls. 'That door leads straight into the kitchen.'

The girls sped off to the house.

'Quite a place,' said Bruce, gazing around through his sunglasses.

'How many rooms has it?' asked Frank.

'Ten bedrooms,' said Bella. 'Plus the annexe over there.' She pointed to a stone building at the end of the orchard stretching beyond the lawn. 'Plenty of room for all. Let's get our bags inside and you can have a look around.'

The girls sped in and out in a state of excitement, exclaiming over everything. 'Dad! Dad! It's got satellite telly! And the swimming pool is massive! Come and have a look!'

'Calm down, you pair,' said Derek, but allowed himself to be dragged outside into the evening sunshine to survey the glories of the swimming pool, at the end of which stood a bar and a barbecue area.

Bella led Frank and Bruce upstairs with their bags. 'You can have your pick of any of the rooms on this floor,' said Bella. 'My room's down the end there.'

Bruce took a room which overlooked the orchard, pushed wide the shutters and leaned out, inhaling the air. 'D'you like it?' asked Bella, following him in. She much enjoyed sharing the pleasures of Montresor, and it gave her a pang to think this might be the last time she would stay here.

'It's amazing,' said Bruce. 'Just amazing.'

Bella smiled. 'I'd better see how Frank's getting on.'

She wandered into the next room and found Frank sitting on the edge of his neatly made-up bed, looking doleful.

She sat down next to him. 'Are you OK?'

Frank gave a sigh. 'I had planned to take Jenny on holiday last year. It was going to be a surprise. Madeira. She'd always wanted to go. Then she got ill. So, of course, we never did go. I just feel so guilty, being on holiday without her.'

'Oh, Frank – don't feel that way. I want you to enjoy yourself.'

Frank smiled and nodded sadly. He looked round the prettily furnished room, and at the fresh flowers in a vase on the bedside table. 'I'm sure I will. Don't worry.'

'Come down and have a glass of wine when you've unpacked. That'll cheer you up.' Bella rose from the bed. 'By the way, there's something I should tell you. Bruce and I haven't really been going out together at all, you know.'

'Oh. Oh?' Frank stared at her in surprise.

'It was just a – well, a sort of stratagem. To get publicity. You know the kind of thing. Not that it did the play much good.'

Frank nodded. 'What a pity. That's how Jenny and I met, you know. In rep. Oh, well. You made a nice couple.'

'I thought I'd better tell you, since we're all going to

be under the same roof for a fortnight. Anyway . . . I'd better go and check that Marianne has got all the groceries I asked her to. I'll see you downstairs later.'

Megan and Adam came downstairs to breakfast in the hotel that morning to find Compton-King already there with Bruno, who looked in many ways worse awake than asleep. His pale-blue eyes were bleary and resentful, his dirty blond dreadlocks even more matted, his stubble denser and his face pastier, with grey shadows below his eyes. He nodded blearily and grunted at Adam and Megan through a mouthful of croissant, and left the table shortly thereafter, heading in the direction of his room.

'Not very companionable,' said Compton-King, pouring coffee. 'My apologies. He'll improve with time. Really quite a nice young man.'

'He looks dreadful,' said Megan.

'Mmm. Could do with a wash and brush-up, admittedly. Have to buy him some clothes at some point. He came with me straight from a gig in Hammersmith.' He looked at his watch. 'Come on, chaps. Get that coffee down you. Time to hit the road.'

The day, like the previous one, was clear and fresh to begin with. Then the sun began to climb. Except for a few cotton-wool drifts on the horizon, the azure sky was untroubled by clouds. By eleven o'clock everyone was very much feeling the absence of air conditioning. The temperature had risen to the mid-twenties, the sun beat down relentlessly, and the air through the open windows as they sped southwards possessed all the refreshing qualities of a humid face flannel. With the absence of conversation or music, everyone became bored and moody. It was an exquisite relief when they stopped off for petrol and were able to luxuriate for fifteen minutes in the air-conditioned interior of the service station. Even then, no one said very much. They were all thinking about the stuffy, tedious hours ahead.

When they went back to the car, the leather seats were unbearably, skin-stickingly hot. Everyone shifted around in discomfort.

'Only another hour to Limoges,' said Compton-King, trying to perk things up, rubbing at his right forearm, which was pink and sunburnt from resting on the open sill. 'And then we can have lunch and cool off properly.'

It was, in fact, another three hours to Limoges. Instead of cruising along at a steady eighty, which had just about made the air in the car bearable, they hit a road-works tailback and slowed to a crawl. The car became an oven. The afternoon was much hotter than the morning. The long line of cars stretching endlessly ahead seemed to shimmer in the heat. Bruno, who hadn't washed or changed his clothes for forty-eight hours, was growing odoriferous. Maps were pulled out, alternatives considered, and after a futile discussion where things threatened to get snappy, they resigned themselves to sitting in the heat, creeping along with the traffic. Even though conversation was now possible, nobody was in the mood to say anything, except for Bruno, who became agitated and swore a lot, which didn't improve the atmosphere. Compton-King rebuked him, and they argued, while Adam and Megan suffered silently in the back.

By the time they reached Limoges, all the restaurants were closed. Spirits sank even lower. They drove on down the autoroute to the next service point and bought ham and salad baguettes and bottled water.

'Should we pick up a few things for the evening?' suggested Megan to Adam, as they climbed back into the car.

'No need,' said Adam. 'Apparently the couple who look after the place are going to leave some things for us. Bread, milk, the makings of dinner, a few bottles of decent wine.' He glanced at Compton-King. 'Where are you staying?'

'I haven't booked anything yet.' He rummaged around, found a Logis guide and chucked it at Bruno. 'Have a look in there – I've marked our area – and get on the mobile and book us something up.'

'I've just had a thought,' said Adam. 'We're probably going to get to Cahors too late for me to pick up our hire car.'

'No problemo,' said Compton-King. 'I'll drive you to wherever you're staying.'

'I was hoping you'd say that. In which case, why don't you stay the night at the gite? It's got four beds. Saves everyone a lot of trouble.'

Compton-King paused, considering. 'Good idea. Come on, let's get motoring.'

The delay outside Limoges meant that they didn't reach Cahors until early evening, and there they hit another patch of slow traffic. By now the air had cooled off, however, and as the journey's end seemed almost in sight, everyone was in a better mood. Bruno sat next to Compton-King with the directions to the gite on his knee. He studied them closely, but failed to mention the first turn-off, so that half an hour later they had to turn back and retrace part of their route. The road was winding and slow. It grew dark, and it was hard to read signs; they lost their bearings twice.

A little after ten, however, they found the sign for Les Pointoises, and in relief and triumph they rolled up the lane towards a huddle of buildings picked out by the beam of the Bentley's headlamps. Compton-King switched off the engine. All was silent.

'It's very dark,' said Megan. 'Which of the gites are we supposed to be using?'

Adam pulled some papers from his pocket and leafed through them, then read out, 'Key to number four under geranium pot next to barbecue.'

There was a thoughtful silence.

'We should have got a torch at the service station,' said Megan.

'I've got a lighter,' said Bruno.

'But we don't know which house it is. There are about six of them.'

'Isn't there anyone else staying here? Someone we can ask?'

'I can't see any lights on.'

'Come on,' said Compton-King, getting out of the car. 'Bring your lighter, Bruno.'

There followed a painful ten minutes during which they groped around in the darkness by the feeble flicker of Bruno's lighter, speaking in low voices until it became evident that the complex was deserted and that there was no need. At last, after Compton-King had barked his shins on a low wall and Adam had almost fallen in the swimming pool, they found the right barbecue, and the right pot. Finding the door, and then the keyhole, took a little while longer.

'I'm dying for a pee,' muttered Megan in the darkness, as Adam prodded at the lock with the key.

'All I want is some food and sleep,' said Adam. 'At least we're here . . . Got it!' There was the sound of a lock turning, and a door opening.

Adam stepped inside, groped for a light switch, and clicked it on.

They stood in the doorway, surveying a low-ceilinged kitchen, illuminated by a naked bulb, and containing cupboards, a small cooker and fridge, a sink, and a cheap table with three chairs. It felt as though nobody had been in for some time, certainly not to dust or lay in provisions. Adam went to the fridge and opened it. Nothing.

'Are you sure it's the right house?' asked Megan.

Adam glanced at the tag on the key. 'Number four. This is the one. Sorry, everyone. Looks like no supper.'

They went through to the living room, which was small and box-like, cheaply furnished with a sofa and two armchairs, a pine coffee table, and some tatty lamps. 'God,' said Adam. 'I had expected something a bit better than this.'

Compton-King glanced at Adam's stricken face. 'Don't worry. We're all exhausted. Maybe we should just get to bed.'

'What makes you think it's going to look any better

in the morning?' muttered Megan. 'It's an absolute dump.'

'I am truly sorry,' said Adam.

Megan shrugged.

With the help of Bruno's lighter, they retrieved their bags from the boot of the Bentley. Trooping upstairs, they were unsurprised to find that the mattresses on each bed were thin and lumpy, with only sheets and one blanket each, and no spare pillows. Notwithstanding the heat of the day, the temperature beneath the clear starry sky had dropped. It was going to be a chilly night.

Adam and Megan took the double bed. Despite the cold, Megan stayed resolutely on her side of the bed, sullen and angry.

'How could you book such a poxy place? It has to be totally the worst gite in all of France!'

'I've said I'm sorry,' said Adam. 'We'll sort it out in the morning. If necessary, we'll find somewhere else.'

'If necessary? I'll say it's necessary. A horrible trip, and a horrible house . . .'

Adam lay in the dark, listening to Megan grumbling, waiting for sleep, envying Bruno his big sheepskin coat. Megan was right. The place was a dump, and he was to blame. He ruminated on the situation, realizing that this was the first occasion on which something had gone wrong for himself and Megan. So far, their existence in London had been untested by disaster, untroubled by anything more than the most minor domestic trauma. This evening her defection had been almost instant, putting him in the wrong, instead of trying to make the best of it and being affectionate and cheerful. Even

Compton-King had tried to be both of those things. He couldn't help wondering if certain other unappealing truths about their relationship were going to surface during this holiday.

12

Adam woke a little before nine. Ready to make the peace with Megan, he rolled over, but found her side of the bed empty. He lay there for some minutes, staring at the thin shafts of light piercing the shutters, trawling over the events of the journey and their arrival last night. Suddenly his thoughts were broken by the sound of high-pitched screaming. He bounded out of bed and down the corridor to the bathroom, from where the screams came. He found Megan dancing around on the tiles in the middle of the bathroom, clutching a towel and emitting squeals of disgust. Behind a plastic shower curtain came the sound of running water.

'What on earth's the matter?' asked Adam.

'Oh, God, just take a look!' Megan, pointing at the shower, retreated to the furthest corner of the bathroom.

Adam advanced on the shower cubicle and pulled back the curtain. Looking down, he saw that the water from the showerhead, which should have been running away, was being regurgitated from the drain in throaty belches of brownish sludge, filling up the cubicle basin and beginning to spill out on to the tiled floor. The smell was revolting.

'Oh, Christ!' said Adam, moving quickly back.

'What is it?' Megan was shivering in horror in the corner, trying to dry herself.

Compton-King's large, unshaven face appeared round the door. 'Trouble, boys and girls?' He looked down and saw the tide of brown liquid seeping quickly over the tiles. 'Shit.'

'Literally,' said Adam. 'It must be the septic tank backing up.'

'Switch the shower off!' squealed Megan. 'It's going to flood the place!'

Adam inched his way barefoot round the brown, spreading tide, pulled back the shower curtain with one hand, and tried to lean over to switch the shower off. In so doing, he put his full weight on the shower curtain, which parted from its rail in a brisk ripping tinkle, and fell over. The edge of the shower basin caught him hard on his ribs, and he found himself wrist-deep in the stuff which was burping from the drain. The combination of the smell from the drain and the pain in his ribs made his gorge rise, and for a moment he thought he might be sick. He struggled to his feet and let the stream of tepid water from the shower rinse the worst of the muck from his hands and arms, then shakily he turned the shower off.

He stood there, T-shirt and boxer shorts clinging to his body, in a pool of sewage, his chest aching. The drain gave a series of deep, effluvial burps, then all was silent. To Megan's yips of disgust, Adam stepped from the burgeoning cesspool and padded over to the washbasin. He teetered around it for a minute or two, rinsing one leg, then the other, keeping a wary eye on the plughole in case it threatened to regurgitate as well. 'I should probably have a typhus injection or something.'

Megan made her way round the creeping puddle and fled to the bedroom.

Adam and Compton-King surveyed the horror. 'Well, that about settles it,' said Adam. 'We can't stay here.' He shivered momentarily. 'Chuck us a towel.'

Compton-King peered into the linen cupboard and pulled out a diminutive guest towel. 'Looks like this'll have to do.'

Adam took the towel and mopped himself ineffectually. 'God, what a mess . . . Maybe Megan and I can move into one of the other villas.'

'Not much point in that, as I imagine they all share this same, wonderful *fosse septique*.'

Adam sighed. 'I'm going to get dressed.'

'I'll drive to the town down the road and get us some breakfast,' said Compton-King, trying to look bright. 'There must be a supermarket.'

'Great. Thanks a lot. I'll ring the people who look after the place and get someone to sort this out.'

Adam came downstairs ten minutes later and rang the caretakers. No reply. He went into the kitchen and found Bruno and Megan sitting at the table. Megan's expression was as miserable as he'd ever seen it. Bruno, on the other hand, looked serene. He was smoking a large spliff, his matted hair dripping water on to the T-shirt which he'd been wearing since Saturday.

'Just been for a swim,' he remarked. 'Pool's not bad.'

'About the only thing round here that isn't,' muttered Megan.

'Yeah.' Bruno gave an otherworldly glance at his surroundings. 'Rick said it would be really cool, but this is tragic. I mean –' he gave a disbelieving laugh, 'I'm a fucking rock star!'

Megan and Adam stared at him wordlessly, then Megan reached out a hand for the spliff. Skank nodded and passed it to her.

That's it, start the day by getting stoned with this moron, thought Adam. He wandered out into the early heat of the day. The swimming pool lay, inert and blue, in the centre of the complex of shabby villas, the rest of which were locked and shuttered. Hardly surprising that no one wanted to rent them. They were shoddy and ugly, with threadbare patches of lawn leading to the pool. Adam wandered from house to house, inspecting the barbecue areas, the shrivelled patches of geraniums which nobody had bothered to water recently, the dilapidated sun loungers and rickety pool umbrellas, wondering how he could possibly have been so unlucky as to finish up renting this. It was clear that they couldn't spend the next two weeks here.

Wandering back to the house twenty minutes later, he could hear the sound of the Bentley's engine in the distance. Food at last. Everybody had been utterly famished since yesterday. He went back to the kitchen to help unload groceries and put some breakfast together.

But Compton-King had returned with nothing more than two baguettes and a bag of croissants. He put them apologetically on the kitchen table.

'Is that it?' Bruno looked dazedly at the bread.

'I couldn't find a supermarket that was open. Managed to find a baker's. Best I could do.'

Megan took a croissant from the bag and began to eat it.

'They're better warmed up,' said Adam in a conciliatory fashion.

'I don't care. I'm too hungry. And fed up. Anyway, the oven probably doesn't work. Nothing else seems to.' She glanced up at Adam, her eyes a little glazed from her smoke, and handed him a croissant. He took it and ate it dejectedly. Bruno broke off a large lump of baguette and chewed it.

'What are we going to do for the rest of the day?' asked Megan. 'We can't live off this.'

'We'll have to go out and find somewhere for lunch,' said Adam. 'And some shops, if possible.'

'And then what?' Megan turned her angry gaze on him. 'Come back here? To this horrible place? You can't go upstairs without wanting to throw up!'

'Megan –' began Adam. But she got up, ignoring him, grabbed another croissant from the bag and stomped from the kitchen.

Adam followed her outside. 'Look,' he said, 'you've made it perfectly clear that you blame me for all of this. But do you really think it helps? Do you think I want to hear you telling me every other second how bad it is, and how fed up you are? Could we try to be a little less selfish, perhaps? How about supporting me, instead of whining on about everything?'

'Don't start having a go at *me*! This was meant to be a pleasant break for both of us, but what happens? First you agree to drive down with two people I've never met in my life, in a bloody awful car that doesn't work properly. Then I find you haven't even bothered to take the time to book somewhere decent – and you expect me to be perfectly fine about it! Do you know what? I wish I'd never agreed to come with you! I wish I'd stayed in London!'

'You don't know how entirely and sincerely I agree with that sentiment,' retorted Adam. He went back into the house.

Compton-King was wearing the insouciant expression of someone pretending not to have overheard someone else's row. 'Look,' said Adam apologetically, 'it was really good of you to drive us down here. But there's not much sense in you hanging around. You'll want to get on.'

'You still have to pick up your hire car,' pointed out Compton-King. 'I'll drive you into Cahors.'

Adam scratched his head. 'I hadn't thought about that. If you're sure you don't mind, that would be great.'

Adam and Compton-King set off for Cahors in the Bentley. Megan and Bruno stayed behind, sitting in the sun by the edge of the swimming pool, their legs dangling in the water.

'You and Adam been going out long?' asked Bruno.

'A couple of years,' said Megan moodily. She had never felt so hostile towards Adam, ever, and it wasn't a feeling she liked. She could tell he felt the same way at the moment, and that merely heightened her own brooding animosity. She should want to make it up with him, but she didn't. She frankly didn't care.

'Right.' Bruno nodded philosophically.

Megan rounded on him. 'What d'you mean – right?'

'Sorry?' Bruno was startled.

'You said it in a certain way. "Right", you said, and then nodded in that significant way.'

'Easy!' Bruno held up a defensive hand. 'Why don't you just chill a bit? Relax. I just meant that two years was probably long enough to start getting on each other's nerves.' Megan said nothing, just stared at the sunlight dancing on the water. Bruno contemplated her expression. He smiled, put out a finger and lifted a lock of hair from her face. 'You look so bloody miserable. Come on, give us a smile.'

Megan sighed, and gave a small smile in spite of herself. She cast a tentative glance at Bruno. He had nice eyes. Smiley eyes. He was young and carefree. Suddenly she wanted to be like that, too.

'That's better,' said Bruno. He dipped his hand in his T-shirt pocket and pulled out a battered spliff and lit it. 'There you go.' He handed it to Megan. 'Now, tell me all about you and Adam.'

After a mellow hour of smoking and talking, Megan began to feel better. Not about Adam, but about herself, about life. It was nice to make a new friend. Her continuing sense of resentment against Adam made her feel justified in having a moan about him. And Bruno was easy to be with. It was a pleasant change to talk to someone with a less serious agenda, not wrapped up in books and literary articles. There was an aimlessness about Bruno which she found quite refreshing.

'How old are you?' she asked.

'Twenty-nine.'

'I thought you were younger.'

'It's my childlike persona,' said Bruno. He shifted himself on to the grass and lay back. 'Nah, actually it's being in the band. In a band you never grow up.'

Megan reflected on this, thinking how pleasant it would be to be able to resist all those pressures to behave like a grown-up. Perhaps it was to do with being in her thirties, perhaps it was to do with being around Adam, so solitary and serious . . . Whatever it was, she liked the idea that it wasn't necessarily too late to have fun.

'What are you going to do?' Compton-King asked Adam, as they drove into Cahors.

'About that wretched house? Try the caretakers again. Not that they're going to be able to make the place habitable, even if I manage to get hold of them. I suppose I'll end up ringing the gite company and telling them I'm going to sue them rotten. What else can I do? I'll just have to try and wring some compensation out of them when we get back to London.' Adam sighed and ran weary fingers through his hair. 'I can think of something to tide us over for today, at least. Harry Day's daughter has a house not far from here. The one who was in the Orton play. She's staying there at the moment. Harry left the house to her and her brother.'

Compton-King nodded. 'Bella. Gorgeous girl.'

'Do you know her?'

'No. Harry and I had drifted apart somewhat by the time she came along. But her face is all over the place.'

Adam nodded. 'We've grown quite – quite friendly since I started the biography. She suggested Megan and I should drop in while we're down here, and I can't think of a better opportunity. At least we'll get some lunch. Then we can sort out somewhere else to stay for the next couple of weeks. I'll ring her when we get back.'

Bella was in the kitchen discussing grocery requirements with Marianne when the phone rang. She had tried to put Adam from her mind since leaving London, and hardly expected to hear from him, so her heart leapt with unexpected pleasure at the sound of his voice.

'Adam! How are you?'

'Well, the trip down was interesting. Richard Compton-King drove us. You remember I mentioned him – an old friend of your father's?'

'Oh, yes.' Her tone was unenthusiastic. 'The one who outed Daddy.'

Adam winced. 'You could say . . . Anyway, the gite we booked has turned out to be a bit of a disaster. My fault. I made a booking at the last minute, took whatever was going. We woke up this morning to find that the septic tank is backing up, and the place is uninhabitable. We're bailing out and trying to find somewhere else to stay, but I wondered if –'

'Come over here for the day. You absolutely must.'

'That's what I was hoping you'd say. It'll only be for a few hours, till we fix up something else. The whole thing is awful.'

'Poor you. How far away are you?'

'I had a look at a map, and it can't be more than an hour or so.'

'Well, put your things together and come over. Ask Mr Compton-King if he'd like to come to lunch, too. I'd be interested to meet him. Since he was such a friend of Daddy's.'

'Right . . .' Adam paused uncertainly. 'He's got a – a young friend with him. A musician. Sort of.'

'The more the merrier. We'll see you around lunchtime.'

Bella hung up. She felt disproportionately happy at the thought of seeing Adam. 'Marianne,' she called, 'we're going to have a few extra people for lunch.'

Adam put the phone down and went into the kitchen, where Compton-King was leaning back in a chair which looked too frail for his large frame, feet up on the table, studying a road map.

'Right, that's all fixed up. Are you and Bruno headed anywhere in particular?'

'Not especially. Just thinking of rolling off in the direction of Bordeaux. Why?'

'Bella wondered if you'd like to come to lunch as well.'

'What's happening?' asked Bruno, strolling into the kitchen.

Compton-King folded the road map. 'We've been invited to lunch by a preposterously pretty young actress. A friend of Adam's called Bella Day. Does that appeal?'

'Cool.'

'I thought it might.'

'Right,' said Adam, 'we might as well get going straight away.'

Megan, wandering moodily in from outside, caught this. 'Get going where?'

'Bella Day's. She's got a house down here,' said Adam.

'You didn't tell me.'

There was an exchange of hostile glances.

'It didn't come up.'

Compton-King, sensing another argument brewing, rose from his chair. 'I suggest we collect our effects and depart.'

They threw things in the back of the Bentley and the hire car, locked up and put the key back under the geranium pot, and drove away in relief.

They reached Montresor just before noon. Bella came out of the house as both cars pulled up on the driveway. She was wearing a thin cotton shirt over a blue bikini, and was barefoot. Adam wished she didn't look so unutterably lovely, and that he didn't smell faintly of raw sewage.

'What a fantastic car,' said Bella.

Compton-King, first out of the Bentley, extended a large hand and smiled fabulously, slipping effortlessly into charm mode. 'Richard Compton-King. Can't tell you how kind it is of you to bail us out of disaster.'

Bella returned the smile and shook his hand, giving him an appraising glance. 'Happy to help.' She moved towards Adam as he got out, prepared to give him a quick kiss of greeting. He held up a hand and stepped back.

'I wouldn't, if I were you,' he said apologetically. 'I was the one who had to deal with the invasion of the septic tank.'

Bella grimaced. 'Well, you can have a bath straight away, if you like. I won't come any closer.' She glanced at Megan, who looked hot, tired and bothered. 'Hi.'

'Hello.' Megan nodded.

'Come into the house. Anybody who needs a shower or bath can have one. Just make yourselves at home. Bring your things. Then I'll introduce you to everyone and we'll have lunch.'

As they went in, Adam and Bella fell behind a little, as though by unspoken agreement.

'Guess who I managed to persuade to come along,' murmured Bella.

'Who?'

'Derek. He's here with his two girls. We've hit it off pretty well so far.'

'Really? That's fantastic.' They paused on the threshold. 'Look,' said Adam, 'it's really good of you – I mean, letting us descend on you like this.'

'Don't be silly. I'm very glad to see you.' Her eyes were expressive, sincerely happy.

'And I'm incredibly glad to see you.'

Showered and changed, Adam wandered through the house to the garden, where he could hear voices. Bella was sitting by the pool, talking to a middle-aged man lying on a sun lounger. He was portly and very hairy, clad in baggy tartan swimming trunks and glistening with sun oil. Bella looked up at Adam through her sunglasses. 'Adam, meet Frank McVeigh, one of our unhappy cast.'

Adam shook hands with Frank, and wondered where Bruce Redmond was. Perhaps he hadn't come. Bella called out introductions to the two girls splashing in the pool, and they waved.

'Where's Derek?' asked Adam.

'Playing table tennis with Bruce,' said Bella. 'They've been at it for the past half-hour. Very competitive.'

Megan and Bruno came out of the house and crossed the lawn to the pool. Bruno, thought Adam with surprise, had cleaned up quite nicely. The matted dreadlocks had been washed and brushed into something more like hair, and now that he had shaved and put on the clean T-shirt and shorts which Adam had lent him, he looked distinctly more appealing than he had on first acquaintance, even to the point of being fairly good looking.

Bella made introductions and poured out cold lemonade from a jug on the poolside trolley.

'This is quite a place,' said Adam.

'It's beautiful,' agreed Megan, whose mood had been much improved by a warm bath and the use of some of Bella's expensive bath oil.

'I love it,' sighed Bella, glancing around. 'I only wish Charlie and I didn't have to sell it.'

'How is Charlie?' asked Adam.

'Fine, as far as I know. He's coming down with Claire at the end of the week.' Her glance met Adam's. She shook her head. 'No, he doesn't know Derek's here.'

At that moment Compton-King emerged from the house, magnificent in a loose, mauve silk shirt, white shorts and canvas espadrilles, his shoulder-length hair swept back, twirling a pair of Raybans. As he crossed the lawn, Frank suddenly reared up in astonishment from his sun lounger. 'Dickie Compton-King!'

'Good God! Frank!' roared Compton-King, and descended on his friend to shake his hand and clap his back.

'Dickie and I go way back,' explained Frank to Bella. 'We were at Marlborough together. How extraordinary that you should turn up here! How many years is it?'

'Ten at least,' said Compton-King. 'That race meeting at Chantilly. Great to see you. Just amazing.'

Bella made the rest of the introductions. Derek and Bruce appeared.

'He's too good for me,' said Bruce, flopping down next to Bella. He noticed the presence of visitors and raised a hand in general greeting. 'Hello.'

'Bruce, meet Adam, Megan, Richard and Bruno.' She turned to them. 'This is Bruce Redmond. And this –' She reached up and caught Derek's hand, 'is my brother Derek.' Derek gave a diffident nod to everyone. 'OK, now we're all here, let's go and have lunch.'

After lunch, Megan and Bruno joined the girls in the swimming pool, and Derek sat under a bean tree at the edge of the garden with a Ken Follett novel. Frank and Compton-King remained at the lunch table on the terrace in the shade of the trellis of vines, polishing off the cheese and the rosé and talking over old times. Adam asked Bella if he could use the phone to try the gite caretakers again. He stood by the kitchen window, phone in hand, listening to the unanswered ringing at the other end. He gazed across the garden to the pool, where Bella and Bruce lay on adjacent sun loungers. They were talking and laughing. They looked perfectly content, perfectly beautiful together. Perfectly perfect. Adam knew he shouldn't care. But he did.

He put the phone down and wandered across the lawn.

Bruce got up and passed him on his way to the house, raising a hand and giving him a casual smile.

Adam sat down on the sun lounger which Bruce had vacated, and glanced at Bella, who was lying with her eyes shut. He let his gaze travel for a few seconds across the satin undulations of her stomach and breasts, then looked away.

Bella opened her eyes a little and looked at Adam. She smiled. 'Isn't it funny, Richard Compton-King and Frank knowing one another?'

'Compton-King knows just about everyone.'

'He's very amusing. I'd like to ask him about when he knew Daddy, but I feel a bit . . . Oh, what's the word?'

'Diffident?'

'Mmm. Sort of.' She closed her eyes again. 'Did you manage to raise the caretakers of the place you're staying at?'

'No,' sighed Adam. 'And I don't suppose there's much they could do, anyway. We'll just have to find somewhere else to stay.' He glanced across at Compton-King, who had his feet up on a chair and looked as though he would happily stay where he was for the rest of the day. 'Time is wearing on. We've got a Logis guide in the car. I'll go and get it.' He stood up.

Bella opened her eyes a little and lifted a hand, stretching it up towards Adam. Uncertainly, Adam touched his fingers to hers.

'It's so nice having you here. Why don't you all stay?' She brushed her fingers back and forth against his. 'For however long you need to.'

Adam put both hands in the pockets of his shorts. No

more of this. It was just a game she liked playing. 'That's kind, but I don't think we could.'

'Why not? Frank and Bruce and Derek are all making a contribution towards the household expenses. You could do the same. What's the point of going off and spending money on a hotel, or trying to find another house? We've got plenty of room, and there's lots to do here. All those silly holiday things, like bikes and tennis and darts . . .' She yawned, let her hand drift back to her side. 'Not if you don't want to, though.'

Time ticked by in the heat, while Adam grappled with this. Much as he wanted to stay, he wasn't sure he could bear watching Bruce Redmond and Bella together.

'Well?' Bella shifted her position, sitting up and leaning her head on one elbow, smiling at him.

'Are you sure?' said Adam. 'I mean, it would be brilliant, but you do have other guests –'

'That's what this place is for. It's much better when there are lots of people around. To be honest, I'm a little bit anxious about what's going to happen when Charlie arrives. No one else understands the situation. You do. You know all about it. It might be a help to me, having you here.'

Adam reflected on this. 'Well –'

'Look, just say yes. I can tell that the rest of your friends would jump at it. For heaven's sake, Frank's found a long-lost friend, Leanne and Emma have got someone else to play with besides each other –' She nodded to where a splashy, noisy game of water volleyball was still going on between the girls and Bruno and Megan, 'and it'll mean you can go off and interview your farmers without having to drag Megan along. I'll bet you'd rather do that on your own, wouldn't you?'

'To be honest, yes.'

'OK then.' Bella lay down once more and closed her eyes. 'That's settled.'

'Seriously?'

'Seriously.' Adam sat down next to Compton-King and plucked a grape from the fruit bowl. 'If we make a contribution to the household expenses, she's more than happy for us to stay here.'

'Highly sociable young thing, is Bella,' remarked Frank, knocking back the remains of his wine. He rose to his feet, his face pink and glossy from heat and wine. 'Think I'll have a little nap now. Glad to know I'll be seeing you both at dinner.' He rolled off in the direction of the house.

'It's bloody decent of her to offer to put us up,' said Compton-King. 'Hasn't she got more people coming at the weekend?'

'That's partly it. I think she hopes having lots of people around will ease certain tensions which might arise with her brother, Charlie.' Adam explained the circumstances of the adoption and Bella's recent discovery of her Deptford family. 'Charlie's backed off from the whole thing, effectively, and I think Bella hopes that putting Charlie and Derek together for a week or so will help the situation.'

'And will it?'

Adam shrugged. 'I don't know either of them well enough to say. They're very alike, in that they both seem to be stubborn buggers, not given to displays of affection.

Anyway, apart from that, Bella thinks that it'll be good for Derek's daughters to have some younger people around. You know, slightly livelier than Frank.'

'If by that you mean my young friend Mr Skeffington-Ancram –' Compton-King lowered his sunglasses from his forehead and gazed through them at Bruno, still splashing around in the pool with Megan and the girls, 'I wouldn't count on him keeping up this clean-cut, big-brother act for long. Surfer Joe is adept at sniffing out illegal substances in any town, in any country, within a matter of hours. Even in rural France. Best if I try to keep him confined to barracks for the duration. Having said that, the boy's got enough Lebanese Red about his person to keep him tranquil most evenings.'

'Megan will be happy, at any rate. I couldn't see myself getting much done on this article otherwise. She's not the easiest of people when she's denied her creature comforts.'

'All worked out very well. Extremely kind of Ms Day. Must go and thank her myself.' Compton-King rose from his chair, pulling in his stomach in preparation for the launch of a full charm offensive. 'Then I'll start earning my keep by popping off to a couple of chateaux and stocking up on enough wine to keep the household ticking over. Fancy joining me?'

'Only if you'll get the air conditioning looked at while we're at it.'

'Good thought. We'll find a local garage and see what they can do.' He headed off to where Bella lay on her sun lounger.

*

After dinner that evening, when the dishes had been cleared away, Adam wandered out into the balmy darkness to where Bruce, Compton-King and Frank were sitting in the garden, drinking wine at the table by the poolside bar. Frank was smoking a cigar, its pungent aroma filling the night air.

Adam sat down, and Compton-King filled a glass and handed it to him.

'I was just explaining to Frank that you're the young man who's writing the definitive biography of Harry Day.'

Frank nodded at Adam, puffing reflectively on his cigar. 'Can't be easy, trying to unravel someone's life, especially someone as admired and revered as dear Bella's father. D'you think you've found out anything about the great man that wasn't already known?'

Adam felt equivocation was called for. 'I'm not entirely sure. It's not so much an unravelling process as a piecing together. It's rather difficult trying to establish the true facts of a life that's only recently been lived.'

'Ah,' Frank nodded, 'the corpse is still too warm.'

'Something like that. I get the feeling it would probably be easier to write the biography of someone who died a century ago.'

'Rotten flesh falls more cleanly from the bone, you mean?'

'Frank, enough of the graveyard analogies, please,' said Compton-King with a grimace.

'It's actually rather a good way of putting it,' said Adam. Then he added, 'My problem lies with people who are still alive, people who knew him. They all have their own agenda, their own reasons for whatever they tell me. It's hard to know what's truth and what isn't.'

Frank leaned back in his chair, tipping the ash from the end of his cigar. 'The dead have no agenda, no excuses. At least, that's my view.' He drew gently on his cigar, the tip glowing red in the darkness. 'I never met Harry Day, but I'll tell you a story I know about him. It was during the years that he was living in India, turning out those Green Juniper books of his. I never went to India, never hit the hippie trail. I was too old by the time that became the thing. But my younger brother travelled there. He went with a schoolfriend when he was just eighteen. I won't name the schoolfriend – he's dead now, anyway – but, like Frank, he'd read the first of those Green Juniper books – what was it called?'

'*Pale Journey*,' said Adam.

Frank nodded. 'That's the one. Anyway, he was an utter devotee of Harry Day. You know what it's like at that age, confusing the man with his art. I think his idea was to find Harry Day and sit at his knee like some kind of supplicant, gazing on the great man's countenance. My brother Gordon simply wanted to travel, and his friend's fixation gave them some sort of purpose, direction. Anyway, Gordon's friend wasn't the only one who wanted to worship at the Harry Day shrine. As Adam doubtless knows, Harry lived in a house up in the hills outside Simla, and the occasional young hippy pilgrim would find his way to Harry's door. He was very hospitable, apparently, and most of them would stay for a couple of days, talking the talk, nourishing Harry's ego, no doubt, and then go on their way. But for Gordon's friend, it was much more than that. He felt he'd found his spiritual home. He wanted nothing more than to become part of Harry's life. We've all been fanatical to that degree, I imagine,' said Frank, glancing at his listeners, 'but most of us just fantasize about it. This boy had actually made his fantasy real. And Harry Day indulged him. The boy offered to help with his work, do research, answer letters, and Harry found that quite useful, since his services were free, so to speak. Gordon didn't want to hang around, though. While his friend was busy insinuating himself into Harry's ramshackle household – there were a couple of young women there, with the same fixation as Gordon's friend – Gordon wanted to move on. He couldn't persuade his friend to leave, so he went off on his own.' Frank paused to draw on his cigar again. 'Two months later he went back. It was perfectly evident to him that his friend had been utterly seduced by Harry Day in more ways than one, enslaved by his own infatuation. He wouldn't leave. It seemed that Harry always had these floating acolytes, sexual playthings, secretaries, gofers, whatever you want to call them. This boy had become one of them. So Gordon set off on some more of his travels – down to Goa, as I recall – and then a few months later he went back again to the house at Simla. By that time Gordon was ready to head home, and he thought his friend should go with him, leave his obsession behind and get a life. But his friend wasn't there. He'd become ill while he was at Harry's – enteritis that turned into dysentery. Harry had grown sick of him by then – he made that pretty clear to Gordon when Gordon showed up – and had had the boy shipped off to a local hospital. Harry wouldn't pay for more than the most basic treatment, didn't try to get in touch with the boy's family, simply discarded him. As he had a right to, no doubt. What was he to this young man, after all? Anyhow, Gordon contacted his friend's family, who hadn't any idea of his whereabouts and were sick with worry, and they wired out money. Gordon and his friend, when he was well enough, went back to Britain. I shouldn't think Harry was ever mentioned. That's about all I know, because Gordon and his friend lost touch, until Gordon heard about ten years ago that his friend had died. He'd become a drug addict, and his end was pretty much the usual squalid story.' Frank took a final drag of his cigar. 'So there's a thing you didn't know about Harry Day.' He crushed the glowing tip out on the grass. 'I've never told anyone that story before.'

There was silence for a moment or two. 'There are often several angles to these things,' said Compton-King. 'That's a third-hand story, told from only one of them.'

Frank shrugged and picked up his wine glass. 'I make no judgements. I only tell you what Gordon knew to be the truth.' He finished the contents of his glass. 'And let's face it, that's all the truth ever can be. One person's version of events.'

'No doubt Adam will want to quote your story,' said Compton-King, glancing at Adam, 'even though it's not exactly to Harry's credit.'

'It's not a question of credit or discredit,' replied Frank. 'If Adam is setting himself up as a biographer, it should all be grist to his mill, as they say.'

Adam set his glass down. 'I don't know. I wish it were

that simple. On the point about Harry's sexuality, I begin to wonder what good it's going to do to publish the truth.'

'What? About his AC/DC tendencies?' Compton-King laughed. 'You've just had corroboration. You can't leave it out. This is painting by numbers, you know, not impressionism.'

'I know. You're absolutely right.' He scratched his head. 'I feel a little odd, having this discussion about Bella's father, while we're sharing her hospitality.'

'I had no idea of any of the things you're talking about,' said Bruce, who had been silent until now. 'Was he really gay?'

'Oh, not entirely. Let's say he liked a bit of both.' Compton-King raised his long arms above his head, stretched and yawned. 'Not that the family cares to acknowledge that.'

'Maybe so,' said Bruce, 'but it's something Adam has a duty to write about, as I see it.'

'Why so?' asked Frank. 'What bearing does it have on anything? I merely ask out of interest.'

Bruce spread his hands. 'People like to know details about their heroes. The more intimate the better. They love it. It's human nature.'

'Even if those details are discreditable?'

'There can be nothing discreditable about a person's sexuality. Not any more.'

'Ah . . .' Frank drew a long breath, and smiled.

'Isn't Frank's story discreditable?' asked Compton-King.

'Well, there's the question. It's up to the reader to

answer it. Adam, as a biographer, merely has a duty to draw as full a picture of the man as he can.'

'And if it hurts people? Living people? If it tarnishes his reputation, diminishes him?' asked Adam musingly.

'That would be down to Harry, and the way he lived his life. Not you.'

'Thanks. Not much comfort.'

'Oh, I'd stick it all in,' said Bruce, getting up from his chair. 'You want to sell your book, don't you?'

'I suppose so.' Adam shrugged, picked up his wine and finished it.

'I'm going in,' said Bruce.

'I think I'll join you,' said Adam. He turned to Frank and Compton-King. 'Goodnight.' He and Bruce crossed the lawn to the house.

'That boy Downing,' said Compton-King, 'is troubled by a conscience.'

'Then he's in the wrong job,' said Frank. 'Shall we open another bottle?'

Bruno and Megan were sprawled on a sofa watching MTV when Adam and Bruce came in, and Derek was sitting at the table, playing solitaire.

Derek glanced up. 'Fancy a hand of poker?'

'Sure,' said Bruce, pulling up a chair.

'No – thanks all the same,' said Adam. He didn't feel like cards. The conversation in the garden had unsettled him. He wandered through to the kitchen, where Bella was clearing dishes away.

'Hi.' She gave him a smile.

'Hi. We left the serious drinkers in the garden.' Adam picked up a cloth and began to dry glasses.

'That wasn't a bad dinner that Derek and Frank cooked, was it?' said Bella.

'Very impressive. I gather it's down to Compton-King and myself tomorrow night?'

'Correct. Can't run a household without rotas.'

'Don't forget I'll be out most of tomorrow talking to an ex-pat farmer. I rang him before dinner and fixed it up.'

'Where is their farm, exactly?'

'Near Lauzerte, about fifty kilometres from here.'

'Oh, I know it. I think they have a market on Tuesdays, so you can pick up some things. We could do with some more melons. We're getting through half a dozen a day. And cheese. We need more cheese.'

The sound of laughter and banter came from the card table. 'Derek and Bruce seem to be getting along pretty well,' said Adam.

'Apart from table tennis, they've discovered they share a passion for poker and football. They both support Chelsea.' Bella put the last of the plates away and closed the cupboard.

Adam nodded. 'Well, I suppose it's good that your brother and your boyfriend get along together. It all helps.'

Bella stared at him in mute surprise as recollection dawned on her – Adam, like the rest of the wide world, thought that she and Bruce were still an item. He had no idea what she and Bruce had been up to. Why should he? As far as he was concerned, she and Bruce were here together, as a couple. She gave a little laugh and laid a hand on Adam's arm. 'Look, there's something I should tell you . . .'

'What?'

'Well,' she said slowly, apprehensive as to what his reaction might be, 'Bruce and I – we haven't really been going out together. In fact, he's not interested in me in that way at all. Or vice versa.'

Some seconds elapsed as Adam tried to make sense of this. 'According to the gossip columns, you've been inseparable for the past two months.'

'Yes, well . . . the gossip columns are why we did it. Why we pretended. It was a publicity stunt, if you like. Bruce's idea. He thought it would raise our profiles, help the play. When the play closed, we just assumed – well, that the gossip would go away, die a natural death. But you didn't know. Sorry.' She gazed at his features, trying to read his expression, and failing.

Adam took a deep breath. 'I see. Well, I have to say you made a very convincing couple.'

'Didn't we? It was good fun while it lasted, actually. I wish all love affairs were as easy. Anyway, I'm sorry if – that is, I'm sorry you were misled.'

'Wasn't that the general intention?'

'I don't want you to go on thinking –'

'Bella, what I think doesn't really matter.'

'I see.' She paused. 'I just happen to remember a certain night, when you came to my flat, and – Well, it seemed like it might have mattered. Once.'

There was a long silence, then Adam said, 'In some ways I'm sorry that you and Bruce weren't for real.'

'Why? Because it would all have been a lot simpler?'

'Something like that. Yes.' Before she could say anything, he added, 'I'm tired. It's been a long and surprising day. I really should get to bed.' He paused. 'I hope you're not regretting inviting us to stay.'

'No, of course I'm not.'

She was so close, so tantalizingly close, her expression so troubled and vulnerable, that he couldn't resist bending to kiss her lightly on one soft cheek. 'Goodnight,' he said, then turned and went upstairs.

Adam lay in bed, thinking it through. It was getting worse and worse. Either he was hopelessly infatuated with Bella, or it was the real thing. He had no idea. He only knew that he was going through the motions with Megan, and it had to stop. He had to tell her. He could almost hear himself doing it. *Look, I'm enormously fond of you* . . . At what point did the depth of love evaporate into the shallowness of 'enormously fond'? Well, it had happened. Regard, affection, friendship – none of these was any substitute for what he felt for Bella, witnessed by his unutterable relief at the fact that she was not having a passionate affair with her leading man. He couldn't go on ignoring it. What was he going to say to Megan? How on earth was he going to do it?

After a while he heard the sounds of laughter and muted conversation as people broke up and went to bed. He very much hoped that Megan wouldn't be feeling especially randy. He closed his eyes as she came in and moved around the room, getting ready for bed. She slid in next to him, but did nothing more than lean over and kiss him gently on the shoulder. Adam pretended to be asleep.

13

The residues of guilt were still with Adam the next morning, driving him to ask Megan if she'd like to come with him on his expedition. She lay in bed, watching him as he dressed.

'No, I don't think so, thanks. I'd rather stay here.' She stretched luxuriously. 'I've always got Bruno to keep me company.'

'Bruno, eh? You mean his interests extend beyond MTV and the Cartoon Network?'

'Don't be rude about him. He's good fun.'

'You just like him because he's a rock star. Or thinks he is.'

Megan smiled. 'Are you jealous?'

'Are you joking?' Adam slipped on his shoes, lifting the curtain to glance out at the early sunshine. He picked up his bag, checking through his notes. 'See you some time this afternoon. Enjoy your day.'

'I will.' Megan rolled over in the empty bed, smiling at her own thoughts.

Compton-King, heading off for an early-morning walk, saw Adam getting into the hired Renault.

'For God's sake, take the Bentley. It's just sitting there. You'll have more fun than in that thing.'

Adam glanced at the Bentley's gleaming contours. 'You mean it?'

'Of course.' Compton-King fished in his pocket for the keys and chucked them to Adam. 'Go on. Enjoy your day.'

Adam had to admit that it was quite a buzz, driving through the French countryside in Compton-King's luxurious silver Bentley. It handled beautifully, the engine purring smoothly and richly along. Now that the air conditioning had been sorted out, any previous sense of animosity towards the car which he may have harboured on the journey down had entirely vanished. He loved this car deeply. It attracted admiring stares, and a small group of children even cheered as he passed through a village, making him feel like a pre-war English adventurer.

Once the novelty of driving the Bentley had subsided a little, he tried to address the two new certainties which had lately made themselves apparent to him. The first was to do with Megan. Since they had come to France with Compton-King, something had happened. And it had happened to both of them, not just himself. He could tell by her voice, her expression, that the faint hostility which had sprung up at the disastrous gite had solidified in some way. Perhaps it was being thrown together with so many new people, or the change of scene. Whatever it was, they were going to have to address the fact that their relationship had altered to the point where it was going nowhere. She knew it, and he knew it. It was now a question of acknowledging it.

And then there was Bella. The certainty of his feelings for her had been brought home to him by the light-headed sense of relief he had felt when Bella had told him there was nothing between her and Bruce. So, was he in love with her? Something of that order. But the world was probably stuffed with men who thought they were in love with Bella Day. He remembered that feeling when she had sat down next to him in the church at Harry's memorial service. Immediate and suffusing infatuation. But the bliss of infatuation, in Adam's experience, was predicated on unattainability. And yet she was, and always had been, utterly vulnerable and entirely available. He could have slept with her nine hours after they'd first met. On the occasion when he'd gone to her flat when she'd just learned about her adoption, she was well on the way to seducing him (with his hesitant cooperation, admittedly), until Charlie had rung and interrupted things. He had no reason to believe that she wanted anything from him other than a casual affair. She lived entirely for the moment. Instant gratification of a casual whim. For him, that wouldn't be enough.

These thoughts occupied him, in a circular and unresolved fashion, all the way to Lauzerte, and he was rather relieved to be rid of them when he reached the Whittingtons' farm. There he spent the day in the company of Roger Whittington and his wife, listening to their story of how they had given up the hard and unprofitable business of farming in North Yorkshire for a new life in south-west France. They showed him round the farm, the thirty acres set aside for hard wheat for pasta, the barley and sunflower fields, the carp and tench ponds, the rows of vines from which they made their own wine, the chestnut trees whose fruit they marketed, and the few acres of oak trees for firewood. The apparently idyllic life was not without its hardships, and they had suffered setbacks and a couple of hard winters early on, when the renovation of the farmhouse was still in progress and temperatures had dropped below fifteen centigrade, but now they seemed content, well settled in with their French neighbours. By mid-afternoon, when he left, Adam knew he had the beginnings of an excellent feature. In the next few days he would pay a visit to the other farmer he had previously contacted and get the thing written by the end of the week.

On the way back he drove up the winding road that led to the medieval hill town of Lauzerte. He had a beer at one of the cafés on the edge of the town square, then wandered around the shops and market stalls, picking up food for the evening. He felt more relaxed than he had done for some weeks, glad to be entirely on his own. That was the problem with his present existence in London. He wanted his life back, his quiet, undisturbed hours, without having to consider anyone else's needs. Then he might be able to work out the confusion of his thoughts and feelings. When he had loaded the melons and chickens into the boot of the Bentley, he walked to the stone wall edging the steep drop down from the road and stood contemplating the gently undulating fields, dotted with farmhouses, broken by distant roads and poplars, stretching to the horizon. He could understand why the Whittingtons were happy with their life, and why Bella loved the house here so much. He stood leaning on the warm stone, constructing a fantasy world, one in which his biography made him enough money to jack in journalism, so that he could turn to full-time writing, and come and live here with Bella in one of the narrow, quaint houses in the streets behind him. Some dream. Whatever the two of them were destined for, it wasn't likely to be that. After a while he walked to the car and drove back to Montresor, no clearer in his mind about any aspect of his life.

Megan was lying in the hammock with her book when Bruno wandered over.

'Fancy a walk?' he asked.

'Where to?' Megan shaded her eyes with a hand as she looked up at him.

'This place I found down the road. It's an old mill, or something. I passed it the other day, went to have a bit of an explore. Completely deserted. Ideal place for a quiet smoke.'

'OK.' She closed her book and got out of the hammock.

'Where's lover boy?' asked Bruno, as they walked down the dusty track.

'Gone to interview some farmers.'

Bruno nodded. 'There it is, just past those trees.' He turned off the track and began to cross the field. Megan followed him. The sun was high and hot.

The millhouse was old and abandoned, the river which had once turned its wheel now no more than an idle stream. Bushes and trees had grown up around it, almost hiding it from the road. Bruno and Megan sat down in the shade, leaning their backs against the warm stone wall. Bruno rolled a joint and lit it. After a few seconds he handed it to Megan. He watched as she drew in the smoke, then took the joint from her.

They sat in the peaceful warmth, the air bright with the lazy sound of crickets, vividly aware of their isolation and closeness. Megan closed her eyes and smiled. It was nice, feeling like this, thoughts floating fluidly and easily, like smoke. This was like being seventeen again. Hiding from the grown-ups. Bruno made her feel like that. Like nothing mattered. Like tomorrow was far away, and you could do what you liked, be totally irresponsible. That was suddenly the way she wanted to be.

'You know what?' Bruno's voice broke the tranquil silence.

'What?'

'You don't want to stay with Adam.'

'No?'

They held one another's gaze for a few seconds. Then, as she'd hoped he would, Bruno kissed her. It was so easy, and she didn't feel guilty about Adam at all. Maybe she wouldn't ever have to. Maybe everything would go back to normal when they got back to London. Maybe this had nothing to do with reality at all, sitting here with her back against a warm wall, being kissed. Whatever. She was simply happy to stay here doing it for the rest of the morning.

The household settled into a pattern. Bruce and Derek, when they weren't continuing their rivalry at the dart-board or table tennis table, were happy to sit around in the sun, drinking cold beers and discussing the coming football season. It was a revelation to Bella to hear Bruce talk about anything other than work, or the lack of it, in the interminable way that actors usually did. Compton-King spent his time either lying on a sun lounger conducting business calls on his mobile, or roaring off in the Bentley with Frank to conduct lengthy *dégustations* at various local vineyards. Leanne and Emma played in the pool, watched satellite television, went out on expeditions on bikes, and spent long, worshipful hours with Megan, looking at her make-up and listening to her talk about her job and the fascinating world of a grown-up media girl. Bruno, when he wasn't lying in the orchard smoking dope, played games of volleyball in the pool with the girls, or lay around tanning his lean, young body a pleasing shade of golden brown and talking about himself to Megan, who seemed drowsily content to lie on a sun lounger next to him and listen. Adam spent much of his time writing up his feature; it was Bella who suggested he use the annexe to do that, and he installed himself in the bedroom there, tapping away at his laptop at a table overlooking the orchard. He used his ostensible work on the biography, too, as a pretext for long, solitary walks, or hours spent swaying in the hammock at the edge of the lawn, pen and paper on his lap. Sometimes Bella would come and lie on a rug on the grass a few feet away, flipping through a small stack of film scripts which her agent had sent her. The warm hours would drift companionably by, and occasionally Adam fed his fantasy by closing his eyes and pretending that no one else existed in this world of sunlight and cricket-song except the two of them.

Cowardice, a wish not to upset the delicate balance of things, prevented him from talking to Megan about where they were going – or rather, not going. There seemed no present need. In the rare moments which they spent alone together, they managed to maintain sufficient kindness and affection to hold things together. But the focus of their concentration was no longer on one another. They made love only once in that week, neither knowing that the other didn't much want to.

Early on Thursday evening, Charlie rang Bella and told her he would be arriving with Claire the next day. When she put the phone down, Bella went out to the garden where Adam lay in the hammock, reading.

'Charlie's arriving tomorrow.' She sat down cross-legged on the warm grass and began to pluck at it.

'Did you tell him Derek was here?'

She shook her head. 'I suppose I was afraid he would react badly. I mean, this house is all about him and me and Dad. You know the way he thinks about the Kinleys. He might regard Derek being here as a kind of intrusion.'

'I thought you saw this as the perfect way to bring them together.'

'I did. Now I'm not so sure.'

'Well, what's the worst that can happen? They've got to get to know each other some time.'

'Not according to Charlie, they don't. That's just it. He'd rather pretend that Derek and the rest of it didn't exist.'

'Relax.' On impulse, Adam reached out a hand and stroked Bella's blonde head lightly. 'They're both civilized human beings.' She looked up and smiled in such a way that Adam felt his heart tighten. He took his hand away.

'When he sees how well you and Derek get on, things will be OK. He'll make an effort.'

She gave a thoughtful smile. 'We are getting along pretty well, aren't we? I think the secret is not to expect any more than that. I did, at the beginning. You know, after the time we first went to Deptford – I thought we would experience some kind of instant, magical bonding. But it doesn't work like that. It's the same with Leanne and Emma. They're just people I have to get to know, gradually. Not that I get on with them as well as Megan does. She seems very good with teenagers.'

'Possibly because she shares a lot of their preoccupations. The world of PR can be somewhat infantilizing.'

'Ouch.'

'No, I'm not being unkind. It's merely an observation.' Adam hesitated, then said, 'The truth is, I've realized in the past week or so that Megan and I aren't going to go the distance. She knows it, too. At least, I think she does. I don't quite know how it happened. Funny how suddenly relationships fall apart.'

Bella gazed at him. She was careful not to register any particular emotion at this news. Why should she feel guilty that he and Megan were breaking up? It was nothing to do with anything she'd done. It had been bound to happen. And now he would be available, hers for the taking. 'You haven't talked to her about it?'

'Not yet.' He shook his head. 'I think we both know it's not a good idea to try to deal with it here and now. We'll sort it out when we get back to London, I suppose.' He glanced down at Bella, trying to read her expression as she continued to pluck at the grass. But it was unfathomable. He swung his legs out of the hammock and stretched. 'Anyway, I'd better not loaf around here much longer. My turn to clean up the barbecue.' She looked up at him and he smiled. 'Don't worry about Charlie and Derek. Remember, it's their problem, not yours. Let them deal with each other on their own terms. I'm sure it'll be fine.'

She sat and watched as he walked across the grass, wishing she shared his confidence.

Charlie and Claire arrived after lunch on Friday, rolling up in their hired Renault. Bella greeted them on the driveway.

'I hope you don't mind there being so many people here,' she said, kissing them both. 'The numbers just built up by accident. Adam Downing and three of his friends had a house not far from here which turned out to be a complete disaster, so I said they could stay here.'

'A bit ultra-hospitable of you,' said Charlie, who looked hot and grumpy. 'Who else is here?'

Bella led the way in, carrying a couple of Claire's many bags. 'Frank and Bruce – two of the people I did the Orton play with.'

They went upstairs and Charlie led the way to his room. As Claire went in ahead of them, Bella put a detaining hand on Charlie's arm. 'And there's someone else here, someone I very much wanted you to meet.'

Charlie stared at her. 'Who?'

'Derek. Derek Kinley. I invited him here with his daughters.'

'Oh, no.' Charlie's expression went dead with disbelief. 'Oh, no.'

'Charlie, what are you so afraid of? You have to meet him some time!'

'I can't believe you've done this. Why didn't you tell me yesterday that he was here?'

'Because you wouldn't have come!'

'Damn right I wouldn't! I told you, I wanted all that left alone! Why do you have to be such a bloody busybody? Why do you have to involve me?'

'Because he's your brother! Because you *are* involved, whether you like it or not! All three of us are!'

Claire came to the door. 'Charlie, this is absolutely marvellous –' She saw his expression. 'What's the matter?'

'You haven't told her, have you?' said Bella. Charlie shook his head. She felt stricken with pity for him. Why was this all so hard for him to face up to? She took her hand from his arm and said gently, 'Look, I'll leave you both to – to get yourselves sorted out. I'll see you later.'

Half an hour later, Claire came downstairs. Bella was in the kitchen alone, peeling prawns for the evening's risotto. She glanced up as Claire came into the kitchen.

'How's Charlie?'

Claire sat down and watched Bella in silence for a moment. 'He's just told me all about you two. About the adoption, everything.'

Bella nodded. 'Right. He should have told you weeks ago.'

'That's what hurts me. Why didn't he?' She turned pained eyes on Bella.

'I don't think you'll like it when I tell you.'

'I wish someone would. Charlie won't.'

'He thought you might think less of him.'

'Less of him?'

'Because he's not who you thought he was. Who *he* thought he was. Charlie's ashamed, he thinks you won't like the idea that he comes from a working-class family in Deptford, that he's not really the son of a famous poet and novelist, that his brother is actually a garage mechanic. In case you hadn't noticed, Charlie has always set great store by who people are, their backgrounds, which school they went to. It's been bred into him. Not surprisingly, he thinks you care about such things, too. Thinks you might not be so keen on marrying him.'

'How could he possibly think that?' Claire's eyes were bright with tears.

'Perhaps it was something you said along the way. Perhaps it's the way you always harp on about the awfully good set of chambers Charlie's in, and the people you know, and the smart dinner parties you go to, and how fantastic your wedding's going to be, and the great big house you're going to live in, as though those are the only things he's good for. Maybe that's where he got the idea.'

Claire rose from her chair, flaring up in anger. 'That is so unfair! And what about you? What's so different and great about you? Turning up at every event going, just hoping to get your photo taken, hoping people will recognize who you are, a second-rate actress who happened to have a famous father!'

'Well, that's where you're wrong. My father was Len Kinley, a complete nobody, a waster and a sponger who apparently never did a good thing in his life, and who talked my mother into giving Charlie and me away in exchange for money. I never got the chance to know him, but I might have loved him if I had. Who knows? The point is, that's the truth, that's who I am, and I don't care what anyone thinks. Poor Charlie does.'

'And you think that's my fault?'

'Not entirely.' Bella sighed, suddenly feeling weary and contrite. 'I'm sorry. I didn't mean to be hurtful. I'm sure you love Charlie anyway, whatever. But I know he was worried about how you'd react.'

'Oh, God . . .' Claire picked up a cloth and dabbed her eyes. 'How could he possibly think it mattered to me? The only thing that concerns me is Charlie, and how he is right now.'

'And how is he?'

'He's just so – so panicky about it. About meeting his brother.'

'It's not easy to come to terms with a past you never knew you had. I've done it, so I know. Charlie hasn't, and he should.'

'Maybe all this is why he's been so difficult over the last few months.'

'Has he?'

'Oh, God, he can be awful. He's moody, he drinks too much . . . He can be quite hard to love sometimes. But I do.' Her gaze met Bella's. 'I genuinely do. Not just those things that you think matter so much to me.'

'Well –' Bella picked up a cloth and wiped her hands, 'I think you'll agree with me that it's important that he meets his brother, and that he begins to accept what's happened, and who he is. What he hasn't realized is that it isn't going to change anything very much. You're who you are. The past is what happened. In many ways, it's helped to reinforce my idea of Cecile and Harry as my parents, knowing they weren't really. That probably sounds stupid.'

'No, it doesn't.' Claire hesitated. 'I'm sorry about what I said before.'

'It doesn't matter. I wasn't very nice either. The important thing is Charlie. I'd like you to help him see that it'll be much better for everyone if he meets Derek and gets to know him. They're very alike.'

'Are they?'

Bella nodded. 'Why don't you come out and meet him?'

Frank and Compton-King had gone out for the day. The others were at the table by the pool, sitting over the remains of lunch. Bella introduced Claire, and left them all together. As she went back into the house, Adam came after her, catching up with her in the hallway.

'Where's Charlie?'

'Still upstairs. Not in a very great frame of mind, I shouldn't think. He hadn't told Claire anything about the adoption or the Kinleys. He's only just told her now.'

'Look, I should have realized this before – you can't just expect to throw them together in front of all the others. Charlie and Derek, I mean.'

'Oh, for God's sake, I don't need you to remind me what a mess I've made of this! And don't tell me what to do!' She put her hands to her face and began to weep. 'This is all so horrible! It's not going to work, and I so wanted it to!'

Her sudden outburst of anger was the last thing he expected. 'Hey, come on, come on . . .' Adam laid his hands on her shoulders. Entirely against his better judgement, he drew her close to him and kissed her hair, stroking her back. It was, he told himself, the best way to comfort her. She wept against him for a few moments. He had never intended that she should lift her face to him to be kissed, merely hoped she would. And she did. He leaned back against the wall in the cool dimness of the hall, holding her against him, as close as was possible, drowning in the pleasure of kissing her. Any doubts he had had about whether or not he was in love with her disappeared. Nothing had ever been so perfect, physically and emotionally – that knowledge, that pure and certain happiness, welled up within him.

Bella drew away at last, but he held on to her, speaking her name in a whisper, over and over, brushing the tracks of her tears from her cheeks with his fingers.

'I'm sorry.' She gave a little shudder, as though suddenly chilled. 'I'm always doing this. It's a comfort thing.' She released herself gently from his embrace. 'I have to go up and see Charlie.'

Adam stood, still leaning against the wall, for some moments. How could she do that? How could she bring him to a pitch of such total certainty, and then just . . . dismiss it as an aberration, a little needy thing of hers? He couldn't go back outside, not in his present state of arousal. He walked into the living room, sat down on one of the sofas amid a clutter of Gameboys and magazines, and closed his eyes.

*

'Charlie?' Bella tapped on the door and opened it, putting her head round. Charlie was lying on the bed, arms folded behind his head, staring at the ceiling.

She came in, closing the door behind her, and sat down on the edge of the bed.

'I've been talking to Claire. I didn't realize you hadn't told her till now.' Charlie said nothing. She stretched out a hand and rubbed his arm affectionately. 'Oh, Charlie, I'm sorry if I've made a pig's ear of things. I did it with the best of intentions, honestly.'

Charlie sighed, took one hand from behind his head and laid it over Bella's. 'I know you did. It's my problem, not yours.' He looked at her closely. 'Have you been crying?'

'Just a little.'

'I'm sorry if I was angry. I'm just such a bloody coward about all this.'

'There's nothing to be frightened of. Derek's lovely.'

'I feel a hell of a sight better having told Claire. I should have done it ages ago.' He sat up and swung his legs round so that he was sitting on the side of the bed next to Bella. 'The thing is, you've been quite fearless about all this. From the beginning you've faced up to it and got your head round it. You went and found them, met them. It's as though I've been dragged along in your wake.'

'I'm so sorry. I didn't think it through properly. I suppose if it had just been you on your own, you would have been happy to leave it all alone. I shouldn't have assumed –'

'Stop blaming yourself. The point is, here we are, and I've just got to get on with it.'

'Look, you can't just come down and meet him in front

of everyone. It's not fair on either of you. I'll send Derek up here.'

Charlie was quiet for a few seconds, then said, 'OK. Tell him to bring a beer up with him.'

Bella went downstairs. As she passed the living room, she didn't notice Adam on the sofa. He had vanished from her thoughts. Halfway across the lawn she called to Derek, who rose and came over.

'Charlie's up in his room. He'd rather not meet you with everyone else around. D'you want to go up?'

Derek nodded. 'Which one is it?'

'Third room on the left, first landing. He asked if you'd bring him a beer.'

'Sure.'

When Bella had gone, Charlie got up from the bed and went to the window, curious in spite of himself. He stood at the edge of the curtain, not wishing to be seen, and watched as Bella crossed the lawn. He saw the tall man with thinning blond hair detach himself from the group by the swimming pool, and walk over to Bella. That was Derek, his brother. A curious sensation of recognition and fearful pleasure filled him. He was big, muscular, like Charlie himself. Prop-forward material, thought Charlie. He watched Derek cross the lawn and enter the house below him, then went to the door and opened it, waiting. After a few moments he heard feet on the stairs, and Derek appeared, holding two bottles of beer. He stopped briefly at the top of the stairs when he saw Charlie in the doorway. Then he came towards him and held out one of the beers. 'Hello, mate.'

'Hi,' said Charlie. He took the beer and stood back to allow Derek to enter the room, then closed the door.

By the poolside, the girls cleared up the dishes from lunch, while Bruce and Bruno went for a game of tennis. Claire had gone for an exploratory walk, leaving Bella to sit anxiously alone, waiting, a half-read book on her lap. She saw Adam emerge from the side of the house through the French windows, heading towards the annexe. He didn't glance in her direction. She was about to call to him, but stopped herself. All in good time. That kiss in the hallway had told her he was hers for the asking, any time she wanted. The trouble was, she almost didn't want to let anything develop between them, half-afraid it would be destined to go the same way as all the other affairs. And she so badly wanted it to be different. She felt tears prickle unexpectedly against her eyelids, and wiped them away. Everything was getting to her lately.

She picked up her book again, but was unable to concentrate. She kept looking at Charlie's window, as though expecting it to tell her something. Then Derek came out of the house. She watched anxiously as he crossed the lawn towards her. He and Charlie had hardly been together for fifteen minutes.

'Where's Charlie?'

Derek sat down on a sun lounger next to her. 'Taking a shower.' He took a swig from his half-finished beer.

'How was it?'

Derek shrugged. 'Not easy.'

'In what way?' Bella closed her book and looked at him tensely.

'I dunno. Just not easy. I thought I might, like, give him a hug or something, but you could tell that wasn't on. He's not like you.'

'No. No, he's not.'

'So I said something about how this was a big thing for both of us. And he said yeah. And so I said, tell us a bit about yourself, we need to get to know one another.'

'And?'

'And he said he was a barrister, and told me a load about what he did. And he asked me about my business. So I told him. And then I asked him if he'd met Joyce, and he said no, he hadn't. Then he asked me if I'd ever played rugby, and I said no. Then I couldn't think of anything to say, and neither could he, and he said he was going to take a shower, he'd see me later, nice meeting me.'

'It doesn't exactly sound like a great emotional reunion,' said Bella.

'It was like standing around at some party talking to someone because you have to, when they don't much want to.' Derek took another swig of his beer. 'That was what it was like.' He glanced at Bella. 'I'm sorry. He didn't exactly make it easy. I would have tried to make it all a bit more friendly, more brotherly and that, but he wasn't having any.' He smiled thoughtfully. 'He's good, though, isn't he? I always used to want a brother.'

'Not a sister?'

'Yeah, well . . .'

'Don't worry. I'm joking. I understand. I just hoped it would be better, that he'd be really glad to meet you at last. I mean, all those years . . .' Her eyes filled with tears again, the tensions of the day rising up in her and spilling over.

Derek leaned over and hugged her, holding her. 'He'll be all right. You've handled all this a lot better than he has. I reckon he's still confused. Don't worry. Don't worry. It'll be all right. Just give it time.'

From his window, Charlie stood looking down, rubbing his wet hair, watching the pair of them, trying to fathom his feelings, wondering jealously whether Bella could finish up caring more about this long-lost brother of theirs than she did about him.

Compton-King and Frank came back late in the afternoon in high spirits. They unloaded the spoils of their trip from the boot of the Bentley, in the shape of more wine and a considerable quantity of groceries.

Compton-King presented Bella with a bottle of parfum des violettes de Toulouse. '"To throw a perfume on the violet is wasteful and ridiculous excess,"' he declaimed. 'Actually, it wasn't terrifically expensive, but we thought you'd like it.'

'If the French police catch you driving over the limit they'll take your car away,' said Bella.

'I didn't drive,' said Compton-King. 'Frank did. Sober as a judge. Now –' He pulled items from carrier bags and spread them on the kitchen table. 'Cheese, fruit, bread, all that heart could desire and more. And two legs of lamb, which I shall personally marinade. Special recipe.' As Megan and Claire put the purchases away, Compton-King began to assemble olive oil, balsamic vinegar, herbs and wine for his marinade, and unwrapped two large butterflied legs of lamb. He glanced up as Charlie came into the kitchen. 'Ah! Bella's brother. We haven't met. Richard Compton-King. Hello!' He extended a hand. Charlie shook it. 'Bloody good of you to let us stay in your fantastic house.'

'Not at all,' said Charlie. He smiled, recognizing something in Compton-King that cheered him up and made him feel more at home. He indicated the lamb and the marinade ingredients. 'Can I give you a hand with that?'

'Of course! Clear the decks, everyone. Charles and I are going to create dinner.' He picked up a bottle and a corkscrew. 'We'll start with a glass of red wine, shall we?'

Half an hour later, while the dinner preparations were underway, Frank and Bruce began to dispense cocktails of their own devising at the poolside bar.

'What's in it?' asked Adam, when Frank offered him one.

'Well, a gin base, plus Cointreau, a dash of fresh orange juice, and a high note of – what was it, Bruce?' Frank turned to Bruce, who was agitating the cocktail shaker in a frenzy.

'Brandy,' replied Bruce.

Adam took one to Bella, who was lying in the hammock with her book. She had just put her book down, as the light was growing too dim to read by, but when she saw Adam approaching she quickly picked it up again.

Adam offered her a glass. 'No thanks,' said Bella. 'I've had Frank's cocktails before, and they're always lethal. Besides, I've got the beginnings of a headache.' She turned to her book again.

Adam lingered, wanting to talk, to broach what had happened before in the hallway. 'Charlie and Compton-King seem to have hit it off.' The sound of Compton-King's voice raised in song, followed by hoots of laughter, came from the kitchen.

'Like calling to like,' said Bella, without looking up. 'Public schoolboys bridging the generation gap. A couple of glasses of wine and the bread rolls start flying.'

Adam crouched down next to the hammock so that his face was level with Bella's. 'What happened earlier –'

'Don't. It was my fault. I'm sorry. I don't want to mess up things between you and Megan.' She closed her book and got out of the hammock. 'I'm going to help the girls put things out for dinner.' And she had crossed the lawn before he could say anything else.

The girls lay the table, lit candles, and Adam and Bruce manned the barbecue while Megan and Claire brought out salads and bread. Then everyone sat down to dinner. Bella watched Charlie uneasily as the evening progressed. He and Compton-King had consumed a good deal of wine during the preparation of the lamb – which, basted with its special marinade and barbecued, was adjudged a great success – and throughout the meal they kept up an effortless, raucous banter. It was amusing and infectious, and everyone seemed to enjoy themselves, but as Charlie got louder and boozier, Derek appeared to grow more withdrawn, as though he couldn't quite find his place in the public-school hilarity. He didn't drink much, and when it was time for the girls to go to bed he disappeared with them into the house and didn't return.

Bella, noticing his departure, went in after a while to

see what had become of him. She found him watching French football on television.

'Aren't you coming back outside?'

'Nah. Not my scene, really. I'm not on their wave-length.'

'Charlie's had too much to drink, I'm afraid. It's all largely defensive, the way he's behaving. It's probably got a lot to do with you, having to meet you.'

'Yeah?' Derek shifted round on the sofa and raised a hand to hers. 'I told you maybe it wasn't a good idea, me coming on holiday with your friends.'

'Oh, Derek, that's rubbish. It's been fine up until tonight. Just Charlie behaving like a hooray. Compton-King's too pissed to see what's going on.'

'Well, anyway –' He looked up as Bruce came in.

'Fancy a hand or two?' said Bruce. 'It's getting too bloody silly out there.'

'Absolutely.' Derek switched off the television and they sat down together at the table in the corner.

Bella went back outside to the noisy dinner table. Frank and Compton-King were singing, swaying together, Charlie banging time on the table with his hands. Megan and Claire looked on in amusement, Claire stifling yawns every now and then. Even Adam seemed to find it uproariously funny. Bruno had long since sloped off to the orchard with a joint to contemplate the stars and his future recording career.

Bella came up behind Charlie and put what she hoped was an unobtrusive hand on his shoulder. 'Charlie, can I talk to you for a moment?'

Charlie looked round. 'Yeah, sure thing.' He got up a

little unsteadily and left the table, following Bella down the steps to the darkness of the garden. Claire watched them go.

'Look, Charlie,' said Bella, when they were out of earshot, 'it isn't going to work if you carry on like this.'

'What d'you mean?'

'You and Derek. You haven't spoken to him all evening. All you've done is get drunk and carry on with Compton-King like you were still in the sixth form.'

'He's a bloody good bloke! I can't help it if my so-called brother doesn't share our sense of humour. Don't know what makes them laugh south of the river, I'm afraid.'

'That is so rotten of you! If you weren't so drunk, you wouldn't say a thing like that. But that's your answer to everything these days, isn't it? Get pissed and hope it'll all have gone away by the morning. Well, it won't have. Derek will still be here, and you're going to have to make more of an effort. He wants to get to know you, Charlie! He likes you.'

'How can he bloody well like me?' Charlie threw his arms wide and stumbled slightly to one side, then steadied himself. 'He doesn't know me! I don't know what to talk to him about! We stood there this afternoon like a couple of prats!'

'Well, I really like him, he's my brother as well as yours, and I want you to try a bit harder!'

'Oh, yeah.' Charlie nodded. 'Yeah, I know you like him. He's a bit of a novelty, isn't he? I'll bet he hasn't got any of my faults. I've heard it all from you before, Bell, how great he is. I bet you wish I was more like him. Fuck it all, you wish I *was* him, don't you?' His eyes suddenly brightened with tears as he leaned drunkenly towards her, yelling, 'Don't you?'

'Sshh! Stop it! Stop shouting!' she hissed. 'Why do you have to feel so sorry for yourself all the time? Why can't you think about other people? God, there's no use talking to you when you're like this. I'm going in. And tell that drunken rabble to keep it down. Emma and Leanne won't be able to get to sleep.'

She went off round the side of the house to avoid the party on the terrace, and through the French windows into the living room, where Derek and Bruce were absorbed in their game of cards. She said goodnight to them and went wearily upstairs to her room. She sat in bed brooding for some time, envying Bruno his blissed-out solitude in the orchard. She could do with some of that. The business of bringing Derek and Charlie together wasn't working. Charlie didn't intend to make it work. At this rate, he and Derek were going to finish up as good as strangers. By behaving the way he had this evening, he'd hoisted up the class barrier and was standing firmly on the other side of it. It was horrible. Still, as Adam had said, it was their problem. It was up to both of them to sort it out between them over the next few days. Not that she thought they possibly could.

When Bella left him in the garden, Charlie stood unsteadily at the edge of the lawn. He heard laughter from the terrace, but had no desire to go back there. Bunch of boozers. The brief conversation with Bella had left him utterly fed up. He just wanted everything to be the way it had been when he and Bella had come on holidays with the old man. He didn't want to stay around here with these people. He wanted it to be the way it was fifteen years ago. Christ, he was pissed . . . Best thing was to go for a walk, clear his head, think things through. He set off across the garden into the orchard, stumbling over a low wall and on to the track which wound down to the village of Sainte Levroux. The moon gleamed palely on the silent melon fields as Charlie made his erratic way, tacking from one side of the track to the other, miraculously avoiding the ditches.

Reaching the sleeping village, he wandered purposelessly through the streets. A cat skittered out of the darkness and across his path, almost causing him to fall over. The fright moved him to childish, drunken tears. He sobbed to himself as he walked along, going nowhere, hating himself. Nobody knew. Nobody could ever understand how much he had wanted, from the moment he had first set eyes on his brother, to be able to show him what it meant to him. He had wanted words, a means of expression for his overwhelming feelings. He had a brother. He had looked at him and been moved, dazed by the realization of what fate had done. But he hadn't the means to say it. Instead, he'd been offhand, snobbish and downright patronizing. Out of nowhere and into his memory came the image of a boy called Jewison, a younger boy at school on whom Charlie had developed an intense crush. Charlie had adored Jewison from afar. Then one day he'd found himself standing next to him in line, and Jewison had said something to him, something friendly and pleasant. Even now, as he leaned drunkenly against a stone wall, Charlie felt burning shame at the memory of how, in his confusion and infatuation, he had been able only to articulate some contemptuous response, lofty and dismissive. He had loathed himself for weeks afterwards. He felt that way now. His behaviour with Derek had been in complete contrast to his own feelings and desires. He badly wanted his brother, wanted to know him, create some manly, brotherly warmth, whatever all that shit was . . . As he thought these things, Charlie snuffled in a maudlin way. Then he looked round, trying to work out where he was. He realized he was cold. He had come out in just his shirtsleeves, and now his drunkenness had ebbed sufficiently for him to appreciate the chill of the night air. He decided he would go back.

As he turned, he caught sight of the church on the other side of the square. He had always liked the Sainte Levroux church. It was small and comforting, without austerity, its Catholic contents ranging from the beautiful to the tawdry, and Charlie, in his unhappiness, was drawn instantly to its familiarity. He crossed the square and tried the handle of the wooden door. It was open. He stepped inside, inhaling the musty perfume of age and incense, feeling his way forward as his eyes grew gradually accustomed to the dim interior. He walked down the flagged aisle, bumped against the side of a pew, and lurched into a stone font with a brass domed lid. The lid shifted with his weight, and he grabbed its cross-shaped handle to stop it clanging to the floor. Ssshhing in admonition, he righted the cover and looked around. The ghostly gleam of the moon through the stained-glass window above the altar painted everything with an eerie light, and he sighed. A serene and drunken peace descended upon him. He walked forward, narrowly missing kicking over a number of small brass pots containing flowers which had been placed on the altar steps. He mounted the shallow steps and felt his way along a row of wooden seats. He knew of old the carved gargoyle faces on the misericordia, and smiled to himself in the dark. He flipped one down and tried to sit on it, but he slipped forward, his feet rucking the thin carpet which covered the stone flags behind the altar. The carpet gave him an idea. He knelt down. It smelt dusty and kind, and so he lay on it, and contrived to roll himself up in it a few times, grunting. He lay there, cocooned, enjoying its canvas-like warmth, not quite sure what he was doing there. He stared into the darkness, his thoughts groggy and confused, and fell asleep.

14

Bella stayed in her room, reading through one of the more promising scripts for a second time, listening to the sounds of the party breaking up and people going to bed. When at last the house seemed silent, she went quietly downstairs to make herself some tea. The events of the day had unsettled her, and she knew she wouldn't sleep for a while.

There was a light on in the kitchen, and there was Claire, in a long cotton robe, sitting at the table, sipping from a mug.

'Can't you sleep?' asked Bella.

Claire shook her head. 'I was waiting for you and Charlie to finish your talk.'

'Charlie? I left him out in the garden ages ago.'

'Oh – I thought he must be up in your room with you.'

'No. When did you last see him?'

'I haven't seen him since he left the dinner table to talk to you.'

'I'll bet he's fallen asleep on the sofa,' said Bella. 'It's not unknown.'

But the living room was devoid of Charlie.

'Is the car still there?' asked Bella. 'He was pretty upset when I left him. He might have gone off somewhere.'

'He can't have. He was too drunk to drive anywhere, surely.'

Bella switched on the outside light and looked through the kitchen window. The hired Renault was still there.

'My guess is that he's gone off to one of the guest rooms and crashed out,' said Bella. 'I'd let him sleep it off.'

'You're probably right.' Claire sighed and ran a tired hand through her hair. 'I wish he didn't think that getting drunk was the answer to everything.'

'I'm not sure it was intentional. I think Richard Compton-King set the pace on the red-wine front, and Charlie felt honour bound to keep up.'

'Maybe. Anyway, see you in the morning.'

'Night.'

Bella made some tea and sat sipping it, thinking about Charlie and Derek.

Charlie opened his eyes, and the first thing he was conscious of was the chill silence of his surroundings. Christ, he was cold. Cold and stiff. He moved his joints against the folds of the carpet, panicking a little, uncertain where he was. Then he remembered. He blinked, his gaze focusing on a woodcut of Saint Sebastian hanging above the choir stalls. He lay for a while, encased in carpet, staring at the saint's tortured body with an acute sense of empathy, the arrows in the flesh echoing the searing pain of his own hangover. Bloody local wine. Worst thing in the world. How on earth had he finished up here? He remembered coming into the church and thinking the carpet looked supremely comfortable – which just showed how off his face he must have been – but he had no clear recollection of walking from the house to the village. He turned his head, and found himself staring at an electrical socket in the back of the altar, just below the cloth, with the words '*micro autel*' printed above it. He yawned hugely, and even this movement made his head thud atrociously. He hadn't felt this hellish in a long time. He prised his elbows free and wriggled into an upright position, pushing back the carpet and rubbing at his legs. He heard a faint sound, and, peering out from behind the altar cloth, he saw an old woman with a bucket and duster at the far end of the church, going about her duties. As quietly as possible, he kicked himself free of the carpet and rearranged it flat on the stone flags. After resting on his hands and knees for a moment or two, breathing heavily, he pulled himself stiffly to his feet, leaning for support on a large candlestick at the side of the altar, and tried to straighten his clothing and hair. God alone knew what he looked like.

He tried to tiptoe down the steps, hoping to head out the side door unnoticed, but the cleaner turned and saw him. He raised a hand and smiled, and called out 'Bonjour!', then gave his surroundings an interested glance, in the hope of being taken for an early-morning sightseer. The cleaner nodded and smiled at him, bemused, and he went out of the side door into the cobbled square and the early-morning sunshine.

Despite getting to bed late, Bella woke early, her mind fogged with the residues of a dream involving Adam and Charlie. She lay there for some moments, trying to recall details, but they had ebbed away. Wondering how Charlie was, she got up and went through the house, looking in each of the spare rooms. There was no sign of him. And no sign of any of the neatly made beds having been slept in. On her way back down the corridor she met Claire.

'Did Charlie come to bed?' asked Bella.

'No – I thought you said he must have gone to sleep in one of the spare rooms.'

'Well, he hasn't. There's no sign of him.' They looked at one another in alarm.

Derek, who had got up for an early swim in the pool, met them as they came downstairs. 'What's up?'

'Charlie's gone missing,' said Claire.

'I had a bit of an argument with him in the garden last night. It was after you'd gone in,' said Bella. 'I left him out there, and that's the last I saw of him. He didn't go to bed, and there's no sign of him anywhere in the house.'

'What about the annexe?' said Derek.

'Oh – of course.' Bella gave a little gasp of relief. 'He must be there.'

She went out and crossed the lawn, then mounted the short flight of stone steps to the annexe. She knocked on the door and looked in. The big room was empty, the bed unslept in, Adam's laptop and papers lying on the table under the window.

She ran back to the house. 'He's not there!'

'Oh, God,' said Claire. 'Where can he have gone?' Her voice was panicky.

'He's a big boy. He can look after himself,' said Derek, about to prepare some coffee.

'He was too pissed to know what he was doing. He could be lying in a ditch somewhere!' said Bella. 'We have to go out and find him!'

Bella and Claire raced upstairs in agitation to get dressed. Derek sauntered outside, looked round speculatively, then set off down the track past the melon and sunflower fields, glancing in ditches for a prone figure, trying to conjecture what he himself might have done in Charlie's shoes.

Charlie walked through the village by the back streets, thankful that no one was around. He glanced at his watch. It was a little before eight. There was always a possibility that he could slip back into the house undetected, but not much of one. He'd bluff it out, say he'd slept in a spare room.

It was when he reached the turning from the main road on to the track leading up to Montresor that he saw Derek. The disused millhouse lay a hundred yards or so from the track, next to a narrow river overhung with trees, and Derek was walking slowly around it. Charlie hesitated, about to head up to the house, then changed his mind and walked across the field to his brother.

Derek glanced up at Charlie in mild surprise. 'Morning.'

'Hi.' Charlie hoped he didn't look as bad as he felt. 'What are you doing down here?'

'Looking for you.'

'Oh . . . right.' Charlie glanced diffidently around, then back at his brother. They stood, hands in pockets, warily contemplating one another, conscious of their similarity of stance and feature.

'I was trying to work out what was going through your head last night, what I'd've done if I'd been you,' said Derek.

'How so?'

'You know – bit pissed, upset after arguing with Bella.' Derek shrugged. 'I reckoned you must have gone for a walk to cool off, then ended up falling asleep somewhere. I was trying to follow in your tracks, so to speak. Thought you might have finished up in there.' He indicated the millhouse.

'Ah. Right. Well, you didn't follow far enough. For some reason, which doubtless struck me as good at the time, I walked into the village. I went into the church and fell asleep behind the altar.'

'What!' Derek laughed. 'Why?'

'I don't know!' said Charlie. He walked a few paces and sat down on the trunk of a partially uprooted oak tree. 'Like I said, it seemed like a good idea at the time.' He put his head in his hands. Wretched as he felt, he realized suddenly that he was glad to be here alone with Derek, who seemed big and safe at that moment. Solid, sane. Charlie himself felt insubstantial, shaky.

Derek walked over slowly and sat down next to Charlie. 'We didn't get off to a very good start yesterday, did we?'

'Not really.'

'It's a weird situation. The thing Bella and I have found is – not to expect too much.'

'I didn't. I don't. I have no expectations. That's the point. I've been trying to avoid everything.' Charlie took his head from his hands and sighed. 'I took the line that it would be better to pretend. Pretend it had all never happened. Pretend everything was just the way I'd always supposed it was.'

Derek nodded. 'I know what you mean. I know what you mean exactly. That first time Bella came to our house . . . When she'd gone, I was in a hell of a state. I finished up wishing she'd never come, that I'd never known. It was bad, I tell you.' They both sat silent for some moments. 'But here we are. What we've got to do is help each other.'

'Help each other?'

'You tell me your story, I tell you mine. That's what Bella and I have been doing. It's a start. It's what people do – people who don't know one another.'

At that moment they heard the sound of a car coming down the road. They looked up and saw the hired Renault go past, Claire at the wheel, Bella next to her. Charlie and Derek were screened from the road by the foliage of the tree on which they sat. Neither of them moved.

'They're looking for you.'

'I suppose so.'

'Not much we can do about it.'

'I didn't mean to worry anyone.'

'Do them good.'

After a few seconds Charlie nodded and said, 'So, you tell me your story. Right from the beginning.'

Three-quarters of an hour later, as they drove back up the track, Claire and Bella caught sight of Derek and Charlie walking ahead of them.

'Charlie!' squealed Bella.

'Oh, thank God!' said Claire.

At the sound of the car engine, the two men stopped and turned. The car pulled up next to them and Bella rolled the window down. 'Where have you been? We've been absolutely frantic!'

'Sorry,' said Charlie. 'I walked into the village last night and kipped in the church.'

'You didn't! Charlie!'

'Don't worry. Nobody found me. No local scandal's about to erupt. I was walking back when I met Derek, looking for me.'

'Well, I thought you might have walked into the village, but I assumed you'd asked Marianne and Pierre to put you up. We've just been there. We scoured the entire village! How come we didn't meet you on the way down?'

'Don't know.' Charlie gave a shrug. 'I didn't think of going to Marianne and Pierre's. Probably just as well, given the state I was in.'

'Well, quite. You look absolutely awful.'

Charlie's glance shifted to Claire, who was sitting silently behind the wheel. 'Sorry,' he murmured.

Claire shook her head. 'Idiot,' she said mildly.

'Come on,' said Bella. 'Get in. You look as though you could do with a bath and some hot coffee.'

'No,' said Charlie. 'You go on. I'll walk up with Derek.'

Bella glanced at Derek. Derek smiled, and she smiled in return. Then she rolled up the window and they drove on.

Bella didn't get the chance to speak to Charlie alone until later that afternoon, when she found him sitting under the bean tree with a book. Claire was sunbathing by the pool with Megan and the girls.

Bella crossed the lawn and sat down on the grass next to Charlie's chair.

'How are you feeling now?'

'Better. Fragile, though.'

'You and Derek had a talk this morning, I gather? You seemed OK at lunchtime.'

'Yeah. Yeah, we had a talk.' Charlie was silent for a moment. 'He's a good man.'

'Yes, he is. He's very –'

'Solid.'

'Yes, he is. And he's funny and nice.'

'Good big-brother material.'

'Right.' Another silence fell.

'It's strange,' said Charlie after a moment. 'I thought learning all about these people, our parents, Len and Doreen –' He paused. 'Len and Doreen. God, imagine what they'd've called us . . . Anyway, I thought finding out about them would make me feel different. I think that's what I was afraid of. That I'd turn into someone else.'

'I know.' She hesitated, then added, 'I imagine it's changed both of us.'

'I suppose. But, I mean, I'm still essentially *me*.'

'Oh, essentially very Charlie.' Bella laughed.

He leaned his head back and sighed. 'I've been crucifying myself these past few months.'

'I know. I've done a lot of soul-searching, too. No doubt a psychiatrist would say it's all very understandable.' She glanced up at him. 'Does that mean you'll try to lay off the booze?'

'Oh, now, hold on a minute.'

'I mean, can you try not to drink quite so much? It worries Claire. It worries me.'

Charlie looked uncomfortable. 'Oh, fine. I know. I know I've been – Well, I suppose I've been trying to get away from this thing, trying to block out finding out I was adopted. Alcohol seems to help.'

'Does it? Well, maybe now you're coming to terms with things, you won't have to rely on it quite so much.'

'I was talking to Derek about that, actually. He was telling me he went through a bad period around the time he got divorced. Started drinking a lot, nearly lost his business . . .'

'He never told me.' Bella looked somewhat piqued.

Charlie smiled. 'Stuff we have in common, you see. Brothers.'

'Huh. Well, if he can knock it on the head, so can you. Anyway, I'm glad you're getting to know one another. It makes me feel vindicated.'

Charlie stretched out a hand to Bella. 'However well I get to know him, I can never feel as close to Derek as I do to you.'

'I know.' She squeezed his hand. 'Shared history. Being related to someone is only part of the story.'

Charlie hesitated, then said, 'I have an awful confession to make.'

'What?'

'I'm rather glad that they – the people who had us, gave us away – aren't around any more. I don't think I could have –' He stopped. 'What I mean is, if I could bring anyone back to life, it would be Harry, not either of our real parents. Is that bad?'

Bella's eyes pricked with tears. 'No, I don't think so. It's just the way things are.'

'When I get back, I'll go and see Mum. I haven't been very pleasant to her of late.'

'I think that's a good idea. It's been as bad for her as for the two of us. Three of us.' She stood up. 'Don't laze around here too long. It's your turn to make dinner tonight.'

As they all sat around after dinner that evening, Frank pulled some leaflets from his pocket. 'I picked these up in the village today. All about local fêtes and activities.' He flipped through them. 'Apparently there's an animal fair tomorrow in Sainte Levroux. It *is* Sunday tomorrow, isn't it? I lose track of time.'

'It's quite good fun, the animal fair,' said Bella. 'They have it every year. All the farmers from the area bring in cattle and goats and horses to be judged, and there are chicks and rabbits, things like that. The girls would like it. You would, too,' she added, nodding at Compton-King. 'They have a local wine-tasting, and a big communal lunch in the square, all laid out on trestle tables. Only a few francs a head. Sorry – euros. Why don't we all go?'

There was general agreement that it would be a novel way of passing a Sunday. Next morning at ten everyone got ready to walk down to the village, except for Bruno, who had sloped off to the orchard with some dope and his mouth organ.

Adam came into the bedroom to pick up his watch, and found Megan lying on the bed.

‘Do you mind if I don’t come with you?’ she said. ‘I’m feeling really lousy. I think I may have had too much sun yesterday.’

Adam sat down on the bed next to her. He had scarcely so much as embraced her or kissed her these past few days. They were hardly ever alone together, which was probably just as well. Something in her very attitude as she lay there seemed expressive of the distance which had grown between them lately. He was sure she was as conscious of it as he was. Maybe now was the moment to say something . . . then again, maybe not. ‘D’you want me to stay here with you? I’m not sure that looking at a lot of Aquitaine cattle is my idea of fun.’

‘No, you go. I just want to rest, honestly. Please – I don’t want to spoil your day.’

‘You’d hardly be doing that.’ But he rose from the bed. ‘If you’re sure you’ll be OK here on your own.’

‘I’ll be fine.’

He bent and kissed her forehead. ‘See you later.’

The normally quiet village was bustling with people, the main roads fenced off and the streets lined with stalls. In the square stood long trestle tables and benches in preparation for lunch, and at the far end workmen were putting the finishing touches to a wooden stage, with microphones and a sound system, in readiness for the local jazz band. A large dusty space behind the tourist office, normally used as a car park, had been turned over to livestock for the day, with a central area fenced off as a judging ring. All around stood rows of cattle, pens of goats, horses and ponies with their manes and tails specially combed and plaited for the occasion, and cages of rabbits and poultry. Adam wandered round with the others for half an hour or so, but without great enthusiasm. He'd spent the previous two days thinking about the biography, trying to work out ways of dealing with the business of Harry's secret sex life. As he stood staring morosely at some goats a couple of ideas came to him – ideas he rather wanted to put down on paper.

He glanced at his watch, and decided he'd had enough of the animal fair, anyway. Unlike Leanne and Emma, he could only spend so long looking at baby chicks. He caught sight of Compton-King's unmistakable tall figure near the judging ring, and went over.

'Listen, I'm going back to the house. I left Megan there – she's rather off-colour and I feel bad about leaving her on her own.'

'OK.' Compton-King gave a nod. 'See you later.'

Adam walked the half-mile or so back to the house, thinking about the biography. He was at the point now where he longed to be back in London and getting on with it. He was grateful for the time and distance which this trip to France had lent him. He was able to see now that any misgivings he'd had about the family's reactions to his revelations had been entirely misplaced. It wasn't his business to worry about Cecile and Briony and the rest of them. Or even Bella, come to that. Harry had lived his life without scruples, and that was the way Adam had to write it. There should be no absolution for fathers who deceived, evaded responsibilities, tried to lead lives that didn't belong to them – Harry, Len, his own father . . .

What was it Tolstoy had said? 'The one thing necessary in life, as in art, is to tell the truth. Truth is my hero . . .' Not the easiest of principles by which to live.

He came in view of Montresor, and tried to shake off the seriousness of his thoughts. High-minded notions apart, in purely commercial terms he was on to an absolute bloody winner with this biography. He couldn't afford to leave anything out. He was still debating whether he was going to use Frank's story about the boy in India, unsubstantiated as it was, and one to which there might be many sides. Harry himself had never mentioned it, and there was nothing about it in the journal which he had kept, on and off, during his time in India. Adam had been able to track down only one of the various young women who'd formed part of Harry's household in Simla, and she'd never mentioned any boy. She still seemed to regard Harry with devoted reverence, so maybe she wouldn't want to remember any such incident. Still, it was worth talking to her again. And to Frank's brother; that would have to be arranged.

Preoccupied with these thoughts, Adam crossed the orchard and went up the stone steps to the annexe and opened the door. It was a moment of acute embarrassment, particularly for Bruno and Megan, who were entirely naked, but too strenuously and intimately involved to notice Adam's presence immediately.

'Oh, bugger,' said Bruno, when he saw Adam standing in the doorway.

Megan just looked at him. It crossed Adam's mind that she looked the sexiest he had ever seen her, naked, hair all over the place, in bed with another man. He felt neither outraged nor upset. Just surprised and rather stupid. He had absolutely no idea how he ought to be reacting, so he decided not to.

'I just came to get a couple of things,' he said, going over to the table and picking up some of his papers, while they watched him wordlessly from the bed. Then he went out, closing the door behind him, and walked back towards the house. He stopped on the terrace, aware of the unpleasant thudding of his heart. Of course he cared. It was a supremely nasty experience to find your girlfriend in bed with some other bloke, even if it was Bruno, and even if you had been intending to end the relationship anyway.

He put his things down on the table near the pool and sat down. After several moments of contemplating his own position, he began to wonder just what was going through Megan's mind. How would she deal with this? He sat with his notes, unable to formulate any of his previous thoughts about the biography. They had fled entirely. He watched a small lizard scuttle up the white-washed wall of the house near the roses, then disappear behind the shadow of a shutter. He looked up as Megan approached. She was wearing Bruno's shirt over her bikini, and her expression was remarkably composed, he thought.

'I didn't want you to find out this way,' she said. The note of apology in her tone was edged with the threat of defiance. She was ready for a scene, if he wanted one. He most definitely didn't.

'How did you want me to find out?'

'I was going to tell you. It's only over the past week or

so that I've realized – well, you know yourself that things haven't been right between us recently.'

'So you decide to hop into bed with the nearest available man?'

'That's got nothing to do with it.'

'I'm afraid it has.'

'These things happen.'

'How true.'

'I wasn't going to say anything until we got back to London. Nothing happened till today. I didn't want it to. Not till I'd told you.'

'Quite convenient, you feeling unwell and wanting to stay behind, when everyone else was going out.'

She was silent for a few moments, then she sighed and sat down. 'If you want me to feel ashamed – well, all right, I do. I didn't know how to let you know, not while we were here . . . I thought you might pick up the signals.'

He looked at her. She was handling this very dispassionately, quite unexpectedly so. 'I did,' said Adam. 'I was going to say something as well when we got back to London. I hadn't quite realized you'd be making a preemptive strike.'

'I told you. Nothing happened till today. Nothing important.' She sat with her hands clasped between her bare knees, looking contrite. He could read relief in every aspect of her body language. 'Bruno says he's going back to London. I think it's best if I go with him. We can get a taxi to Bordeaux. I'll ring and see if there's a flight this afternoon.'

'That's very organized of you. What would you like me to tell Bella?'

‘I don’t know. Just thank her for a great time. I’ll send her some flowers or something when I get back to London. You know, to say thank you. It’d be embarrassing if either of us stuck around . . .’

‘It might,’ agreed Adam.

She stood up. ‘Right . . . I’m sorry, things happening like this. I’ll move my stuff out of the flat when I get back.’ She hesitated, looking down at him. ‘We had quite a good time, didn’t we?’

‘Not bad. We should congratulate ourselves on ending things in such a civilized way.’

She smiled shakily, looking a little moist round the eyes. Adam was not unfamiliar with the female inability to leave any break-up untouched by sentiment. A kind of emotional embroidery carried out at the last moment. To forestall it, he looked back fixedly at his notes and said, ‘I’d go and ring the airport, if I were you.’

When she was gone, he fell to wondering what exactly she would expect of Bruno once he was back in his natural hedonistic environment. Not too much, he hoped, holiday romances being what they were. Then again, he told himself, it simply wasn’t his problem.

The others came back around mid-afternoon. No one noticed the absence of Megan and Bruno. Adam, however, thought it best to mention to Compton-King that his protégé was heading back to London.

‘Surprised he stayed as long as he did,’ said Compton-King, who was lounging in a chair beneath an umbrella by the poolside bar. ‘Doubtless his stash ran out. At least he got some proper food and a dose of Vitamin D. Boy generally never sees the light of day, so far as I can tell. I'll have to be getting back myself, in a day or two. Mucho business to attend to. What about you?'

'I've done what I came to do. Ready when you are.'

'What about Megan? She seems to be rather enjoying herself.'

'Ah, well . . . Here's something I didn't mention. She's flown back to London with Bruno.'

Compton-King raised his sunglasses. He gave Adam a penetrating and inquisitive stare. 'As in –?'

'As in – I went to the annexe to pick up some papers and found them in bed together.'

Compton-King gave a low whistle. 'God, I'm sorry. I was the one who brought him along. I do feel somewhat responsible.'

'Don't. It was pretty much over between us, anyway.'

Compton-King settled his glasses back on his nose. 'Randy little bastard.'

'It takes two.' After a moment Adam asked, 'So, when do you want to go?'

'Where are we now? Sunday? What about Tuesday?'

'Fine. I'll go and give Bella advance warning.'

Bella was in the hammock with her script. She glanced up as Adam came across the grass.

'I like this one,' she said. 'It's a good part. Not very big, but it's a step closer to Hollywood.'

Adam sat down on the grass. 'Is that what you want?'

Bella let the script flop on to her chest and sighed. 'I suppose. Ultimately. I'd be lying if I said I had a great and abiding love for the English theatre. That's not my particular pose. I like being in movies.'

'What's the part?'

'Girlfriend of a small-time drug dealer. The drug dealer becomes a police informant, but she doesn't know this, and – well, it's complicated, but quite funny. As I said, a small part, but it's got some good lines.'

'So you'll be off to Hollywood.'

'I don't know. We'll have to see.'

Adam lay back on the warm grass and gazed upwards, narrowing his eyes against the sunlight breaking through the shifting leaves. 'Megan and I have split up. She's gone back to London.'

It was several seconds before Bella spoke. 'That was a bit sudden.'

'Not so very. I told you, we hadn't been getting on for a while.'

'Did you have a major row?'

'No, nothing like that. It appears she's found true love with Bruno –'

'Bruno!'

'– so they've flown back together.'

'Whew.'

'She says goodbye and thank you and all that stuff. Anyway, it breaks the party up somewhat, and I've decided to head back with Compton-King on Tuesday.'

Bella put her script to one side and leaned over the edge of the hammock, so that she was looking directly at Adam. 'It's been fun having you here. I'm sorry you have to go so soon.'

'I've finished my article. I have to get it in by the end

of next week. Besides, I need to do some work on the biography. I want to see your stepmother and tie a few loose ends together, and then I can start turning it into a proper book. I still haven't talked to you about your father, not properly. Nor Charlie. Maybe that's best left till we all get back to London.'

'Oh, I don't know. Now is probably as good a time as any to tackle Charlie. He's been having heart-to-heart talks with Derek, exchanging childhoods. I'd catch him while he's in confessional mode, if I were you. You'll have all tomorrow.'

'You could be right.' He glanced at her. 'What about you?'

She crinkled her eyes. 'I think I've probably told you all there is to tell, one way or another.'

'I still need to get it on tape.'

She nodded. 'I was thinking – would you be interested in having all the letters he wrote me while I was away at school, and while he was in prison? There are quite a lot of them.'

'I had no idea. Yes, I'd love to see them.' He hoped she didn't have the idea that there might be some sort of trade-off, that he might submit to pressure not to publish certain details of Harry's life in return for a few letters, interesting though they might be.

'Just so long as you tell me which bits you're going to use, if any. Just so that I know.' She smiled. 'I do trust you.'

To this, Adam found he could say nothing.

The next day Charlie sat down with Adam at one of the small tables on the lawn beneath the trees and talked about his father. It was unexceptional stuff – childhood reminiscences, recollections of teenage holidays with Harry, occasional incidents and arguments between father and son. Adam knew he would use only fragments by way of illumination of Harry's character as a father, but he could tell from the way that Charlie talked that the exercise was greatly therapeutic for him.

'It's funny,' said Charlie, when they seemed to have exhausted most of his memories, 'but knowing that I'm adopted throws light on some of the things Dad did, the way he was . . . At least, I think it does. Maybe I'm wrong. Maybe it makes no difference. He was never very authoritarian, never particularly paternal, in any strict sense. Treated us like equals. Maybe that's why my friends liked him so much. He used to spend a lot of time talking to them. He liked me to invite them over in the holidays.'

'Really?'

'He seemed to enjoy having teenagers around, said he found our conversation amusing. There was one friend in particular, James Gifford. His people lived in Venezuela, so he used to spend most half-terms with us.'

'Where was that?'

'At Gandercleugh. Bella and I spent Christmas, Easter and half the summer holidays with Mum, and the rest of the summer and all our half-terms with Dad. He really liked James. I remember I had to spend one half-term in hospital with appendicitis, but he invited James down for the holiday on his own, anyway.'

Adam told himself not to be so damned stupid. It could have been nothing untoward. Just friendly behaviour towards one of his son's friends. None the less, he found himself saying, 'Have you kept in touch with James? It might be interesting to hear what he remembers about Harry.'

'I haven't seen him since we left school. I'm sure I could put you in touch with him, though.'

'That might be interesting,' said Adam.

Bella strolled across the lawn. She was wearing denim shorts and a linen blouse so thin that Adam could trace the outline of her breasts. She smiled at Adam and Charlie. 'You realize you've been out here for two hours?'

'It's been very useful,' said Adam. 'I think we're about done.' He leaned forward and switched off the tape.

Charlie rose and stretched. 'I'd better go and find Claire. See you later.'

'Bye,' said Adam. 'And thanks.'

Bella sat down in Charlie's chair.

'How did that go? Was he forthcoming?'

'Very. Tell me, did any of your friends spend the holidays at Harry's house when you were a teenager?'

'Not that I can think of. Why?'

'Charlie said Harry liked having teenagers around, that he would encourage Charlie to invite schoolfriends to Gandercleugh for the holidays.'

'Mmm. Sometimes. They were always Charlie's Uppingham friends, though. Dad used to like getting a group of them together to talk about politics and art, get some great heated discussion going. He was always very interested in what young people were thinking and doing. Perhaps he just found boys more stimulating than girls. He never talked much to my friends.'

'Charlie mentioned one boy in particular, someone called James Gifford. Do you remember him?'

'Oh, James. Yes, I had a real crush on him,' laughed Bella. 'He was *very* good-looking, looked just like George Michael. He came to Gandercleugh quite a lot. I think his parents lived abroad. He and Dad got on very well. I remember getting jealous of the fact that James used to go off and have long walks and conversations with Dad, but not with me. Charlie found the politics and art bit rather boring, I think. Why do you mention James in particular?'

It didn't remotely cross her mind, Adam realized. He felt a pang of conscience. 'Just that I thought he might be someone else to talk to. You know, how a young person outside the family saw Harry.'

'If you can track him down. I don't think Charlie's seen him in a few years.' She stood up. 'I'm going into the village to pick up some things for tonight. Richard's cooking a special going-away dinner of *magret de canard*, by the way, and I rather think he expects you to be on hand in the kitchen.'

'Right, I'll go and don my apron. See you later.'

Dinner, which was entirely of Compton-King's devising and extremely good, went on until very late. Adam, knowing he had to be up early the following day to make the journey home, didn't drink a great deal. He felt a certain diffidence in the company of the others. Megan's abrupt departure with Bruno had left him feeling somewhat self-conscious, and he was more subdued than usual. He was preoccupied, too, by thoughts of the biography, anxious for the opportunity to talk to Compton-King alone about it. That would come tomorrow in the car, he supposed. He sat quietly, observing the dynamics of the little party, struck by the difference a few days had made. Charlie's abrasiveness had mellowed. His conversation, though boisterous as ever, now included Derek, took account of him, and he and Derek and Bruce seemed to have formed an easy triumvirate. Bella had achieved some sort of rapport with Derek's daughters, and she was making a distinct effort to get on better with Claire. Adam suspected that her original animosity towards Claire had been born out of nothing greater than jealousy that her beloved twin brother had found someone to marry, and no doubt that would sort itself out with time.

Compton-King proposed a toast to Bella and Charlie, and then announced that he proposed to mark his departure with a midnight swim. Everyone else helped to clear up the dishes, then Emma and Leanne went to bed. Bruce, Derek, Charlie and Claire retired to the house for a game of poker, while Frank took himself off to the bar at the end of the pool to drink a nightcap and shout encouragement to Compton-King, by now on his eighteenth length.

Adam left the kitchen and went into the garden, where he found Bella snuffing out the candles on the dinner table. Without their soft illumination the night air was ghostly and dim.

'I just wanted to thank you, in case I don't see you in the morning,' said Adam. 'I've had a great time.'

'Except for Megan leaving.'

'Up to and including that.'

She said nothing for a moment, just picked at some wax on the table. 'It's been a strange week,' she said at last. 'Not at all the holiday I'd expected.'

'I hope having extra guests hasn't been a problem.'

'Not at all.' She smiled.

'At any rate, it's been a success as far as Derek and Charlie are concerned.' Small talk, standing there saying something for the sake of it.

She nodded. 'I think so. I hope so. I don't know where it goes once we all get back to London. I just hope they both continue to make the effort.'

'I think they will. I think it's done them both a lot of good.'

'I suppose we should all be grateful to you, really. You were the one who brought it about, with your spirit of journalistic enterprise. Just think how it might have been if you hadn't found out. Charlie and I could have gone on forever not knowing we had another family, thinking what was false was true.'

'Would it have been so false?'

'Of course. Don't you think so?'

'Well, I have very confused notions about truth at the moment, and its uses. I'm just glad it's worked out for you.' He paused. 'Anyway, I'd better get to bed.' He nodded in the direction of the pool, from which shouts and splashes could be heard. 'I have a suspicion that I'm going to have to do most of the driving tomorrow. I'm not sure Compton-King's going to be in a fit state.'

Bella laughed. 'He's wonderful.'

He gazed at her for a moment, then said, 'So are you.' He leaned forward and kissed her gently. She responded, putting a hand around his neck and drawing him towards her. It lasted only a moment.

'Goodnight,' said Adam, and left her standing in the darkness of the garden.

Adam went upstairs, cleaned his teeth, threw his belongings into his bag, then undressed. He took his most recent notes to bed with him and lay there, reading. There was a light knock at the door, and he looked up. Was he expecting her? He wasn't sure. Perhaps it was just the recollection of that first time she had come to his room that made it seem so natural. He watched her come in. Unlike that first time, she was still dressed. She closed the door and leaned against it.

'Déjà vu,' said Adam.

'Not quite,' said Bella. She crossed the room, sat down on the edge of the bed, took his notes from his hand and laid them on the bedside table.

'This definitely rings a bell,' said Adam.

She leaned forward, and he drew her into his arms and kissed her thoroughly and absorbedly for a long time.

When at last they drew apart, she asked softly, 'Why don't you send me packing? What's so different about this time from the first time?'

Adam contemplated her face, drew a line with his finger along each of her cheekbones. 'The difference is that I didn't know you before. Though I probably loved you.'

'Even then?'

'Even then. From the moment you came into your father's study, and ever since.'

'I think it took me a bit longer.' She smiled, gazing into his eyes.

She loved him. Every ambiguous moment, every uncertain instant, was made secure in those few words. He kissed her again.

'Back then,' said Adam, 'I was worried that I might become just another one-night stand.'

'And now?'

'You tell me.' He unbuttoned the top two buttons of her blouse and slid his hands against the delicious warmth of her breasts, making her shudder.

'I promise,' said Bella, as he began to undress her, 'that I'll still respect you in the morning.'

Adam woke at six to the beeping of the alarm on his mobile. Bella lay in the crook of his arm. She opened her eyes drowsily as he stirred.

'Oh, don't go yet,' she murmured.

'I have to. Richard wants to make the journey in one day.' He untangled himself gently from her warm embrace and sat up. He gave his head a shake. 'God, I could have done with a bit more sleep.'

She smiled. 'Got to make the most of these one-night stands, you know.'

'Don't make me feel insecure.' He leaned down and kissed her, then got out of bed.

She lay watching as Adam dressed. 'Do you remember what you said that night I came to your room at Gandercleugh?'

'Not with any great clarity. I was a bit busy trying to get the better of my natural inclinations, as I recall.'

'You said you had hoped to elevate me to pedestal status and leave me there.'

'Did I say that?'

'Mmm. Did you prefer me as some kind of fantasy?'

'Hardly. It was fun while it lasted, but the real thing is much better.' He smiled and bent to kiss her. 'I'll call you when I get back to London.'

Compton-King wasn't easy to rouse, but his bags had been packed the previous day, and he and Adam were in the car by six forty-five, and well on their way to Limoges by nine. Adam was happy to drive, entirely occupied by his own thoughts, while Compton-King lay reclined in the passenger seat, his Panama tipped over his eyes, sleeping off his hangover.

They stopped briefly for lunch then headed off again, this time with Compton-King at the wheel.

'Not a bad ten days. My batteries feel totally recharged. Must send the lovely Bella a thank-you present when we get back.'

'I got more work done than I expected,' said Adam. 'Apart from the article, I got Charlie Day down on tape.'

'Any startling revelations?'

'Only inadvertently. Then again, it depends on one's interpretation.' And Adam told Compton-King what Charlie had said about his schoolfriend, using Charlie's words as exactly as he could recall them, and then what Bella, independently, had said. 'Possibly it was all perfectly harmless,' concluded Adam. 'That story of Frank's was still relatively fresh in my mind, though, hence my train of thought. I wouldn't have put Harry down as a molester of teenage boys.'

'You never know. Honesty compels me to say that I wouldn't put it past Harry. A great man, but not a nice one. Whatever Cecile may think, I don't believe old Harry ever changed his ways. Just went well under cover.' He gave Adam a glance. 'Can you follow it up?'

'Charlie's schoolfriend? I doubt it. Even if I managed to track him down, I could hardly ask him if he'd been molested at the age of fifteen, or whatever.'

'No, I can see that.'

'And suppose I did find out that Harry had done something like that – where would it take me?'

'That would depend.'

There was a pause, then Adam said, 'D'you know what I think?'

'What?'

'I think Harry wanted to get the biography underway while he was still alive in the hope that I wouldn't find out these things after his death. That I wouldn't go to much trouble to carry on researching, because he'd given me so much material. For instance, of all the people he put me in touch with, he never mentioned you. I reckon he only gave me the names of people he regarded as safe. Not Cecile, one imagines, but he knew there was no way round that. He must simply have hoped she would want to protect herself as much as him.' He sighed.

There was silence for some moments. Then Compton-King said, 'I realize now that I never knew the real

Harry. He was an amusing friend, excellent company, but I think I always knew deep down that he simply wasn't much of a human being.' He sighed. 'I don't know how much you know about the circumstances surrounding Joe's death, Halliwell topping himself, all that horror . . .'

'Just what I've read.'

Compton-King nodded. 'No one knows the truth, of course. No one ever will. But Harry was instrumental. I know that now, looking back. I remember being there on a couple of occasions in the spring of that year, 1967, when Harry did a pretty good job of belittling Kenneth, reminding Joe that he was the real playwright, and Kenneth just a hanger-on. Harry knew how much Halliwell envied Joe's success – even resented it, in a funny way – and worked that up. Mischief-making. Anyone could see Kenneth wasn't well, that he was depressed, but Harry still goaded him. Whatever sense of worthlessness, or envy, desperation – call it what you like – drove Halliwell to do what he did, Harry was part of it.' He turned and glanced at Adam. 'We're all bound up with other people, all part of their fate, but the fact remains that Harry deliberately damaged people.'

Adam reflected on this for some moments. 'The question that occurs is whether one's perception of an artist as a moral being alters one's view of their work. You know – Wagner's music, that kind of thing. And the answer seems to be that it does. Whether or not you think it should is neither here nor there, it just does. It's human nature. You can't help it.'

'And you're worried that if you write the unvarnished

truth about Harry Day, no one will ever regard his work in quite the same way?'

'Something like that. I don't think he was a monster, exactly. But if you believe that the man and the artist are an indissoluble whole, that the nature of the man permeates his work as an artist, then – well, knowing the truth about him must affect the way people come to regard Harry's work. Which makes writing a truthful biography a big responsibility.'

'You could stop, if you wanted. You don't have to publish it.'

'Leaving aside the small matter of repaying the advance, I now feel absolutely driven to publish this book. Nothing matters more to me at the present moment. Not one thing.'

'Then you have to tell it like it is.'

'Would you be prepared to explore the Orton–Halliwell thing with me? Go back over the conversations when Harry was there? Let me quote you?'

Compton-King drove for some moments without saying anything. Then he gave Adam a glance. 'Since you're so determined to do a thorough job – yes. I can't vouch for perfect recall, though.'

Some hours later, the Bentley pulled up outside Adam's flat in Baron's Court.

'Well driven,' said Adam.

'And you.'

'Want to come in for a drink?'

Richard shook his head. 'I need some sleep. Back to the funky world of music-making tomorrow.'

Adam surveyed the worn, preternaturally handsome features. 'Don't you ever feel like giving it up?'

'No. I might start to grow old. Besides, bills to pay, parties to throw. You know.'

Adam got out and fetched his bags from the boot. He leaned through the passenger window. 'Thanks for the ride. And for listening to all my problems concerning the biography.'

'Old Uncle Richard, ever ready with a sympathetic ear. We had a blast.'

'I'll call you soon.'

Compton-King raised a hand in salute, then roared off down the road.

Adam went upstairs to his flat. It was blissfully silent. The cupboards were empty of Megan's clothes, except for one or two small items. How quickly a woman could disappear from one's life. Not even a trace left in his heart. He went to his bag and took out the piece of paper on which he'd written the number of Bella's house in France, then picked up the phone.

It was wonderful just to hear her voice again.

'I'm missing you already,' said Adam.

'I wish you could have stayed longer. It's strange without you. Charlie asked me what I was moping about this morning, so I told him.'

'About us?'

'Yes. I had to tell someone. You know that feeling.'

'Yes.'

'So my brother seemed like the best person.'

'Not your other brother?'

'Derek's different . . . It won't always be like that, I

hope, but no – for the moment I just told Charlie. He said that anyone whose absence made me this miserable must be good for me.'

Adam smiled. 'Ring me as soon as you get back to London.'

15

The next day Adam sat down with the sheaf of notes he'd compiled during his stay in France. He re-examined Frank's India story, then rang Leila, one of the women who had formed part of Harry's household in Simla many long years ago, in the days of flower power and swamis and the dream of universal love, and whom he'd managed to track down a couple of months previously. She was a housewife now, living in Croydon with three children and a husband who ran a chain of dry-cleaning shops. Though not much good on detail, in her initial interview with Adam she'd provided him with some good insights into Harry's character. Adam knew it was probably against the odds that she would have any specific recollection of Frank McVeigh's brother's friend after all this time, but it was worth a try.

'Leila, this is Adam Downing. We spoke a couple of months ago about Harry Day.'

'Oh, yes.'

'Look, I've been speaking to someone who mentioned a specific incident which occurred while Harry was living in India, and I wondered if you had any recollection of it.' Adam sketched out the story which Frank had told him.

'To be honest,' said Leila, 'it's so long ago, and so many people came to visit . . . I can't remember them all.'

'Yes, of course. But this boy stayed for some months. It seems he may have become – well, sexually involved with Harry.' He waited. Nothing of this kind had ever been mentioned in his previous conversation with Leila, no suggestion that Harry was anything more than a benign, paternal figure in the household in India. The silence stretched out. 'Leila? Is that true?'

'Yes,' replied Leila slowly. 'But I still can't help you.'

'Why not? If you know that, then you must remember the boy.'

He waited several seconds for her answer.

'There was more than one. It could have been any one of them. I don't know what happened after Harry got tired of them, got rid of them.'

Adam struggled to absorb this. 'But – you didn't mention any of this when we last spoke . . .'

She sighed a deep, dispirited sigh. 'I didn't want anyone thinking badly of Harry. He was such a great man, you can't understand . . . The things he taught me, all that wisdom.' Her voice shook with all the earnest wistfulness of the gullible young woman she had once been. 'It wasn't his fault.'

'So there were young men who came to visit, whom Harry seduced –'

'They were stupid, they got into something they didn't understand. Harry wasn't like other people. He had his own rules, his own standards. People just couldn't measure up to them . . . Look, I didn't say anything about this before because I didn't want you to write about it, or people to read about it. They'd just get the wrong idea about Harry. It's impossible to explain how things were then. No one would understand. I don't want you to quote anything I've said. I'll just deny it.'

'But –'

'I really don't want to talk to you any more. That time was very special to me. I don't want to destroy the memory of it. Please don't call me again.'

And she hung up.

Bella came back at the weekend, and Adam went round to see her as soon as she got back.

'It seems like weeks since last Tuesday,' she said, kissing him.

He marvelled at how inadequate and imperfect his recollected thoughts of her had been. The reality of her was so fresh, so vivid and lovely. He kissed her. 'So, how have the last few days been?'

'Good. It's been worthwhile. A crowded couple of weeks, but worthwhile.' She smiled. 'Derek and the girls enjoyed themselves. They may come out again next summer.'

'I thought you and Charlie were selling the house?'

'That was before Claire saw it. She's rather fallen in love with the place, and is apparently not quite so keen on Charlie selling up his share just to fund a mansion in Surrey. No doubt she's already combing *Country Life* for something more modest, but still sufficiently poncy.'

'She's not too bad.'

'No, she's all right, I suppose. A bit too aspirational and class-conscious. Charlie has the same tendencies.'

'Maybe Derek will be a good influence.'

'Mmm. Meeting Derek has had quite an effect on

Charlie. I think, for the first time in his life, Charlie's looked outside himself and seen how it could be, where he came from, and how lucky he is. He hasn't said a great deal to me, but I get the feeling he rather looks up to Derek. He likes that, the big-brother thing.'

'And what does Derek think about Charlie?'

'That I don't know. I'll find out when I see him next week. After that, when we meet up, I hope it'll always be the three of us.' Bella glanced at Adam. 'Don't worry. I'm realistic. I don't hope for great things. Just enough. Just enough not to lose the connection. So, how's the biography going? Unearthed any more dark secrets?'

'It's progressing,' said Adam. What else could he say? He gazed at her fixedly for a moment. He hadn't really given any thought over the past few days to the possible effect of his work on their new relationship. But the way things were going . . . The outrage and wrath of Briony and Cecile – those were things he could distance himself from. But Bella's reaction? She was the one person he should be able to sit down and discuss this with, but that seemed impossible. Not now, and not in the foreseeable future.

Adam was sitting in his study the next day, wondering whether he could interest the *Sunday Times* in a feature on Aldous Huxley and drugs, when the phone rang. It was Charlie.

'Adam? Hi, listen, I'm just on my way into court, so I'll keep this short. Remember that schoolfriend of mine I told you about, James Gifford? Well, I've managed to track him down. He's teaching at a boarding school near

Slough, called – hold on, I've got it here . . . Ravensbourne College. I'll give you the number.' Adam reached for a pen and took down the number. 'A friend gave me the information, so if you do get in touch, he won't know who you are. I have to dash. Bye.'

'Bye.' Adam put the phone down and stared at the paper on which he'd written down the number. There was probably nothing in it, mere base speculation on his own part, and he would doubtless be wasting his time. None the less, fifteen minutes later, he picked up the telephone, rang the number, and was put through to the Masters' Common Room.

At Gifford's invitation, Adam drove to Slough later that day, wondering what kind of questions he was going to ask. *Tell me, were you ever sexually molested by the great Harry Day? My readers would like to know.* The fact was, he thought, if the man had any dark secrets concerning Harry Day, he probably wouldn't have agreed to see Adam in the first place.

It was the end of August, and the school was still deserted. James Gifford greeted Adam and led him down echoing corridors to his study.

'Somewhat spartan, I'm afraid. I think of it as my monastic cell.' Gifford, tall, soft-faced and dark-eyed, looking not a great deal like George Michael, showed Adam in. The study was small and austere, the walls lined with books, with no more furniture than an old leather-topped desk and a swivel chair, and a low coffee table in front of a squat sofa. None the less, the room possessed a certain charm, an old-fashioned and mournful quality. The open window looked out across playing fields and a line of summer trees.

'School's quiet, of course,' said Gifford. 'The boys don't come back till Wednesday. Please –' He gestured towards the sofa, and Adam sat down and drew his tape recorder from his pocket. James Gifford sat in the swivel chair and gazed at Adam with mild interest.

'It's good of you to see me,' said Adam. 'I've been working on this biography for a year now, but your name only came up the other day.' Adam placed his tape recorder on the table in front of him. 'Mind if I switch this on?'

James Gifford glanced at it with what seemed like faint apprehension, then nodded. 'Go ahead.'

'You were at school with Harry Day's son, Charlie, I believe?'

'That's right. I was at Uppingham from '83 to '88. Charlie came around '84, '5, something like that.'

'And you spent several half-term holidays at Gandercleugh?'

'Yes. I think I must have been there six or seven times, in all.'

'Tell me what you remember about those holidays, particularly about Harry. Charlie says you had quite a close relationship with his father?'

Gifford glanced down at his fingers. They were long and white, the nails not quite clean. 'Yes. He was a very charismatic man. I was rather star-struck, I think, when I first met him. I'd read all his books. He'd just been shortlisted for the Booker Prize. *Adventures Of* . . .'

'How old were you then?'

'Fourteen. I mean, looking back, I'm not sure I could really have understood the themes he was dealing with in that book – not properly, as an adult would.' Gifford gave a little laugh. 'But he was incredibly patient. I would sit expounding all my half-baked adolescent theories about literature and writing, and he never patronized me. We talked a lot about politics, I recall. He'd been a member of the Communist party, just like Amis, but he never quite lost the faith, as Amis did. My God, I blush to recall how I actually had the temerity to accuse him of political hypocrisy, enjoying fame and wealth and at the same time espousing the socialist cause, while I ate his food and played on his tennis court.' Gifford shook his head. 'That was later, though, when I knew him somewhat better. When I was sixteen or so . . .'

The tape wound on, reeling in Gifford's hazy account of conversations, meals, outings, acts of kindness, heated discussions about politics and drugs, none of it startling or revelatory. Adam watched Gifford, whose drifting gaze never touched Adam's, but now and then fell meditatively upon the tape recorder; he watched the odd twitch which touched his mouth whenever he smiled, the pale fingers twisting as he spoke. The words came out, a prosaic but charming account of adolescent hero worship, marked with self-deprecation and wistful sentiment. Adam listened, asking the odd question, letting the story unfold, and realized as he did so how much this man wanted to talk about Harry – and how little of it had anything to do with whatever it was that lay, dark and still, at the core of Gifford's memory. Twenty minutes ticked by; forty. There came a pause, a loss of momentum, as though whatever had impelled Gifford to invite Adam here had suddenly wound down, broken. There was just silence. The tape spun.

Adam, when they had begun this conversation, had not expected to be able to ask the question which he asked now.

'Tell me –' began Adam, watching as James Gifford wound his fingers together, over and over, '– was there ever anything inappropriate in your relationship with Charlie Day's father?'

Gifford fixed his gaze on the view from the window, as though straining to see something in the far distance. Trying not to let someone see your tears, thought Adam. Gifford shook his head, as though he didn't trust himself to speak. Still the fingers went on folding, twisting. He suddenly reached down and, fumbling for a second, pressed the 'stop' button on Adam's recorder.

'Is that the kind of question a biographer asks?' Gifford's voice was unsteady, but he let his gaze meet Adam's.

'There's no question I can't ask. People needn't always answer.'

For some seconds James Gifford struggled to find words. 'Harry Day did a great deal for me. He – he read my poems. He pushed me to believe in myself, my ideas. I didn't have a lot of self-confidence in those days. Not a great deal now . . .' Gifford's laugh was almost soundless. He paused, frowning. 'He made me see that literature is something incandescent, absolutely transforming, that it can change people for good or ill. He introduced me to writers, ideas, gave me a perspective on the world which no one else had ever done.' There was a new undercurrent of passion in Gifford's voice. 'That is a great deal to give a boy, someone who was essentially quite lonely, far from home . . .' Again he fastened his gaze on something far beyond the window. 'I was impressed, naturally, overwhelmed. Overwhelmed with kindness. I was grateful. One doesn't wish to offend. At fifteen, one is –' He stopped. There was a long silence, stretching out over minutes.

In the end Adam said gently, 'Were you afraid I might ask?'

Gifford, whose eyes were now fixed on the floor, one hand shading them, nodded. Then he looked up at Adam. 'You will write nothing about this.' His voice was low, quite firm. 'You will write nothing, because I've said nothing. And if you do, I will deny it. I might even sue you. I won't let anyone destroy Harry Day's reputation. He was a great, great man, who instilled in me a love of everything I hold dear today, every aspect of my work and my teaching. Do you understand that?'

Adam had the feeling he didn't understand a thing. 'Why did you agree to see me today?'

Gifford said nothing. Adam, watching the bleak, expressionless face, had never felt so close to a stranger in his life.

'Was it because you wanted someone to know the truth?'

Gifford clasped his fingers together. 'I haven't told you anything.'

Adam nodded, reached out and picked up his tape

recorder, checked it, put it in his pocket. He did it slowly, giving Gifford a few seconds in which to collect himself.

'Thank you for your time,' said Adam, getting up.

Gifford rose and went to the door. He paused, a hand on the doorknob, his self-possession somewhat recovered. 'Harry wasn't a bad man, you know.'

'You don't think so?'

'I think he was a genius. A creative genius. I stood in awe of him then. I still do.'

Adam said nothing. Glancing round the small study before leaving, he noticed for the first time the volumes of Harry's books lining a section of shelving – poetry, plays, novels. Everything Harry had ever written was probably there.

Bella lay across her bed, phone in hand, listening as her agent, Carla, elaborated the career possibilities for the coming year.

'It's a six-part dramatization of *Northanger Abbey*,' said Carla. 'Jane Austen. Have you read it?'

'The only Austen I've read is *Pride and Prejudice*, when I was at school,' said Bella.

'Roughly the same, but different plot, and a bit more gothic. They want you for the heroine, Catherine Morland. It's a lovely big, juicy part.'

'Lots of hanging round stately homes in period costume. And those bloody carriages. I've been there before,' said Bella. 'Anyway, in costume dramas the heroine is usually totally bland, utterly unmemorable.'

'Well, you'd have to read the book.'

'I really liked the *Hard Sell* script. I'd rather be a

drug-dealer's moll than simper around in sprigged muslin. Besides, it's Hollywood.'

'Well, if you do that, you'd be away for a good six months. They're talking about starting shooting this autumn. The director's anxious to get going, so we'd have to tie it up in the next two weeks.'

Bella gave a little moan, agonized by indecision. 'The Jane Austen thing would be good, though, wouldn't it? Oh, Carla, I don't know.'

'Think about it for a couple of days. No immediate hurry, but I do need to know by the end of the week. Let's have lunch on Friday, and you can tell me then.'

'OK,' said Bella. 'Let's do that.'

That night she lay in bed with Adam and talked to him about the film part, and the costume drama.

'If I take the film, I'll be in the States for a while. They'll start shooting this autumn.'

'Which do you want to do?'

Her gaze, which had been fixed on some remote, speculative point in the corner of the room, travelled to his. She shook her head. 'I don't know.'

'I wish I could make your mind up for you. I wish I could simply say – forget Hollywood, stay here with me. But that's an entirely selfish perspective. You've got your career to think about. Anyway, when do you have to decide?'

She sighed. 'Friday.' There was silence for a moment, then she said, 'Oh, sod it, I don't want to think about that any more. Let's talk about something else. Tell me about the biography. When will it be finished? I'm dying to read it.'

'I don't know. I'm hung up on certain aspects.'

'Such as?'

For a few seconds he thought of telling her everything, but somehow couldn't bring himself to. By way of evasion, he said, 'Aspects of his past that Harry didn't touch on in all the time I spent with him.'

'His gay days in Soho?' She sighed. 'I know I said a while ago that I'd rather you didn't mention that, but I've changed my mind. I mean, it was when he was fairly young, and going a bit AC/DC is hardly scandalous by today's standards. It's practically expected.'

'I don't think your mother feels that way.' That was putting it mildly. Just wait till she got wind of what he was really going to tell the world. 'And most biographers like to keep their subject's family on board.'

'Truth must win. Otherwise life is impossible,' said Bella.

'Sorry?'

'One of my lines from *Funeral Games*. I think it's so right. You should keep your integrity, write the unvarnished truth.'

He looked at her, and she smiled to show she meant it, she was easy with him writing what he liked. How little she understood, thought Adam. She had no idea of what he'd uncovered, what the unvarnished truth was turning out to be. The biography would be just the beginning. Once it was published, other people would come forward, silent voices would begin to speak, and Harry Day and his family would suffer for ever. Except that Harry was dead and it couldn't hurt him. Not the way it could hurt Cecile and Charlie and Bella, along with others. *Truth must win*. What did any of them really know about truth? He didn't have a clue himself.

Adam and Compton-King spent a long evening together, mulling over Compton-King's recollections of times spent with Orton and Halliwell and Harry. At the end of it, Adam told Compton-King about his conversation with Leila, and his meeting with Gifford.

'He wasn't just a closet homosexual,' said Adam, 'he was a serial seducer of young men. Boys. It's one thing revealing to the world that Harry was gay, or at any rate bisexual, but the rest?' Adam shook his head in disbelief. 'And the thing is, Cecile and Briony must have known. They *must* have known.'

'Cecile does have a way of turning a blind eye to things,' said Compton-King.

'Exactly. Look at the business of the adoption. Rather than address it, deal with it by telling Bella and Charlie, she pretended it hadn't happened. And the way she talks about Harry, his affairs with men – she still pretends it was nothing more than a passing phase.' He thought about what George Meacher had said that day in Soho – *Thirty years on, and still keeping up appearances. Only nowadays they call it being in denial* . . . How right he had been. And Meacher himself – he knew more than he'd let on. Adam knew he was going to have to talk to him again. That would probably cost him another lunch. But it would be worth it. No doubt about it this time. He sat reflecting for some moments. 'It's Briony's part in this that I don't fully understand. Why did she marry him? I know Harry's connections were useful to her career, but why marry a geriatric poet who was into little boys?'

'I suspect the answer to that one is rather complex,' said Compton-King. 'I can enlighten you in one regard, however. The word is that dear Briony goes like an express train, to coin a phrase. I've done a little digging around on your behalf, and a chap at the BBC told me. She sleeps with just about everyone she works with, the younger the better, and keeps it well under wraps. After all, it doesn't quite fit with her public persona. So she probably married Harry for a variety of reasons, not least of which would be money, a nice house in the country, and a wonderful façade for her clandestine love life. I suspect that she and Harry probably struck a little deal right at the outset.'

'So both Briony and Cecile turned a blind eye to the things that Harry got up to?'

'Quite. The difference being that while Cecile was deeply humiliated and pretended they weren't happening, Briony probably couldn't have cared less.'

Adam let out a deep sigh. 'This means talking to Briony again. I have to tell her what I know. See how she reacts.'

'Good luck,' said Compton-King.

'You know, I've come a long way in a year. I remember the first time I talked to Harry, saying something along the lines that I thought that too many biographers had a habit these days of delving into the murkiest corners of the lives of their subjects, trying to find something salacious to help sell their book.'

'I wouldn't say that that's what you've done, exactly.'

'Do you know what amazes me?' said Adam after a

short silence. 'The way nobody blames Harry for any of it. Nobody thinks ill of him. Even people that he patently damaged, like Gifford. I suppose that's what worries me most about writing the biography. There is so *much* to an individual, no one is all good or all bad . . . I have to deal with the ugly side of Harry's character, tell the world things they never knew before, and still try to convey –' Adam stopped and sighed.

'What?'

'How much he was loved. Which seems, in the circumstances, an odd thing to have to do.'

Adam rang Gandercleugh and told Peter that he wanted to talk to Briony. He half-expected that after their last conversation she might refuse to talk to him, but she came on the line within seconds. Her tone was chilly, none the less.

'What can I do for you?'

'I wondered if you could spare some time to talk to me. There's something we need to discuss.'

Briony hesitated. The last time she had spoken to Adam she had had the unpleasant feeling that things were slipping out of her control. She didn't like that one little bit. She had devoted some considerable time to thinking of ways to stop Adam, to prevent this biography ever seeing the light of day. But she could see none. She had consulted her lawyer, but he'd pointed out to her that they could take no action until they knew exactly what Adam intended to say. If she were to remain on top of things, it was important for her to know what information Adam possessed at any given moment.

'Very well. I can spare you a couple of hours tomorrow.'

'I'll be there around ten,' said Adam.

The first thing that struck Adam when he arrived at Gandercleugh was how little of Harry's presence remained. Briony was in the throes of renovation, the old-fashioned grandeur of the rooms, the rich, deep colours which Harry had loved, being replaced by pastels, pale curtains and fabrics, new, sleek furniture. Peter showed him into the morning room, where he and Harry had often sat. The big desk where Harry had worked and answered correspondence was gone, and the large, deep sofa with its tartan rugs, the battered leather footstool. In their place stood new armchairs upholstered in cream-coloured silk, and a glass-topped table with a bowl of fresh roses in its centre. Straw-coloured curtains flanked the open French windows, lifting slightly in the breeze, instead of the heavy, wine-coloured velvet drapes of Harry's day.

After a few minutes, Briony came in from the garden through the French windows. She was dressed as if for a celebrity interview in a smart blue linen dress, her hair tied back with a matching scarf, a cardigan thrown over her shoulders. Her jewellery and shoes were perfectly accessorized. Her manner was poised, guarded.

'You've made a few changes,' he said, glancing round.

'I've had every room redone. I simply couldn't bear the gloom.' She went over to a cushioned window seat and sat down, tucking her legs up neatly beneath her, and Adam sat in an armchair opposite. 'Let's dispense with pleasantries, Adam. Just say what you've come to say.'

'Last time we met,' said Adam, 'I told you that I'd found out about Harry's homosexuality –'

'Which was a minor incident, relegated to the past. I can't see why you're intent on making so much of it,' interrupted Briony.

'Well, that's where I have to disagree. I've found out a number of things, and they all point to the probability that Harry was actively gay throughout his entire life, and that he had a particular penchant for seducing young men, a lot of them underage.' Briony's gaze didn't flinch. Her lovely face was mask-like. 'I know, for instance, that he seduced a schoolfriend of Charlie's who used to come here in the school holidays. He was only fifteen. I've spoken to him. There was a teenager who came to stay at Harry's house in India, whom Harry made his lover, and subsequently kicked out, even though the boy was ill, in need of hospital treatment. Harry just discarded him. As he apparently did many others.'

Briony's expression was cool, unmoved. 'If any of that were remotely true, which I don't accept for one second, I can't see what comment you expect me to make on events which occurred long before I married Harry.'

'The point is, I think it was still going on while you were married to Harry. And that you knew about it.'

She stood up, drawing her thin cardigan around her. At that moment Peter opened the door on cue, about to ask if they were ready for coffee. 'Not right now, Peter!' flashed Briony, and Peter retreated.

Briony paced across the pale, new carpet. 'I can assure you there was nothing like that in Harry's life. If you think I'm going to give you some version of our marriage other than the one you already know, then I'm not.'

'Was it just for convenience, for the kudos, that you married Harry?' Before she could answer, he added, 'It's why Cecile did.' Was that true? At this very moment, it didn't matter.

She's going to burst a blood vessel, thought Adam. Briony's eyes blazed, but her face remained impassive. She had her arms folded, and he could see the slim fingers pressing down hard on the flesh of either arm.

'Was it that way for you and Harry? A domestic camouflage, so that you could both do exactly as you pleased and still live respectably in the public eye?'

She can't kick me out, thought Adam. She needs to know what I'm going to do with the things I'm telling her.

It was enough pressure. 'Everybody is entitled to a private life,' she said, her voice even and cold. 'I made it my business to know nothing about what he did while I was away. He respected my privacy, too.'

She's as good as confirmed it, thought Adam. He wondered how many affairs she'd had during her marriage. If Compton-King's information was reliable, the figure probably ran to dozens.

'I know nothing about underage boys,' she added.

'I do. I have facts and witnesses.' Not true, but it would do.

Her steeliness broke. 'You're not going to publish this, are you?' Her eyes were beseeching, disbelieving. 'What good would it do anyone? A life, a reputation thrown away! Why would you do that? Just to sell a book?

You were Harry's friend. He confided in you, trusted you –'

'No, he didn't. He trusted no one. Except perhaps you.'

She switched her tack to one of outrage. 'You self-righteous bastard! You want to destroy someone who was a far greater person than you ever will be, just to sell your rotten book and have your moment of triumph and fame!' She sat down on the window seat again, breathing rapidly. 'As far as this conversation goes, I haven't told you a thing. I don't care what Cecile may have told you about her marriage. But if you write one word that doesn't accord with what Harry and I told you about us, then I'll sue you.'

He gazed at her speculatively. This indignation, this outrage, had nothing to do with Harry's reputation. Just like Cecile, she didn't want her private life explored and exposed. The papers being what they were these days, that would probably happen eventually, anyway, biography or no biography.

'I want to tell the truth, because I think the truth is important. Don't you?'

When she spoke again, her manner was contained, her voice low. 'No, I don't. I think what's important is that living people shouldn't be made to suffer. That's what's going to happen, Adam. If you have any conscience, then I beg you – leave it alone.' Her voice was frank in its appeal. The taut, pretty features had slackened and aged a little. 'Our marriage was more real than you imagine. He was just a complicated man.' She put a hand to her forehead. 'I can't see it would do anyone any good for it to be known. Apart from the damage it would do to me, think of the hurt it would cause Bella and Charlie.' To this he said nothing. She'd touched on the one aspect of this whole thing which remained unresolved in his heart. After a few seconds she asked, 'Well? What do you intend to do?'

'I don't know,' said Adam. He rose from the chair.

'I promise you,' said Briony, 'I will do everything in my power to make sure none of this sees the light of day. Don't underestimate me.'

Adam, who had reached the door, turned and regarded her. 'It's always a pity when people do that. Underestimate others, I mean.'

And with that he left and drove back to London. A long journey for such a short visit, but to have his speculations confirmed, it had been worth it.

Briony's subsequent phone call to Cecile was terse and to the point. Cecile made an initial show of dignified elderly bewilderment, but Briony was having none of it. 'Oh, come off it. You've known about Harry's little goings-on for as long as I have. Longer.' Silence at the other end. 'Haven't you?'

Cecile sighed. 'Why do you think I divorced him? I actually had to pay that wretched model to lie.'

They discussed it for a few minutes, but neither could see what there was to be done about Adam and the book. 'We'll just have to wait until we see the proofs,' said Briony. 'Then talk to our lawyers.'

'What makes you think we're going to get to see them?'

'Because when they read the manuscript, Downing's

publishers will realize they've got a time bomb on their hands. It's in their interests to be as circumspect as possible. They won't particularly welcome a lawsuit. Better to find out in advance what you're likely to be up against. That's why we'll see the proofs.'

'I suppose you're right . . . By the way – it's only just occurred to me – something that might be of interest.'

'What?'

'Charlie told me a few days ago that Bella and Adam Downing have a bit of a thing going. Not that Bella's said anything to me yet.'

'Well, now,' said Briony thoughtfully, 'that *is* interesting. And useful. Don't you think?'

Cecile rang Bella and asked her to drop round, ostensibly for a fitting for the dress she was to wear as one of Claire's bridesmaids.

At the end of the trying-on session, when pinning and measuring had been completed, Cecile said to Bella, 'Darling, there's something I need to discuss with you.'

Bella laid the half-finished dress across Cecile's work table. 'What is it?'

'It's about your father's biography.'

'What about it?' Her mind shifted to Adam. She wondered whether she should tell her mother about herself and Adam. Perhaps not yet. She sat down at the table and took the mug of tea which her mother handed to her.

Cecile sat down on the other side of the table. 'Well, Briony and I have decided to withdraw our cooperation.'

'It's a bit late for that, isn't it? Why, for heaven's sake?'

'It turns out that Adam Downing intends to embark on some quite unnecessary and unpleasant speculation about your father. It's unfounded, of course, and we have done our best to persuade him not to print it, but –' She lifted a hand and let it fall. 'I thought it best to tell you, and Charlie.'

Bella gave an embarrassed smile and sipped her tea. 'Mummy, if this is about stuff that Harry got up to before you and he were married – well, I do know about it. Adam's told me. And I don't think the revelation that he had a passing gay phase is going to cause a great sensation. I imagine it's not an unusual thing among creative geniuses. I don't think you and Briony should let it worry you.'

'We wouldn't – if that was the extent of what he intends to say. Unfortunately it's far worse than that.'

'Worse? Worse – how?' Bella couldn't believe that Adam hadn't confided in her, whatever it was. Not after everything that had happened.

'Oh, you know how it is when someone famous dies. Scandal-mongers turn up ten a penny, envious people from the past, possibly some with grudges . . .' Cecile sighed. 'People are prepared to tell all kinds of lies – who knows why? Anyway, what was, as you rightly say, a trivial instance in Harry's past has been blown into something more than that. There are people who are apparently prepared to say that it went on far longer – that he went on having affairs with men, that he went around seducing schoolboys –' Cecile broke off, shaking her head.

'What?'

'I know – horrible, and quite fantastical. The suggestion

is that he led some appalling double life that neither Briony nor I knew about. It's simply staggering.'

'That's unbelievable! And you say Adam's actually going to put this in his book?'

'So he says. I hate to say this, because I know he's your friend, but I suspect his reasons are mercenary. He seems prepared to believe anything sensational, if it's going to help to sell his book. When someone's dead, they can't defend themselves, after all.'

'I can't believe he didn't tell me this . . . Are you quite certain?'

'Oh, yes. Briony had a rather unpleasant confrontation with him. She pointed out the kind of distress it was going to cause all of us, but he didn't seem unduly concerned.'

'He wouldn't deliberately hurt any of us. I know he wouldn't.'

'Who knows what his priorities are, darling?' Cecile sipped her tea, eyeing Bella.

'I'll speak to him. Don't worry. Just leave it with me.'

Adam had arranged to meet Bella for dinner that evening, and he was surprised when she rang him late-afternoon.

'You sound upset,' said Adam. 'What's up?'

'Why didn't you tell me?'

'Tell you what?' asked Adam, with a sinking heart. He thought he had a fair idea.

'These things – these unbelievable things you've been planning to write about my father.'

'Who told you?'

'Cecile. She rang me. Said she thought I had a right to

know what you intended to say. Which is more than you did.'

He hadn't discussed anything with Cecile beyond Harry's early life in Soho. Evidently she and Briony were in contact. He had had an idea they might close ranks in an attempt to stop him from publishing what he knew. Here was the real, the ultimate pressure. He closed his eyes for a moment.

'I was going to talk to you about it. The right moment just hadn't come up. Apart from which, I'm still checking facts.'

'Facts? Adam, how can you believe *any* of it?'

What was he supposed to say to her? Above all, he wanted her to go on believing all the things she had ever believed about Harry. They were still true. Just as it was probably true that Cecile had once been in love with Harry, despite all that came after. Just as it was true that James Gifford really was the man he was today because of Harry. How could he tell her that there was more to it than that, without destroying her ideal?

'It's true. So far as I can verify, it's all true. That's what happened. That was who he was. I'm sorry. The last thing in the world I wanted was for you to be hurt.'

'It's too late for that. It's not just that I don't *want* to believe those things about my father. You're telling me they're true, but I know they're not. It's all rumour, conjecture, the kind of horrible stuff that people come up with after someone like that dies. Chuck a bit of dirt, see if it sticks.'

'Do you think I'd seriously write about it if I didn't believe it?'

'That's the point, Adam.' He could hear her voice tremble, then break. 'You can't write about it. Not if you love me. Please.'

Long seconds ticked away. At last Adam said quietly, 'Bella, I have no choice.'

'Oh yes, you do.' Tears shook her voice; he longed to hold her, to calm her. 'I'm giving you a choice, Adam. Either you give it up, the entire project, or everything's over between us.'

'Please, don't say that,' said Adam. 'I love you – more than you know. But I can't just abandon this book.'

'Why not? What good is it going to do? Who's going to benefit from it? Not me, not Charlie, not Briony or Cecile, not anybody that ever knew and loved my father. All you're going to do is ruin the reputation of a great person. Is that what you want your book to do? If you have to write it, leave those things out. You could if you wanted. Then no one has to suffer.'

'This isn't the way you were talking last time we spoke about this.'

'Because I didn't have any idea of what you really intended to say!'

'I can't just be selective with the truth. I'd rather give the book up than do that.'

'Then will you?'

Adam found himself recalling that day when she'd come into Harry's study when he and Harry were discussing the very beginnings of the biography. She'd come a long way since then, found out a great deal that perhaps she'd never wanted to, thanks to him. Now he was proposing to put her through more pain, and lose her into the bargain. For what? Was it just for the sake of a book which, as she said, would probably do no one any good in the long run? Or was it something more than that?

He tried to make his tone rational, placatory. 'Bella, look, I know you're upset, but you can't just call up like this, issue ultimatums, and expect me to – to give in. This is my work, a whole year's work, something I've dedicated myself to.'

'It's my *father*! My *family*! You expect me to believe that you love me, when you're prepared to sacrifice our happiness, our peace of mind, for your *work*? My mother says there's absolutely no truth in any of it, anyway!'

'Look,' said Adam, his voice as heavy as his heart, 'this was never going to be easy to talk about. Whatever Cecile may have said, I can justify every –'

'I don't want justification! You seem to forget that we are his family! We knew Harry better than anyone! I don't want to hear any of the lies you've been peddled!'

'Bella, we can't talk about this over the phone. I'm seeing you tonight. Why don't you just give it a bit more thought between now and then? Don't be so quick to condemn. Try to see it from my point of view –'

'Adam, there is no point of view. It's not open to debate. This isn't emotional blackmail. It's a simple statement of fact. If you're prepared to go ahead with this, then we have nothing left to say to one another. Nothing.'

He hesitated for a moment, then asked quietly, 'Do you love me?'

He could hear her take a deep, ragged breath before

answering. 'I don't know. I thought I did. I want to. But I can't if you do this.'

'We'll talk tonight. Sort something out.'

She clicked the phone off and put it down slowly. What kind of compromise did he think there was to be reached? Bella dried her eyes and paced around the flat. How odd, that she had spent months looking for her family, looking for some imagined reality, only to find that her first and fiercest loyalties lay – had always lain – with Charlie, Cecile and Harry. She shut her mind to the possibility that there might be some truth in what Adam had discovered. That wasn't the issue. The issue was that Adam was threatening to destroy her father's reputation, and she would defend that with every breath in her body, truth or no truth.

She sat down and stared bleakly at the traffic in the street below. The irony of finding a man she thought she could love – not just for a fleeting instant, but properly, enduringly – only to find he was bent on the destruction of everything and everyone dear to her. In spite of all that, he loved her. Of that she was convinced. He was bound to see the impossibility of the situation. And if he loved her as much as she thought he did, surely he would come to the conclusion that what they could have together was worth more than any book.

The phone rang and she reached for it quickly, half-expecting it to be Adam. But it was Carla, her agent.

'Bella, darling, sorry to hustle you, but I need a decision. The people at Carlton need to know one way or another about the Jane Austen.'

'Oh, God . . . I don't know. I think it's yes, but I'm still trying to decide.' If, as she felt he would, Adam gave in, then everything would be fine, she could forget the Hollywood thing. But in the unlikely event that he refused to compromise, insisted on going ahead, then she wanted to be as far away from him, and this whole, horrible situation, as possible. Tears stung her eyes at the thought that it might happen. No, she refused to accept the possibility. Not if he cared. 'Carla, give me till this evening. I'm sure it's going to be OK, but let me call you later. You said you didn't need to know till tomorrow.'

'Well, tomorrow's the deadline, but they've been pressing me. It would help if I could say something today.' She sighed. 'All right. Call me this evening.'

At quarter past eight that evening, Adam sat waiting for Bella in the bar of the restaurant he had booked for dinner. She came in late, breathless, beautiful. He felt his throat tighten at the sight of her.

She pulled off her jacket. 'Sorry I'm late. I had trouble getting a cab.'

'It doesn't matter.' She sat down and he leaned across and kissed her cheek, taking in the perfume, the softness of her skin. 'Drink?'

'Just mineral water, thanks.' She smiled, but her eyes were clouded, troubled.

They gazed tentatively at one another.

'Have you been working hard?' she asked. Adam nodded. 'I managed to do a bit of serious shopping myself,' said Bella, and gave another quick smile. Her mineral water came. She sipped it, then set it down. 'OK, then.' He watched the rapid pulse which beat in her throat. She is so anxious, she loves me so much, thought Adam. He waited to hear what she would say next. 'I hope I didn't sound too – well . . . too dictatorial on the phone this morning.' Adam shook his head. 'It's just – it's just so important to me, Adam. You do understand that, don't you?'

He nodded. 'Yes, I understand that.'

'So . . . You said we would sort something out.'

He leaned forward, gazing intently at her. 'Before we say anything else, there's one thing you have to understand. I love you, and I would do nothing to hurt you. Nothing you say or think can change that.' He stroked her cheek once with his finger. 'But as for sorting something out, that's up to you.'

'What do you mean – it's up to me?'

'Whether or not this book makes any difference to us. It's up to you to decide whether or not you can accept what I'm going to write.'

Bella drew a long breath. 'You're going ahead with it?' He nodded. She looked away for a few seconds, then asked, 'How can you possibly pretend to love me?'

'You once quoted something to me,' said Adam. 'From your play. "Truth must win. Otherwise life is impossible."'

She shook her head. 'All you have to do is compromise.'

'But it's right. I have to say what I know to be the truth, or say nothing at all.'

'Then say nothing. Forget compromise. Just abandon the biography. Please, Adam.'

He gazed at her, as if trying to fix the moment, to recall every precious, shared instant. He could hardly comprehend what it was he was about to lose.

'I can't.'

There was a silence. 'At least we know where we stand. I know now what matters more to you.'

'No, you don't. It's not the simple choice you make it out to be.'

'Yes, it is. And you've chosen. You're on the other side now. I have to stick by my family.' Her eyes were bright with tears. 'It's all pointless, this – you do realize that? We won't let you publish it. We'll do everything possible to stop you. And so no one will be any the better off – not you, or me, or anyone.'

He could think of nothing to say to this. He watched as she rose, picked up her jacket, put it on. As she was about to leave, Adam said, 'Whatever happens, remember – he was a great man. A great writer.'

She walked out of the bar, and Adam was left alone. He sat there for some time. At last he got up, paid, went down to the street and hailed a cab to take him home. When he turned the key in the lock of his door and went in, it was as though the silence had been waiting for him, to welcome him. He walked into his study and stood by the window, watching the beginnings of the late-summer dusk creep across the London sky. He sat down at his desk and began to work.